HOLLYHOCK RIDGE

HOLLYHOCK RIDGE

Pamela Grandstaff

Books by Pamela Grandstaff:

Rose Hill Mystery Series:

Rose Hill

Morning Glory Circle

Iris Avenue

Peony Street

Daisy Lane

Lilac Avenue

Hollyhock Ridge

Sunflower Street

Viola Avenue

Pumpkin Ridge

For Betsy

CHAPTER 1

The sky was still as black as the bottom of a coal mine at 5:05 a.m. when Ed Harrison delivered the *Pendletonion* newspaper to the residents of Rose Hill, but Diedre Delvecchio had already smoked her first five cigarettes of the day. The ceramic ashtray, a Myrtle Beach souvenir from her sister's vacation, had three packs worth of butts in it from the previous day. Unless her husband, Matt, emptied it while she was out of the house, the butts would continue to pile up until they overflowed onto the kitchen table.

Diedre scoured the classified pages' yard sale section like a four-star general studying battle maps in a war room. She had to prioritize the most desirable locations in order to outmaneuver her competition.

There was one out on Hollyhock Ridge described as a moving sale. There was nothing like facing the daunting prospect of packing up all your worldly goods and then paying by the pound to have them transported long distance to make a family a lot less sentimental about their possessions. It was a little way outside of her comfort zone as far as driving was concerned, but for Diedre, a moving sale was like an open bar to an alcoholic. Tired, stressed, and preoccupied, those poor suckers would just want the stuff gone and were likely to let it go cheap.

Diedre left the newspaper on the table, where her husband, Matt, would read it while he ate his cereal before he left for his job managing Delvecchio's IGA, the business his father began back in the 1940s. After he read the newspaper, he would place it on top of the newest stack, now five feet high, that was accumulating in the dining room. He wouldn't dare try to sneak it out of the house. Matthew hated a fuss, and Diedre could kick up a fuss like nobody's business.

They didn't use the dining room anymore; no point, really. They didn't invite people over. Matt's family stayed away. Diedre's sister, Sadie, sometimes stopped by, but Diedre always slid out the front door and spoke to her on the front porch. Matt and Diedre's daughter had stopped coming home for visits years ago. Tina was embarrassed, she said, for her husband to see the house, and didn't think it was safe for her children to be in it. Frankly, Diedre found her daughter to be a prissy prig who overdramatized everything, her son-in-law a sneering snob, and their whiny children exhausting. If they did come, they would just complain about the house, or worse, try to sneak things out when Diedre wasn't looking. People thought she had so much that she wouldn't miss a thing. They were wrong.

The kitchen table was fine for eating, and there was still room left on top for two people to put down two plates. Stacks of broken down cardboard milk cartons that Matt had tied with twine took up the rest of the space.

A toaster oven sat on top of the broken range; they didn't need the full-size oven just to heat up frozen dinners and make toast. The kitchen counters were covered in nested stacks of used plastic containers, the sizes sorted from large to small, from cottage cheese down to yogurt singles. The defunct dishwasher contained all the good dishes they no longer used, kept there since they were last washed three years before, after a disastrous Thanksgiving dinner with her daughter's family that ended in a volley of recriminations that couldn't be taken back.

If Diedre was the hunter/gatherer, it was Matt who was the compulsive cleaner/organizer; Diedre thought it must be from a lifetime of stocking shelves at the IGA. She was a saver, just like her mother and father, who grew up during the Great Depression. You never knew when you might need something, but when the time came, she would have it. That was what she always said, anyway; the truth was something long-buried under the tall stacks of clutter in her head.

Diedre made sure she had her smokes and a lighter before getting into her twenty-year-old Buick Roadmaster station wagon with the fake wood panel sides. Garbage bags full of plastic bags took up the whole back seat, right where she could get to them when she needed them. On the passenger side front seat she kept her purse, a large tote bag filled with extra things she might need, including pens, notepads, maps, a half carton of cigarettes, spare lighters in case one ran out of fuel, packets of tissues, several small bottles of hand sanitizer, multiple packets of sugar and sugar-free sweeteners, a plastic bag full of quarters, and several rubber-banded rolls of one, five, and ten dollar bills.

Three years ago her husband had issued an ultimatum: she could only bring home things they ate or otherwise consumed, or he was leaving her. No amount of fuss could back him down, so determined was he to gain control. Diedre couldn't imagine life without collecting things. What would she have to look forward to? Why even get up in the morning?

Shortly after Matt's declaration of war, Diedre went to work at her brother-in-law's hardware store, ostensibly to help out after his wife left him. If she used cash he didn't know she had, and if she didn't bring home what she purchased, she reasoned, her husband would think he'd won and get off her back.

In the back of the station wagon were several milk crates, a stack of newspapers with which she could pack breakables, a laundry basket full of bungee cords, and a handcart she could use for heavier things. There was a roof rack on top of the car she could bungee things to if her finds took up all the cargo area.

Diedre loved this car. It was her best friend.

"Let's get this show on the road, Beulah Mae," she said, patting the dashboard, where a bean-bag weighted ashtray held all the butts from the previous day's hunt.

When Diedre pulled off the road just across from the house on Hollyhock Ridge, she was gratified to see she was the first to arrive. There was a junk man who sometimes got there before she did, and a few amateurs who had the nerve to knock on doors, waking up the homeowners and asking to see what they had before anyone else could. Diedre preferred to bide her time, and didn't consider it fair game until the front door opened or the garage door went up.

She rolled down a window and lit her next cigarette off of the first. She took the last sip of her third can of diet soda, and then tossed it in the passenger side floor well, where thirty or forty others were already attracting bees.

The advertisement had said "8:00 a.m. to noon."

It was 6:00 a.m.

It turned out to be well worth her wait.

She got over ten years' worth of Mary Engelbreit magazines for ten dollars.

"I hate to part with them," the woman said, "but I just keep moving them from house to house, and although I mean to, I never go back and reread them."

Diedre had found it was best to say as little as possible when people are parting with something that has great sentimental value. You never knew what could trigger them to change their minds about selling. Instead, she pressed her lips together and turned up the outside corners in what passed for a smile, and quickly loaded the magazines into the back of her station wagon.

Among other things, she also acquired five dozen Mason jars without lids for fifty cents a dozen, a raggedy patchwork quilt made from feed sacks for ten dollars, a chipped McCoy Pottery planter for a quarter, and a plastic jack-o'-lantern full of nails and screws for fifty cents.

"How much for the child's wagon?" she asked the man, who looked as if he was nursing a wicked hangover.

"I was going to throw that away," he said. "You can have it."

It was missing a wheel and one of the wooden side guards, but it reminded Diedre of one that she had coveted when she was a little girl.

Other people started to arrive, and Diedre felt that familiar, panicky feeling.

What had she missed?

What if someone else got something she might need?

Quickly she inventoried the offerings, and although the back of the station wagon was full, she had the feeling she was leaving something valuable behind.

"Do you have anything you were thinking about selling that you haven't brought out yet?" she asked the woman.

"Well," the woman said, and Diedre's heart rate sped up. This was how you got the thing no one else knew was available. "Dave's been after me to sell an old treadle sewing machine that was my grandmother's. I don't sew, and it's real heavy, and he says he's not paying to move it one more time."

"I sew," Diedre said. "I just love old sewing machines; I'll give it a good home."

The husband helped her strap it to the top of her car.

"Will you have someone to help you on the other end?" he asked her.

"Sure," Diedre said. "No problem."

Diedre pulled back onto the narrow two-lane road that wound around Hollyhock Ridge, anxious to get away before the woman changed her mind. Although the reflection in her rearview mirror was now full of her new things, in the side-view mirror she could see the woman still standing in her driveway, holding the fifty dollars Diedre had paid her for the sewing machine, looking as if she was already regretting letting it go.

Diedre trembled with the adrenaline revved up by the sale. This was a great haul. Many of the items were dear to the heart of that woman, and those feelings were now Diedre's to enjoy.

Diedre preferred a storage unit on the back side of the lot, where she could unload in private without passersby seeing her station wagon. She removed the padlock and pulled up the garage-style door to reveal a thirty-foot deep by ten-foot wide concrete pad and cinder block walls with a ten-foot-high ceiling.

None of her husband's compulsive organizing took place here. It was stuffed full, floor to ceiling. As she surveyed her treasures, a feeling of calm, much like the nicotine wave from her first cigarette of the day, flooded her body with a feeling of well-being. To Diedre, this was a comforting nest of her secret things. She could come here and be with them every day, to admire them, to feel the safety and security they provided.

Although it looked as if she couldn't cram in one more item, there were still pockets of space available. She unloaded and stowed everything except for the sewing machine strapped to the roof of her car, and was standing there regarding it when a truck came around the side of her section of units and parked nearby.

Diedre didn't like people looking at her things.

She watched two men get out of the truck. With their shaved heads, scraggly beards, and heavily tattooed skin, they looked to her like drug dealers; probably did business out of here. It wouldn't surprise her. People were always up to no good. One man lifted his head in a greeting, but Diedre pretended as if she hadn't seen it.

Diedre removed the bungee cords holding the sewing machine to the roof rack and eased it down the side of the station wagon to the ground. It was much too heavy for her and crashed to the ground, scratching the side of the car. She tugged it into the storage space, and then pushed as hard as she could to get it all the way in so she could roll down the door behind her. But it was no use; she couldn't get it all the way inside.

To the right of the door was a tall metal filing cabinet. If she could get the sewing machine up on top of that, she would still have room for some more things.

One of the men came up behind her.

"You need some help?" he asked. "Man, you got a lot of junk in here."

Diedre didn't like people looking at her things, or touching her things, but she knew she couldn't lift it on her own.

"I can't pay you," she said. "I don't have any money."

"Don't worry about it," he said. "No charge."

He smiled and revealed brownish teeth, and there were scabs on his face from a multitude of sores, but his eyes were the scariest part of his appearance. Diedre didn't like to look in them for very long. Those eyes didn't care about anything or anybody.

"Can you get it up there?" she asked, pointing to the top of the filing cabinet.

"Sure," he said, and then turned and called out to the other man. "Hey, Ricky, come help me a minute."

The two men took either end of the sewing machine, heaved it up to shoulder height, rested a moment, and then pushed it up on top of the filing cabinet. It teetered a little.

"That don't look safe," Ricky said.

"It's fine," Diedre said, anxious to get them out of the storage unit. "Thanks for your help."

"No problem," the first man said. "Have a nice day."

As they walked away, Ricky said, "What a load of junk," and they laughed.

Diedre pulled the door down, turned around, and leaned back against the filing cabinet. Whatever was behind it shifted, the cabinet scooted backward, Diedre fell back with it, and the sewing machine came down on top of her.

It was odd.

Diedre found herself floating up near the ceiling of the storage unit. All she could see of her body beneath the sewing machine were her pink sweatpants-covered legs and her tennis shoe-covered feet.

She didn't feel particularly upset; in fact, she felt calm and detached. She floated up through the roof of the storage unit, and watched as one of the men raised the garage door to her unit, and then quickly lowered it again. He opened the driver's side door of the station wagon, looked inside, and then shouted something to Ricky. The first man then drove off in her station wagon, with Ricky following in the truck.

Diedre floated upwards, above the storage unit facility and the hillside next to which it sat, and looked down on her station wagon as it rolled along the narrow two-lane road. As she rose even higher, she could see all the way north to the four-lane highway, and all the way south to Rose Hill. The higher she rose, the more peaceful she felt, as calm and serene as the puffy white clouds floating in the beautiful blue sky. The sun was shining so brightly she felt enveloped in its warm, brilliant light. It felt a lot like how she felt in her storage unit, in her nest of things.

Safe.

Secure.

Loved.

CHAPTER 2

K ay Templeton woke to the sound of someone outside her bedroom window. She looked at the clock; it was 5:35 a.m. Her house had recently been vandalized with spray paint, and she was not going to let that happen again. She got out of bed and pulled on her robe as she stuck her feet into her slippers. She grabbed her cell phone off the bedside table, and thinking she might need a weapon, picked up her umbrella as she went out the front door.

As she rounded the house, umbrella raised, ready to do battle with what she presumed were juvenile miscreants, she was surprised to find Sonny Delvecchio on a ladder, painting the side of her house with white paint. He had covered the orange letters spelling out "DYKE" and was just starting on "WITCH."

"Sonny!" she said. "What are you doing?"

Sonny was a big man, clad in paint-spattered coveralls and scuffed work boots. He leaned back and looked her up and down.

"Good morning, Mary Poppins," he said. "Nice getup."

Kay lowered her umbrella, adjusted her robe, and smoothed down her hair as she walked through the tall, dew-soaked grass. The morning fog from the Little Bear River was thick in the air, and she could only see about half a block in any direction.

"That's evidence," Kay said. "I don't think I'm allowed to paint over it, yet."

"Well, now, I asked that substitute chief of police if he thought it'd be all right, cause it makes me so doggone mad every time I see it, and he said if you didn't know anything about it you couldn't be blamed. Think of it as a random act of reverse vandalism. I figure there've been enough pictures taken of it that nobody's likely to forget what it looked like."

"That's very kind of you, Sonny," Kay said. "It's been three weeks, but every time I look at it, it feels as bad as the first time."

"There's not a person worth anything who could believe you'd have anything to do with black magic, and I'm pretty sure you don't prefer the ladies; not that there's anything wrong with that. I prefer the ladies myself."

He gave Kay an appreciative look that flustered her.

"Jumbo wrote it about my foster daughter," Kay said. "She's on vacation with friends in Florida, so I'm glad she won't have to see it when she gets back."

"Grace Branduff is a pip," Sonny said. "Jacob Branduff was an ornery cuss, but she's a good 'un. Matt says Grace is the best worker he's ever had at the IGA."

Sonny was the oldest brother of four in the Delvecchio family, and owned Delvecchio's Hardware; Matt ran the IGA, Paul and his wife, Julie, owned PJ's Pizza, and Anthony owned an insurance agency. Their mother was a tall, statuesque Italian beauty named Antonia; their father, Sal, was a tiny man who suffered from horrible emphysema.

"I'll leave you to get on with it," Kay said. "Come in for some coffee when you're done."

As Kay walked back toward the front of her house, she saw Diedre Delvecchio driving down Peony Street in her shabby station wagon. Kay waved, but of course, Diedre pretended not to see her. Diedre liked to pretend Kay didn't exist, and Kay was glad to accommodate her.

Diedre's husband, Matt Delvecchio, had been Kay's first boyfriend. They had started going together in 7th grade, which meant Matt carried her books, hung out by her locker between classes, and talked to her on the phone for hours every evening. The devoted Kay sat in the stands to watch

Matt play football and baseball, and beamed up at him as he pinned a corsage on her dress before every school dance.

There were no cell phones or Internet back then. Computers were business machines that took up whole rooms and calculators represented the most sophisticated technology they used. Both were children of strict parents and as such were never allowed to be alone together.

By his senior and her junior year, they had made plans: after she graduated they would get married and have a bunch of kids. He would work in the family business; she would stay home and be a full-time mother and homemaker. Although her parents were not happy about it, she agreed to convert to Catholicism and had begun taking R.C.I.A. classes at Sacred Heart. They were as committed to each other as teenagers could be, and they were also committed to waiting until they were married to have sex.

In the spring semester of her junior year, Kay contracted Mononucleosis and missed a month of school. During that time little Diedre Brennan got her braces removed, traded her thick glasses for contact lenses, had her hair frosted, and bought a padded push-up bra. Even after all that devoted abstaining, it had not been difficult to seduce Matthew. Kay had no doubts about who was the aggressor; Diedre had rubbed her nose in it.

But Matthew could have said, "No."

Kay cooked Sonny a full breakfast of eggs, bacon, toast, and hot coffee. He took his boots off on the front porch before he came inside. He seemed to tower over everything in Kay's tiny cottage and took up every bit of one side of the breakfast nook. He tucked his napkin in the neck of his coveralls and ate with gusto.

Kay sat on the other side of the booth, sipped her tea, and enjoyed watching him eat with such pleasure.

"This is so good," he said. "I can't tell you the last time I had a breakfast like this. You shouldn't have gone to the trouble."

"I enjoy cooking and baking," Kay said, "as anyone can plainly see."

"Don't you put yourself down," Sonny said while pointing his fork at her. "You're just as pretty as you were in high school. Besides, I like a womanly woman."

Sonny's eyes twinkled mischievously. Kay felt her face flush with both embarrassment and pleasure.

"My little brother was an idiot to let you get away," Sonny said.

"That was a hundred years ago," Kay said.

"If I hadn't had the stupid idea that it was wrong to go after my brother's girl, I would have snagged you for myself."

Kay remembered Sonny as a tall, athletic teenager who was loud and boisterous with his friends but awkward and shy around girls. He had always gone out of his way to be kind to her over the years, and she was always glad to see him. He was the kind of person you could call in the middle of a freezing winter night because your furnace had quit working and he would arrive within minutes, toolbox in hand, a good-natured-smile on his sleepy face.

"Things have a way of turning out like they ought to," Kay said.

"His wife's crazier than a bee-stung bobcat," he said. "You should see their house."

"I've heard there's a bit of a clutter issue."

"I don't know how he lives with her," he said. "She smokes like a fiend, she won't cook or clean, and she's trashed that house. She doesn't care about her daughter or her grandkids; can't be bothered to help my mother, even when my dad's so sick ..."

"But doesn't she help out at the store?"

"She runs the cash register two afternoons per week, with plenty of smoke breaks," he said. "But just between you and me and this breakfast here, she also helps herself to the cash."

"That's terrible! What does she say when you confront her about it?"

"I never have," he said. "I just quit giving her paychecks; I figure she takes what she thinks she's owed. I don't need another reason to fight with her."

"Can't you talk to Matt about it?"

"Matt and I were never what you'd call close to begin with," he said with a shrug. "Plus he thinks I'm going straight to hell for being divorced."

"I'm sorry to hear that."

Kay got up and retrieved second helpings of everything for Sonny.

"Do you ever hear from your ex-wife?"

"Karla only calls when she wants something," he said. "I gave her the house, the car, and everything we had in savings, but that boyfriend of hers is out of work, and he owes child support for the three kids from his second marriage. They're living in a big house on the golf course down by the Cheat River, which is the perfect place for those two if you ask me. They're both driving luxury cars and taking expensive vacations; meanwhile, I'm living over the store and driving a ten-year-old truck."

"I'm sorry you had to go through that," Kay said. "How're your girls handling it?"

"They're still not talking to her," he said. "I tell them 'She's your mother, you should treat her with respect no matter what fool thing she does,' but they can't get over it."

"It will get better with time."

"I don't know," he said. "I'm still pretty mad about it, and it's been three years."

"It doesn't sound like she's any happier," Kay said. "Maybe she'll come back."

"What's done is done," Sonny said, shaking his head. "She broke my heart, bled me dry, and sacrificed our family. You can't undo a thing like that. I may have to forgive her because God says I have to, but I will never forget what she did, and I will never give her the chance to do it again."

"Maybe you'll meet someone else," Kay said. "You're only what, fifty-four, fifty-five?"

"You keep on cooking like this, and I'll be back on your porch every morning like a stray dog."

"You're good company," Kay said. "Come over anytime."

"You shouldn't have fed me," he said. "I'm not kidding."

He smiled at her, and she felt a ripple of something run through her body; it had been a while, but Kay could still remember what it felt like to be attracted to someone who was flirting with her.

"Nice little place you got here," he said, as he looked around. "Built in the 30s probably, and solid as a rock, but with the original plumbing and electric. You got anything needs to be worked on?"

"Now that you mention it," Kay said, "my toilet's been running nonstop for over a month. I had Elbie come look at it, and he did something to it, said it needed a part, but I expect he's forgotten about it."

"I've fixed plenty of Elbie's handiwork over the years," Sonny said. "I'll look at it."

Kay washed the dishes while Sonny looked at the toilet. When he returned, he was shaking his head. He held up the paperclip and rubber band that had been holding things together.

"This evening I'll bring over the part you need," he said. "Please just call me next time you need something fixed. Elbie has good intentions, but he hasn't got a clue what he's doing."

"I appreciate it," Kay said. "I know how busy you are."

"I'd like to get up in your crawl space," he said.

"I beg your pardon," Kay said.

"I bet you don't have near enough insulation under the house, in the walls, or up in the attic."

"Probably not," Kay said. "I just haven't had the money to do all the work that's needed. Right now every extra penny I have is going to pay Sean Fitzpatrick for legal work, and he's giving me a huge discount."

"It seems to me you shouldn't have to pay to protect yourself when Machalvie and Rodefeffer are the ones who broke the law."

"They'd love to make me the scapegoat," she said. "Sean's just making sure they can't."

The former mayor of Rose Hill and the former bank president were being investigated for various schemes they were involved in, and as town administrator, Kay was being required to provide documents and information to federal agents.

"Sean's a good boy," Sonny said. "I wish my brother would quit trying to fool everybody and just be himself."

"I didn't know you knew about that," Kay said.

"I don't see what all the fuss is about. It's just two people loving each other, and isn't that what we're supposed to do? The rest of the family doesn't want to know; they're happy for Anthony to keep pretending so they won't be embarrassed."

"It's sad," Kay said. "I hate to see anybody throw away the chance to be loved and be happy."

"Who knows? Maybe they'll work it out," Sonny said. "Meanwhile, let's get your house ready for winter."

"But it's only July," Kay said.

"Which means we only have three months until the snow flies."

"I really can't afford it right now."

"I'll do a little at a time," Sonny said. "We'll work something out."

Before he left, Sonny mowed the lawn and fixed a loose shutter.

As she got ready for work, Kay found herself singing a song that was stuck in her head. She laughed as she realized it was "Handyman," by James Taylor. It felt good to have someone so competent concern himself about her house. His compliments toward her and her cooking had been sweet as well.

'He's one of the few eligible heterosexual men of a certain age left in this town,' she thought. 'It probably doesn't mean anything, but why not enjoy it?'

Kay stopped by the post office to pick up the mail for City Hall as well as her own. Diedre's sister, Sadie, was the postmistress. Even though she knew how much animosity Diedre felt toward Kay, she was still friendly. She asked about Kay's foster daughter, Grace.

"Grace and her friend, Tommy, went on vacation with my friend Jane and her son," Kay said. "I guess they're having such a good time they don't want it to end."

"That poor child deserves some happiness after the life she's had," Sadie said. "Jacob Branduff was a mean old coot."

"Jane has been wonderful to her," Kay said.

"Jane's still young and energetic," Sadie said. "She can keep up with them. Plus she understands all that social media stuff they do. Not like you and me. Give us a comfy chair and a good book, and we're happy."

Kay felt a pang at that. It so closely mirrored her insecure feelings about doing what was best for Grace. She worried that she was too old to be a good mother to her and that Grace would suffer because of it.

In addition to one addressed to Grace, there was an envelope addressed to Kay from a bank in Pittsburgh, where Grace's family trust account was held. Curious, she stood outside on the sidewalk in front of the post office and opened hers. It was a check made out to her for what was to Kay an enormous amount of money. On the attached stub was written, "Third quarter child care expenses."

Kay felt a little light-headed. She slid the check back in the envelope and tucked it down into her quilted tote. She would call them when she got to work. Surely this was a mistake.

But it was no mistake.

"That's the amount you'll be paid quarterly to cover all expenses related to Grace's care," the trust officer informed her. "You can use it for your mortgage payment, home improvements, a car, food, clothing, school supplies; anything that goes toward Grace's comfort and well-being. Just keep your receipts for your accountant, and we'll send you a 1099 after the first of the year."

"Can I pay her an allowance out of it?" Kay asked.

"Grace will have her own check every quarter," he said. "You should have received that, as well."

Altogether, the quarterly expense checks would add up to more than Kay made in a year. She'd have Grace for at least two more years until she graduated from high school. Kay thought of all the things she could do with the money during that time. All those little things that needed to be done to the house, the list of which at times seemed overwhelming compared to her meager salary.

She could get a new roof, have the foundation repaired, and replace her old, cantankerous appliances. She could turn up the heat in the winter and not worry about the utility bills. Heck, she could get a new, more energy-efficient furnace. She could buy a new car with all-wheel-drive, so, come winter, she wouldn't slide all over the place in her old clunker with the starter that was beginning to act up.

Everything could be taken care of with this money.

Ashamed of her selfish thoughts, Kay reminded herself that this was actually Grace's money, to be used to make her comfortable, healthy, and safe, but her initial feeling of excitement could not be quelled. It felt as if she'd won the lottery.

One problem was that she didn't want to deposit the check in the local bank; within the hour everyone in town would know about it. She would have to consult with Sean about what to do. As a mayoral candidate, she didn't want to be found to be hiding anything, yet she wanted to hide it!

It's amazing what having some newly found financial security could do for one's mood. Kay felt like a weight she hadn't known she was carrying had been lifted. Between the breakfast with Sonny and the check she'd received, Kay was feeling something she hadn't felt in a while – hopeful.

The Pine County prosecutor stopped by City Hall to gossip with Kay and shared some confidential information about Jared "Jumbo" Lawson, the boy who had vandalized her house.

"He's going to plead guilty to the lesser charge of vandalism," he said, "in exchange for us dropping the hate crime charges. He's more likely to get into college with what looks like a youthful indiscretion rather than a terrorist act."

"Will he receive any counseling?" Kay asked.

"Community service," he said.

"It's a pity," Kay said. "What the boy actually needs is some mental health assistance."

"It's been my experience that you can't counsel the bigotry out of a person," he said. "If someone feels justified in their actions, it's almost impossible to convince them they're wrong. Jumbo's not likely to change anytime soon, not in any meaningful way."

"He'll just get bigger," Kay said, "and more dangerous."

"He'll be in trouble again before too long," he said. "I spent some time in a room with him. He's about as dumb as he is angry."

"His poor mother," Kay said.

"Marigold's still determined to run for mayor, I hear," he said. "Should be a cakewalk for you."

"I feel sorry for her," Kay said.

"I've spent some time in a room with her as well," he said. "If you ask me, he's a chip off the old block."

Later on, Chief Lawrence Purcell, known as "Laurie," the man serving as temporary chief of police while the current chief was on a much-deserved vacation/honeymoon, stopped by her office and plopped into a chair in front of her desk. He was a tall, loose-limbed man with a care-worn face and sad blue eyes.

"Hello, Chief Purcell," she said. "To what do I owe the honor of this visit?"

"I'm bored, Kay," he said. "Nothing ever seems to happen in this town. Where are the drug dealers and blackmailers I was promised?"

"You caught us during a lull," Kay said. "The college students are off for the summer, and the tourists are staying up on top of the mountain, where it's cooler."

"I need something to do," he said. "Starsky and Hutch play on their phones all day when they aren't eating massive quantities of food, or sleeping. I feel like the father of two teenage boys."

Kay assumed he was referring to deputies Frank and Skip.

"They're nice boys," she said. "Don't be too hard on them."

"Don't you have any deep suspicions you'd like me to follow up on?" he asked. "Isn't there somebody you'd like me to haul in for questioning?"

"Someone did paint my house this morning," she said.

"That was probably an angel," Laurie said, "rewarding you for being so good."

"You've only got one week until you start your new job in Pendleton," Kay said. "Consider yourself lucky."

"I'm telling you I need some crime, Kay," he said. "I'm going soft. Those crafty crooks in Pendleton will eat me alive if I don't exercise my deductin' and detectin' skills."

"Be careful what you ask for."

"I'm also a little sick of pizza," he said. "PJ's is good, but not as a steady diet."

"There's a perfectly good diner at the end of the next block," she said. "Plus there's the Mountain Laurel Depot."

"I saw the diner menu; there were several words on it I didn't understand," he said. "What is chervil and why do I want it in my fingerling potato salad? Plus, the word 'fingerling' is unappetizing to me. Why doesn't anybody fry chicken anymore?"

"They serve fried chicken at the Depot."

"I ate their greasy spoon special my first day on the job," he said. "I paid for it all night."

"What do you want to eat?"

"Fried chicken," he said, "mashed potatoes with gravy, green beans, dinner rolls the size of a cat's head, and all-American apple pie."

"I think I can handle that," she said. "Why don't you come over for dinner tonight?"

"Excellent," he said. "I'm not the greatest company, but if you have a piano, I will gladly play for my supper."

"I don't have a piano," she said. "How about I invite some people to entertain you?"

"Shady people," he said. "Make sure they have a lot to hide."

"I'll do my best," Kay said.

When Kay went home for lunch, she found several large rolls of pink insulation on her front porch and a note from Sonny that read: "Be back for dinner."

Kay checked her kitchen cupboards and refrigerator in order to make a store list and then used the rest of her lunch hour to shop at Delvecchio's IGA.

As soon as Matt Delvecchio saw her, he came out of the back room to greet her.

Kay's heart fluttered, as it had for more than 30 years, whenever she saw Matt. He may have acquired several gray strands among his dark curls, some deep laugh lines on his face, thicker lenses in his glasses, and an extra chin, but to Kay, he was still her first love, and so far, the only man she'd ever felt that way about. She had dated a few other men over the years and had even gone so far as to get engaged to one of them, but ultimately she hadn't been able to go through with it. She told people she was just too set in her ways to accommodate a husband, but in her heart of hearts, she blamed Matt.

"Hey, gal," he said. "Whatcha lookin' for?"

"I'm cooking fried chicken for some friends," she said. "Do you have any pole beans?"

"I do," he said. "I've also got some beefsteak tomatoes and new potatoes that look good."

"I'll take them," she said.

"I'll get you a fresh chicken out of the walk-in," he said.

"Better get me two," Kay said. "I've invited some big eaters."

"I wish I could be there," Matt said. "There haven't been any home-cooked meals in my house for a long time."

Kay let that go, just like she did all his woebegone statements. It was his fault, after all. He could have had all his meals at her house every day, slept in her bed every night, and sat next to her in church every Sunday; but Diedre had shaken her tiny rear end, and he had thrown it all away.

To say she had been humiliated and heartbroken was an understatement. At the time, to her teenage heart, it had felt like attempted murder.

Today, Matt made sure she had the best of everything, and once she was in line at the front registers, he sighed.

"You take care," he said.

His big brown eyes bore a wistful expression.

"Thanks," was all Kay said.

It was embarrassing how he acted, and Kay hoped no one would say anything about it. As soon as it was her turn to check out, the clerk shook her head.

"He's like a big, sad puppy dog whenever you're in here," she said.

Kay felt her face redden, but she just smiled a tight-lipped smile in response.

"Biggest mistake that man ever made," the clerk said. "Have you heard about their house?"

Kay nodded but kept adding her groceries to the moving conveyer belt, hoping to get this over with as quickly as possible.

"I was up there last winter, making a delivery, and even though she wouldn't let me past the front door, I could tell what it was like in there. The front porch is covered with old lawnmower parts, bicycles; you name it, they've got it, rusting in the rain."

Kay didn't want to be unfriendly, but she also didn't want to talk about Diedre and Matt.

"How's your son?" Kay asked the woman and was rewarded with a long humblebrag about how the woman never saw him because he was so good at school and sports, and so popular with the girls.

"I'm voting for you," the clerk said as Kay prepared to leave. "We can't let Marigold take over or we'll, none of us, be good enough to live in Rose Hill."

Kay thanked her and left. If it wouldn't look so bad, and if she wasn't running for mayor, she'd do her grocery shopping in Pendleton.

Back at work, as Kay passed the conference room where the FBI team was working, she realized she was holding her breath and walking softly. Someone dropped something behind her, and the loud noise made her jump and scream.

"Sorry," the mailman said.

He had dropped a heavy package on the floor just inside the door.

A female FBI agent, the one named Terese, opened the door to the conference room and looked out, her hand on the gun she wore concealed under her suit jacket.

"Don't shoot," laughed the postman.

Terese frowned and then nodded at Kay.

"Good afternoon," Kay said, her heart still pounding from being startled.

Kay hoped that seeing her wouldn't remind Terese that they needed something else from her, wanted to ask more questions. Kay was so rattled by every interaction with them that she always made stupid mistakes in her own work during the rest of the day. She reassured herself, as she always did that she hadn't done anything wrong, but still, she worried.

The FBI was investigating the most recent mayor of Rose Hill, Stuart Machalvie, for various underhanded and illegal activities he and his cohort, ex-bank president Knox Rodefeffer, had cooked up over the past few years. Although

Kay had partial knowledge of several of the schemes they were involved in, she hadn't been involved in any of them nor done anything illegal. That hadn't stopped Stuart from trying to implicate her; or his wife, Peg, from slandering her in an effort to undermine her credibility and derail her mayoral campaign. The whole situation was like a dark cloud that followed her around, and she was looking forward to the day when it was gone.

Later that afternoon, City Council Member Ruthie Postlethwaite stopped by. She handed Kay a jar of her homemade strawberry preserves and helped herself to a cup of coffee from the service cart in the hallway. She settled herself in the chair by Kay's desk and took a sip of the coffee.

"Thank you for the preserves," Kay said. "I enjoyed the hot pepper jelly you made last month."

"The berries are from the IGA," Ruthie said, "so they're probably from Peru or Mexico. Hard to believe we can't grow perfectly good strawberries in this country."

"I'm sure they'll be delicious."

"I heard you went grocery shopping today."

"Such a small town, and with so many other more important things to talk about," Kay said.

"If it's any consolation, Matt Delvecchio is as miserable of a man as you're likely to meet."

"That all happened ages ago," Kay said. "It's ancient history."

"I remember it like it was yesterday," Ruthie said. "I was the one who held you while you cried in the girl's bathroom."

"I've always appreciated your friendship," Kay said. "We've been through a lot together."

"Shug and Doreen are living in Sarasota, next to a golf course," she said. 'That could've been you, you know."

Shug, short for Bert Sugarman, was the man Kay had been engaged to but had broken it off.

"Shug would not have been happy with me in the long run," Kay said. "He's better off with Doreen. She loves to golf and eat salads for every meal. All those vitamins and protein shakes that man lives on; I couldn't have stood it."

"But where's your security, Kay? Who's going to take care of you in your old age? I've got old Pudge and my kids, and who've you got?"

Kay knew that Ruthie didn't mean to be cruel; she just didn't have the sensitivity filter that most people are born with or develop over time. Ruthie loved Kay and was concerned about her, so blunt observations were how she communicated it.

"I'll be all right," Kay said.

"I'm sure Grace will appreciate you taking her in, but I doubt she'll take care of you in your old age. She's not your blood relative, after all, and she'll only be with you a couple of years before she's off to college. You won't be able to count on her long-term, you know."

"I'm glad to have her for as long as she needs me," Kay said. "She should go on and have her own life. I want her to do whatever makes her happy. There's no guarantee children will take care of their parents, anyway. You're just lucky."

"Have you heard from that last one, that rotten Tiffany?"

Tiffany was the previous foster child Kay had hosted.

"No, I haven't heard from her; nor am I likely to."

"She had the prettiest voice, just like an angel. She didn't turn out to be an angel, though, did she?"

"Addiction can happen to anyone," Kay said. "It breaks my heart when I think of the potential that child had. She was bright; she could have gone on to college."

"The apple didn't fall far from the tree, is all."

"That's not necessarily always true," Kay said. "She could still turn her life around with the right help."

"You did all you could for her, and how did she repay you? Stealing from you and running away."

"Let's talk about your new grandbaby," Kay said. "I know you have pictures and I'm dying to see how much she's grown."

Kay was thus able to distract Ruthie from depressing subjects and awkward walks down Memory Lane.

An hour later, as Ruthie packed up her photo albums and prepared to leave, it was all Kay could do not to sigh with relief. She loved Ruthie, but it wasn't always easy.

"Oh, one more thing," Ruthie said. "Have you seen Hannah's campaign posters?"

"I have," Kay said. "I think they're funny."

Animal Control Officer Hannah Campbell's City Council campaign poster featured a photo of herself dressed in a white choir robe, surrounded by a veritable ark-full of animals that had been digitally added to the photograph, holding her deceptively-cherubic-looking son, who had a tinsel halo affixed to his head. The caption was "Beloved by animals and children, trusted by all, vote for Hannah Campbell for Rose Hill City Council."

"She's not taking it seriously if you ask me," Ruthie said. "If she was, she'd be here campaigning instead of gallivanting off to Myrtle Beach to horn in on her cousin's honeymoon."

"Maggie and Scott invited the family for the last week of their month in Myrtle Beach," Kay said. "No one in that family has gone on a vacation for years. It's good for people to get away."

"I don't see why the town should have to pay for the chief of police to have a month off *and* pay for someone to cover for him," Ruthie said. "It just doesn't seem right to use taxpayer money that way."

"You missed the meeting where we voted on that," Kay said. "Scott's earned more than enough vacation days; he just never gets to take them. Laurie's being paid out of the contingency fund, which Stuart never used for anything legitimate; just whatever cockamamie scheme he was involved in at the time."

"Like the time he sold our only good snowplow to Pendleton, in the middle of the winter, and then didn't have enough money to replace it."

"So he could pay for a new, heated bandstand for the winter festival, so his wife wouldn't have cold feet in her high heels and fur coat."

"That man is a piece of work," Ruthie said. "Do you think he'll serve any time?"

"I'm sorry, but I can't talk about it."

"Oh, I know," Ruthie said. "Someday, when this is all over, you owe me a good, long chinwag. Just don't go forgetting all the details."

"We'll see," Kay said, who wished she could forget.

Kay had to put the leaves in her dining room table in order to accommodate her many guests. She covered the table with her best linen tablecloth, and set each place with her mother's Virginia Rose pattern china. The final touches were ivory tapers in pink Depression glass holders, and a green McCoy Pottery vase full of over-bloomed pink peonies she had purchased on sale from Erma at Sunshine Florist. She just hoped the petals would stay attached until dinner was over.

The *Rose Hill Sentinel* owner and editor, Ed Harrison, arrived first, carrying a bottle of wine. Kay rarely drank anything stronger than coffee and had to dig out some wine glasses in order to accommodate the gift.

Ed was tall with the lean frame of a runner, had bright blue eyes behind wire-frame glasses, and kept what hair he had left shaved close to his head.

"I appreciated the invitation," Ed said. "I haven't seen Claire much these past few weeks, since the wedding. We've both been too busy, I guess."

"The wedding was beautiful," Kay said. "Claire did an amazing job on such short notice."

"I'm just glad Maggie didn't leave Scott at the altar."

"There was no fear of that," Kay said. "Those two belong together. You and Claire looked good together, walking down the aisle afterward. I noticed you disappeared for a while."

"We're just friends," Ed said. "Maggie says she needs time to adjust to being back here, and I need to be patient."

"Easier said than done," Kay said. "I think it might be hard for Claire to adjust to small-town life after traveling all over the world. Rose Hill is as far from Hollywood life as you can get."

"She says she's ready to settle down, and her parents need her."

"How's Ian doing?"

"His dementia's getting worse. He's upset about Delia going to the beach for a week. He keeps telling people she's left him."

Ian and Delia were Claire's parents.

"Poor Delia, she needs the time away. How is Claire coping?"

"We're all pitching in," Ed said. "I take him to breakfast and then to the service station, where Patrick watches him all morning. Patrick then takes him to the Rose and Thorn for the afternoon, and Melissa takes him home for dinner. Claire gets off work at five and then watches him all evening."

"How's Claire's new job?"

"It's just temporary," he said. "She interviewed for an associate professor position in the drama department at Eldridge. They want her; they just need board approval in order to hire her."

"Meanwhile, I'm sure Sean appreciates her running his new office while he gets on his feet."

"I'm not sure how suited Claire is to a desk job," he said. "I think she'll be happier at Eldridge."

"As will you be, too, I'm sure."

"I'm nervous about it," Ed said. "It's one thing to edit a small town newspaper, and quite another thing to teach journalism to college kids."

"You'll be a great teacher," Kay said. "How's Melissa coping with the bakery while Bonnie's at the beach?"

"She's doing great," Ed said. "I think Bonnie might resent how well she's doing without her. She's added some things to the menu that Bonnie would never allow."

"I'll have to go down there," Kay said. "I'd love to support her, and I never pass up the opportunity to try a new treat."

"Anything I can do to help with dinner?" he asked

"You're my guest," Kay said. "I wouldn't hear of it."

Laurie arrived with another bottle of wine, and the two men settled into Kay's deep armchairs in the small living room. Kay tended to dinner as she enjoyed hearing them get to know each other. It felt so good to have people in the house; why didn't she do this more often?

Sonny arrived bearing an apple pie from Fitzpatrick's bakery.

"It's apple streusel," he said.

"Sounds delicious," Kay said.

"It was the prettiest," he said, and then more quietly, "just like you."

Kay felt herself blush.

"I saw my big pink present out on the front porch," she said.

"I came over this afternoon and had a peek under the house," he said. "There's a drainage issue I need to address right away. After that, I'll work on your roof and gutters, and then get up in the attic and insulate. After everything above it is ship-shape, I'll winterize the crawl space."

"Just between you and me, I may be able to pay you for your work after all," Kay said. "I found out today that Grace's trust is going to pay me for taking care of her."

"So they should," he said. "It won't be expensive; you can pay for the supplies, and I'll do the labor for free."

"I should pay for your labor," Kay said.

"It's easy for me," he said. "Plus your house is so small, there's not a lot of square footage to work on."

"I appreciate it," Kay said. "I'm ashamed at how I've let things go."

"Don't give it another thought," Sonny said. "This is what I'm good at. You've got a whole town to run."

Claire arrived, and Kay was immediately struck by her facial expression when she saw Laurie and Ed together in the living room. She didn't seem glad to see Ed but seemed downright dismayed to see Laurie. She immediately covered this up with a bright smile, but Kay had seen how she felt and wondered.

"Hello everybody," Claire said. "Sorry I'm late; I put the rolls in but forgot to turn on the oven, so I had to start over. Melissa's staying with Dad tonight, but she's also taking care of everyone's pets while they're at the beach, so I had to take him back to the Thorn to wait until she's done."

Claire was a tall, striking woman with a fair complexion, blue eyes, and long dark hair. She was dressed, as usual, in form-fitting, fashionable clothing, and high heels, her hair perfectly done and makeup expertly applied. To Kay, she looked like someone more fittingly attired for attendance at a fashion show in New York, rather than a quaint, home-cooked supper in the tiny town of Rose Hill.

Claire brought the tray full of rolls to the kitchen and Kay put them in a basket lined with a white tea towel. Sonny had pulled the ottoman out and was seated upon it, talking to Ed and Laurie. Kay watched with interest as Claire peeked in at them and then chewed her lip.

"I didn't know Laurie was going to be here," she whispered to Kay.

"Don't you like him?" Kay asked.

"It's not that," Claire said. "I was just surprised, is all."

It was obviously more than that, but Kay let it go.

Dottie and Georgia arrived. Dottie was the head librarian at the Rose Hill Library, and Georgia was a retired schoolteacher. Kay considered them her closest friends.

As soon as Kay relieved them of their covered dishes, she and Claire hugged them both.

"I haven't seen you two since I was in high school," Claire said.

"We're old ladies now," Georgia said. "I'm surprised you recognized us."

"Speak for yourself," Dottie said.

Georgia's dark hair was now shot with gray and white, Dottie's fingers were knobby with arthritis, and there were many more lines on both of their faces, but since Kay had seen the changes come along gradually, it was hard for her to picture them any differently. Georgia was dressed for the summer in capris, a pink breast cancer fundraiser T-shirt, athletic shoes and white socks, and Dottie wore a chambray jumper over a white T-shirt with sandals.

You rarely saw one without the other, taking a morning or evening walk, shopping for groceries, attending church, or sitting together on the porch of Dottie's house on Lilac Avenue. Active members of the Interdenominational Women's Society and avid gardeners, they also made weekend deliveries for the Sacred Heart Food Bank, even though they were Methodists.

31

In the way that close friends and family members have, they often finished each other's sentences and enjoyed an almost psychic communication method made up of cryptic comments and facial expressions. Kay watched them now, as both noted the presence of Ed and Claire, and an amused expression flitted between them like a badminton birdie being popped back and forth.

"I have a bone to pick with you, Claire," Georgia said. "You've been back for months; why haven't you been to see us?"

"I've been busy, but that's no excuse," Claire said.

"Working for movie stars and traveling the world," Dottie said. "You probably have a lot of juicy stories you could tell."

Claire didn't look as if she wanted to revisit her past anytime soon.

"Let's eat," Kay said.

At the table, Kay directed everyone to join hands and bow their heads.

"Bless us, Father, and bless this food," Kay said. "We thank you for good friends old and new, for the food that nourishes our bodies, and the love that nourishes our souls. Amen."

"Short and sweet," Sonny said. "Just like I like it."

"My father used to say a funny grace," Claire said. "Praise the Lord and Holy Ghost; who eats the fastest gets the most."

"We sing our grace," Georgia said, and then she and Dottie treated everyone to a harmonized rendition of it.

"Oh, the Lord is good to me,
And so I thank the Lord,
For giving me the things I need,
The sun, the rain, and the apple seed.
The Lord is good to me.
Hallelujah, Amen."

"That was beautiful," Kay said.

"This looks delicious," Sonny said, as he passed the big platter of fried chicken.

"All diets are off," Georgia said. "I hereby declare all assembled to be in a state of grace where no calories will adhere to our hips."

"Here, here," Dottie said. "So mote it be."

"Was your father a Freemason?" Laurie asked Dottie.

"He was," Dottie said. "Here in Rose Hill."

"Mine, too," Laurie said. "I believe the lodge in Familysburg was in amity with Rose Hill; so they probably knew each other."

"What are you talking about?" Claire asked.

"It's a secret," Laurie said. "If we told you, we'd have to kill you."

Claire rolled her eyes and turned to talk to Georgia while Dottie and Laurie discussed people they had in common.

"What are you doing, nowadays?" Georgia asked her.

"Looking for a job," Claire said. "I applied for an associate professor position in the theater arts department at Eldridge, but I haven't heard back yet."

"I wouldn't hold my breath if I were you," Georgia said. "They tend to hire alumni for professorial positions and keep the townies in lowly staff positions."

"I'm well qualified for the job," Claire said. "I went to a professional theater arts school and have hair and makeup experience in theater and film."

"But who are your parents and where did you get that degree?" Georgia asked. "That's all they care about over there."

"I've been hired," Ed said. "My father wasn't rich, and I grew up below Rose Hill Avenue."

"But you graduated from The Annenberg School of Communication at the University of Pennsylvania," Georgia said. "That makes a huge difference."

"And you're a man," Dottie said. "Don't look at me like that; I didn't invent sexual discrimination, I just testify to its pernicious infestation, like knotweed. And look what they're getting in the bargain: the *Sentinel* and your cheap labor."

"I think Claire will get the job," Ed said.

"From your mouth to the college president's ear," Georgia said, but she didn't look optimistic.

"What are you working on?" Kay asked Georgia. "You're always busy researching something or other."

"Addiction," Georgia said.

"A timely subject," Ed said. "There's an epidemic of opiate addiction in Pine County right now. There were more fatal overdoses from heroin this year than all together in the last ten."

"It's cheaper than OxyContin and easier to get," Laurie said.

"There's been a surge in the number of break-ins and robberies as well," Ed said.

"And more meth labs and crack houses," Laurie said.

"What do you do with your research?" Claire asked.

"I learn from it," Georgia said, "and then I bore other people with it."

"It was neurological medical research last year," Dottie said. "I know more about Oliver Sacks than his own mother."

"I'd be interested to hear what you've learned," Ed said. "I, myself, am completely addicted to the Internet. It's scary to me how fast news is disseminated, especially when it's inaccurate and inflammatory."

"There are several schools of thought," Georgia said. "You won't be surprised to learn they each relate to the physical, mental, and spiritual state of a person."

"I thought it was established that addiction is an illness," Kay said.

"But is it a mental or physical illness?" Georgia asked.

"Could it be both?" Kay asked.

"Possibly," Georgia said.

"Tell them about the discarnates," Dottie said. "It's amazing to me what people come up with."

"Later," Georgia said. "Some researchers believe addiction begins as a reaction to a mental state, but quickly becomes physical through an adaptation of brain chemistry. Conversely, there's also research indicating that individuals can be born with addiction-prone brain chemistry, and the mental processes then adapt to that."

"Which came first, the junkie chicken or its egg?" Ed asked.

"Is light a wave or a particle?" Laurie asked. "I believe the answer to that question turned out to be 'whatever gets the job done.' "

"Exactly," Georgia said. "Put simply, addiction is the insatiable craving for something that temporarily fulfills a need, whether that's for pleasure, escape, or relief from physical, mental, or psychic pain. When under the influence of the addictive substance or behavior, the addict finds relief from feeling, perceiving, or remembering the addiction stimulus. Ultimately, however, the addictive experience does not nourish the mind, body, or soul in any meaningful, lasting way."

"Can anything?" Laurie asked.

"Good question," Georgia said, and then nodded at him with a compassionate look on her face.

"What about spiritual nourishment?" Kay asked.

"That's another addictive substance, if you ask me," Laurie asked. "The story is we're watched over by some omnificent being, but where's this cosmic Santa Claus when we need him? Plenty of horrible things happen to innocent people, and plenty of evil hoodlums live long, wealthy lives. Hard to believe it can be real."

"Is anything real?" Georgia said. "How would we even know?"

"That's too existential for me," Kay said.

"It's a question of faith," Sonny said. "It seems to me you gotta believe in something or what's the point?"

"How do you keep believing in God's infinite love when bad things happen?" Dottie asked. "That's when faith is tested."

"We're supposed to accept that there are some things we just can't understand," Sonny said. "Only God knows the reason."

"Further along we'll know all about it," Georgia sang, and then Dottie joined in,

"Further along we'll understand why.
Cheer up my brother, live in the sunshine;
We'll understand it, oh by and by."

"You two could take your show on the road," Sonny said. "You're good."

"So basically people get addicted because something hurts, or is missing inside," Ed said.

"Or outside," Laurie said.

"Or just perceived to be missing," Dottie said.

"Anything that causes pain," Georgia said. "Physical, mental, or existential."

"If you think you've got a reason to be depressed, you will be, whether it's true or not," Ed said.

"It can be anything," Georgia said. "Or it can be everything; a tipping point is reached, and pain, sadness, anger, guilt, or shame overwhelm the mind."

"Isn't guilt the same thing as shame?" Claire asked.

"Guilt is about things you've done or failed to do," Georgia said. "Shame is about who you are."

36

"Pain, sadness, anger, guilt, and shame," Laurie said. "The Royal Flush of addiction."

"Some folks'll do anything to escape their feelings," Dottie said.

"Even if it's only a temporary distraction," Claire said. "Like shopping."

"Or web surfing," Ed said as he raised his hand.

"Or television," Sonny said, raising his.

"Or eating," Kay said, raising her fork.

"Or gossip," Dottie said and pointed to herself.

"Or research," Georgia said.

"Or adrenaline rushes," Laurie said. "I mean, I've heard that can happen."

"So how can any of it be treated?" Ed said. "It seems like drug addiction is almost impossible to beat."

"It's tough," Georgia said. "Especially when complicated by socio-economic conditions that are less than favorable."

"The what are what?" Claire asked.

"When you're poor, sweetie," Kay said. "Everything's harder when you're poor."

"This is a depressing subject," Dottie said. "Tell them about the discarnates and then let's talk about something else."

"Discarnates," Claire said.

"There is an esoteric line of thought, that I do not agree with, by the way," Georgia said. "But it is interesting. Some folks believe that the world is full of discarnate entities ..."

"Ghosts," Dottie said.

"Spirits," Georgia said. "These entities are supposedly all around us, some mischievous, some helpful, some benign ..."

"Because they don't know they're dead," Dottie said.

"Or they don't want to move on, to, well, wherever," Georgia said. "The belief is that if a living person is weak or incapacitated in some way, one of these spirits can attach itself to that person and influence their behavior so that the entity can experience something it enjoyed while incarnate."

"Hungry ghosts," Laurie said. "That's a Buddhist concept, isn't it?"

"Very good, Laurie," Georgia said. "You are correct."

"Sounds like demonic possession," Sonny said.

"But the word 'demonic' connotes evil," Georgia said. "We're just talking about random lost spirits who used to be human and miss having sex or getting drunk."

"I think that's just a way to avoid taking responsibility," Ed said. "Anyone can say the devil made me do it, or discarnates made me do it, or my disease made me do it. It's just denying that the addiction is your responsibility, that you have some accountability."

"Ultimately, addiction is not a moral issue," Georgia said and was rewarded with a chorus of disagreement. "Now, hear me out. The fallout from addiction often has negative consequences, but the physical, mental, or spiritual need to experience something in order to relieve suffering is just a human imperative."

"In other words, we are all addicted to something," Dottie said. "So we should all have compassion."

"Love can be an addiction," Claire said

She seemed surprised to find she had spoken her thoughts aloud and blushed.

"It can indeed," Georgia said and patted Claire's hand.

"My mother told me this years ago," Dottie said.

"Oh no, here we go," Georgia said.

"Shush," Dottie said. "Love is caring plus competence."

"You can't stop her once she gets started," Georgia said.

"Leave me alone," Dottie said. "You've been talking since we sat down."

"Go on," Claire said. "I want to hear this."

"Any two blockheads can have romantic or sexual attraction," Dottie said. "The real deal is caring for someone over the long haul, after the sexy stuff is, not gone, exactly, but let's just say it's not as strong as it used to be. That's when putting someone else's needs ahead of your own is more important than a dozen roses."

"That comes with maturity," Kay said.

"Or when you have children," Sonny said.

"That's the caring part," Dottie said. "Competence is having the wisdom to care in a healthy way. That means treating your loved ones with respect and requiring you be treated with respect. It means you accept human flaws but don't enable destructive behavior. It means you don't spoil your kids; you teach them how to care with competence. It also means not giving in to the demands of your loved one to the point where you're sacrificing your own well-being."

"I wish they'd teach that in school," Georgia said. "It's more important than arithmetic, as far as I'm concerned."

"What about the husbands and wives of self-destructive people?" Sonny asked. "How can they be caring and competent and stay married?"

"Sometimes you can't," Dottie said. "You shouldn't stay in a marriage to the point it causes harm to yourself or your children. Sometimes the most competent, caring thing you can do is remove yourself from a situation that is no longer healthy, that you can tell is not going to get any better."

"Tell that to the Pope," Sonny said.

"My discarnate wants more mashed potatoes," Laurie said. "Will you pass them, please?"

"New topic!" Georgia said. "Kay, what's going on with your campaign?"

CHAPTER 3

Dinner was a success as far as her guests' appreciation of the food went, and Dottie and Georgia did their part to entertain everyone. Now Dottie was telling stories about her grandkids.

"So then little Jessie says, 'That was too much tater and not enough tot, Mamaw,'" Dottie said. "Can you believe that little punkin'? He's only five."

After Georgia told a story about an elderly couple she knew who were taking ballroom dancing lessons, Laurie said to Claire, "You're quite an accomplished dancer, yourself, aren't you, Claire?"

Claire blushed, and then said, "I don't know why you would think that," before abruptly changing the subject.

Laurie smiled in amusement and Kay noted that Ed didn't seem to notice the exchange.

After they discussed the phenomena of having songs stuck in their heads, Laurie brought up the subject of favorite songs, said his was "Claire de Lune" by Debussy, and asked each person at the table to name their favorite. When he got to Claire, she said, "I don't have a favorite."

Laurie turned to Ed.

"Surely you know Claire's favorite song, Ed."

"Nope," Ed said. "I'm sorry to say I don't."

"If I were you, I'd make it a point to find out what it is, and then dance with her while it plays," Laurie said. "That's what I'd do, anyway, if she were my sweetheart."

"Oh, for heaven's sake," Claire said. "What a silly thing to say. Kay, let's eat that delicious looking pie you've got in the kitchen. You sit still. I'll go get it."

"I'll help you," Laurie said and jumped up to follow her into the kitchen.

41

There was no doubt in Kay's mind that there was something going on between Laurie and Claire. She could also plainly see that poor Ed hadn't a clue.

Kay made a point of asking Claire to stay behind when everyone began to make noises about leaving. After everyone else had gone, Claire carried dishes to the kitchen while Kay filled the sink with hot sudsy water and put on some rubber gloves.

"Everything was so good," Claire said. "I feel like I've gained five pounds."

"You could use it," Kay said. "You're looking a little peaked. Are you still having bouts of nausea and dizziness?"

"Yes, but I'm not pregnant," Claire said. "I've peed on about ten dozen of those test sticks, and they all say the same thing: I'm getting old, so it must be menopause."

"Forty is not old."

"I'm still thirty-nine for another two weeks, thank you very much."

"Did you go to the doctor?"

"I saw Doc Machalvie, who thinks it's probably just stress, but he wants me to go to a specialist in Morgantown," Claire said. "Before you say anything, I promise that as soon as my mother gets back, I will."

"Have you heard from them?"

"They're having a blast, apparently," Claire said. "Hannah said even Aunt Bonnie was having a good time, and cooking every meal. She doesn't see why they should waste good money going out to eat when there are grocery stores full of anything you could possibly want."

"How're the men holding up?"

"Scott and Sean are taking Hannah's dad and Maggie's dad fishing on the pier every day, so they're as happy as clams. My mom, Aunt Bonnie, Maggie, and Hannah are all taking turns keeping an eye on little Sammy, and you know that's a full-time job. He likes to fling himself into the deep end of the pool and run right into the ocean.

That child has no fear of water except at bath time. Scott's going to teach him to swim before they come home."

"What about Hannah's mother?"

"Aunt Alice relaxes on the beach all morning, naps in her bedroom all afternoon, and then reclines in a lawn chair on the veranda all evening. She has to take her 'nerve pills,' of course, and they make her sleepy."

"Do you think there's anything actually wrong with Alice?"

"She's had every medical test there is, and no one can find anything physically wrong with her. When we were growing up, she was always dumping her kids on Aunt Bonnie or my mom. It's like she can't cope with real life."

"She's always been an introverted kind of person; hard to get to know."

"She's my aunt, and I love her, but she's a difficult person to be around."

"I was surprised Maggie and Scott invited everyone down there. Everything all right?"

"Maggie said they've had a great time; they were just getting homesick. Hannah invited herself down, and before you knew it, they were renting a van and taking everybody."

"Well, not you, Patrick, or Melissa."

"Somebody's got to run the family businesses, take care of all the pets, and I have to look after Dad. Mom needed a vacation more than anyone."

"As long as I'm stirring up trouble," Kay said. "What's going on between you and Laurie?"

Claire's face flushed and had the guiltiest look.

"Oh my," Kay said. "You better tell me about it, so I don't invite you both to dinner again."

"It's so stupid," Claire said. "Stupid of me, that is. You know after Maggie and Scott's wedding I got caught up in that awful FBI thing with Knox and Anne Marie."

"You must have been scared to death," Kay said. "I'm not sure if the federal agents are making things better or worse."

"After Sean and I got back from the State Park, everyone had already left the party at the Rose and Thorn. We missed the whole thing. I was too wound up to go home, and Patrick was worn out, so I offered to bartend for him until closing. There were just a few locals left, you know, Pudge and his pals, and someone I didn't know was sitting down at the end of the bar. Patrick said if anyone gave me any trouble I should ask him for help, that he was a good guy."

"Laurie?"

"Uh huh."

"What happened?"

"Nothing much. He teased me about the mud on my shirt and my scraped knees, and tried to guess what I did for a living by reading my palm."

"He flirted with you," Kay said. "No harm in that."

"We talked a while, and then we danced a little."

"Which is what he was alluding to at dinner."

"It was my favorite song, you see," Claire said. "Chris Isaac's 'Wicked Game.' Do you know it?"

"I do," Kay said. "Kind of dark but terribly romantic."

"We danced, he walked me home, we looked at the moon; it was that big moon we had in June, the whatsit?"

"Supermoon."

"That's the one," Claire said. "He kissed my hand and then later sent me a text with a link to "Claire De Lune," by Debussy."

"Which he also worked into the conversation tonight."

"He's torturing me."

"He's got a crush on you," Kay said. "But he knows you're dating Ed so he won't take it any further."

"Except on the walk home that night I may have shared a few doubts I have on that subject."

"You have doubts about Ed?"

"I have a personality disorder," Claire said. "I have one perfectly lovely almost-boyfriend who is a stand-up, dependable man, and yet I would risk that for a recently divorced widower cop with a drinking problem."

"You must have heard gossip about that."

"Please," Claire said. "I grew up with a cop for a father in a family that owns a bar. I know all the signs. Plus, he as much as told me."

"His first wife was a lovely woman."

"So he said."

"He was devastated when she died."

"So much so that he dove into a bottle and came back up with wife number two."

"Daphne," Kay said. "She's way too young for him, and cheated on him with his best friend, who also worked for him."

"So he quit rather than fire the guy."

"He was honest with me when I interviewed him for the temp job," Kay said. "He assured me he had his drinking under control."

"Maybe he does," Claire said. "I've been avoiding him since that night. He didn't tell me he was a policeman or that he was subbing for Scott. He said he was starting a new job in a month, working for the city of Pendleton."

"Which wasn't a lie."

"You're defending him."

"I hired him," Kay said, "and that was all true."

"If he had said what he did for a living, I would not have continued to flirt with him."

"What concerns me most are these reservations you have about Ed."

"Ed is still married to Eve."

"Legally, maybe, but they haven't lived together for over a decade," Kay said. "Everybody knows that."

"I didn't know until right before Maggie's wedding."

"Doesn't Eve live in Atlanta?"

"She works for a 24-hour news channel now, so she's headed this way to cover the FBI investigation. Ed says Congressman Green and Senator Bayard are involved, so it's a national news story."

"I've never met her," Kay said. "I hear she's very pretty."

"I hate her already," Claire said. "The bottom line is Ed's not an option until he's legally divorced and I know she's out of his life for good."

"But what about Laurie?"

"I've given myself a thorough talking-to on that subject, every day for three weeks. I just have to take myself firmly by the hand and lead myself away from danger. I can do it if I keep focused and stay away from him. In only one more week he'll be gone."

"Pendleton's not that far away."

"He won't have any reason to come back here, and I've made it clear that I have no interest in getting involved with him."

"He's infatuated," Kay said. "It almost doesn't matter what you say when someone feels that way."

"Any two blockheads," Claire said. "Isn't that what Dottie said?"

"He's a good man," Kay said. "He and his first wife had one of those caring, competent marriages."

"Speaking of good men," Claire said. "I saw Sonny giving you the adoring looks over dinner. That man is sweet on you."

"Nonsense," Kay said. "He's just being kind to an old family friend."

"He's single and ready to mingle," Claire said.

"Hush," Kay said. "He's just a good friend."

"He'd be perfect for you," Claire said. "He's a big ole handyman who can see to things around here, and I don't just mean the house."

"Stop it," Kay said. "It probably doesn't mean anything."

But secretly, Kay hoped it did.

Earlier, Claire had been unhappy to find Laurie had followed her into the kitchen to get dessert.

"What are you doing?" she asked him.

"I'm attempting to talk to you alone, which is the last thing you want if the past few weeks are any indication. It's enough to make a man feel unwanted. It's lowering my already rock-bottom self-esteem."

"There's nothing to say," Claire said. "You're leaving in a week and whatever happened between us is not going to be repeated."

"You think it was just a transient lunar phenomenon," he said. "I think it was the beginning of something beautiful."

"I'm not interested," she said.

"Liar," he said.

"You remind me of Pepe le Pew," Claire said. "It was funny when I was little, but that was before I knew about sexual harassment."

"Mon chéri," he said with a French accent. "Let us flee to Capri."

He took a step closer, effectively trapping her against the sink.

"Stop it, Laurie," she said and pushed him away.

"Flirt," he said.

Later on, as she was walking home from Kay's house, Claire ran into Professor Alan Richmond, the drama department chair who was ostensibly helping her get hired to teach theater and film hair and makeup at Eldridge College.

"Good even, my dainty primrose," he said. "I am looking much forward to the pub quiz this evening."

"Did you assemble a team?"

"I have," he said. "And what jovial, nimble-pinioned lads they be. I think you'll like them and I know they'll like you."

"Have you heard anything about the position?"

"Nary a whisper," he said. "But remember, the wheels of academia move slowly, and little is accomplished quickly."

"See you tonight," she said.

"Good night, good night! Parting is such sweet sorrow that I shall say good night till it be pub quiz hour."

Claire left her father in Melissa's capable hands and arrived at the Rose and Thorn fifteen minutes early for game night. Her cousin Patrick, a big, blue-eyed, dark-haired charmer, was bartending. He was also flirting with a slender young woman with a pixie haircut who wore a peasant blouse and heavy, black-framed glasses. Among other visible tattoos on her body, she had a large owl on her chest, and multiple piercings in her ears, nose, and eyebrows.

The young woman looked Claire up and down in a not-too-friendly way but then thawed a little as soon as Patrick introduced Claire as his cousin.

"Arwyn Abramowicz," the woman said as she stuck out her hand.

Claire shook her tiny hand, and as she did so, noticed multiple scars on the young woman's wrist and arms. Arwyn saw her notice.

"I'm a professional chef," she said. "Those are my war wounds."

Claire thought the burn scars were probably related to the woman's profession, but the profusion of small cuts might symbolize something much more disturbing. She had once been acquainted with a young actress who cut herself in order to deal with the post-traumatic stress disorder she had acquired from submitting to so many demeaning casting couch experiences. Before filming each day, it had taken the better part of an hour to cover up her cuts, just like those on Arwyn's arms, and had required thick, waterproof makeup. This same actress had used Adderall to stay thin, cocaine to stay awake, and Trazodone to sleep.

"Arwyn owns the Pine Mountain Diner," Patrick said and opened his eyes wide at Claire behind Arwyn's back.

Claire knew he was begging her not to mention how much he hated everything on their menu.

"That's great," said Claire. "I've eaten there several times, but I've never seen you. You must stay busy in the kitchen."

Arwyn raised an eyebrow at Claire as if what she'd just said was too idiotic and obvious to require a response, and then abruptly turned around to resume flirting with Patrick.

'Okay,' Claire said to herself. 'There were two bitch indicators in under one minute; I think we're done here.'

Claire turned as Professor Richmond came in with what looked very much like two more Eldridge professors. They did not wear pocket protectors, nor were their pants too short, but they emitted that indefinable something that instantly told Claire they were not from Rose Hill.

"May I present Torbjörn Vilhelmsdotter-Holjer," Dr. Richmond said. "Doctor of Philosophy."

"Please call me Torby," the man said, with a shy smile, as he shook Claire's hand.

He looked like a blond, Scandinavian giant, and his accent confirmed it.

"I am from Sweden," he said.

"And this is Professor Ulrich Von Nedermyer," Dr. Richmond said. "He teaches physics."

"Please call me Ned," he said, as he shook Claire's hand.

Ned was short, with a balding head and a full beard. He was wearing dark socks with his sandals, and his German accent was pronounced.

"Are you from Germany?" Clair asked.

"My mother is from West Switzerland and my father from the North, so I speak French with a German accent," Ned said. "It is confusing for me as well."

Claire introduced the trio to Patrick, and then Arwyn, who scanned them, seemed to decide they weren't worthy of her notice, and abruptly turned her attention to her phone instead of making conversation.

"We're here to play," Professor Richmond said. "Such is a game we play, and so we test our strength. Shakespeare."

"Time is a game played beautifully by children," Torby said. "Heraclitus."

"The distinction between the past, present, and future is only a stubbornly persistent illusion," Ned said. "Einstein."

"You never know what day could pick you, baby, out of the air, out of nowhere," said Arwyn, without looking up from her phone. "Sun Kil Moon."

There was a pause while everyone digested that.

"Oh," said Arwyn, looking up. "I thought anyone could play. Guess not."

"Have a seat," Claire said to the Eldridge professors. "We'll get started as soon as everyone's here."

"You need to choose your team name," Patrick said. "What can I get you to drink?"

The professors placed their drink orders and got settled in a booth just as Laurie and veterinarian Drew Rosen came in.

Drew looked more like a tourist, dressed as he was in hiking clothes. He had longish brown hair and the burnished look of someone who spent a lot of time in the sun. Arwyn perked up when she saw him and immediately transferred her focus from Patrick to Drew.

Patrick introduced them to Arwyn, who merely glanced at Laurie before commandeering Drew and steering him toward a booth.

"You're obviously not from here," she said to him as they walked away. "What's your story?"

Laurie stood a little too close to Claire, and she stepped away.

"Don't worry," he said. "I'll behave."

"I didn't know you were playing," Claire said.

"I left Gonzo and Fozzie in charge at the station," Laurie said, "in case there are any jaywalking incidents to be investigated."

"They're trained deputies," Claire said.

"Children shouldn't be allowed to carry guns," Laurie said.

"Maybe you'll have a seasoned crew in Pendleton," she said.

"They couldn't be any worse," he said.

Drew beckoned him over, so Laurie went to join the others.

"I guess my team isn't coming," Claire said.

"They'll be here," Patrick said. "I talked to Sam earlier, and you know Ed never misses a game. What in the hell else does he have to do?"

Claire served everyone their drinks and then sat at the bar next to Pudge.

"I guess you heard Matt Delvecchio's wife's gone missin'," Pudge said.

He spoke low as if he didn't want anyone else to hear.

"No, I hadn't heard that," Claire said. "What happened?"

"Left the house this morning before the sun came up and never came back."

"That's odd," Claire said. "I thought she was afraid to leave the house."

"Oh, she'll go out if it suits her," he said. "She never misses a flea market or a tag sale. She only takes a fit of being a-feared if it's somewhere she don't wanna go, like her only daughter's wedding, or to see her grandchildren. That woman's selfish, cold, and turned funny, and that's a fact."

"Maybe she'll come back," Claire said. "It hasn't been twenty-four hours, yet so the police can't get involved."

"Kay was the last person to see her alive," Pudge said and raised his eyebrows as if that was alarming news. "Saw Diedre driving down Peony Street, 'round five-thirty this morning."

"So she saw her drive by," Claire said. "That doesn't mean anything."

"What people are asking is what was Kay Templeton doing outside that early in the morning?" Pudge said.

"Surely no one thinks Kay had anything to do with Diedre's disappearance."

"Kay's been carrying a torch for Matt Delvecchio since high school," Pudge said. "It's kind of interesting that she'd be the last person to see his wife alive."

"Diedre may not be dead," Claire said. "She may have just run off somewhere."

Pudge shook his head.

"Diedre Delvecchio's an odd duck, that's for sure," he said. "But she is not the type to run off. She just wouldn't. Mark my word: that woman is dead."

"Matt must be frantic," Claire said.

"Oh, I don't know," Pudge said. "He might be kind of relieved. You ever see the inside of that house?"

"No," Claire said. "But I've heard."

"They had a plumbing problem a couple years back, and Matt called me rather than his own brother; there's some bad blood there, on account of Sonny's divorce. I tell you that house would give a pack rat claustrophobia. I've never seen anything like it. Stuff piled up to the ceiling, with just enough space to walk through each room. It's just like on one of those shows."

"Well, Kay had nothing to do with her disappearance," Claire said. "You know that, right?"

Pudge shrugged.

"All I know is what I hear," he said. "And I hear Sonny was there, too, which makes it all the more interesting."

"Why is that?"

"Everyone knows Sonny's got a grudge against Diedre," Pudge said. "Diedre helped Karla hide her affair for months before she left Sonny. They pretended to go places together when Karla was meeting her boyfriend."

"Doesn't Diedre work for Sonny?"

"That she does," Pudge said. "Now ain't that interesting?"

"I assume all these people are your friends?" Claire asked.

"Why, sure," Pudge said. "I grew up with the Delvecchio boys."

"Then I'd hate to hear how you talk about your enemies," Claire said.

"I'm just a-telling you all this so you can warn Kay," Pudge said. "My wife tried to talk to her this evening, but she won't listen."

"Warn her about what?"

"That rich harpy she's a-runnin' against has started spreading the lies far and wide," he said. "She as much as accused Kay of murder."

Sam and Ed walked in together, and Claire took a pitcher of beer and three glasses to their table. Sam, an Iraqi war vet turned technology genius with recurring PTSD issues, had the usual inscrutable expression on his face, but Ed looked worried.

"I've been calling you all evening," Ed said.

"My phone ringer must be off," Claire said.

That wasn't true; she'd just been ignoring his calls.

"There's something I need to discuss with you," he said.

"Excuse me," Sam said and went up to the bar.

"Go ahead," Claire said.

"I'm sorry I ran off right after dinner," Ed said. "Something came up."

"No problem," Claire said. "I wanted to talk to Kay."

"Eve's in town," he said. "You remember me saying she's doing a story on the federal investigation."

"I do remember," Claire said. "I also remember you saying you were going to have Sean draw up your divorce papers so she could sign them when she got here."

"Something's happened," Ed said. "There's no easy way to tell you this …"

The door opened and Eve walked in. She was pretty and petite, with expertly streaked blonde hair, outfitted in a fashionable ensemble perfectly proportioned to her figure, except for the pronounced baby bump she was sporting out in front.

"No need to," Claire said.

Eve lit up at the sight of Ed, who jumped up to pull a chair out for her. She made a show of kissing his cheek and then wiping away the lipstick in a very familiar manner. She barely glanced at Claire, but waved at Patrick and smiled as if they were the best of friends.

"Good to see you," she called out to Patrick. "We need to catch up later."

"Eve, you remember Claire," Ed said.

Claire did not offer to shake hands, and neither did Eve.

"Nope, sorry," Eve said. "It's been a long time since I was in Rose Hill."

She said the name of the town in the same way one might say, "Alcatraz."

"Congratulations," Claire said.

Eve reached out and squeezed Ed's hand.

"We're so excited," she said.

"It's such a surprise, Claire said. "I didn't know you two were back together."

"Back in March," Ed said, "when I took Tommy to see his mother in Florida, we had a layover in Atlanta."

"I can see that," Claire said.

Sam came back to the table, sat down, saw where Eve's hand was, and his eyebrows went up.

"I need your team names," Patrick called out.

"Team Tardis," Professor Richmond said.

"Cop, Doc, and Pole," Laurie said.

"What about you guys?" Patrick called out to Claire.

No one spoke. Eve was looking at Ed, Ed was looking at Claire, and Claire was looking at Sam.

"Team Awkward," Claire finally responded.

Sam, who was taking a sip of beer, choked on it, and Claire patted his back.

Team Cop, Doc, and Pole won, Team Tardis got loudly drunk, and Team Awkward lived up to its name. Now, after the game, Laurie was playing the old upright piano while leading the professors in singing a Monty Python song about lumberjacks. Arwyn and Drew were acting cozy in a corner, and Patrick was collecting his cut of the bet money from the locals.

Ed and Eve had departed as soon as the game was over. Claire, who had succeeded in not looking at either one of them since Eve put her hand over Ed's, could feel herself relax as soon as they were gone.

"Surprising turn of events," Sam said.

"Not for me," Claire said. "I'm used to men promising one thing and doing another."

"You've had a little too much to drink," Sam said. "Come on and let me walk you home."

"Piss off, you," Claire said. "I don't need some man to take care of me."

"Be careful, Claire," Sam said, put a twenty on the table, and left.

Laurie immediately slid into the vacant chair to the left of Claire. Claire looked around to find Professor Richmond had taken his place at the piano and was playing what sounded like a Cole Porter tune.

"You're either the most open-minded person I've ever met," Laurie said, "or your definition of an exclusive relationship needs to be revised."

"There is no relationship between Ed and me," Claire said, "if there ever was."

"Can I buy you a drink?" Laurie asked.

"You can buy me many drinks," Claire said. "You can buy me all the drinks."

Laurie went to the bar and returned with a tray bearing six shots of whiskey and a fresh pitcher of beer.

"On the house, your bar-keeping cousin says."

"He's a man among men," Claire said. "Despicable, horny men who can't keep it in their pants, but I love him, nonetheless."

"Bottoms up," Laurie said.

Although Claire tipped up a shot glass and swallowed the fiery liquid, she noticed Laurie did not.

"On the wagon?" she asked.

"I'm working the early shift tomorrow," he said.

After three shots, Claire was ready to unburden herself and told him everything that had happened since she quit her job working for movie star Sloan Merryweather and moved back to Rose Hill. The whole time, Laurie tended to her shot glasses and kept the pitcher filled.

"So this thing with Ed's wife happened before you came back to stay."

"He's Tommy's guardian," Claire said. "Melissa was in prison down in Florida ..."

"For kidnapping him as an infant from his drug-addicted mother and assuming her identity," Laurie said. "Patrick filled me in."

"Yes," Claire said. "She served three years of a ten-year sentence, and Ed took Tommy down there to see her one weekend every month."

"So you immediately suspect that Eve was already pregnant and just needed to hook up with Ed to make it seem like it might be his."

"Yes!" she said. "They hadn't been together for ten years. Why now, all of a sudden?"

"I admit it does get my spidey senses tingling."

"It's just like him to take whatever she says at face value," she said. "He's so ..."

"Stupid? Thick-headed? Slow-witted? Moronic?"

"Shut up," she said. "He's too trusting, is all. He thinks the best of people. It's a good quality; it just gets him in situations like this."

"Name another situation he's been in that's like this."

"He got involved with Melissa, who's always been in love with Patrick. She wanted to get married and have a father for her kid, and Patrick was in love with someone else, so she seduced Ed."

"I've met Melissa," he said. "I can see the appeal."

"But she's all wrong for Ed, and didn't love him."

"I have to speak up for the rest of my brethren to say Ed is not the first man to be blinded by lust, nor will he be the last."

"He knew it was not going to work out but did it anyway because it was what she wanted."

"Poor old Ed, at the mercy of the wicked womanly wiles of your underhanded gender."

"He's kind of naïve."

"I think you've got it all wrong," Laurie said. "Ed's not stupid, he's just human. It's you who always thinks the worst of everyone."

"I do not," she said.

"Ah, but you do," he said. "I've done nothing to deserve the continual mistreatment you dish out, and yet, you cannot stop lambasting me with your bitter misgivings."

"Because you're an alcoholic in denial," she said. "Being in a relationship with an addict is like watching a slow-motion suicide."

"Dammit, woman," Laurie said. "I demand that you be married to me for at least two years before you speak to me like that."

"It's true," she said. "Don't deny it. It's like your self-destruct button is stuck in the on position."

"What you need are more drinks," Laurie said. "You'll like me much better in a little while; just wait and see."

They continued talking, and Claire continued drinking. When Patrick called time at 1:30, Claire was feeling more than a little fuzzy-headed. Parts of her were actually numb; not the lusty, romantic parts, but for sure the thinking clearly parts.

"Why was I mad at you again?" she asked Laurie.

"You aren't mad at me," he said. "You're mad at yourself for liking me so much but being so mean to me."

"That sounds true," she said. "I do like you and I can be mean."

"I knew it was just a matter of a few more shots," he said. "Now we're friends again."

Patrick picked up their glasses and wiped the table.

"Time to go, folks," he said. "Unless you're helping me mop."

"Nope, not tonight," Claire said.

She attempted to stand, but the room whirled.

"Whoa, there, young lady," Laurie said. "I think you need to get home to bed."

"If you wait around I'll walk you home," Patrick said to Claire.

"I'll take her," Laurie said.

"All right," Patrick said. "You know she's my cousin, right?"

"And her pop's a cop," Laurie said. "Don't worry; I'll see that she comes to no harm."

"I don't want to go home," Claire said to Laurie.

"Fine with me," Laurie said.

When Claire awoke, through one squinted eye she could detect that she was not in her own bed, and upon opening the other eye, which had a hard time coordinating with the first, she ascertained she was not in her parents' house. Upon further investigation, she found she was not wearing her own clothes, nor, as it turned out, anyone else's.

She attempted to turn her head, which felt as if someone inside it was using a sledgehammer to try to escape. Very carefully, she turned over and found Laurie sleeping next to her.

"Oh, crap," she croaked.

The digital alarm clock on his bedside table displayed 7:15 a.m.

"Oh, no," she said

She slithered out of bed and landed on the floor with a thump.

She used the edge of the night table to get to her feet. Steadying herself against the wall, she wobbled over to the bedroom door, took a flannel robe off the hook, and put it on.

"Good morning," Laurie said.

Claire felt the contents of her stomach rise but thankfully made it to the bathroom before everything exited the way it had come in.

Seated on the cool tile floor with the commode lid as a headrest, Claire frantically searched her memory for a timeline of the previous evening's events.

It was no use.

Even thinking hurt.

"Here," Laurie said.

He was wearing sweatpants and nothing else.

He handed her a glass of water and what looked like two aspirin. He then sat on the edge of the tub and regarded her with affection.

"I called Melissa," he said. "She stayed with your Dad last night, and took him to work at the bakery this morning."

"He'll be worried," she said. "He doesn't like any change in his routine."

"She said he's fine," he said. "Ed picked him up at the bakery and took him to breakfast. No harm done."

"I wouldn't say that."

"No point in regretting anything," he said, "when there's nothing to regret."

"I was naked in your bed," she said.

"You threw up all over your clothes," he said. "I washed them; they're in the dryer."

"They're dry clean only," she said. "You may as well have set them on fire."

"Sorry," he said. "I didn't think of that."

"You didn't have any pajamas you could lend me?"

"I did offer," he said. "You refused."

"You could have slept on the couch," she said.

"I wanted to be nearby in case you got sick again," he said. "Anything happens to you, I'd have three burly Irishmen busting my kneecaps with their shillalies."

"That's offensive," she said. "For sure there were no shenanigans?"

"If I've learned anything over the past two years, it's not to have intimate relations with pretty drunken ladies, no matter how ardently they insist."

"I insisted?"

"Avidly," he said. "I was as surprised as I was flattered."

"Sorry."

"In all honesty, the smell of whiskey and beer vomit is not the aphrodisiac it's claimed to be."

"Kill me now," she said.

"I'd rather draw you a nice hot bath and scrub your back," he said. "Alas, I will be late for work if I don't shower and get out of here in the next twenty minutes."

"Do you mind if I stay here?" she said. "I don't think everything's out yet."

"Be my guest," he said and stood up.

He hooked his thumbs in the elastic waist of his sweatpants.

"Don't peek," he said. "I know how you beauticians are."

Claire lay her head back down on her arms and closed her eyes. After Laurie had showered, shaved, and vacated the bathroom, Claire dragged herself into the shower and hoped the hot water could somehow rinse away the events of the previous evening.

Once out of the shower, Claire got dressed in the same bathrobe, because her clothes were now shrunken rags, and not in the cool Bohemian sense. She was sitting at the kitchen table, drinking black coffee, and toying with a dry piece of toast, when she heard her phone ringing. She followed the noise to where she'd dropped her purse, in the foyer. It was Ed. She let it go to voicemail.

She called Melissa at the bakery.

"You ornery catbird," Melissa said. "I don't blame you; that was one awful thing Ed done to you, and that Laurie's a sweetie."

"Who all knows?"

"Everybody who was still in the bar knows you left with him," Melissa said, "but only me and Patrick know you didn't come home last night. I swore him to secrecy, and he can keep a secret if'n I make him."

"I'm so sorry I didn't call," Claire said. "Laurie said he talked to you."

"Don't worry 'bout it none," Melissa said. "You been due a night to cut loose so I was glad to help out. Me and your dad played checkers and watched big time wrasslin'. Why don't you let me stay with him every night this week so you can enjoy yourself?"

"I appreciate that Melissa, thank you. Right now I'm hoping you'll do me another favor," Claire said. "My clothes and shoes from last night are ruined; could you bring me something to wear?"

"Where are you?"

"Laurie's staying at Scott's house while Scott and Maggie are on their honeymoon."

"I'll put yer clothes in a garbage bag and leave 'em on the back porch," Melissa said. "That way maybe the neighbors won't see."

"Thank you," Claire said. "I owe you so big."

"No biggie," Melissa said. "Just tell me, what's Ed's excuse for knockin' up his ex-wife?"

Claire told Melissa what she knew.

"I don't know anything else about it," Claire said. "I hadn't come back to Rose Hill yet, so it's not like he was cheating on me. It was probably just one of those things that happen. Sex with an ex."

"It might not even be his," Melissa said.

"That's what I think."

"I hardly know the woman," Melissa said, "but Patrick said she hit on him real hard way back when she first moved here with Ed. He said he weren't the only one, neither. I kinda doubt she's been going without all these years. Ed may not be that baby's daddy, but it might be better for her to say he is."

"If the real father's married, or her boss."

"She's a fancy news reporter now; thinks she's famous 'cause she's on the TV," Melissa said. "It would probably be better if the baby's daddy was the man she was married to instead of whatever gray cat she done hooked up with."

Melissa dropped off a most interesting ensemble that Claire would not have put together, but she could hardly complain. After she got dressed, Claire put her previous night's clothes in the same bag and stuffed them in the garbage can on her way out the back door, where she immediately ran into Pudge's wife, Ruthie Postlethwaite. Ruthie was walking their little dog up the alley, almost as if she had been doing so repeatedly in order to catch Claire leaving the house.

"Good morning," Ruthie said with a smirk. "Late night last night?"

"Yep," Claire said, as she felt her face flush. "I guess Pudge told you."

"He said you really tied one on," Ruthie said. "I guess I can't blame you after finding out about Ed's wife that way."

"Oh, I knew he was married," Claire said. "Ed and I were only ever just friends."

"Kind of like you and Chief Purcell are friends?"

"No matter what it looks like, we're just friends," Claire said. "I had a little too much to drink last night, and Chief Purcell looked after me, that's all."

"He's married, too, I guess you know."

"Nope, he's divorced now," Claire said.

"Well, that's a sight better," Ruthie said. "Although it doesn't look too good, you sneaking out the back door like that."

"Then I'll just have to count on you not to spread gossip about me," Claire said. "On account of there's nothing going on."

Ruthie lifted an eyebrow but did not affirm that intention.

"I guess you heard all about Diedre disappearing," she said instead. "The police are involved now."

"I did," Claire said. "Is Marigold telling people Kay had something to do with it?"

"She's not coming right out and saying it," Ruthie said. "She's just implying it; you know how folks like that are."

"I certainly do," Claire said, waved good-bye, and headed off in the other direction.

Claire went home to change clothes, and before she left again, she chugged a tall glass of water, took another couple aspirin, and put a sleeve of soda crackers in her purse for later.

In front of Sean's new family law office, up on Rose Hill Avenue next to the bookstore, Claire's ex-husband, Pip Deacon, was sitting on the sidewalk, smoking a joint. He wore white painter overalls, work boots, and nothing else. With his long golden dreadlocks and tanned, muscular arms, he looked and smelled the part of the beach bum pothead he had always aspired to be.

"You're late," he said. "I'm charging Sean from the time I show up here."

"You're not fooling anyone," Claire said as she unlocked the door. "No one palms a tobacco cigarette and smokes it like that."

Pip just shrugged and followed her inside.

Claire turned on the computer, checked Sean's emails, and then checked the voicemail. There were no new emails or messages, so her work was now done. There was nothing left to do but babysit the quiet office. She sighed, and then made some coffee. Meanwhile, Pip got to work, and she was relieved that he didn't try to chat her up while he did so.

About an hour later, Ed came in.

"Mr. Harrison," she said. "How may I help you?"

Ed sat down in the chair next to her desk.

"Are you busy?" he asked.

"Terribly," she said, as she shuffled some papers.

"I just wanted to apologize for you finding out about Eve the way you did," he said. "I was as surprised as you were, just earlier in the day. I did try to reach you."

"So you hooked up in Atlanta this past March, and she's just now letting you know she's pregnant," Claire said. "Any reason why she waited so long to tell you?"

"She didn't want to deal with it," he said. "It was an accident; she thought the contraceptive she was on would prevent that. I guess nothing's one hundred percent."

"And it's for sure yours?"

"She said it was, based on the timing," Ed said, "and I believe her. She didn't realize she was pregnant until she was too far along to do anything about it. She's never wanted children, so it's been traumatic for her."

"Poor lamb."

"I am sorry," Ed said. "She's asked me to stand by her, and I said I would. I couldn't do anything less."

"Of course not," Claire said. "I wish you both well."

"We're not getting back together," Ed said. "We're going to see this pregnancy through, and then after an appropriate amount of time passes, we'll get divorced."

"Appropriate in what context?"

"Eve's getting more high profile assignments now that her career's heating up," Ed said. "She can't afford a scandal right now. She doesn't want it to be made into a tabloid thing, but she's made enemies at every tabloid. I know it seems shallow and self-serving, but she's worked so hard to build her career, and something like this, if spun the wrong way, could destroy everything."

"It may be better family values for the minivan demographic if she says it's her husband's child, but is it the truth?"

"I'm choosing to believe her."

"And what about the kid? What about afterward?"

"We haven't discussed that yet."

"Hadn't you better?"

"I just found out yesterday, Claire. Today she's working. I'm sure we'll iron out all the details as we have time to do so."

Claire's head still hurt, and she was the grouchiest she'd felt in a long time.

"All right," she said. "Consider me informed."

"The timing could not be worse as far as you and I are concerned."

"We're just friends," Claire said. "Besides, you're married to her."

"I heard you got a little drunk last night."

"Ix-nay on the ossip-gay," Claire said. "If we are to remain friends, we must agree never to speak of last night."

"Fair enough," Ed said. "I guess you heard about Diedre Delvecchio."

"I heard Marigold's virtually accused Kay of murder."

"She better be careful," Ed said. "That could backfire on her."

"Do you know anything about hoarding?"

"No," Ed said. "I've never been in their house, but I hear it's bad."

After Ed left, Claire sent an email to a makeup artist who worked for one of the morning news shows in New York. Claire had helped her get started in the business, so the woman owed her a favor. What Claire wanted was information, and she was pretty sure this woman could get it for her.

After that, she did some Internet research on hoarding. She also remembered what Pudge Postlethwaite had said about Diedre going to yard sales and flea markets. She made some notes in case she ran into Laurie later. Not that she planned to. But he might stop by. He would probably come around later and tease her about the previous night. It would be embarrassing, and she'd have to put a stop to it.

But he didn't.

At lunchtime, Claire walked up to the city building and glanced oh so casually into the police station as she passed it, but she didn't see Laurie. Kay was in her office, but Laurie was not visiting.

"Morning, Sunshine," Kay said.

Claire got Kay caught up on the events of the previous evening.

"My Lord," Kay said. "Your life is like a soap opera."

"I know, right?"

"What are you going to do about Laurie?"

"Not a blessed thing," Claire said. "I need to stop worrying about romance and start focusing on my life."

"But you are attracted to him."

"Laurie's a mess right now. He would just be the next in my long line of terrible romantic mistakes. Remember, I am very firmly taking myself by the hand and walking away from the man."

"Only when sober, apparently."

"I want my life to be able to pass the Bechdel test."

"What's that?"

"There's this really talented cartoonist named Alison Bechdel. One of the characters in her comic strip says she only goes to see films where two female characters talk to each other about something other than some man. That's the Bechdel test," Claire said. "I want there to be more important things in my life than worrying about romance."

"Relationships are important," Kay said. "It would be a sad, lonely world if no one cared about romance."

"What about work? What about doing something meaningful for other people? I've led a selfish, self-indulgent life up to now, and I'm ashamed of myself. There has to be something more worthwhile I could spend my time doing."

"If you're serious, I can probably find you something meaningful to do," Kay said. "Just remember it's not healthy to make work your only reason for living. You're liable to end up a lonely old lady."

"I do get lonely, and I do miss the affection, certainly the sex, but dammit, I'm tired of worrying about it all the time. It's mentally and emotionally exhausting, and I'm tired of being disappointed."

"I blame Pip," Kay said. "He soured you on relationships, I think."

"That was my fault for trying to turn a bad dating accident into a marriage. If it hadn't been me, it would have been the next random teenage girl with low self-esteem and poor decision-making skills. Pip just needs to be with somebody, anybody. He's a master at acting helpless, which is just the good-looking version of bone-idle-lazy. Women love to rescue Pip, and he can be very obliging when he wants to be."

"Haven't you ever dated someone you thought could be the one?"

"I fell for a struggling actor once, and then proceeded to fall for every line he fed me. It was spellbinding the way that panty-dropper could manipulate me; all he had to do was smile, and I'd reach for my credit card. He was a master of the big romantic gestures. I finally had to physically remove myself from his zip code because he was such heroin to my romance addiction."

"Good for you for rescuing yourself."

"Oh no, out of the frying pan into the fire, that's my motto. Next, there was this Indy film director I called 'the pale poet.' His emotional development was arrested in high school. Being a director finally gave him power over the cheerleaders."

"What about the Scottish actor? What was his name?'

"Carlysle was a drama teacher; Maggie says that one's my fault for ignoring the accuracy of his position description. He was funny and clever and had the sexiest accent. He laughed me right into bed. Turns out, he was more ambitious than in love; come to think of it, they all were."

"Which is the opposite of Pip."

"You're right; I never thought of it that way."

"Ed's a good person in a bad situation."

"Ed doesn't even know me, and I think when he finally does he won't be so interested. Plus, he has his hands full now with Eve and the baby. They have history, and she's vulnerable right now in an attractive way. He's trying to save her, I think."

"You think it's his?"

"I don't know," Claire said. "But I do know some people that work in her world who will find out."

"What if you found out it wasn't?" Kay asked. "Would you tell him?"

"No," said Claire. "I'd find some way to make her tell him."

"Be careful," Kay said.

"Hey," Claire said. "There's some scurrilous gossip going around about you concerning Diedre's disappearance."

"Ruthie called me last night," Kay said. "There's nothing I can do about it."

"We could find her," Claire said. "Or find out what happened to her."

"How?"

"Pudge said Diedre liked to shop yard sales and flea markets. Let's look at what ones were advertised yesterday. Then we can ask those people if she was there. Maybe we can find out where she went and who saw her last."

"I've got this week's papers here in the recycling," Kay said. "But I can't go around asking about Diedre. Think of how that would look."

"But I can," Claire said.

CHAPTER 4

Claire was walking back down Rose Hill Avenue and had just crossed Peony Street when she smelled a familiar Pip-like smell. A van with a Colorado license plate was parked out in front of the Rose and Thorn. The back end was covered in bumper stickers urging the legalization of marijuana and memorializing Bob Marley. There were also multiple, blue marijuana-leaf-shaped stickers with the words "Smoked Grass" on them. The windows of the van were partially down, and smoke was rolling out as thick as if the interior were on fire.

Laurie was standing outside the Thorn, leaning back against the brick façade next to the entryway.

"Who are they?" she asked, gesturing toward the van.

"Tonight's entertainment, I gather," he said. "According to your cousin Patrick, they are a bluegrass ska fusion band."

"Lemme guess," she said. "Smoked Grass."

"Uh huh," he said.

"Are you going to arrest them?"

"I haven't decided," Laurie said. "On the one hand they aren't actually harming anyone but themselves, they aren't driving under the influence, they aren't selling it, and they are technically partaking inside their own private property."

"But ..."

"It's still illegal in this state," Laurie said. "If they were knocking back beers, I could arrest them for having open containers, but I probably wouldn't as long as they didn't then attempt to drive. It's not for me to decide what's legal because the law is clear, but the real question is why do I even care?"

71

"My father often said it's not always black and white."

"I've been in charge here for three weeks, and so far I haven't arrested anyone," Laurie said. "I've only got a few more days to go. The real questions are: do I want to inconvenience these young people, deprive the Thorn of its musical entertainment, and then do paperwork all afternoon?"

"What can I do to help?"

"You could politely point out the proximity of law enforcement, and encourage them to extinguish their potent potables."

Claire walked around to the driver's side of the van and greeted the dread-locked occupant. He smiled a stoned grin as he lowered the window the rest of the way down. His eyes were red and glassy. Before he even spoke he offered her a hit off the water pipe he was holding.

"No thanks," Claire said, and then coughed.

"What's shaking, Mamacita?"

"I just wanted to warn you that there's a policeman nearby," she said. "You might want to stop smoking that right here on the main drag."

Mr. Dreadlocks reached over to the dashboard and then handed Claire a card that proclaimed he was legally prescribed medical marijuana.

"You all have these?" she asked.

He nodded, waggled his eyebrows, and then winked.

"Carry on, then," she said. "Godspeed."

The occupants of the van all giggled like schoolboys as she walked back around to where Laurie was standing. She reported her discovery.

Laurie shook his head.

"I had more respect for them before I knew that," he said. "Now I want to hassle them just for being so crafty."

"You're a strange man," Claire said.

"I'm also a gentleman," he said. "But then, you already knew that."

"I know you are," she said, "and a gracious host."

"It will be our secret," Laurie said. "Just two ships that got drunk, took off their clothes, and passed out in the night. Well, technically your ship was the one that got drunk, naked, and then passed out. I was more like the lonely lighthouse of frustration."

"It's complicated," she said.

"Not at all; it's quite simple," he said. "Soon I'll be off to woo the beautiful daughters of the former police chiefs of Pendleton. I only hope they are half as charming and entertaining as you are."

"See, when you talk like that I begin to question my resolve."

"Have dinner with me this evening. We will soberly explore ways to remove the remaining barriers to the fulfillment of your deepest desires."

"I'm kinda sorta committed to an evening of watching television with my dad," she said. "I feel bad about abandoning him last night."

"How can I argue with that?"

"Thanks for the offer."

"It stands," he said. "Keep that in mind if anything changes."

"I will."

"It's not that far to Pendleton."

"I know."

"Ah, fair Claire, just when I thought it was impossible to break such small pieces as remained of my heart," he said.

"Bye, Laurie," she said.

"I am taking myself firmly by the hand," she quietly said to herself as she walked away. "I am walking away from trouble."

"There's a full moon this week," he called after her. "I'll be thinking of you."

As Claire walked past the tea room, a movement inside caught her eye. She looked in but didn't see anyone, and the "Closed" sign was still on the door. She decided it must have been a reflection in the window from a car driving past.

Back at Sean's office, Pip was not waiting to be let in. Claire wondered if he had skipped out on this job, as he had so many others.

When the phone rang, Claire answered it, "Fitzpatrick Family Law office."

"Fancy," her cousin Hannah said. "I'll be sure and tell Sean you showed up for work."

"Hey, how's the beach?"

"Wonderful," Hannah said. "I'd be happy to stay here and never come back."

"Your husband might not like that."

"It might do him good to miss us a little," Hannah said. "Right now he's probably basking in the lack of Sammy-related chaos."

"What about your campaign for City Council?"

"That's a lock," Hannah said. "I'm kind of a superhero in Rose Hill, you know; the Masked Muttcatcher, fighting the forces of evil and rescuing kittens from telephone poles."

"Your posters are funny."

"My computer genius husband helped me do that," she said. "He thinks it's hilarious that I might actually be elected to help govern our bug-sized burg."

"You've got my vote," Claire said. "How's everybody?"

"The old men are fishing, the old ladies are shopping at the outlet mall, and Sammy's out here on the beach with me, feeding popcorn to seagulls," she said. "Maggie, that lily-white, freckled freak, is lubed up in SPF ten thousand, hiding out with a book on the condo balcony."

"Sounds good to me."

"We heard Diedre disappeared. What's up with that?"

Claire told her all she knew.

"You need to get on that," Hannah said. "Find out where she went and who she talked to."

"I was thinking about it."

"Listen, you amateur, me and Maggie would've cracked this case by now. Get up off your ass and investigate ... what? No, Sammy, that was not swearing; your Aunt Claire is riding a donkey ... I don't know its name; Claire, what's your donkey's name? She says its name is Baron Von Stinkle .... Yes, you can ride it when we get home, but only if you take a bath first. Lord, save me from my son, the swearing police. Listen, Claire. Go see Diedre's sister at the post office. They hate each other, but I bet Sadie knows something. She hears everything down there."

"Yes, ma'am, I'll get right on it," Claire said. "You can't see it, but I'm saluting."

"As you should," Hannah said. "Get a picture of that crazy nut and show it to people, ask questions, be nosy. Geez, do I have to tell you how to be a Fitzpatrick?"

"I'm on it," Claire said. "Tell Maggie I won't let you guys down."

From the Pendleton paper website, Claire printed the photo of Diedre that Ed had submitted along with the article about her disappearance. Along with that, she took the directions and the list of yard sales from that day's newspaper and set off to investigate Diedre's disappearance.

Claire first stopped at the post office, where Diedre's sister, Sadie, worked.

"I was so sorry to hear about Diedre," Claire said. "You must be worried sick."

"My sister and I are not close," Sadie said. "She couldn't be bothered to help out when my husband got home from having open heart surgery, and I still had to work full-time. I had to hire nurses to come sit with him while she sat on her bony ass in that filthy house of hers."

"I'm so sorry," Claire said. "Do you have any idea where she might have gone?"

"Not a clue," Sadie said. "She only leaves home long enough to work at the hardware store a couple afternoons a week, or to hit every yard sale in the tri-state area."

"Well, I hope she comes home soon so everyone can breathe easy."

"She's my sister, I mean, I don't want anything bad to happen to her," Sadie said. "I just can't afford to take time off from work to look for her."

Claire went to the flea market site out near the highway, found it closed, and then visited the three home addresses mentioned in the classifieds. No one recognized the photo until she came to the last address, out on Hollyhock Ridge. A large rental moving van was parked outside, and a harried-looking man and woman were loading their belongings into it. The woman gave Claire a list of what she had sold to Diedre and described her station wagon.

"Her car was packed so full she had to put the treadle sewing machine on top. My husband helped her put it on the roof rack," she said. "She would have needed someone to help her unload it."

Claire drove back down Hollyhock Ridge, wondering what could have happened to Diedre between there and Rose Hill. Could she have missed a curve and gone over the hill at some point? Claire paid attention but didn't notice any guardrails missing or broken. After she got back to town and dropped the car off at home, she called Laurie and left a voicemail with what she'd found out, along with the woman's name and phone number.

Back at Sean's office, she could see Pip waiting outside.

"You need to give me a key," he said.

"Not gonna happen," she said.

Claire sat back down at her desk in Sean's office and looked longingly through the window to outside, where the sun was shining in a cloudless blue sky.

She considered looking at clothes online but reminded herself she was supposed to be conserving money and not spending it, at least until she had a new job. She went to one of her favorite celebrity gossip sites, where she was immediately assaulted with a photo of her ex-employer frolicking on a beach in an exotic locale, along with Claire's ex-boyfriend, Carlysle. Claire quickly clicked off the site and exited the Internet.

Her head still ached, not only from the death-grip of her lingering hangover but from hearing Pip bang away with a hammer in Sean's office, where he was installing built-in bookcases.

Her phone trilled that she had a text message, and it was from her make-up artist friend. It was just as Claire suspected; Eve was rumored to have had an affair with a married senator. The pregnancy wasn't mentioned, but Eve had probably been able to hide it up until recently.

There was no doubt in Claire's mind that Eve needed Ed to be the father in order to cover up that affair. Eve must have known about the pregnancy before she arranged to meet with Ed in Atlanta. Claire didn't know anything about being pregnant, but she knew quite a bit about actresses faking pregnancies. Eve looked further along than four months. Too bad her mother was in Myrtle Beach; Claire would like to have the former nurse and mother look at Eve and give her opinion about how far along she actually was.

Now, how to get Eve to confess this to Ed?

She needed some serious think time.

Claire went to the front door and used a piece of scrap wood to wedge it open. Fresh air whirled through the open doorway and stirred the papers on the desk. Claire breathed in deeply and made an executive decision.

Ten minutes later she was sitting right outside the office at a small table she had carried out there, with Sean's cordless office phone and an iced coffee from Little Bear Books. She gathered her hair up into a messy knot and shed the cardigan she wore over her sleeveless top, the better to feel the delicious breeze on her bare arms and neck. She closed her eyes behind her sunglasses, in preparation to have a good, long think.

A little while later, she heard a noise, and when she opened her eyes, Ed was standing there.

"Working hard?" he asked her.

Claire showed him the stack of Sean's business cards on the table, weighted down with a rock. She offered him one, which he declined.

"Public relations, huh?"

"Mm-hmm," she replied.

"It looks more like basking in the sunshine," he said. "Mind if I join you?"

Claire gestured with her hand to show that he was welcome. Ed went inside, carried out a chair, and sat down across from her.

The banging in the back of the office stopped, and then the whine of a circular saw could be heard.

"That Pip?" he asked.

"The one and only," she replied.

"I was so caught up in my own drama this morning I forgot to ask, how are you?"

"At loose ends," she said. "I haven't been offered the Eldridge job, and this is only temporary until Sean comes back from the beach and hires someone permanent."

"Melissa took secretarial training in prison," he said. "She'd probably appreciate the opportunity."

"We talked about that," Claire said. "We all love Melissa but here's the thing: he's concerned about her grammar, which is atrocious, and he's not sure how his clients would feel about her being an ex-con. She could work on the grammar, but the federal record is not going to go away."

"Valid concerns," Ed said. "I wish it wasn't that way, but here we are."

"Let me tell you what I did all day yesterday," she said. "I had Cameron Crowe's website open on one browser tab, where I could read his interviews with seventies rock stars, and I had a video website open on another tab, so I could watch performances of the music they talked about in the interviews."

"Sounds like fun," Ed said.

"And it was," she said, "but that's all I did all day long. I need to be working. I need a project, a challenge."

"You're like a bird dog that needs to hunt," Ed said.

"I'm not sure I like that comparison," Claire said.

"See, some dogs are bred to be active and hunt, and other dogs are bred to be companion animals and are more laid back. If you try to make a hunting dog be a house dog, he'll go nuts, tear up the furniture, and chew the table legs. It frustrates him. If you try to make housedog hunt, it scares the hell out of him, and the first time he hears a gunshot he'll run off, and you'll never see him again."

"You're not making it any better by elaborating," Claire said. "Don't you have any analogies where I'm a beautiful caged songbird or a brilliant, crime-solving cat?"

"Why don't you write a book?" Ed said. "People seem to love tell-all books about celebrities."

"Not gonna happen," Claire said.

"I thought your confidentiality contract disappeared," he said.

"I've thought about it," she said. "There's a literary agent who still calls to make offers. I like celebrity gossip as much as the next person, but it's like eating junk food; I don't always feel so good afterward. I could write a book so salacious it would ruin careers and get a hit put out on me, but what would I have accomplished? I don't want to look back on my life and have to face that kind of book as the biggest contribution I made to the world."

"Well said."

"I don't know that teaching rich kids how to apply theater makeup is going to be all that worthwhile, but at least I'd be teaching someone how to do something constructive instead of destructive."

"I hope it works out."

"When do you start?"

"August first," he said. "I'm a little nervous."

"Oh, you'll do fine," Claire said. "You're a born teacher, and you love journalism."

"A dying art," he said. "I may as well teach them how to make the paper and ink."

Pip came out, greeted Ed, and then lit up a joint.

"You can't do that out here," Claire said.

"All right, Mom," Pip said.

He licked his fingers, pinched out the end he had just lit, and tucked it back into the chest pocket of his overalls.

"I'll see you later," Ed said and left.

Claire watched him go. A sitting duck, that man, too naïve for his own good. She hadn't come up with a plan yet, but she wasn't through thinking.

Pip took the seat Ed had just vacated. He reached for Claire's cup, so she scooped it out of his way.

"I just want a sip," he said.

"Get your own," she said.

"Can't, I'm broke."

"You're always broke," she said. "Stick with a job more than two minutes, and you'll have money."

"Don't lecture me, Claire," he said. "We're not married anymore."

"And yet you still come to me with your hand out, expecting me to take care of you."

"You owe me for that condo."

"I paid every payment," Claire said. "You saddled me with that ludicrous mortgage and then took off."

"My name was on the deed."

"You signed away your rights in the divorce settlement."

"I didn't read that thing. It was, like, a gazillion pages long."

"And yet you signed it."

"Ten bucks," Pip said. "Please, Claire. I'll pay you back as soon as Sean pays me."

"No," Claire said. "No, no, no, no, a thousand times no."

"I hate you, Claire."

"Prove it," she said. "Cut me out of your life forever."

Pip's eyes filled with tears.

"You're all the time busting my balls," he said. "I'm trying, Claire, I'm really trying."

"Your hot, salty tears no longer have an effect on my cold, icy heart."

"They killed Courtenay," he said. "She was the only one who understood me. She was the only one who ever really loved me."

"That was awful," Claire said. "I know you miss her."

"Knox did it," he said. "He had her killed to shut her up."

"He was implicated but not arrested," Claire said. "Anne Marie's assistant said Knox conspired with her, but there's no proof."

"Where's Anne Marie now?"

"Back in California," Claire said.

"But Knox is still around here somewhere," Pip said. "He owes me."

"Leave him alone," Claire said. "People seem to have accidents or drop dead all around that guy."

Pip got up and went off down the street. Claire wondered if he would come back that day, but she didn't bother to ask; he'd just say he would and then not show up. Claire sipped her drink, closed her eyes again, and tried to get back to the deep-thinking place.

"Excuse me, Miss."

She opened her eyes. It was Laurie.

"Did you procure a permit to put this table out here on the sidewalk?"

"No, but I did sleep with the chief of police last night," Claire said.

"Well, all right, then," he said as he sat down, "even with no hanky panky involved I think this is still covered."

"What could I get with hanky panky?"

"The key to the city," he said, "and quite possibly a street named after you."

"I'll bear that in mind."

"How's your head?"

"Better," she said. "I plan to drink four more of these before my very busy workday ends. I've got so much to do, as you can plainly see."

"How about some lunch?" he asked. "I could go fetch us something to eat out here, all alfresco-like. Très parisien, très déjeuner à l'extérieur."

"Plan approved," she said.

He cocked his head to the side and regarded her with a wry smile.

"I'd like a do-over some night this week," he said. "This time a little less inebriated."

"Plan denied," she said.

"All right," he said. "Let's get you fed and hydrated and then I'll try again."

"Off with you," she said. "I'll have sparkling water and the Salad Niçoise, dressing on the side."

When Laurie returned, with a salad for her and a club sandwich for himself, he spread out their lunch on the table as if he were a waiter, and draped a paper napkin over her lap.

"I hope madam will enjoy her repast," he said. "Bon appétit."

"Merci," she said and removed her sunglasses.

"Quelle horreur!" he said. "I take back my dinner offer. Je refuse."

"Your French is decent," she said, "but it's cruel to taunt a hung-over person, don't you know that?"

"I saw the expectant father over here earlier, pestering you," he said. "I almost arrested him for loitering with the intent to bore you to death."

"He's too busy crocheting baby blankets to bother with me," Claire said.

"Are we entirely convinced it's actually his impending bundle of joy?"

"The latest information from my confidential sources indicates it is not."

"Oh well," he said. "If it hadn't been the not-so-ex-wife showing up pregnant it would have been something else. Kidnapping, false arrest, amnesia ..."

"What do you mean?"

"Why, that you and Monsieur Éditorialiste are star-crossed lovers, doomed to stay apart until the third act. You can't get together now; it's too soon. Meanwhile, you're free to waste time with me."

"He had a big crush on me in high school," Claire said. "I didn't know that until I came back this year. If I had stayed in Rose Hill and not run off with King Dipshit to California, Ed and I might be married with a bunch of kids by now."

"So time-travel, why don't you? Go back to high school, back old Ed up against a locker, and rock his world. You wouldn't have stayed with him; he'd have lost you at J-school, where all that rarified hubris lit the righteous fire in his belly. Just think of all the earnest protesting you'd have had to do against anything the slightest bit unfair. Think of all the recycling and volunteering; all those poor people you'd have to care about. It gives me hives just thinking about it."

"I oughta slug you," she said.

"Yet you're smiling."

"How is it that you can encapsulate all the things that irritate me about Ed, but you completely miss the point of why I'm attracted to him?"

"Enlighten me," he said. "I'm eager to learn."

"He's steady," she said. "He'd never run off and leave me for some twenty-year-old floozy he met in a bar."

"Ouch."

"He'd be loyal and faithful, and I could count on him."

"Sounds more like a dog than a man," he said. "Tell me this, Claire. Does he make your knees weak when he kisses you?"

"Yes," she said. "As a matter of fact, he does."

"Still too boring," he said. "Wouldn't you rather fight crime with me?"

"Speaking of which," she said.

"To change the subject," he said.

"Did you get my message about Diedre?"

"If you're going to do my job for me, you should also have to fill out my paperwork."

"She's a hoarder," Claire said. "Every day she scouts out yard sales in the newspaper and then goes from one to the other, buying things."

"Except her husband says she's reformed," he said. "Three years ago he gave her an ultimatum: either stop acquiring things or he was leaving. Not anything as drastic as a divorce, mind you, because their religion precludes that, but he was planning to move back home to live with his parents."

"I didn't know that," Claire said.

"He came in to file the missing person's report," Laurie said. "I did ask questions. I'm not completely disinterested in your local domestic disturbances."

"But the lady out on Hollyhock Ridge said Diedre bought quite a bit of stuff the day she disappeared."

"So where's she putting it?"

"Someone else's garage?" Claire mused. "Not her sister's; they're barely speaking."

"A storage unit," he said.

"Give me two minutes, and I can print out a list of every place within a fifty-mile radius. Care to accompany me?"

"Sure," he said. "I've got nothing better to do."

"You're supposed to warn me to stay out of it," Claire said.

"I've only got a few more days in Rose Hill," he said. "I'd like to spend as much of that time as I can with you."

They took Laurie's truck. Claire immediately searched the radio stations until she found a pop music setting.

"How can you stand that drivel?" he asked her.

"Normally, I love it," she said. "Today it makes my head hurt."

Laurie changed it to a traditional vocal jazz program on Public Radio and then sang along.

"Who is that?" she asked.

"Rosemary Clooney," he said. "She also wants me to straighten up and fly right. You women and your demands."

"Is that the music your dad listened to?"

"No, my dad was a Merle Haggard and George Jones man," he said. "My mother preferred classical music. I found this all on my own."

"I like it," Claire said. "It's sweet."

"It can be heartbreaking," he said. "It can be everything all at once."

"My cousin Maggie listens to this kind of music," Claire said. "Billie Holiday and Dinah Washington. She plays it in her bookstore."

"Do you mean to tell me that I've been pursuing the wrong Fitzpatrick all along?"

"I used to work in a strip club," Claire said.

"All right," Laurie said. "That was a bit of a non sequitur, but do tell."

"When I moved to California, I couldn't afford to take the additional training hours required to get a license to do hair, so the only place that would employ me without a license was a strip club. I didn't take off my clothes; I did the strippers' hair and makeup."

"Sounds reasonable enough."

"That's how I met the woman who I worked for, for the next twenty years. She started as a stripper, became a dominatrix, then a porn actress, had plastic surgery, changed her name, and became a famous film actress."

"As one so often does," he said.

"She paid me an enormous amount of money to do her hair and makeup, plus menial, personal assistant-type things," Claire said. "Mostly I was paid to keep her secrets, which are quite valuable, as you can imagine. In Rose Hill terms I am filthy rich."

"Why'd you quit?"

"My dad got sick," she said. "My mom needed me."

"Do you miss it?"

"No," Claire said. "I kept expecting my life to get better, to be happier, and sometimes I thought I had found it, but it never lasted. You can get tired of luxury and first-class travel when you're lonely all the time. I wasted twenty years of my life getting rich on the coattails of someone else's fame instead of having a family and putting down roots."

"So, what you're telling me is that you practiced cosmetology in Rose Hill without a license? I'm going to have to arrest you now. I hate to do it, but like your married boyfriend, Ed, I'm so honorable and full of integrity that I have no choice."

"Ed doesn't know any of that."

"I see," Laurie said. "So why tell me?"

Claire shrugged and looked out the window.

"It's either one of two things," he said. "Either you care so little what I think, or you care so much. I know what my preference is, but I'd hate to delude myself."

Claire continued to watch the scenery fly by, and for a little while, Laurie was content not to talk. Finally, after about ten minutes of what felt to Claire like companionable silence, he reached out and pushed her shoulder.

"Hey," he said. "I'm an alcoholic. I got drunk after my wife died, because losing her felt like getting blasted in the chest with a double-barreled shotgun, and I stayed drunk until last October. While I was drunk, I married the most inappropriate person I could find and made a huge mess of everything. I couldn't have self-destructed more neatly if I'd poured gasoline all over my life and lit a match. I've let down everyone who ever loved me or counted on me. My mother died disappointed in how I turned out. I lost my best friend, I quit my job, and I never liked being a police officer to begin with; I just didn't know how to do anything else, and it's what my old man wanted me to do. How's that for honesty?"

"So what you're saying is you're not exactly excited about your new job."

"Obviously," he said. "What I'm also saying is life is messy, and people screw up, but the beauty is you can also be redeemed. I don't mean as in 'go to church and get saved.'

I mean you can decide things are going to be different, and then make it so."

"Is that what you're doing?"

"It's what we're both doing," he said. "I think you can only have real compassion for someone like you or me if you've been someone like you or me. The Scoopster has never been anything but an upstanding model citizen. How could he understand?"

"I wanted to tell him," she said. "I started to more than once."

"Don't tell him," Laurie said. "Don't tell him and don't pine for him. He's not the guy for you, Claire. If you can't be yourself, it's no good even trying."

"And you are the guy for me, I suppose."

"I'm probably the worst person you could choose," he said, "and yet I desperately want to call you 'sweetheart.' I don't understand your penchant for huge handbags and insanely elevated footwear, but I'm willing to accept those quirks as part of the package. I don't want to hurt you, Claire, but I'm bound to do so, sooner or later. I know all this about myself, and yet I can't seem to quit following you around town like some lovesick teenager."

"You still drink," Claire said. "I've seen you in the Thorn."

"It's under control."

"I didn't think that was possible for alcoholics."

"It's possible for me."

"Here it is," she said, as they came upon the first storage unit facility on the list.

"So we've concluded it would be a huge mistake, you and me," he said, as they parked by the office. "A catastrophe of epic proportions."

She turned to face him and was struck by his pained expression.

"Let's not have sex," she said. "Let's just be friends instead."

He shook his head.

"No offense, Claire, but I don't think I could bear the proximity without the intimacy."

"So we won't be anything to each other," Claire said.

"Except we already are," he said. "We're only human, after all. What more can we expect?"

Diedre did not have a unit rented in this first place. At the third place they came to, the manager recognized her photo. He led them to a storage unit on the back side of the property, unlocked the garage door, and rolled it up.

"Oh my goodness," Claire said.

"Will you look at that," the manager said.

The unit was packed from floor to ceiling, wall to wall, with every kind of thing you could collect. Boxes, furniture, rolled-up rugs, toys, bicycles; you name it, it was crammed into this space. But there was no treadle sewing machine.

"When was the last time you saw Mrs. Delvecchio?" Laurie asked him.

"Several months ago," he said. "There was still snow on the ground. Her station wagon got stuck in the mud, and we had to pull her out."

"Let's press on," Laurie said.

"What do you mean?" Claire said. "We found it."

"We found one," Laurie said, "and it's full. There'll be more."

At the fourth place on the list they found another unit Diedre had rented, and at the fifth place, they found Diedre.

Claire sat in the truck with the windows rolled down while the county morgue staff took away Diedre's body. She was feeling pretty queasy, having just thrown up her Salad Niçoise in the bushes at the edge of the property.

She recognized County Investigator Sarah Albright when she arrived and hoped to avoid her. Unfortunately, she wasn't so lucky. Sarah followed Laurie over to the truck.

"Good afternoon, Miss Fitzpatrick," she said.

"Good afternoon, Ms. Albright," Claire said.

"Chief Purcell, here, tells me he gave you a ride to this facility out of the goodness of his heart, and that in the process of speaking to the manager about procuring a unit for yourself, you happened to mention the deceased."

Claire didn't understand why Laurie wasn't telling Sarah the truth, but she instantly backed him up.

"That's right," Claire said. "I'm having my things shipped from California, and I need a storage unit."

"Decided to stick around, huh?"

"Mm-hmm."

"I guess Chief Gordon's still on his honeymoon."

"That's right."

"Old Maggie finally got the matrimonial noose around his neck," she said with a smirk.

Claire just stared at Sarah until the woman flushed and looked away. Laurie cleared his throat and tried not to smile. Fire Chief Malcolm Behr arrived, and Laurie walked away to greet him.

"He still on the sauce?" Sarah asked.

"I beg your pardon," Claire said.

"Changing jobs won't change anything," Sarah said. "Until he hits rock bottom and gets some help he'll just keep making the same mistakes."

"None of your business, really."

"You'll see," Sarah said. "He'll take you down with him if you're not careful."

"You seem to think you know everything there is to know."

"I do," Sarah said. "I was one of the people he hurt on his way down."

"Excuse me?"

"After his wife died, I eased his pain, so to speak, for a little while. Smart guy, Laurie; he's a lot of fun to talk to but rubbish in the sack. That's the problem with alkies, you know. They can't keep it up."

"I don't want to hear anymore," Claire said. "Please stop."

"I'm just sayin' ..." she said. "Watch yourself."

Claire turned away, rolled up the window to the truck, and tried not to visualize everything Sarah had just told her, but it was too late.

On the way back to Rose Hill, Claire's head was so full of conflicting thoughts she had lost the ability to form a sentence.

"Mystery solved," Laurie said, finally. "Thank you for your capable assistance."

"Where's her car?" Claire said.

"What?"

"Where's the station wagon?"

"Good point," he said. "You think someone murdered her by dropping a sewing machine on her head in order to steal her vintage station wagon."

Claire shrugged.

"It's a loose end."

"What happened back there?" he asked. "Did good ole Sarah fill your head full of nonsense about me?"

"She warned me about you."

"So concerned was she about your emotional well-being, that, as a caring, compassionate woman-friend, she felt compelled to alert you to my unworthiness as a potential partner."

"I dislike Sarah, and I don't trust her," Claire said. "But it's one thing for you to say you were a reckless drunk for a couple years, and another to talk to one of the women you fooled around with during that time."

"There were more than a few," he said. "I could give you a list."

"I don't like this about myself," Claire said. "I'm jealous even though I know it's petty and mean."

"I'm just glad you care," he said.

"I'll have to introduce you to my ex-husband, Pip," Claire said. "Then you might understand why I'm so screwed up."

"Pip Deacon is your ex-husband? Stoner dude Pip Deacon is Prince Shit-for-brains?"

"King Dipshit is his formal title," Claire said. "You know him?"

"Oh, Lord," Laurie said, and then laughed a little too long and loud for Claire's taste.

"I'd say we're even," he finally sputtered, and then smothered some more laughter.

"I was only seventeen when we met," Claire said.

"And I was forty-two when I met Daphne," Laurie said and shrugged. "It just goes to show you can be a fool at any age."

"Why didn't you want Sarah to know you were investigating Diedre's disappearance?"

"You change subjects with rapier-like speed."

"Tell me."

"Less paperwork," he said, with a shrug. "This way, Sarah gets credit for finding the missing woman, and gets her name in the paper, but she also has to do all the heavy lifting. All I had to do was give her my statement, and now I'm done. Her work just got started."

"I think it's because you feel bad about the way you treated her."

"Part of some kind of atonement initiative, you presume."

"Isn't that one of the steps?"

Laurie gave a Claire a look that could have cut glass. It was the first time she'd been at the receiving end of his anger and contempt, and she could feel her face flush.

"I wouldn't know," he said.

"It seems to work for other people."

"Other people can believe in a higher power," he said.

"C'mon," Claire said. "You don't believe in any kind of creator."

"Intelligent or otherwise," he said.

"Just nothing."

"I believe human existence is a long, lonely slog through pain and sorrow, experiencing loss after loss, only to end up mentally and physically crippled before dying an undignified death."

"That's the saddest thing I ever heard."

"And I wonder why everyone doesn't drink."

As soon as they got back to town, Claire walked up Peony Street toward Kay's house, intending to give Kay the news about Diedre. As she passed Machalvie's Funeral Home, she noticed the former mayor, Stuart Machalvie, former bank president, Knox Rodefeffer, and Knox's brother, Realtor Trick Rodefeffer, having an argument in the back parking lot. As soon as they saw Claire, they stopped talking, so when Claire reached Kay's house, the back of which was shielded from Machalvie's parking lot by thick hedges on the other side of the alley, she quickly skirted around to the backyard of the house and knelt down by the hedges to listen.

"Congressman Green is no longer returning my phone calls," Stuart said. "I can't even get his personal secretary on the phone."

"Senator Bayard's staff is doing the same thing to me," Knox said. "I guess they're hanging us out to dry."

"I've got reporters calling me all hours of the day and night, and the feds came to my office yesterday," Trick said. "I don't know about you guys, but I'm scared."

"I've got one piece of advice for you two," Stuart said. "Listen to your attorneys. If they say keep your mouth shut, keep it shut. Don't talk to anybody without their approval, and don't say anything they haven't advised you to say."

"Easy for you to say," Knox said. "You're not being accused of murder."

"Because you told Courtenay to give Aunt Mamie the tea," Trick said. "That's what killed her, Knox."

"I had no way of knowing that tea would interact with all the medications she was taking. I'm telling you, I thought I was doing something nice for the old bat."

"So why didn't you take it to her?" Trick asked. "Why send your mistress?"

"I knew Mamie would just ask me for money," Knox said. "I was tired of hearing it."

"What happened to all her money?" Trick asked. "Sandy heard you were embezzling it through the bank."

"Boys, I don't want to hear this," Stuart said. "This is your family's business. I'll see you later."

Claire heard Stuart walk away, get in his car, and drive off.

"You need to lay off the sauce," Knox said. "You're gonna get us all arrested."

"Just tell me," Trick said. "Did you mean to kill Aunt Mamie?"

"No, of course not," Knox said.

"Where's her trust money?"

"All gone," Knox said. "She put it up as collateral on a second mortgage, and she defaulted. She was broke."

"That's not what people are saying ..."

"I don't care what people are saying, and if you had any sense, you'd tell that wife of yours to keep her mouth shut."

"So why did Courtenay get murdered?"

"That crazy assistant of Anne Marie's did that," Knox said.

"But he says Anne Marie was working with you."

"He's lying," Knox asked. "I'd hardly go into business with my ex-wife, and I ended the affair with Courtenay back in the spring, so I had no reason to cause her harm. It's more likely that my current wife would try to kill Courtenay; she's the homicidal maniac in the family."

"Where is Meredith?"

"Gone for good, I hope," Knox said. "Listen, my life's on the line, Trick; my freedom's in jeopardy. We've got to form a united front on this. You'll be expected to testify on my behalf. We've got to get our stories straight."

"The truth, you mean."

"Yes, of course, that's what I mean."

"It looked bad," Trick said. "You didn't see Aunt Mamie. It was like something out of a horror movie. It looked like she died in pain."

"I didn't mean to hurt her," Knox said. "I'm sick of going over this with you. You've got to pull yourself together, little brother."

"The FBI wants to interview me."

"Call the attorneys," Knox said. "They'll prep you and go with you."

"I just want it all to go away."

"You and me both," said Knox. "I've got to get on the road. Are you all right to drive?"

"I'm fine," Trick said. "You go on."

"Just keep it together a little while longer," Knox said. "And for God's sake don't drink so much. You look terrible."

Claire heard them get in their cars and leave. When she stood up and turned around, Kay was standing right behind her. Startled, she jumped and clasped her hand to her heart.

"You shouldn't sneak up on a hungover person," Claire said. "I'm liable to puke on you."

"That was certainly an interesting conversation," Kay said. "Come inside. I've got something to show you."

Once inside the house, Kay went back to the bedroom and returned with a thick file folder full of documents. She sat down at the dining room table and patted the folder.

"Trick mentioned Knox had been accused of embezzling from his Aunt Mamie," Kay said. "I think I know where the money went."

Kay took out a sheaf of what looked like bank statements paper-clipped together.

"The city has a contingency fund," Kay said. "For years, Stuart has siphoned money off of that fund to pour into his many schemes. For the past two years, he's been depositing money from the fund into a bank account in Pittsburgh. He reported it to the City Council as fees paid to a consulting firm. However, the documents I just happened to have intercepted have his name, Knox's name, and one other interesting name listed as owners of this account."

"Interesting how?"

Kay held out one of the statements for Claire to look at.

"Marigold Lawson?" Claire asked. "What is she doing mixed up with Stuart and Knox?"

"Well, from what I can tell, Knox and Stuart have been paying into this account for two years, but only Marigold has taken any money out."

"Campaign slush fund?"

"Except I don't think that two years ago Marigold was planning to run for mayor," Kay said. "Stuart's wife, Peg, was slated to run because they always alternated their four-year terms."

"So what kind of dirt did Marigold have on Stuart and Knox that would compel them to pay her this kind of blackmail money?"

Kay shrugged.

"It's interesting, isn't it?"

"I bet she didn't disclose it when she signed up to run for mayor."

"Probably not," Kay said, "which puts me in sort of a ticklish spot."

"Did you tell the feds about this?"

She shook her head.

"Before he left office, I snagged these out of Stuart's briefcase and copied them," Kay said. "I couldn't very well admit that, could I?"

"You sneaky devil."

"Listen," Kay said. "Stuart and Knox are facing federal charges. They would love nothing better than for me to take the fall. Nobody's going to protect me, so I have to take care of myself; and if that means I have to play their game better than they do, well ..."

"You want me to find out what the bank account's for."

"It's a lot to ask."

"I'll do it," Claire said. "Evidently, I'm a bird dog that needs to hunt."

"What?"

"Nothing," Claire said. "Listen, I have some bad news about Diedre."

"I already heard about it," Kay said. "What a terrible way to die; all alone with no one knowing where she was."

"You should have seen those storage units," Claire said. "You wouldn't believe how much that woman had in there; no rhyme nor reason, just stuffed in there like garbage."

"Some sort of obsession, I guess," Kay said. "My grandparents never threw away anything useful because they had been through the Great Depression. Papaw bent old nails back straight, put them in a coffee can, and Mamaw kept used buttons in a jar. She used the fabric from old clothes for quilts and canned everything grown in their garden."

"This is different," Claire said. "I'm kind of a shopaholic, but I take good care of what I buy: clothes, shoes, handbags, jewelry, accessories, makeup ... listen to me; even talking about shopping gets me excited. But my point is, my closet in the L.A. condo was more of a shrine than clothes storage. Diedre's stuff looked like a mass of junk."

"It's a shame," Kay said. "I feel sorry for her family."

"Well, I'm just going to say it," Claire said. "This means Matt's free."

"Nope," Kay said. "I'm not going there."

"All right," Claire said. "But I know you've thought about it."

CHAPTER 5

Once again, Kay woke up to the sound of someone doing something to her house. It was six a.m. This time, she took care to brush her hair and put on some clothes before she ventured outside.

Sonny's truck was parked outside, and his feet were sticking out between the hollyhocks and foxglove, from underneath the crawlspace of the house. Kay stooped down and tapped his boot.

"You want some coffee?" she asked.

"Yes, in a minute," he responded.

"Come in whenever you're ready," she told him.

Kay sang as she started preparing breakfast for him, noticed what she was singing, and rolled her eyes at herself. There was something about making a big breakfast for a big man she knew would appreciate it that tickled her, and she was amused by that. Although she vociferously defended the rights of women to do anything men did and get paid the same for doing it, and she wouldn't want to make taking care of a man the central focus of her life, still she was enjoying this little taste of domesticity.

When Sonny came in, he unlaced his boots and pulled them off. She noticed he had a hole in the toe of one of his socks. Although she noticed, she did not offer to sew it up for him. There were limits, apparently, to this homemaking urge she was feeling.

"That smells wonderful," he said and rubbed his hands together.

"Wash your hands, please," she said.

He went down the hall to the bathroom, and when he came back, he said, "I'll bring you a new refill valve assembly this evening."

"That's very kind of you," Kay said. "Be sure to add that to my tab."

He tucked a napkin into the neck of his blue work shirt, took up his knife and fork, and then looked at Kay.

"I could get used to this," he said and winked at her.

"Oh, go on," Kay said, but she could feel her face flush.

He made multiple happy sounds as he consumed everything on his plate, and was pleased to accept seconds of everything.

"I guess you heard about Diedre," he said.

"It's an awful thing to have happen," Kay said. "I planned to send a box from the bakery over to Matt's later today."

"Three storage units, that woman had; filled to the ceiling with other people's junk. Laurie said she must have been trying to get a treadle sewing machine up on top of something and it fell on her."

"I hope she didn't suffer."

"They said she died almost instantly."

"That's a small blessing, then."

"I can say this to you because you know the situation: they did not have a happy marriage. Never did."

"I'm sorry to hear that."

"With our church, you know how it is; Matty couldn't do anything but what he did, which was bear it as best he could. There's no way out for us, no full pardons for good behavior. My name is mud over there, on account of Karla, and that wasn't even my fault. My mother wanted me to get an annulment, but what would that say to my girls? Me and your mother were only kidding about our marriage, we didn't mean it? No, thank you, I said. I haven't been back to Mass since then."

"I'm sorry to hear that," Kay said. "I can't imagine giving up my church; it would be like divorcing my family."

"They'll be lining up for Matty, though," Sonny said. "There'll be casseroles and homemade preserves as far as the eye can see. That's the difference between death and divorce."

"He will need the support of his church family," Kay said. "It may help him."

"I hope he can have some peace now," Sonny said. "The best thing he can do for that house is set it on fire. The cigarette smoke is in the plaster; he'll never get it out. The junk can be hauled away, but if I were him, I'd tear it down and build a new house. Or sell it. There can't be any good memories there."

"But their daughter might have some."

"No," Sonny said as he shook his head. "Nobody was ever happy in that house."

"When's the funeral?"

"Tomorrow," Sonny said. "You going?"

"No, I don't think I will," Kay said. "I'll send some flowers."

"You know, this makes my brother a single man, a widower."

"That was over a long time ago."

"I wondered."

"That's ancient history," Kay said. "We're all different people now."

"I like how you turned out," Sonny said. "I hope you don't mind me saying."

"I don't mind it," Kay said. "I like how you turned out, too."

"I'm gonna make a list of everything that's wrong with your house, and you and I can prioritize it," he said. "Maybe over dinner some night, somewhere nice."

"I'd like that," Kay said.

"Good," he said and thumped the table for emphasis. "I'll have my people call your people."

Kay laughed.

"Now that's what I like to hear," he said.

Kay liked it, too.

There they were.

Claire had scoured the Internet for over an hour and finally beheld them, the perfect shoes; impossibly steep, wickedly black, plenty of toe cleavage, with the requisite red sole. Not likely to be invited to a gala event or premiere any time soon, Claire, of course, had no place to wear them, but that hardly mattered. What mattered was the time it took to search for them, the thrill of finding them so heavily discounted, with free shipping, in her size, in the color she wanted, and the surge of pleasure she got when she clicked on the red rectangle marked "place order."

If she were a smoker, she would have lit up afterward. Now what?

Despite her intention not to, she had already caught up on all the latest celebrity gossip that didn't concern her previous employer. It had only been a few months since she was employed as the assistant to that aging Hollywood she-devil, Sloan Merryweather, and already there were names she didn't recognize slated to perform in films she'd never heard of. She would soon be just like everyone else, with no insider knowledge or connections.

It didn't take long to become irrelevant in that world; it could happen over a weekend during which your latest film tanked, or the morning after an ill-advised drunken post on a social media site. Fans were fickle and apt to turn on you, and industry power players only cared about the bottom line, either the insatiable one in their pants or the career-making one on the profit and loss spreadsheet. If you weren't making them rich, you had better be young, attractive, and willing to do anything, *absolutely anything,* to make it.

Claire looked around Sean's office, where every flat surface was covered in sawdust from Pip's circular saw. Pip hadn't bothered to show up yet, probably wouldn't now, especially since the cloudless sky was bright blue and the temperature hovered in the mid-seventies. Just as well, she thought. She was kind of glad for a reprieve from the whine of the power tools and the whine of Pip begging her for more money.

Claire closed the web browser, stood up and went out the open front door. Right before noon, the streets and sidewalks of Rose Hill Avenue were busy, with plenty of tourists dressed in the expensive designer version of outdoor sporting apparel, and wealthy parents shepherding their teenagers to Eldridge College orientation events. Claire recognized the frustrated sense of entitlement on display as the impatient parents negotiated the tiny town, so lacking in valet parking, chain coffee shops, and expensive antique stores, and not nearly quaint enough to warrant a longer stay than was absolutely necessary.

She considered dragging the table outside again to watch the parade but felt too deflated, too lethargic to bother.

'Am I depressed?' she wondered.

Bored was more accurate.

She still hadn't heard from the human resources office at Eldridge, and although she loved her cousin Sean, she regretted her offer to babysit his office space until he returned from the beach. More than anything, she missed Maggie and Hannah, more like best friends than first cousins.

"You look like you want to kick someone," Laurie said, interrupting her brooding. "I hope it's not me."

"No," Claire said. "I'm bored."

"Good," he said. "Close up shop and come have lunch with me."

"Did you find Diedre's car?"

"Is lunch conditional upon that?"

"No, I was just wondering."

"Why you are so worried about that poor woman's car, I'm sure I don't know."

"It bothers me," Claire said. "Doesn't it bother you?"

"Not in the least," Laurie said. "Stolen, probably, or rolled over the hill behind the storage unit; I didn't bother to look. Found or not, she's still dead, killed by her addiction to acquiring other people's junk, for feck's sake, and I don't think finding her ratty old clunker is a good use of my staff's time, even if Itchy or Scratchy had a clue how to go about it."

"I don't know why it bothers me," Claire said. "It just does."

"You should be an investigative reporter," Laurie said. "Maybe your boyfriend, Mr. Pulitzer, could employ you as an intern at the erstwhile *Sentinel*. Considering the average age of his subscribers, it should be called *The Incontinent*."

"I'm used to being much busier than I am right now," she said. "I need a project."

He spread his arms wide.

"And here I am, desperately in need of organizing."

"No, really," she said.

"But I'm completely serious," he said. "I'm starting a new job on Monday, and I need somewhere to live, some decent clothing, and a haircut."

"Scott will probably let you rent his place as long as you want," she said. "I can help you with the clothes and the haircut."

"So let us convene in yonder bistro, where I'll buy you a well-organized salad with the dreaded dressing on the side," he said. "We'll make a list and then prioritize it."

"You're patronizing me," she said.

"Only a little," he said.

"I'm having lunch with Kay," she said.

"Then dinner," he said.

"I have to stay in with Dad tonight," she said. "Melissa has been generous, but I don't want to take advantage of her."

"Then let me bring dinner to you and your father," he said. "Say sixish?"

"You don't know how he is now," she said. "He's not the man you remember, and he may not remember you."

"I'll go with the flow," he said. "If it upsets him for me to be there, I'll leave."

There was a screech of tires and a bang as two vehicles collided at the sole traffic light in town. Laurie closed his eyes and groaned.

"Is it bad?" he asked her. "You look. I don't want to."

"It's tourist on tourist, not local," she said. "Out-of-state plates, luxury car, and SUV."

"I guess I better get involved," he said. "No sense in bothering Miss Marple or Monsieur Poirot."

"Sorry you hate your job so much."

"I wish with all my heart I had become a history professor," he said. "See you later."

Kay had a small table set for lunch on her front porch. A steady breeze carried with it the scent of honeysuckle and newly mown grass, and the sky was a brilliant blue. Bees were hovering around the flowers she had planted by the porch; they especially seemed to love the purple coneflower and Shasta daisies. Multi-colored hollyhocks waved in the breeze; the Heavenly Blue morning glories that twined up the trellis were just about to close for the day.

Kay took a deep breath of fresh air and allowed herself a moment to enjoy the simple pleasures of a good front porch. She wished she could curl up on the glider with a book and an iced tea and not have to go back to work this afternoon.

As soon as Kay went back to the kitchen to fetch the iced tea, there was a knock on the front door.

"You're early," she called out, as she wiped her hands on her apron and went to greet Claire.

But it was Matt Delvecchio peering in through the screened door.

Kay's heart beat faster, as it always did when she saw him. She had been thinking about him more than usual since his wife disappeared, and even more so after word came that Diedre had died. She had always been careful to maintain a cordial distance between Matt and herself since everybody above a certain age in Rose Hill knew what had happened between them in high school; in a small town, no news was old news. You were your past, for better or worse, as long as you lived there.

"I guess you were expecting someone else," he said, and Kay thought she detected an accusation in his tone.

"Claire is coming for lunch," she said, as she opened the screen door.

Matt stepped in, and Kay realized she had been holding her breath.

"I'm sorry to intrude," he said.

"Don't be silly," Kay said. "Come in and have some iced tea; I was about to pour myself some, and there's plenty."

Matt sat down on one side of her kitchen booth, and Kay poured some Blackberry Sage tea over cubes in a glass.

"This is good," he said after he tasted it.

"It's decaf," she said. "I had to give up the good stuff when I got high blood pressure."

"It's hell getting old, isn't it?"

"It is," she said as she sat down across from him. "How're you doing, Matt?"

"It was a shock," he said. "Not knowing where she was, and then, well ..."

He looked out the window, his eyes shiny with tears. It was all Kay could do not to put her hand over his. She handed him a tissue instead.

"How's Tina doing?" Kay asked him.

"She's on her way," he said. "My mother's taking care of everything."

"I'm so sorry," Kay said. "It's a terrible thing to have happen."

"She was a pack rat, you know that," he said. "Everybody knew it. She couldn't help herself. I tried everything; she wouldn't talk to Father Stephen about it, and if I tried to get rid of anything she'd just about have a stroke. A few years ago one of her stacks of junk fell over and killed our cat. After that happened I gave her an ultimatum; not one more thing could come into that house that we didn't eat or wear. It seemed to get better after that. I didn't know she had found other places to put it all. I had no idea she had rented those storage units. It's embarrassing. It looks like I didn't know my own wife."

"It's an illness," Kay said. "She couldn't help it."

"If you want to know what I think, it was the devil," he said.

"Oh, now," Kay said. "You don't really believe that."

"I do," he said. "Or it was God punishing us for the sin we committed when Tina was conceived out of wedlock."

"I don't believe that," Kay said. "Young people are not mature enough to make sensible decisions, what with all those raging hormones. It's only natural that mistakes are made."

"I've never forgiven myself for what I did to you," he said. "And I never forgave her, either."

"The Bible says we're supposed to forgive those who trespass against us," Kay said. "You can't hold hatred in your heart like that; it will poison your whole life."

"I never cheated on her," he said. "Our marriage was never good, was barely tolerable, but I didn't run out on her and Tina, even though I wanted to."

"Of course you didn't," Kay said.

"We were never a real family," he said. "She didn't seem to like being a mother, and Tina certainly felt that. My daughter was closer to my mother than she was to her own mother."

"I'm sorry to hear you were so unhappy."

"You never married."

"I should have left Rose Hill," Kay said. "I might have met someone then."

"You dated that guy from Pendleton for a long time," he said. "I thought you might marry him."

"After Shug retired, he wanted to move to Florida," Kay said. "It basically came down to the facts that I don't like golf, and I can't leave Rose Hill. I'm like a plant with deep roots; it would probably kill me to transplant me."

"I've never stopped thinking of you," he said. "All these years, it should have been you and me together."

"I think things turn out like they should."

"They can now, you mean."

"I'm sorry," Kay said. "That wasn't what I meant. I've accepted what happened. I've had a good life."

"Alone, though."

"I took care of my parents for many years, and I've taken care of the town. I've had my foster kids, and now I have Grace," she said. "That's enough for me."

"It's a shame you've had to work," he said. "If you'd married me, you could have stayed home and taken care of our house and our children."

"Even if I had married, I would've expected my husband would want me to do what made me happy. Many women enjoy caring for children and a home, and I might have been one of them. As it turned out, I had to work. I'm not sorry about that. I've enjoyed taking care of this town, and I'm damn good at it. I wouldn't give that up for any man."

"Sonny wouldn't mind," Matt said with contempt. "He's what they call a progressive. If it were up to him, we'd have homosexuals running around flaunting themselves in front of decent people and innocent children. No one would stay married; Rose Hill would be like Sodom and Gomorrah."

"I'm not going to talk about Sonny with you," Kay said. "But I am disappointed to hear you talk that way. Gay or straight, all people have the potential to be good, bad, or indifferent. Sexual preference is just one aspect of a person's personality."

"But they're depraved."

"Homosexuals don't do anything in the bedroom that heterosexual people don't do, and if you don't believe me, look it up on the Internet," Kay said. "Just because you're squeamish about someone else's sex life doesn't give you the right to condemn it. As long as it's between consenting adults, it's no one's business but their own."

"The Bible says homosexuality is an abomination."

"The Bible says eating shellfish is an abomination," Kay said, "but I notice you sell a lot of shrimp at the IGA."

Kay took a deep breath and attempted to calm herself. Of all the things she didn't expect to do today, debating LGBT rights with her high school sweetheart had to be near the top of the list. It was pointless. Besides the fact that their confirmation bias was like a brick wall between them, arguing about Bible interpretation never swayed anyone.

"Let's stop this," she said. "I don't want to argue with you."

"You didn't use to be like this," he said. "You used to look up to me."

"I was sixteen years old, for goodness sake," Kay said. "Over the years I've learned to make up my own mind rather than let someone else make it up for me."

"Don't marry Sonny."

"Who says I'm going to marry Sonny?"

"I know he's going to ask you," Matt said. "He told our mother that he thought you'd make a wonderful wife."

"And I would," she said, "but I don't have plans to marry anybody right now. My life is complicated enough."

"Just wait six months," Matt said. "Enough time so that it won't look bad if we start to see each other. I never stopped loving you, Kay. Don't you still love me?"

There was a knock on the door, and Kay was relieved that she didn't have to answer him.

"I hope I'm not late," Claire said as she entered the house.

As soon as she saw Matt, Claire stopped, and her eyes widened.

"I'm sorry," she said. "I can come back later."

"No," Kay said. "It's fine. Matt was just leaving."

Matt didn't look as if he planned on leaving, and his frown indicated he wasn't happy to be interrupted. He stood up and used the tissue Kay had provided to wipe his eyes and blow his nose.

"I'll talk to you later," he said to Kay.

"I'm so sorry for your loss," Claire said as he passed her on his way out.

Matt compressed his lips, nodded, and then left.

Kay put her hand on her stomach and took a deep breath.

"Thank you, Claire, for showing up when you did," she said.

"What's going on?"

"He needed to talk," Kay said, "and as his friend, I'm happy to listen, but he's got some pretty unrealistic expectations."

"What did he say?"

Kay shook her head.

"Let's eat," she said.

Kay had assembled some delicious-looking chicken salad-filled croissants along with a colorful green lettuce salad. They carried their food, along with two glasses of iced tea, to the front porch. They sat down, and Kay took another deep breath.

"I don't know if I can eat," she said. "He's got me that riled up."

"This is so good," Claire said, as soon as she had swallowed her first bite. "If it would help to talk about it, I'd be glad to listen."

"As far as Matt's concerned," Kay said, "we're still the same people we were in high school."

"You mean his wife just died, and he's already asked you out?"

"Pretty much," Kay said.

"Oh, my Lord," Claire said. "They haven't even buried her yet."

"I know," Kay said. "It looks terrible, doesn't it? He wants me to promise to wait six months so that a decent period of time can pass before we date."

"What do you think?"

"Quite frankly, I'm appalled," Kay said. "It made me sick at my stomach, and all I could think was that I wanted him to leave. Then we argued about Sonny, and also, I think, about his brother, Anthony, although he wasn't explicitly mentioned. I was so glad to see you. It saved me from having to hurt his feelings."

"It does seem kind of tacky that he ran right over here the day after they found his wife's body," Claire said.

"Grief hits people in different ways," Kay said. "Maybe this is temporary insanity."

"That's very generous of you," Claire said. "It sounds more to me like he's missing a sensitivity gene in his DNA."

"I've spent years telling myself that if it weren't for Diedre, Matt and I could have been happy together," Kay said. "Now that it's a real possibility, I should feel something positive, shouldn't I?"

"I don't know," Claire said. "I'd have trouble getting past the tacky part, myself."

"That was unfortunate," Kay said. "He couldn't have waited a while?"

"Except his brother would have the jump on him."

"Sonny may not be interested in me that way."

"I saw the way he looked at you at dinner," Claire said. "He's smitten."

"I don't kid myself about things like that," Kay said. "Look at me."

She gestured to her body's generous proportions.

"You're too hard on yourself, so you think everyone else is, too," Claire said. "I'm telling you, I know smitten when I see it, and Sonny Delvecchio's got it bad."

"He's always been so sweet to me," Kay said. "I just never thought of him in that way until this past week. Now I expect him to show up every morning."

"And he keeps coming back," Claire said. "See?"

"There's too much going on right now," Kay said. "I can't deal with this, as well."

"That's how life is," Claire said. "You've heard about the calm before the storm? Well, smell the ozone, sweetie."

"People are already spreading less than flattering gossip about me, thanks to Marigold," Kay said. "This would delight her no end."

"So tell them both to back off," Claire said. "You don't have to decide anything right now."

"You're right," Kay said. "I know you're right."

"Don't let Matt pressure you," Claire said. "If he's half the man you've imagined him to be, he'll honor your request."

"You're absolutely right," Kay said. "I do feel better, thank you, Claire."

Kay took a big bite of her croissant and rolled her eyes over how good it tasted.

"I do love my own cooking," she said. "Thanks for giving me an excuse to cook and for listening to all my silly problems."

"Glad to be of service," Claire said. "Now it's my turn; let's do me."

"Have you heard any more about Eve's, um, delicate condition?"

"It's not his," Claire said, and then told her what she had found out about Eve's affair.

"What are you going to do?"

"I haven't completely solidified my plans," Claire said. "Somehow I've got to get her to confess it to him. Otherwise, she'll deny it, and I'll just look like a sore loser."

"He's got to know she wasn't celibate while they've been apart."

"But he never bothered to get divorced from her, so maybe this is fulfilling some subconscious wish he had."

"Until he knows the truth, Ed will stand by her, right or wrong," Kay said.

"Don't I know it," Claire said. "That's the reason it will probably never work out for us."

"Why is that?"

Claire paused.

"I had kind of an adventurous life after I left Rose Hill," Claire said.

"Well, of course, you did," Kay said. "You weren't living in a convent. I imagine life in Hollywood is pretty wild sometimes."

"Wild doesn't even begin to describe it," Claire said. "Even so, I think Ed has kind of an unrealistically romantic view of women in general, and of me, in particular."

"Sounds familiar," Kay said. "You could be describing most men over the age of forty in this town."

"He had kind of a crush on me in high school."

"I'm not surprised."

"I know that was a long time ago, and people change, but I meant something to him then, and it's like I'm finally in a place where I'm ready to reciprocate his feelings."

"It's wonderful you found each other again after all this time," Kay said. "It's very romantic, very chick lit."

"Let me ask you this," Claire said. "Do you think you owe the entire truth about your history to the man you love?"

"That's not an easy question," Kay said. "I don't have much of a history, so I can't say it has ever come up."

"I truly believe that if I told Ed everything I did after I left Rose Hill, the people I was involved with and the situations I got into, he would think less of me."

"The more important question is how do you think of you?"

"I wish I had done some things differently," Claire said. "But honest to God, I was just doing the best I could with the brains I had at the time."

"You were so young."

"And naive," Claire said. "I thought I could be in that world but not of it, do you know what I mean?"

"I think so," Kay said. "If you believe that about Ed, he probably isn't the one for you. But are you absolutely sure?"

Claire shrugged.

"Meanwhile," she said. "I told Laurie the whole story, and he didn't even blink."

"I wondered how that was going."

"He's coming over for dinner tonight," Claire said. "I told him Dad probably wouldn't remember him, but he wants to come."

"I've known Laurie for a long time," Kay said. "He was so sweet with his first wife, the one who died. They had their problems, like everyone, but they were so devoted to each other."

"No wonder he went off the deep end after she died."

"I have faith in Laurie," Kay said. "It seems like he has the drinking under control, and I think this new job will be good for him. A new start in a new place is sometimes the best medicine for a broken heart."

"That's a dangerous stage for a man to be in," Claire said. "I don't want to be his transitional woman."

"He just divorced his transitional woman," Kay said. "I think you might be right on time."

When Claire got back to the office, Pip was not waiting outside, but Eldridge Inn owner Gwyneth Eldridge was. Dressed like the wealthy high society lady she considered herself to be, Gwyneth was attired in the currently popular style of preppy clothes that looked too small for her already gaunt frame. From her small, tailored handbag to her tassled two-tone loafers, Gwyneth could have passed for one of the visiting Eldridge students' irritated, self-entitled mothers.

"I suppose it's too much to ask for you to post when you'll be back when you leave for lunch," Gwyneth said in her snide nasal whine, as she looked at her small, tasteful watch. "I've been waiting quite a while."

"What can I do for you, Gwyneth?"

Claire unlocked the door and held it open for her. Gwyneth walked past with an exaggerated lean away from Claire, as if she were terrified of catching river cooties. She then wrinkled up her nose at the interior of the office, looked for a place to sit, and when nothing was deemed clean enough to place her rear upon, she crossed her arms and cocked her hip instead.

"I'm looking for someone to set up and manage a real spa in the basement of the Inn," she said. "I thought you might be interested in the position."

"No, but thank you for considering me," Claire said, as politely as she could.

"You'd rather do this, then," Gwyneth stated, with a curled lip.

"I'm doing this as a favor to my cousin," Clair said. "I've applied for a position at Eldridge, so I'm waiting to hear from them."

"As a secretary?"

Her incredulity was insulting, as was her obviously low opinion of secretaries.

"In the drama department," Claire said. "Teaching theater students how to do hair and makeup."

"Oh," Gwyneth said. "I guess that makes sense."

"I'm looking forward to it," Claire said.

"I could pay you more," Gwyneth said.

"I appreciate the offer," Claire said, "but I'm committed to Eldridge."

"I need someone immediately," Gwyneth said. "I've got a writer's group coming in September for a retreat, and I told them I had a spa. That temporary tent thing in the basement is not going to cut it with these people. They're expecting walls."

Last month Claire had designed and erected a temporary spa space in the Inn's basement for a weekend seminar Gwyneth was hosting. With only twenty-four hours of advance notice, Claire had created what she thought looked like an ethereal angel camp, using white sheets and mood lighting to create private individual massage spaces. It was fine for a weekend but wasn't meant to be used long term. A scandal had interrupted the seminar, and as if it had somehow been her fault, Gwyneth had never paid Claire for the work.

"I'm sorry," Claire said. "I've committed to do this until Sean comes back and then I'll start at the college. I don't have time to do it for you."

"You could work in the evenings."

"I'm sorry, Gwyneth, but I can't do it," Claire said. "I hope you can find someone."

"I don't see why you couldn't work on it in the evenings and on weekends," Gwyneth said. "I could pay you quite a bit."

"I'm turning you down, Gwyneth," Claire said. "I know that's not what you want to hear, but it's not about money. I just flat out don't want to do it."

"I can't believe you people," Gwyneth said before she left in a huff. "You can't even pay people to work in this town."

Claire bit her lip and resisted the urge to follow her out in order to tell her exactly what she thought of rich brats who return to Rose Hill and expect everyone to bow down and lick their loafers.

'You people,' Claire thought. 'What nerve. I wouldn't work for that woman if I were flat broke and she had the last job in town.'

Claire then had another thought. What if Gwyneth sabotaged her job prospects at Eldridge? She was on the board of trustees, after all. Claire called the human resources department and left another message, asking them to call her. She wanted some reassurance that this position was actually going to happen.

Claire had quite a bit of money saved and invested, both from the sale of her California condo and the large sum she had earned while working for Sloan Merryweather. If she was careful about spending, she could live on the interest, probably for the rest of her life. That is, if she quit ordering expensive shoes that she would probably never wear; that wasn't going to be easy. Just thinking about not shopping made her want to shop, made her feel deprived and pitiful. There was no harm in looking around for a while, she thought, as she opened the browser on the computer. She didn't have to buy anything. Besides, she might have missed a new mark-down while she was at lunch.

When Kay returned to work, her thoughts were still churning over Matt's visit. She stopped long enough to exchange pleasantries with the security guard downstairs, the maintenance man leaning on his mop, the woman working at the utility board office, and the three people standing in line to pay their water bills. Upstairs, she popped into the city treasurer's office, which was across the hall from hers, to let Lucille know she was back from lunch, and they enthused about the great weather.

She had left the door to her office open while she was out, and when she reached her desk, she found something curious on top of it. It was made from a long metal bolt with a wing nut screwed on at the top and a fat nut at the bottom. To that wingnut, someone had welded on two more wings. The wings had been dabbed with white paint and the flat top of the screw with yellow. The bolt itself was painted green, and the nut was painted a terra cotta color.

It was a miniature daisy in a tiny flower pot.

Kay felt her face grow warm, and a flush of something like happiness spread throughout her. She had no doubt who had made the thing and placed it on the middle of her desk.

What a dear man.

'But what am I going to do about it?' she asked herself.

Matt was not going to be happy if she and Sonny got together, and the town gossip machine could run for months on the fuel that situation would provide. It could, in fact, have a negative effect on her campaign. How could she let Matt down gently, encourage Sonny, albeit slowly, and maintain peaceful relations with the whole Delvecchio family?

And who was to say Sonny had serious intentions? He hadn't actually professed his undying love to her, and how could he, so early in their so recently developed close friendship? It could all go completely south, she could end up with neither man and be humiliated in front of the entire town.

Kay felt hungry. She had just eaten a big lunch, but the urge to consume food was powerful. She knew there would be donuts on the coffee cart in the hallway, left there for staff and visitors. Without questioning her motives, Kay picked up her tea mug and walked briskly down the hallway to the small kitchen at the end. As she passed the coffee cart she noted muffins on a plate, but no donuts. On the kitchen counter sat the Fitzpatrick's Bakery box, but it held only muffins, not donuts. She was craving a donut. A glazed chocolate ring, in particular. The muffins looked fine and were probably good, but they weren't what she wanted.

Back in her office with her tea, she called Fitzpatrick's Bakery.

Melissa answered.

"Good afternoon," Kay said. "I notice we have muffins today. Did someone change our standing order?"

"Bonnie's at the beach and I'm afraid of the deep fat fryer," Melissa answered. "I got burnt once and I ain't doing it again. Are the muffins bad?"

"I'm sure they're fine," Kay said. "Not to worry; I was just curious."

After she hung up, Kay looked at the stack of invoices on her desk that needed to be approved and passed on to the city treasurer. She also needed to review the minutes from the last City Council meeting in order to prepare an agenda for the next one. A light was blinking on her phone, notifying her of waiting voicemail messages. Her daily to-do list was paper-clipped to her desk blotter, with only half of the items crossed off.

She considered the flower Sonny had made for her, and then put it in her desk drawer.

She thought about donuts.

Donuts and cold milk.

On impulse, she picked up her handbag and walked across the hall.

"I have to drive to Pendleton," she said with an exaggerated sigh.

"The courthouse will be a nightmare at this time of day," Lucille said. "You probably won't get back by closing time."

"Maybe I'll get lucky," Kay said. "See you in a bit."

She said good-bye to everyone downstairs, relating loudly that she had to go to the Pendleton courthouse, and then she walked up the hill to her house. She was out of breath by the time she reached her car and had to lean on it for a minute to rest.

'I'm the last person who needs to eat a donut,' she thought.

Once she was in her car, she caught a glimpse of herself in the rearview mirror.

"I don't care," she said. "I want them."

Twenty minutes later she was alone in her car in the parking lot outside the Pendleton Megamart, with six chocolate iced glazed donuts and a pint of cold whole milk. It was heavenly. By the time she returned to her office she felt full, overfull, actually, and sleepy, but most importantly, she wasn't afraid or worried. She felt sated, comforted, and relaxed. Very relaxed. The rest of the afternoon passed in a pleasant haze, her thoughts insulated from anxiety by the sugary comforter wrapped around her nerves.

By four o'clock she had a headache, felt sick at her stomach, and had begun the next emotional stage of coming down from a fatty sugar high, which was reproach and disgust. This was followed by worrying Sonny would show up at her house in the evening, or that Matt would, or that they both would.

She called her friend Dottie at the library and arranged dinner out and a movie in Morgantown with her and Georgia. She would enjoy their company, but more importantly, she could avoid having to anticipate anything awkward happening or having to deal with uncomfortable feelings.

Plus there'd be candy at the theater, and her friends didn't judge or scold.

Claire was walking down Rose Hill Avenue when she saw the most peculiar thing: Knox Rodefeffer, dressed in his daily uniform of navy blazer and khaki pants, was standing on the grassy verge between Fitzpatrick's Service Station and the Dairy Chef, picking up and throwing rocks at a large black sedan with darkly tinted windows and a Maryland license plate, that was idling at the curb.

People on the street had stopped to stare. Across the street, her cousin Patrick was watching from the front stoop of the Rose and Thorn, and customers in the Dairy Chef were watching through the window.

"Leave me alone!" Knox screamed as he threw a small rock that bounced off the car's exterior. "Stop following me!"

As he picked up another rock, the front wheels of the car turned, and the car rolled up over the curb toward him. Knox screamed, turned, and ran away, between the Dairy Chef and the service station, to the alley behind it. Claire was amazed to see how fast the tall, ungainly man could move.

The car backed out onto the road, rolled forward, and took a right at the corner of Peony Street and Rose Hill Avenue. The driver didn't seem to be in a hurry, and the slowness of the car's pursuit of Knox was somehow more sinister than if the tires had screeched and they had sped away. It was as if the driver knew Knox couldn't sustain his run all the way up the hill to his house, so there was no hurry.

Claire looked at Patrick, who was shaking his head as he went back inside the bar. Even though she disliked Knox with a fervor usually reserved for hairy-legged spiders and cat-calling construction workers, she was concerned for him.

And she was curious.

Her shoes precluded running, so she slipped them off and put them in her handbag. She started off at a trot, but when she got to the corner of Peony Street, she saw the car turn right onto Morning Glory Avenue at the top of the hill, where Knox lived, and started to run.

She decided to cut up through the alley behind Sunflower Street, where she thought she'd see Knox ahead of her. He was, however, nowhere in sight. Surely he couldn't have made it home already. She watched as the sedan cruised by the end of the alley up on Morning Glory Avenue.

She slowed to a fast walk in order to look for where Knox must be hiding, somewhere along the alley. She found him behind some bushes near Lilac Avenue.

"What's going on, Knox?" she asked him.

"Do you see a black car anywhere nearby?" he asked her.

He was trembling so hard the branches of the bush were trembling. His face was pale, and he was sweating profusely.

"They're cruising down Morning Glory Avenue, looking for you," she said. "Do you owe somebody money or something?"

Knox stood up and brushed himself off, trying to look important and indignant, which was hard to do with leaves in your hair, or what passed for hair in his toupee.

"What, are you spying on me?" Knox said. "Hoping to get some dirt to tell your federal agent friends?"

"You're welcome," Claire said. "I was concerned for your safety, but now, not so much."

Just then, the sedan turned onto Lilac Avenue and rolled toward them. Before Claire knew what was happening, Knox had shoved her out into the street in front of the car and took off up the alley on the other side.

Luckily for Claire, the car was rolling so slowly that it was able to stop before it hit her. Claire removed her hands from the front of the hood and stepped out of its way, but not before she'd got a good look at the man in dark glasses behind the wheel. As the car sped away, Claire cursed Knox loud and long, using as many course adjectives as she could think of to modify the words "son of a bitch."

In the midst of her rant, she heard someone nearby clear her throat and turned to find Sister Mary Margrethe standing in a flower bed in front of Sacred Heart Catholic Church. Sister M-squared, as she was called, shook her head and waggled her garden-gloved finger at Claire.

"Sorry," Claire said, feeling her face heat up with mortification, mostly because it was not the first time she had been caught swearing by this particular nun.

When Claire arrived home at six o'clock, Laurie's truck was parked in front of her house. In the living room, Laurie had the front cover off of the old upright piano and was tuning it. Her father was sitting in his recliner, with her Boston terrier, Mackie Pea, and the black kitten she'd been calling "Junior" curled up on his lap.

"Hi," Claire said.

"Hey there, Claire Bear," her father, Ian, said. "Do you know Laurie? He's Chief Purcell's son. You know Larry Purcell. He's the chief over to Familysburg."

Claire gave her most sympathetic look to Laurie, and he smiled in response. His father had died a few years ago, from complications caused by his alcoholism. Laurie had been the chief for more than ten years by that time.

"I do know Laurie," Claire said. "He's having dinner with us tonight."

"Well, that's good," Ian said to Claire. To Laurie, he said, "Last time I saw you, you were headed to college. You went somewhere real smart. Where was it?"

"Yale," Laurie said. "I had a scholarship."

"What'd you study up there?"

"History," Laurie said.

"Now, what can you do with a history degree besides teach it?" Ian asked him.

"Become a police officer," Laurie said.

"Are you now?" Ian said. "Your old man must be very proud."

"He is," Laurie said. "I've just about got this old wreck tuned."

"Where are you working?" her father asked.

"I start over in Pendleton on Monday," Laurie said.

"You'll be working for Shep, then. He's a fine man; you'll learn a lot from him."

"I hope to," Laurie said. "I'll do my best."

"The thing to remember is that police work is as much of an art as a science," Ian said. "It's delicate work in a small town; you can't just stomp around enforcing the letter of the law all the time, like some big police robot. You've got to take everything into consideration; the context of the crime, the likelihood that it will be committed again, the personalities of the people involved, and what you would want to be done if it was your kin who committed the same crime."

Claire stood in shock as her father spoke like he used to, like himself, someone she hadn't heard speak since she returned in the spring.

"I'll keep that in mind," Laurie said. "Thanks, Chief."

Moving as quietly as she could, Claire sat down on the edge of the couch, as if her father were operating under a sanity spell, one she could break with too much noise.

"That's all behind me now," Ian said. "I'm happy just to drive the school bus."

He sat up, dislodging the sleeping cat and dog, and turned to Claire.

"I've forgotten the kids," he said. "They'll be waiting for me."

"Pudge Postlethwaite took over your route, Dad," Claire said. "Don't worry."

"Pudge?" he said. "But Pudge works at the power plant."

His eyes clouded with confusion. The spell had broken.

"He's retired now," Claire said. "You just forgot; no big deal."

"I've forgotten a lot of things," he said.

Claire's heart broke for him like it did every day.

"My dad forgets things all the time," Laurie said. "It comes with age, he says; it happens to us all."

"He's right," Ian said. "It's a good thing you young folks are around to look after us."

"It's the best thing," Laurie said and looked at Claire. "It's the most important thing."

Laurie had brought a big bucket of fried chicken and all the side dishes offered by the colonel's chain store in Pendleton. Claire used paper plates, which she had deemed the tableware du jour while her mother was at the beach. Laurie was gracious and accommodating to her father, and didn't seem to notice when her dad dropped more bites on his stained shirt than went in his mouth and then talked with his mouth full.

Mackie Pea had stationed herself beneath Ian's chair, the better to catch falling snackies, and Junior grabbed anything the little dog missed. Claire caught Laurie surreptitiously supplementing these snacks with pieces of his chicken.

Tentatively, Claire allowed herself to relax and enjoy the meal. The chicken skin was crunchy, greasy, and delicious. She added up the carbs in her head and rationalized to herself that the protein balanced them out. She'd skip the mashed potatoes, mac and cheese, and biscuits, and then exercise longer tomorrow to make up for it.

After dinner, Laurie helped Ian back to the living room and then proceeded to play any song the older man requested on the newly tuned piano. Claire was amazed at how many songs her father remembered. Singing along with Laurie, he nodded his head to the music (that everyone else could hear, for a change), and seemed content.

Eventually, he got sleepy, and Laurie played some beautiful, peaceful melodies. When he began playing "Claire de Lune," he turned around and looked at her.

"Remember this?" he asked her.

"I do," she said.

When her father began to snore, Laurie stopped, shook out his hands and whispered, "I was rusty."

Claire and Laurie convened in the kitchen, where he ate some blackberry cobbler, and Claire made him some coffee.

"Thanks for that," she said. "You play so beautifully."

"My mother insisted on lessons. I hated it then, but I enjoyed it immensely tonight," he said. "I used to play for my own father. I miss it."

Claire sighed.

"I keep telling myself I need to enjoy him while I have him, but it isn't easy. He has these delusions, about my mother, about me. It's hard. I saw a glimpse of my dad in there tonight, but he's mostly someone I don't know, and I don't always like."

Laurie didn't say anything, but his sympathy was palpable.

"And now for the haircut," she said.

Claire retrieved her haircutting equipment from the bathroom, along with a towel. Laurie obediently sat where she told him to, held still, and allowed her to move his head as she needed to. When she was done, she gave him a hand mirror so he could look at her work. It was then that she noticed his hands were trembling. He saw her notice, and their eyes met in the mirror.

"Is that from playing so long?" she asked.

He smiled that wry, sad smile that she was coming to know so well.

"Oh," she said.

He nodded.

"I have some whiskey," she said.

He took her hand, kissed it, and then clasped it to his heart.

From the cabinet over the refrigerator, Claire retrieved the bottle of Jameson's that her cousin Patrick had given her father many years before. Her father had forgotten it was there, and her mother didn't drink anything stronger than the occasional glass of wine, so it had never been opened. Claire only knew it was there because she found it when she was searching for the paper plates.

She hooked her fingernail under the seal to remove it and then unscrewed the lid. She placed the bottle on the table next to his coffee cup.

"I'll be right back," she said. "Help yourself."

Claire went to the bathroom and closed the door behind her. Now her hands were the ones shaking.

She had just given whiskey to an alcoholic.

At the moment, she had just wanted to relieve his suffering; she wasn't thinking about anything else.

He said he had it under control; maybe a little was all he needed.

But she knew better.

She washed her hands and then counted to twenty before she went back to the kitchen. Laurie was clearing the table. On top of the fridge sat the bottle of whiskey, the level showing very little had been poured out, and his coffee cup was upside down in the dish drainer on the counter by the sink.

"Thank you for dinner," Claire said.

"It was a lovely evening," Laurie said.

He embraced her and kissed the side of her forehead.

Claire put her arms around him and hugged him. He loosened his grip, and she tipped her head back.

"Is there anything I can do to help?" she asked him.

"Probably not," he said.

"I don't know what to do," she said. "I'm worried about you."

"I've kicked it before," he said. "I can do it again."

"Have you tried AA?"

"It's not a good place for the chief of police to be seen," he said. "I would lose my job."

"You say you have it under control," Claire said, "but it gives me pause."

"As in, let's take a step back and reassess?"

"I care about you," she said. "I wish it could work out."

He grasped the back of her shirt and pulled her close. His kiss had fire and passion in it, but all Claire could taste was the whiskey and coffee.

The thought came to her, 'It's like kissing a dying man,' but she pushed it away.

After Laurie stopped kissing her, he kept her in a close embrace for a few moments, then kissed her temple, let go, and left, without saying another word.

Claire went to the back door and looked west, where the sun was setting behind the mountains. She wanted to cry, but she also wanted to believe he could change, could deal with the grief that drove him to self-medicate, and that they could have something, if not exactly like what he had with his first wife, maybe a sort of approximation, a balm strong enough to soothe them both.

When Kay returned from Morgantown, it was almost midnight. Sonny Delvecchio was sitting on her porch swing, smoking a cigarette.

"I didn't know you smoked," she said.

"Only when I'm nervous about something," he said. "It calms me down."

She sat down on the top step.

"That was a lovely gift you left on my desk," she said.

"I felt stupid after I did it," he said. "I almost went back and got it before you could see it."

"I loved it," she said. "I'm glad you made it for me."

"This thing with Diedre," he said. "Does it change anything for you?"

"It's a horrible thing," she said. "I feel so sorry for your family."

"That's not what I asked you," he said.

"There's this wonderful phrase that I learned from that scoundrel boss of mine, the former mayor," she said. "When someone asked him to comment on something, and he wasn't sure how to respond, he would say, 'I'm still processing that, and I'll get back to you.' "

"Has Matt been by?"

"He stopped in briefly today," she said.

"I didn't get the good looks in our family," Sonny said. "That was Anthony's gift, straight from our beautiful mother. I didn't get her full head of hair like Pauly and Matty, either, that's for sure. I got my height from my mother's side of the family, but I got my father's bald head and this big honkin' schnoz. But along with that, I also got his big heart. If my wife hadn't left me, I would never have stopped trying to make her happy. I'm not saying you couldn't be happy with Matty, and if you two end up together, I'll raise a toast to you at your wedding and dance with you the appropriate number of times. I won't make a fool of myself. I'll be disappointed, but I'll be all right."

"It's too soon after Diedre's death for that kind of speculation," she said. "It's dishonorable to her memory."

"I know it's what my brother wants," he said.

"But what about what I want?"

"You take your time and consider your options. As long as I'm one of them, I don't care what anybody thinks but you."

"You're so sweet," Kay said. "I don't know what you see in me."

"I see myself in you," he said. "You got a big heart, too, the kind that gets stomped on. We saps oughta stick together."

"I'll give it my deepest consideration," Kay said. "Thank you for being so kind."

"You got any pie left?"

"One thing you can always be sure of," Kay said, "is that I'll have something sweet in my kitchen. Come on in."

"You know," he said as he followed her inside, "you got some boards on this porch could use replacing. I'll bring my tools over on Saturday and work on that for you."

CHAPTER 6

Claire rested her head on the desk and considered taking a nap. How did people do it? Working at the same desk, looking at the same computer, the same view, day after day?

Claire thought of how often she had complained about her job when she worked for Sloan; the travel hassles, the temper tantrums, and the movie sets in far-flung places where any inconvenience was always Claire's problem to solve. At least it was different every day and often interesting, even when it was brutal.

There were occasions when she felt boredom while waiting on film shoots for shots to be set up or the light to be right, or while waiting in the VIP lounge in a foreign airport, listening to Sloan berate someone over the phone. At least there was always something to do while she waited, or some bitchy assistant-something-or-other to gossip with.

This, this forced *containment*, was pure torture.

She had once again sworn off shopping, so of course, all she wanted to do was look at the pretty shoes and handbags online. She had also sworn off any gossip site that might accidentally tell her something new about her ex-boss's fake engagement to her ex-boyfriend. Without constantly anticipating the needs of an insanely entitled she-devil, shopping, processing Hollywood gossip, or obsessing about some man, Claire didn't know how to be.

'Shallow,' she thought. 'The shallow concerns of a shallow person.'

She wanted to become someone better than that; someone who cared about important things. It was no wonder Ed was still married to Eve; at least she could talk to him about the things in which he was interested.

Maybe she could get better informed about world events.

She opened an Internet browser and went to a world news site, but after five minutes she shut the browser with a pounding heart. Terror, murder, torture, earthquakes, tsunamis, hurricanes, irreparable ecological decay, political parties accusing each other of atrocious behavior, children suffering from incurable diseases, loved ones killed in heartbreaking accidents, abandoned animals, homeless elderly, and on every page: death, death, and more death. Reading the vicious reader comments on every page only made everything seem worse.

She was reminded of what Laurie had said about life being a long slog of sorrow.

Now she was depressed.

As an antidote, Claire got back online and went to her favorite female-centric, aspirational-themed website where the young women who hosted it posted funny photos, celebrity gossip, and photos of beautiful rooms in expensive homes, as well as encouraging posts about keeping in shape and losing weight. Today, however, she noticed a proselytizing post on achieving the "thigh gap" situated right above a post filled with photos of and recipes for high-calorie desserts.

'It's crazy-making,' Claire thought, 'what we do to ourselves.'

She recognized the urge to do something to feel better: to eat something, to shop for something, or to saturate herself with celebrity baby photos. Maybe she could slip out early and go for a long run, work off the calories she consumed the day before.

All addictive behaviors, she realized.

What else was there to do?

She considered calling the nice woman in the human resources department at Eldridge College, but she had already left her several messages, and by not returning her calls, Claire suspected the woman might be avoiding her, even though it was more likely she just didn't have anything new to tell her.

Claire called Professor Richmond instead. She rolled her eyes at his voicemail message.

What a ham.

"Hell is empty, and all the devils are here," he intoned, as if from a stage in London's West End. "Record a message, if you must."

"Hi, Professor Richmond," Claire said. "This is Claire Fitzpatrick; I was just wondering if you had heard anything about the position and if we're still on for Scrabble tonight. Give me a call when you have time."

Claire ended the call and looked around. She realized she was slumped in her rolling office chair, so she sat up straight. She realized she was frowning, so she smoothed her facial features into what she thought was a cheerful, pleasant expression.

"Who are you making faces at?" Melissa said from the doorway.

"I have resting bitch face," Claire said. "So I'm working on it."

"That's the silliest thing I ever heard," Melissa said.

"I'm so bored," Claire said. "How do people stand this?"

"I know it," Melissa said. "I took today off but I woke up at the regular time, cleaned the whole trailer, and now I'm antsy."

"I'm stuck here until they deliver Sean's copier printer thingy," Claire said. "Let's take the table out front and get some ice coffees from the bookstore."

Once seated outside with their beverages, they got caught up on family gossip.

"I guess Bonny's bossing everyone around something terrible down at the beach," Melissa said.

"Better them than you," Claire said. "Sean said he was basically serving as chauffeur and manservant to all the old people."

"If you get the job at the college, do you think Sean would give me the secretary job?"

"I don't know what Sean's going to do," Claire said. "Have you tried anywhere else?"

"I have, but I got a feeling that prison record's all they see when they look at my resume."

"I'm sorry," Claire said. "I know you're a good person and you didn't deserve to go to prison; I wish everyone else knew that, too."

Melissa shrugged.

"I kidnapped a baby out of a meth house," she said. "I pretended to be his mama and let everyone think the real me died when the place blew up. I know I done wrong, but I'd do it again in a heartbeat."

"Tommy has you to thank that he's alive and well," Claire said. "Everyone seems to love that kid."

"I wish he was home," Melissa said. "I like knowing where he is, even if he ain't with me."

"Kay heard from them," Claire said. "They're having a great time."

"She done told me," Melissa said. "Kay's a good egg."

"I guess you heard about Diedre Delvecchio dying."

"That's all anybody's talking about," Melissa said.

"They never found her car; don't you think that's odd?"

Melissa shrugged.

"I guess that don't hardly matter since she's dead."

"After they deliver the copier thingy, I'm going to go look for her car," Claire said. "Do you want to go with me?"

"Why?" Melissa said. "The police should do that."

"Because I don't have anything else to do," Claire said. "Because sitting in this office every day all day is driving me mad."

"I'd give anything to have a job like this," Melissa said with a wistful look on her face. "Somebody with a job like this is respectful-like. You get to wear nice clothes and don't get flour all over you. No hot kitchen, no hot grease. Nobody looks down on you if have a job like this."

Claire knew that wasn't true, but she didn't say it. No matter what you did, or how experienced or well-educated you were, there was always somebody who would enjoy looking down on you.

She wanted to help Melissa; how could she do that?

"You know," Claire said. "If you work on your grammar, it will help you get a better job."

"You sayin' I sound stupid?" Melissa said, with a raised eyebrow. "I ain't as dumb as I look."

"I know you're not dumb," Claire said. "You just need to sound as smart as you are. Would you like that?"

"I dunno," Melissa said. "I don't wanna sound like no big fake."

"Actresses have to learn to speak in different ways so they can get better parts," Claire said. "That's part of the job; how would this be any different? You'd be playing the part of a smart secretary to get a job as a smart secretary."

"How would I even go about doing something like that?" she asked.

"There's bound to be an online class," Claire said. "We can enroll you, and then you can go online in the evenings and do the lessons. It'll be super easy. Then you practice what you learn every day. Bad grammar's just a habit; it can be broken if you want to do it."

"I think I might be Tennessee to the bone," Melissa said. "I might be able to get the words right, but I'll still sound like Chattanooga's in my veins."

"The grammar is more important than the accent," Claire said. "We still want you to sound like Melissa, but Melissa, the professional-sounding secretary."

"If you think it will help," Melissa said. "I'm willing to try anything."

Claire helped Melissa enroll in an online grammar class, and while they were looking over the lesson plans, a man delivered the printer. He set it up and then showed them how to make copies, scan documents to save as PDFs on the computer, and to fax documents. When he left, they printed out Melissa's lessons from the online class, and then scanned and emailed them to each other.

"If you already know how to run all the office machines and improve your grammar," Claire said, "you'll be way ahead of the game."

"I can keyboard 100 words per minute," Melissa said, "but I don't spell too good."

"Well," Claire said.

"What?"

"Never mind," Claire said. "That's what spell check is for."

Claire put up a "be back in an hour" sign on the door and locked the office behind her.

"Pip's supposed to be doing finishing work on Sean's office," Claire said, "but since he didn't show up this morning I don't imagine he'll show up now."

Since Melissa's car was parked out front, they took it to the storage unit complex where Diedre's body had been found.

"I do need to rent a storage unit for all the stuff that will be shipped from California," Claire said. "That will get us in the gates, and then we can nose around."

Melissa sat on the hood of the car and texted while Claire went inside the office. She asked if they had something on the back side of the lot and the woman didn't seem to think that was odd.

"I got one needs cleaned out," she said, consulting her chart. "It'll be ready in about a week."

"Is that the one they found the body in?"

"I don't know anything about that, and I'm not supposed to talk about it."

"I don't mind taking that one," Claire said. "Can I at least drive back there and look at the outside of it?"

The woman showed her on the map where it was, but Claire already knew.

"If you don't tell anybody I gave it to you, I'll give you the key," the woman said. "Just be sure and bring it back here before you leave."

"That's okay," Claire said, and her distaste must have shown on her face.

"There's no blood or anything," the woman said. "We got a company that cleans that stuff up for us."

"This has happened more than once?" Claire asked.

"People do crazy things in those units," the woman said. "We had one guy living in his for a couple of months before we figured it out. When you're homeless, it's cheaper than an apartment."

Claire accepted the key and promised to bring it right back.

She and Melissa drove around to the back of the property and parked next to the chain link fence across from Diedre's unit.

"I'll pass," Melissa said when Claire told her she had the key.

Claire braced herself for a bad smell, but it smelled like someone's musty basement full of junk, plus a bleach smell from the big clean spot on the floor. Claire looked around the small section of floor space that was clean, but she didn't know what she was looking for.

'What am I even doing here?' she asked herself. 'This is silly.'

A truck drove past slowly, and two shady-looking characters gave Claire up-and-down looks and sly smiles. They drove on down to the unit at the end, and Claire rolled the door down and locked it. She definitely didn't want her stuff to be kept back here with those guys nearby.

Melissa was standing outside of the car, leaning back against it, texting again. As Claire walked up to her, she could hear the door to the unit at the end roll up. She watched the men go in and immediately roll the door down behind them.

"I think I got all wound up for nothing," she said to Melissa. "Let's go home."

Melissa stopped texting and lifted her head, but she wasn't looking at Claire.

"Do you smell that?" she asked.

Claire sniffed the air, and there was something, a chemical smell, acrid but faint.

"I guess, why?"

"I know that smell," Melissa said.

Melissa hurriedly walked over to Diedre's storage unit, flattened her back against it, and then edged her way down closer to the end unit. Claire watched in amazement as Melissa reached the garage door of the end unit, sniffed the crack between it and the cement block wall, and then ran all the way back to the car.

"We gotta get outta here," she said as she opened the driver's side door. "Get in, get in, get in!"

Claire scurried around the car and got in right as Melissa started backing up. She was still closing the door as the car moved.

"What's going on?" she asked.

Melissa zoomed up the driveway and screeched to a halt in front of the office.

"Tell 'er you changed your mind," Melissa said. "You don't want it. Hurry!"

Claire went inside, told the woman she wasn't sure yet, but would get back to her, and gave her the key. The woman shrugged, irritated but obviously disinterested.

When Claire got back in the car, Melissa was sunk down low in the seat, had sunglasses on and had stuffed her hair up in one of Patrick's ball caps. She pulled out of the parking lot so fast the tires screeched.

Claire was still trying to put on her seatbelt.

"What in the hell just happened?"

Melissa's face was pale, and she was driving very fast.

"Slow down," Claire said. "The county keeps a car on this road, and you don't want to get pulled over while you're on parole."

Melissa slowed down to the speed limit.

"You think that woman could identify me in a lineup?"

"I think she's already forgotten me," Claire said. "What's going on?"

"They're making meth in that storage unit," Melissa said. "Long as I live I'll never forget that smell. That's what they was making when they blowed up the house after I got Tommy out."

"We need to call the police."

"You can do whatever you want long as you leave my name out of it."

"I will, don't worry."

"They're evil, them meth-heads," Melissa said. "All they want is more meth; they don't care who they have to steal from, or hurt to get more. They're like walking dead people with no souls; like zombies."

"You drop me off in town, and I'll call from a payphone," Claire said. "Are there still payphones?"

"Them meth-heads are the ones you wanna avoid when you're locked up," Melissa said. "Them and the crackheads are the worst. They'll snort drain cleaner if they can get hold of it; they'd sooner gut you as look at you."

Claire couldn't think of any response that wouldn't sound feeble or patronizing. She was just sorry Melissa had come to know such things. They were quiet until Melissa dropped her off in front of the office. Claire started to say something, but Melissa pulled away from the curb before she could.

When Claire reached the door to the office, she found a note from Pip.

"Call me" was all it said.

Claire unlocked the door and went inside. She dialed the number to the Rose Hill Police Station, and it went to voicemail.

"Lovely," she said, and ended the call rather than leave a message.

"Are you working?" she texted Laurie.

She waited five minutes, but there was no response.

She called Pip, using his mother's house phone number. Pip could never keep a cell phone, either because he lost them or the service was disconnected for non-payment. His mother, Frieda, answered.

"Haylo," she said.

"Frieda, this is Claire, is Pip around?"

"You just missed him," Frieda said. "He's gone up to Knox's house to have it out with him."

"Well, that's stupid."

"I told him he was gonna get himself in trouble with the law again, but he's got this fool idea that Knox owes him money for killing Courtenay."

"Is he planning to blackmail Knox?"

"I don't know what he's doing."

"Well, crap," Claire said. "How long ago did he leave?"

"Five minutes, maybe," Frieda said. "If you'd give that boy some of that money you owe him, he wouldn't have to go begging Knox for it."

Claire ended the call rather than argue.

'I'm not going to get involved,' she told herself. 'This is not my problem.'

She tried to turn her mind to something else. She needed to call some law authority and report the meth lab at the storage unit. She didn't want to call 911 from Sean's office phone; she would have to look around town for a payphone.

But her mind kept wandering up to Morning Glory Avenue. She thought about the dark sedan. What if Knox was paranoid enough to shoot whoever knocked on his front door? Or what if Knox's house was currently infested with armed thugs?

She was up and moving before she could talk herself out of it. She locked the office door behind her and called Laurie as she walked.

Where was he?

By the time she reached Morning Glory Avenue, hiking up the steep driveway to Knox's house, she was out of breath. She desperately needed to start running again. Knox's big Lincoln was parked in the driveway with Pip's rickety old pickup behind it. There was no dark sedan in sight.

Claire rang the doorbell and waited. She rang it again, and then knocked on the door. She waited a moment, pounded on the door, and then was surprised when it swung open.

Claire's pulse quickened. Despite the alarm bells sounding in her head, she pushed the door open and stepped inside.

"Knox?" she called out. "Pip? Are you in there?"

Her ex-husband was standing in the foyer, looking up at Knox, who was lying on his side facing the wall in the middle of the lower portion of the wide staircase. There was a huge gash across the back of his head, and the back of his shirt was soaked with blood. He was so still, and there was such an absence of Knoxness in the atmosphere, that Claire had no doubt that he was dead.

"Pip," she gasped. "What happened?"

"I don't know," he said. "He was like this when I got here. Claire, what'll we do?"

Pip's eyes were open so wide the whites were showing all around the irises. His face was pale. He was breathing so hard he was almost hyperventilating.

"We call the police," Claire said, taking out her cell phone.

"They'll arrest me," Pip said. "I can't go back to jail."

"Wait a minute," Claire said. "Don't panic or you'll do something stupid. Well, more stupid, anyway."

Pip pushed Claire out of the way and ran out of the house. He jumped in his truck and then backed it down the driveway, turning so sharply at the end that the truck tires screeched. He gunned it and was gone.

Claire called the police station again, left a frantic message, and then she called the County Sheriff's Office dispatcher. Once that was done, she turned back to look at Knox.

The polished wooden stairs were carpeted with a plush, multicolored Oriental runner, held down with brass rods fastened at the back of every step. The carpet stopped halfway up the stairs at a marble landing before continuing on the other side up to the second floor. Knox's head was resting on the third step down from the marble landing; below it, down to around mid-chest level, the carpet behind the body was stained a deep dark red. His left arm was beneath him and the other hung limp from the shoulder that was rolled toward the wall. His jacket was missing, exposing his big belly straining the buttons of his blue oxford shirt. The legs of his khakis rode up a little where he must have slid down a step or two after he fell, revealing argyle socks and brown penny loafers.

A piece of paper was stuck to the bottom of one of his shoes. Claire took a closer look; it was a hundred-dollar bill. From the open front door a stiff wind whipped up the staircase; the bill detached and flipped in the breeze, coming to rest near the bottom step. Claire left it where it landed.

Claire had been on enough movie sets where violence and gore were so cleverly faked that, when faced with actual blood and a dead body, it didn't seem quite real to her. It also seemed impossible that someone she knew, albeit someone she disliked intensely, could be gone, just like that.

A scant few weeks previously, she had socked Knox in the face for trying to swindle her parents out of their home and then had watched, horrified, as his wife, Meredith, tried to bludgeon him to death with a collector's coin box. There was no doubt Knox Rodefeffer had been a power-hungry, underhanded, low-down bastard, so there were plenty of people who might want him dead. Claire wondered which one he had finally pushed over the edge.

Knox's first wife, now a famous psychic, had allegedly conspired with him to frame and then get rid of his last mistress, Pip's ex-girlfriend, Courtenay. His brother Trick suspected him of embezzling from and killing their aunt. His business partner, former Mayor Stuart Machalvie, was the focus of a federal investigation due to the schemes he and Knox had cooked up to line their pockets and get Knox elected senator. There were also a couple of high-level politicians who would be relieved if Knox Rodefeffer could no longer testify against them in order to save his own hide.

Claire thought it was obvious someone hit him from behind, but if so, wouldn't he have fallen forward? How could he have died from a wound on the back of the head, yet be lying on his side on the stairs, facing the wall? Maybe he was dazed at first, and attempted to flee up the stairs, only to pass out and fall. But his position didn't jibe with that scenario. It was certainly a puzzle.

She had the thought that maybe she would just look around a little before someone from the sheriff's office arrived. She probably had at least ten minutes.

She went back through the hallway next to the stairway, which led to the kitchen. Everything was spotless and neat in there. The door from the kitchen to the mudroom was open, and in the mudroom, there were muddy footprints on the floor. Claire could see that the deadbolt was drawn back on the door to the outside.

There was a set of stairs on the other side of the kitchen that led to the second floor. Claire listened, but it didn't seem like there was anyone else in the house. She didn't imagine whoever killed Knox would want to hang around to see what happened.

Claire went up the back stairs, which led to a long hallway. All of the doors were closed except one to what looked like Knox's office. Inside, it looked as if Knox had just stepped away from his desk. His cell phone lay on the desk next to the documents he'd been looking at. There was a stack of bills, and the amount due on each made Claire whistle. There were also several overdue notices and a checkbook register that displayed a negative number as the balance.

Knox was in deep debt, no doubt about it.

Claire plucked a tissue from a box on the desk and covered the end of her finger with it. Pressing his cell phone buttons through the tissue, she went to the call history for the day and photographed the screen with her own phone.

Claire looked around the room, and noticed a painting on the floor, leaned against the wall. Above it, the door to Knox's safe was wide open. Claire peered in; it was empty.

In the distance, she heard a siren as the first county car entered the city limits. She shoved the tissue and her phone in her pocket, ran back down the hall, and down the back stairs. She ran through the kitchen, the hallway next to the stairs, and out the front door. Out of breath, her heart pounding, she sat down on the front steps and tried Laurie again.

It went to voicemail.

She watched as a county car careened up Peony Street and slid around the corner of Morning Glory Avenue. After it pulled up the driveway and parked, Sarah got out of the driver's side door. She was frowning as she walked up the path to where Claire was sitting.

"Where's Purcell?" Sarah asked.

"He must be off today," Claire said. "He's not answering my calls."

"Passed out drunk's more like it," Sarah said, shaking her head.

"Even a police chief gets a day off," Claire insisted, but Sarah rolled her eyes.

Another county car arrived, and Sarah turned to greet her team. Claire watched as they dressed in crime scene suits and paper booties.

"Don't leave," she told Claire before they went inside.

"Don't worry," Claire said.

She figured Sarah would be preoccupied for a while, so she took out her phone and opened a browser. She did a search for each phone number she had found in Knox's phone and added the numbers and names to her contact list.

At 8:00 a.m., Knox called the bank in Rose Hill

At 8:19 a.m., Knox called a bank in Pittsburgh.

At 8:32 a.m., Knox called his first wife, Anne Marie, when it would have been 5:30 a.m. in California.

At 9:14 a.m., Knox called an attorney's office in Morgantown.

At 10:12 a.m., Marigold Lawson called Knox.

At 10:28 a.m., Knox called Stuart Machalvie.

At 12:20 p.m., Knox called Rodefeffer Realty.

At 12:52 p.m., Pip called Knox from Frieda's house.

Claire wanted to write it all out and analyze the data, but she didn't dare do that while Sarah was so close by.

By calling his mother, she was able to find Skip, Scott's youngest deputy, and a few minutes later he drove up in the town's only cruiser but seemed reluctant to come up the stairs.

"Frank's in Pendleton at the courthouse," he said.

"Sarah's inside," Claire said.

He started to enter the house, but Claire stopped him.

"I wouldn't go in there without a crime scene suit on if I were you."

"Oh, yeah, right," he said.

He looked toward the cruiser as if he longed to jump in it and drive away.

"What do you think I ought to do?" he asked her.

"Just wait for Sarah," Claire said. "Keep an eye on me."

Skip's eyes widened.

"Are you a witness to the crime?" he asked her.

"I don't know what happened to Knox," Claire said. "Pip found him."

Skip cleared his throat, and his voice jumped an octave as he spoke.

"A blow to the back of the head," he said. "They were talking about it on the radio as I came up the hill."

"Pip didn't do it," Claire said. "You know Pip; he's too much of a coward to kill anybody. He's more of a pot-head than a hot-head."

Skip shrugged.

"I guess I'm just crowd control," he said.

"I guess I'm the crowd," Claire said. "What would you like me to do?"

"You're a person of interest," Skip said, "so don't go anywhere."

"Don't worry," Claire said. "Have you seen Laurie today?"

Skip couldn't look her in the eye. He cleared his throat.

"He's off today," he said.

"I know he's got a drinking problem."

"He's never come to work drunk," Skip said. "My dad's an alcoholic, so I'd know. They think vodka doesn't smell, but it does; I know that smell. He might be drinking, but not when he's working. Laurie's a good guy; we all like him."

"I like him, too," Claire said.

"How's your dad?" Skip asked.

"About the same."

"The chief was always good to me; he paid the tuition my last semester at the community college after my old man stole my student loan money."

While they waited, they talked about her dad and other people they knew. Skip still seemed like the same shy, gawky grade-schooler he had been when Claire was a teenager, just much taller. After Claire moved back, Skip's mother had taken a liking to her Boston terrier, Mackie Pea, and had knitted her a little coat, which the little dog had almost immediately drug through the mud.

By the time Sarah came back outside, Claire and Skip were in the front yard, passing a football he had found in the bushes. Sarah took one look at them and threw her hands up in the air. Claire had thrown a pass right as she came out; the football hit Skip in the chest and bounced off. He looked petrified; Claire wished Laurie was there to protect him.

"You," Sarah said as she pointed to Skip. "Get that car out of the driveway and wait for the morgue van."

Skip ran to the car like his shirttail was on fire.

"You," she pointed at Claire. "Come with me."

"Pip didn't do it," Claire said. "He found Knox. The front door was open when I got here. His truck was parked in the driveway; he wasn't trying to hide that he was here."

Sarah waved that away.

"I was with the State Police when they questioned your ex-husband after his girlfriend was murdered. He's a beautiful specimen of manhood, but he's got the brains of a golden retriever."

"Are you going to question me soon?" Claire asked. "I need to pick up my dad."

"Your father was a gentleman and a damn good policeman," Sarah said. "It's a shame what's happened to him."

Claire was not used to Sarah being this personable, and it made her suspicious.

"Let's go sit in my car," Sarah said. "We'll record your interview, and then later one of these yahoos will type it out for you to sign. Off the record, why were you up here?"

Claire knew nothing she said was off the record; what was Sarah up to?

"I called Pip's mother, and she said he had come up here to ask Knox for money. I knew it wouldn't go well, and I wanted to ..."

What had she wanted to do?

"Rescue him," Sarah filled in.

It almost seemed as if Sarah understood and empathized.

That couldn't be true.

"I guess," Claire said. "After you have a relationship with somebody ... even when it ends badly ..."

"I get it," Sarah said, and Claire could swear she looked as if she empathized. "You never quit wanting to look out for them."

Claire nodded, while thinking, 'I cannot trust her. It's got to be a trap, but it doesn't feel fake. Is Sarah that good of an actress?'

The questioning was straightforward, and Sarah didn't throw any curve balls. Claire told her about Knox's altercation with the dark sedan and regretted she hadn't thought to record the plate number. She told Sarah about Knox pushing her in front of the car and named Sister M-Squared as a witness.

Claire studied the woman as they talked. Claire could see how tired she was; there were dark circles underneath her eyes, and she looked a little haggard.

Claire guessed even bitches could have sorrows.

Afterward, Sarah gave her a ride down the hill but detoured to Sunflower Street. She parked in front of Scott's house, where Laurie was staying. His truck was parked out front.

"Huh," Claire said. "He must be home."

"He is," Sarah said, and to Claire's surprise, Sarah's eyes filled with tears. "If you would check on him, I'd appreciate it."

Claire's mouth fell open, and she stared at Sarah.

"Just make sure he's okay," Sarah said. "And if he's not, take care of it as discreetly as possible. I can't help you, but text me and let me know if he's okay."

Claire took Sarah's number and watched from the curb as she drove away. She knew Sarah and Laurie had a fling after his wife died, but it now seemed like it had meant much more to Sarah.

What the hell?

Claire pounded on the front door, but no one answered. It was locked with a deadbolt. She went around to the back and pounded on that door, but there was no answer. The doorknob was locked, but when she rattled the door, it felt like the deadbolt was not engaged. Claire took out a credit card and slid it between the door jam and door, where it caught the slanted edge of the flimsy doorknob bolt; she wriggled it back and forth until she disengaged it, and then pushed the door open.

'Only a cop in Rose Hill would have such a piss-poor security system,' she thought.

"Laurie," she called out, but he didn't answer.

She smelled him before she found him. He was passed out on the bed, snoring like a sleep apnea patient, with a large empty vodka bottle next to him. He had spilled the vodka and pissed the bed. He was lucky he hadn't vomited and asphyxiated.

Claire regarded him. What she felt, other than disappointment, sadness, and pity, was disgust. Okay, he wasn't on duty, and he wasn't driving; he was in the privacy of his temporary home, and the only thing he had hurt belonging to anyone else was the urine-soaked bed. Well, that and Sarah's heart, now that Claire knew she had one. And her own heart? Claire didn't want to think about that.

Did this happen because of the whiskey she'd given him the night before? Claire felt a deep sense of shame. Whatever would or would not eventually happen between them, she felt she owed him the effort of making sure he was okay.

Claire called Patrick, the only person she knew who could advise her and be trusted. He said he would come up as soon as he got someone to watch the bar. She offered. Her dad was there, and it wouldn't hurt to feed him pizza and let him watch a game on the big screen while she tended bar. She left the back door unlocked and ran down to the Rose and Thorn, gladly handing off the responsibility for Laurie to her cousin.

"It's a shame," is all Patrick said.

Claire put an apron on, and the locals at the bar immediately started razzing her.

"Shut up, or you're cut off," she said.

They grumbled but returned to watching the baseball game on the huge, flat-screen television.

She texted Sarah: "alive and asleep."

Sarah did not text back.

Claire gave the locals each a free shot and a beer. It wasn't their fault she was in such a bad mood; bitches have sorrows, too.

While she was working at the Thorn, Professor Richmond called and asked if she was still planning to join them that evening for the Scrabble game. Claire didn't feel like it, but she thought she better play nice with her prospective boss.

After Claire delivered her father home, it was past seven, and he was sleepy. She knew he would immediately fall asleep in the recliner, but she waited for Melissa to show up before she left.

"Thank you for giving me all these evenings off while my mom is out of town," Claire said.

"You deserve the break," Melissa said. "I don't mind it; I brought Patrick's laptop so I could do my lessons."

"That's great," Claire said.

"What did they say when you called?" Melissa asked.

"Who?"

"The po-po," Melissa said. "What did they say about the you-know-what at the you-know-where?"

"Oh crap, I completely forgot," Claire said. "Walk me outside."

Out front, where her father could not hear, Claire filled her in on what had happened at Knox's house.

"That man was lower than a worm's willy," Melissa said. "He never done nothin' to me, personal-like, but he done pissed off a lot of other people in this town."

Claire hoped Melissa's grammar lessons would help, but she could see it would be a tough row to hoe.

Claire walked up the steps to Professor Richmond's apartment, which was over the garage behind the Rose Hill Bed and Breakfast. She could hear them before the door opened; it sounded like they were arguing. When Professor Richmond opened the door, he had a glass of what smelled like gin in one hand and was wearing his half-moon reading glasses.

"Claire's here!" he told the people inside, and Claire heard the other two men cheer.

"My good gentlewoman," he said, as he stood aside to let her in. "The pretty cousin of Mary Margaret; how fares your good cousin on her trip to the seaside?"

"I think she regrets inviting so many family members to join them," Claire said.

Both men, who were seated, jumped up as she entered. The Scandinavian giant she remembered as "Torby" enveloped her slender hand between his two giant paws and gently pressed it.

"Nice to see you again," Claire said.

"The pleasure is all mine," he said.

The short, round, bald one with the glasses, "Ned," bowed at the waist.

"Welcome," he said.

"We're just about to finish a game," Professor Richmond said. "Afterward, we'll take a break so Ned can smoke one of his loathsome cigarettes, and then we'll begin again with you."

"Claire can be the judge," Torby said.

"Yes, Claire, you decide for us," Ned said.

"The bone of contention, as it were," Professor Richmond said, "is the word 'weltschmerz.' "

"I thought Scrabble was played with only seven letter tiles," Claire said.

"We play our own version, with three sets of tiles, and everyone gets twenty letters," Ned said.

"The rule is we only choose words from everyday modern American English usage," Professor Richmond said.

"Such as it is," Ned said, and chuckled.

"No one I have met in this country would use that word but you," Torby said to Ned.

"What does it mean?" Claire asked.

"It means to be disappointed because the world is not what you wish it to be," Ned explained to Claire. "I have many American friends who use this word. They all know what it means."

"Ned wishes the world used more German words," Torby told Claire. "He is presently experiencing weltschmerz."

Ned didn't seem insulted by that; he merely nodded and smiled as he shrugged as if to say he couldn't disagree.

"I've never heard that word used before," Claire said. "But I know exactly what that feels like."

"Denied," Professor Richmond said. "Pick it up, Ned; try again. Claire, make yourself at home, do. There are nibbly things in the kitchen if you're hungry. Help yourself to a drink."

The small studio apartment was made up of a galley kitchen, living room, bathroom, and bedroom, all tucked into 600 square feet. He had furnished the living room for comfort, with four club chairs surrounding a low round table, on which was placed the Scrabble board. There was a dart board on one wall, with multiple darts stuck in it.

On another wall was a framed poster promoting the Royal Shakespeare Theater's *The Merry Wives of Windsor* from 2007. Judi Dench played Mistress Quickly, and Simon Callow played Falstaff; theirs were the only names she recognized. The requisite bust of the bard was on top of the fridge, where it wore novelty glasses sporting a mustache and big nose as well as a bright red fez with a gold tassel.

The small cart serving as his bar was well-stocked with good liquor, but, thinking that staying sober was the prudent choice, Claire poured a club soda for herself and dropped in a wedge of lime.

She looked at the photos on the refrigerator, thinking it must be a universal habit to use that surface as a gallery. There were faculty group photos and one of a young group of actors dressed in Elizabethan garb, lined up on a stage. There was one of a handsome young man holding up a skull; she didn't have to guess what role he was playing. He had signed it, 'with love and thanks, Rafe.'

Rafe. So refined. So not a Rose Hill name. Here it would be Ralphie, and if he hated that he would use his middle name instead, unless that was worse, in which case he could go by any number of nicknames, including Buddy, Bubba, Bubby, or some horrible name assigned to him by vicious schoolmates, like Fatty, Farty, Beanpole, or Stretch.

Claire wandered over to a nearby bookshelf, filled with the expected Shakespeare collections and other classics she recognized from having been made to read them in high school.

"All done," Professor Richmond said. "I am victorious, for once."

"I am out for a smoke," Ned said and went outside.

"I am out for a piss," Torby said and went down the short hallway to the bathroom.

"Professor Richmond," Claire said.

"Please, Claire, I've told you, call me Alan."

"Alan," she said. "Have you heard anything about the position?"

"No, love," he said, and Claire was surprised to hear him use such a common endearment, but he quickly reverted to his upper-class British speaking voice. "Not to worry, my dear. There is nothing either good or bad but thinking makes it so."

"Do you think Gwyneth Eldridge could blackball me with the committee?"

"I suppose so, as she is on the board, but why would she?"

"I turned down a job working for her. She doesn't like to be told no."

"Arch-villain, she," he said. "Despised, distressed, hated, martyr'd, kill'd!"

"Not quite that bad," Claire said. "Unless she screws up this job for me. Then all bets are off."

"I don't think you have anything to worry about," he said. "I told the committee you could get Sloan Merryweather for the film festival, and they're all panting to meet her. More of a scenery chewer than an actress, to my mind, but to each his own."

"I couldn't, though," Claire said. "Even if I asked her she wouldn't do it. We didn't part on the best of terms."

"Is that so?"

"I would be great at this job," Claire protested. "I graduated from a prestigious film and theater arts hair and makeup school in Los Angeles. There's a copy of my diploma in my application packet."

Claire's hope level dropped to the bottom of the barrel as a look of disappointment and irritation replaced Alan's previously patronizing smile. Why hadn't he asked her earlier about getting Sloan? She would have told him that was impossible. It was apparent he hadn't even looked at her application or resume. They didn't care about her qualifications; they only cared about the movie star. It had so often been that way. Why did she think this situation would be any different?

"I'm sorry," Claire said. "I hope this doesn't mean I won't get the job."

He waved her away as if he were already bored with the topic.

"Fortune brings in some boats that are not steered," he said. "Leave it to fate."

"Do you have a quote for every occasion?"

He gave her a stern look.

"Irritating you, is it?"

"No, I like it," Claire said. "It's a pleasure to hear you speak."

"It intimidates the students and amuses their parents," he said. "I like to give good value for the obscene cost of tuition."

"What about 'This above all; to thine own self be true,'" Claire asked.

"Truth doesn't always pay the rent, though, does it, pet?"

"No," Claire said. "It doesn't."

"Are you in financial distress?"

"Nothing like that," Claire said. "I'm just bored."

"That is a statement I simply will not allow," he said. "There is no earthly reason for anyone to be bored, especially not one living in a country where for most people matters of life and death are not a daily consideration. You could read, for example, one of about a thousand books I could name off the tip of my tongue, easily accessible through two libraries and one excellent bookstore–owned by your fair cousin, no less–or by using one of the many infernal contraptions the students attach to their persons like external pacemakers ..."

"It's not that I don't like to read," Claire protested. "It's more that I hate to begin a book and know immediately how it will end; it's like there are three plots available and a thousand ways to rehash them."

"What about the pleasure of the words, my dear? What about the pure rhapsodic joy one may experience when language is wrought by the hands of a genius? The bard often stole, no, borrowed his plots; hell, he even sometimes borrowed the speeches from other plays, but all is forgiven when you hear it spoken aloud. Never does the English language sing as it does when performed well as written by Shakespeare."

"I see why you're such a great professor."

"I merely play the role of professor, but my sentiment, although dramatically conveyed, is humbly sincere," he said. "One who can turn up a nose at Shakespeare has no soul, at least not an English soul."

"I love to hear it spoken, to see it acted," Claire said. "It makes sense to me then. But I fall asleep when I read it. It's hard to comprehend it when I'm the one interpreting it."

"I shall take you on as a student," he said. "A private student. I shall convert your soul to English; nay, I shall save it."

'Good luck with that,' Claire thought but did not say.

Torby and Ned returned, and a new game commenced. Claire was an average player and no match for the intellects of her opponents, but to them, she was a valuable expert on common American English usage. It was a dubious honor, but one she accepted, nonetheless.

Throughout the game, Claire listened as the three professors also played a verbal game of quotes. Whatever word had been placed on the board, the player who put it there would share a quote that related to its meaning, and then the other two professors would share a quote that related to the same word, or to a random word in the first player's quote. She realized now that's what they had been doing on pub night in the Thorn.

After listening to several of these without participating, Claire decided to try to join in. The word she placed on the board was "ruin."

"We are here to ruin ourselves, to break our hearts, love the wrong people, and die," she said. "John Patrick Shanley wrote that; it's from the movie *Moonstruck*."

The three professors were looking at her as if surprised to find that not only was she still in the room but that she could speak. Claire found she got a little thrill from shocking them.

"I often think I should have that tattooed on my ass," she said, and then worried she had gone too far.

After a brief pause they laughed, or more accurately, Professor Richmond smirked, Ned guffawed, and Torby giggled. Claire was relieved.

"Well done, you," Professor Richmond said. "If it is true that there are as many minds as there are heads, then there are as many kinds of love as there are hearts. Tolstoy."

"It is not a lack of love, but a lack of friendship that makes unhappy marriages," Torby said. "Friedrich Nietzsche."

"Imagination, on the contrary, which is ever wandering beyond the bounds of truth, joined to self-love and that self-confidence we are so apt to indulge, prompt us to draw conclusions which are not immediately derived from facts," Ned said. "Antoine-Laurent Lavoisier."

"That's not very romantic, Ned," Torby said.

"Romance is a lie told to propagate the species and sell deodorant," Ned said. "You can quote *me* on that."

Claire now wished she had not attempted to play this additional game. It added another layer of stress to an already challenging situation.

Torby set down the word "reason" off of the letter *n* in Claire's word.

He smiled at Claire.

"There is always some madness in love. But there is also always some reason in madness," Torby said. "Nietzsche, again."

"The heart has its reasons which reason knows not," Ned said. "Blaise Pascal."

"Much improved, Ned," Professor Richmond said. "Faith consists in believing when it is beyond the power of reason to believe. Voltaire. You could substitute the word 'love' for faith, and it would still be accurate."

"What, no Shakespeare?" Ned said as if shocked. "That's two in a row."

"Very well," Professor Richmond said. "And yet, to say the truth, reason and love keep little company together nowadays."

They all looked at Claire.

Her heart was racing as she tried to think of a quote using the word 'reason' or 'love.' She could think of any number of song lyrics, but here she was claiming her area of expertise was film, and she wanted to stick with that. She thought of Laurie, and a quote immediately came to her, as easily as if the temperamental actress who once said it had just lit a cigarette and raised a heavily-penciled-on eyebrow.

"Love is a fire. But whether it is going to warm your hearth or burn down your house, you can never tell," she said. "Joan Crawford."

"Wonderful," Torby said.

"She is an old-time film actress," Ned said. "Correct?"

"Correct," Claire said.

"I want to thank you, Claire, for throwing up the sash to allow some fresh air into our musty room," Professor Richmond said. "You must never miss a game night."

Two hours later, as Claire left the professor's apartment, warmed by their flattering attention and buzzed by their clever banter, she thought, 'What odd friends I'm collecting.'

They wanted her to learn to play Whist; it sounded too difficult to her, but for them, she said she would try. Alan had given her a reading list and a stack of books; it was daunting, but she wanted to please him.

She hoped the position at the college would work out. She also hoped her experience and skill would be more valuable than who she knew, and yet, even as she cheered herself with these thoughts, deep down she realized she was hoping it would all work out in the face of all the evidence to the contrary. She was old enough to know that the world did not reward merit as often as it did connections.

Her mother, who was known for her positive outlook, still could be heard to say, "When has the world ever been fair to this family?"

'I'm ass-deep in weltschmerz,' she thought.

She crossed the street to the Rose and Thorn and stopped in. Patrick was polishing glasses. He raised his head in a greeting. When he'd returned from Laurie's earlier in the evening, he had pronounced him passed out but in no danger; Patrick was better than an EMT in diagnosing degrees of drunkenness.

Claire set her stack of books on the bar and took a seat at the end, near the front door, the seat her father used to sit in and the one Laurie always chose: back to the wall, the best position from which to observe the entrance and the whole bar.

At her request, Patrick brought her a club soda with lime.

"You want a shot in that?" he asked her.

"I'd rather face my troubles than drown them," she said.

"What's up?"

"I don't think I got that job working at the college," she said.

"I don't know why you'd want to work with that bunch of snobs, anyway," he said.

"I like the people I've met," she said. "I would be great at that job; I'm good at what I do, and I think I would be a good teacher."

"So what's the snag?"

"They want me to get Sloan Merryweather for their film festival."

"So ask her."

"I can't afford to," Claire said.

"Why? What's it gonna cost ya?"

"My soul, probably. And even if she agreed, she'd probably cancel at the last minute just to spite me."

"So work for Sean."

"It's so boring," she said. "Plus Melissa wants the job."

"She told me about the online class," he said and shook his head.

"You don't think it's a good idea?"

"I think trying to be somebody you're not is always a mistake."

"It's okay to improve yourself to make something more of your life."

"Except you got her hopes up," he said. "Now if she doesn't get the job she'll feel worse than she did to begin with; plus things will be weird between her and my brother."

"I'm sorry," Claire said. "I thought it would help."

"Maybe it will," Patrick said. "I just don't want her to get hurt."

"I wish I had someone like you on my side," Claire said. "I could use the support."

"Laurie's a good guy," he said. "You could stand to be patient with him for a little while."

Claire shrugged. She thought of Laurie lying there in a pool of piss and vodka, snoring his head off.

"Looks like old Ed's got himself a little family now," Patrick said. "That Eve's a piece of work."

"Even bitches have sorrows."

"What's that supposed to mean?"

"It's something I've been thinking about," Claire said. "I'm going to try to cut everyone some slack. We all have our troubles."

"Listen," Patrick said. "I could use a partner here, and Melissa can't do it on account of her parole. I heard Meredith's been to see Trick; she's so broke she has to sell the tea room. I wanna buy it to expand this place, but I haven't got the dough for the down payment. Whadda ya say?"

"I'll think about it," she said. "Did you hear about Knox?"

"Of course," he said. "The scanner grannies knew before the police did."

"That's probably my fault," Claire said, thinking of her frantic cell phone call to the station.

The scanner grannies were a group of elderly people in town who kept their ears glued to their old-school police scanners, now illegal, which could pick up on even more than radio transmissions. Claire had taken to doing more texting than calling since she'd been home on account of the likelihood that any cell phone calls she made were being monitored by the local blue-haired version of the NSA.

"What are you hearing?" she asked him.

"They're after your ex," he said. "The idiot shouldn't have run off like he did; makes him look guilty."

"I don't think Pip did it," Claire said. "Not that it matters what I think."

"The back door was unlocked, and they found footprints in the mud to and from the woods.

"Pip went in and left through the front door."

"Poor old Pip; always in the wrong place at the wrong time; like that time he married you."

Claire balled up the cocktail napkin and threw it at him.

"He's probably halfway to Mexico," Claire said. "That's his usual response."

"Well, Knox's wife number two is in town, so she might have done it; Anne Marie's in California, so wife number one is in the clear."

"Unless she hired it out," Claire said. "I overheard Trick and Knox having an argument behind Machalvie's. You think Trick would kill his brother?"

"A few years ago I would happily have killed my eldest brother, but someone else did me the favor," he said. "Nothing would surprise me."

"The ex-mayor was worried about Knox talking too much," Claire said. "There's a federal case being built against them."

"Another fine suspect," Patrick said.

"Plus whoever was in that car Knox was throwing rocks at."

"That was entertaining," Patrick said.

"Are there any payphones in town?"

"Why?"

"I need to report something to the police, anonymously."

"Care to share?"

"No," she said. "The fewer people who know, the better."

"There's a payphone down at the post office," he said.

"Thanks for the drink."

"Think about what I said. You could manage the events and food. You'd be great at it. You could also sing anytime you wanted. I remember when you used to want to do that for a living."

"Not anymore," she said. "I'm done traveling, and I'm too old for the band bullshit."

"You could team up with Laurie," he said. "Piano and vocals."

"I don't think I can depend on Laurie," she said. "I will keep the partner idea in mind, though, thanks, Patrick."

As Claire got up to leave, she was surprised to see Eve enter the bar.

"Do you have a minute?" Eve asked.

"Sure," Claire said, dismayed to find her heart racing.

She hadn't done anything wrong; why was she so scared of Eve?

They sat down at a table by the window, the furthest from the eavesdropping locals. Eve waved away Patrick's offer of something to drink.

"I thought it would be good for us to have a talk," Eve said. "My husband told me how fond he is of you and how close you've become, so I imagine you weren't too happy to see his pregnant wife come back to town."

"I don't think of you two as husband and wife," Claire said. "Obviously, for the past ten years, neither have you."

Eve dropped any semblance of friendliness.

"Listen," she said. "I can't help what happened. We're just trying to do what's right for our baby."

"Your baby, obviously," Claire said. "But I'm guessing the father must be somebody pretty inconvenient."

"I strongly suggest," Eve said, "that you back off and leave Ed alone. You don't know me very well, because if you did, you'd be much more careful."

"What exactly are you threatening to do to me, Eve?" Claire said. "You obviously think I'm pretty stupid, so you can't be surprised you have to spell it out for me."

"I have connections in Hollywood," Eve said. "I made a few phone calls this afternoon, and one of them was to a private investigator. If there's anything you wouldn't want Ed to know about your time out there, or that you wouldn't want the board of trustees at Eldridge to know, I suggest you watch your step."

The look on Eve's face was pure malice spiked with self-entitlement. Luckily for Claire, she had twenty years of experience dealing with rich, powerful sociopaths.

"Here's the thing I learned in the film industry about blackmail," Claire said. "The only way to stop a blackmailer is to hit them back hard with your own blackmail. I know quite a few people in your industry, the kind nobody pays attention to, the ones who see and hear everything because they're not considered important enough to be discreet around. If you wanna play that game with me, Eve, then you should know who *you're* dealing with. You may wound me, but I can destroy you."

Claire said what she did with a friendly smile, using the same tone she would've used if she were sharing an amusing anecdote. The achievement of her intended effect was evident in the micro-expression of fear that flitted across Eve's face. It was gone quickly, but it was proof that Claire's counterpunch had landed.

"So here we are," Eve said, "at an impasse."

"Except that, I have little to lose compared to you," Claire said. "I can always go back to cutting hair, and I can always find another boyfriend. I wonder, however, if you could afford to bear what I could do to your career. Not blatantly, of course, but through my connections at all the tabloid magazines, gossip sites, and entertainment television shows. Think of all the media mileage they could get out of guessing who the real baby daddy is. You better hope that kid has blue eyes and a bald head instead of the brown eyes and dark hair of a certain senator."

An expression of blatant fear was now firmly established on Eve's face, along with the fury of one used to getting her way through guile and intimidation being thwarted by an opponent she has fatally underestimated.

"How much is it going to cost to make you go away?" Eve asked.

"Confess to Ed before I get to him," Claire said.

"I'll see you in hell first," Eve hissed as she struggled to get up.

In her haste to leave, she knocked over a chair, and everyone in the bar turned around to look.

"Let me know when the baby shower is," Claire called out after her. "I can't wait to see the sonogram pictures!"

"What was that about?" Patrick asked as he righted the chair that had fallen.

"Just another clever bitch who thought I must be stupid because I'm from here," Claire said.

"Yeah, I hate when that happens," Patrick said.

Claire walked down Rose Hill Avenue toward the post office. She was all wound up from her fight with Eve and feeling queasy about how vicious she had been, even if it was in self-defense. Claire tried to put herself in Eve's place, and imagine what she would do in the same situation, but she had nothing to lose compared to Eve, with her public image and nascent media career threatened by a scandalous affair with a married politician. Claire couldn't imagine being in that situation. It must feel awful, though, after all Eve went through to get where she was.

It was so common it was a cliché to fall in love with the wrong person, and then do even more stupid things as a result. Claire could easily imagine doing that because she so often had.

Claire decided that Eve's predicament was the most convincing evidence yet that bitches could indeed have sorrows. They were still bitches, though, even if they were pregnant.

As she crossed the street, she looked down Pine Mountain Road toward the river and saw the lights were on in Ed's office. She did an about-face and walked down there. He was sitting at the computer, typing something. She tapped on the window. He smiled and jumped up to let her in.

"How goes the newspaper business?" she asked him.

"I've been calling you," Ed said. "I thought maybe you weren't speaking to me."

Claire took a seat on the other side of the work table and refused the beer he offered.

"I'm sorry I've been such a bitch about the baby," Claire said.

"I don't blame you for being sore," Ed said.

"Is Eve going to stay here in Rose Hill for a while?"

"No," he said. "She wants to have the baby in Atlanta, where she thinks the hospitals are better. She's going back next week. I'll go down there when she's due so I can be there when it's born."

"Are you thinking about moving to Atlanta?"

"No," he said. "I'm a Rose Hillian, born and bred. Besides, Tommy's in school here, and I've got the job at Eldridge and the *Sentinel* to think about. Eve will go wherever her career takes her, and I'm not cut out to be a camp follower. We'll work something out."

"You could bring up the child here," Claire said. "It takes a village, I hear, and Rose Hill's one of the finest."

"Eve wants more than we can give it here," Ed says. "Private schools, you know, a college covered in ivy, and so forth."

"Last I looked Eldridge was covered in something, but it may be kudzu."

"I think she has something more prestigious in mind."

"Like Hogwarts."

"That's the one."

"So what will your role be, exactly?"

"Father as needed, I guess," he said. "Daddy on call."

Claire started to say something and then shut her mouth.

"It's convenient, you were going to say," he said. "You think she's using me."

"What's it matter?" Claire said. "The child will have a great father; that's more important than any baby mama drama."

"That's what I think," he said. "I know it's more about what's best for her career than having any kind of real relationship with me. I know all that, but there's a chance it's mine, you know? And even if it isn't, it will be. I love Tommy, but we both know I'm only a stand-in for Melissa. This could be my only shot at having a child of my own."

Claire stood up, more as a response to that last comment stabbing her in the heart than anything else. Tears stung at the back of her eyes but she sniffed them back.

"I'll let you get back to work," she said. "Are you writing about Knox?"

"Yeah," he said. "Trying to get it in tomorrow's Pendleton paper. Do you mind telling me what happened?"

Claire sat back down, told Ed everything that happened, and he took notes. She took out her phone and gave him the times of the calls and the owners of the phone numbers.

"Sarah doesn't know I have this information," she told him. "I can call Anne Marie; she may be willing to tell me what Knox's call was about. I'll let you know what she says."

"I won't put any of this in the *Pendletonian*," he said. "I'll follow up on all of the other calls and use what I find out in Sunday's *Sentinel*. That should give Sarah enough time to disseminate the information among the ranks, which will clear you, and still give the *Sentinel* the scoop."

"Pip didn't kill him," Claire said.

"I'm calling him a person of interest," Ed said. "Sorry, but that's as innocent as I can make it sound when he took off like that."

"Pip's an idiot, but he's a passive idiot," Claire said. "He doesn't have it in him to kill anyone."

"I hope you're right."

Claire was irritated by Ed's refusal to take her word for it, that Pip did not kill Knox. It felt as if the chasm between them, created by Eve's pregnancy, was widening further by the minute. Claire now felt like an old girlfriend Ed was distantly fond of, instead of the role she had played a few weeks ago when he was pledging to see her through what turned out to be a pregnancy false alarm of her own. He was already driving down the road to fatherhood with Eve riding shotgun, and she was left behind, coughing in the dust as they sped away.

Claire had the ammunition to shoot the tires off of that car, but there was a baby to consider. It was bad enough she had just verbally threatened a pregnant woman, albeit one who had tried to blackmail her. That kid might be born with a lightning bolt on its forehead, and it would be all Claire's fault.

Claire left Ed's office and walked up the hill to the crossroads of Pine Mountain Road and Rose Hill Avenue. The lights were on in the Little Bear Bookstore, and Eldridge orientation attendees were congregating in groups on the sidewalk between there and the college. The air was crisp and clean smelling, a steady breeze coming off the Little Bear River. There were bright stars in the dark sky, and an almost full moon had crested the hills to the south-east.

Claire felt as lonely as she had ever felt, even more so than when she was on the other side of the earth from what she thought of as home. Now she was home, but with her mother and cousins away at the beach, Ed working things out with Eve, Laurie drunk to the point of unconsciousness, one ex on the run from the law and another in the arms of her ex-employer, who cared where she was or what she was doing?

Melissa had Patrick, Eve had Ed, Maggie had Scott, and Hannah had Sam. Even Kay, who hadn't had a date in years, now had two brothers vying for her heart.

'I don't have anybody,' Claire thought.

She knew she was sinking into the quicksand of self-pity, but she didn't care. She felt a kind of perverse satisfaction in being proved unworthy. At least you knew where you stood in the scheme of things, instead of hoping life would somehow miraculously get better.

Some days being optimistic took too much effort.

Claire used the pay phone to dial 911, gave the operator all the information she had about the meth lab, refused to supply her identity, and then headed home. As she passed Ed's house, she avoided looking through the uncovered window into the lighted front room.

Why didn't people draw their curtains at night? Didn't they know the effect their belly cupping and supportive hugging could have on an old spinster? Well, technically, a divorcee, but she felt more like a spinster.

She even had the requisite cat.

Barren.

Unloved.

Unemployable.

Willing to stoop low enough to threaten a pregnant blackmailer.

And she couldn't even shop online lest she go broke before her lonely old age set in. It was pitiful. All she needed now was a hearing aid, and she could be a junior scanner granny.

Inside her parents' house, her father was snoring in his recliner. Melissa was working on the laptop and waved hello. Mackie Pea was curled up beside her, and Junior the cat was stretched out on the carpet near them.

"I saw the cat chase the dog," Melissa said.

"What?"

"I always say 'I seen' when I should say 'I saw.' "

"That's right," Claire said. "How's it going?"

"It's hard," she said. "There's a lot to remember."

"You'll get there," Claire said.

"Listen to this," she said. "Fitzpatrick Legal Services, Melissa speaking; how may I help you?"

"Very good."

"Mr. Fitzpatrick is not available," Melissa said. "May I take a message?"

"Melissa," Claire said. "Did it hurt your feelings that I suggested you improve your grammar."

"Course it did," she said. "Nobody likes to be told they're not good enough for something."

"I'm sorry," Claire said. "I stuck my nose in where I shouldn't have."

"I ain't mad at you," Melissa said. "I'm thinking of it like you said; I can pretend to be a secretary who talks good all day, and then talk like myself the rest of the time. It'll be my job to talk good."

"Well," Claire said.

"What?"

"Never mind," Claire said. "Just so you know, I love you just the way you are, as does everyone else."

"Thanks, Claire. I love y'all, too."

Claire considered the list of phone numbers she had given Ed. She knew anyone in Rose Hill wouldn't hesitate to share all they knew with Ed; they'd known him all his life or theirs. This didn't include Marigold Lawson, whose run for mayor was not supported by the local paper. The attorneys would claim client privilege until they received legal proof of Knox's death and a subpoena.

She knew Anne Marie from way back in the Hollywood days when Claire was Sloan's assistant. Anne Marie had been Sloan's go-to psychic, and Sloan had promoted her services to the Hollywood contingent of the California New Age community. Claire wasn't sure who's side Anne Marie was currently on visa vie the murder of Courtenay by her assistant, Jeremy. She probably still blamed Claire for helping the FBI nab Jeremy, and for helping Ed write an unflattering article about her bogus ministry, but it was worth a try.

"Claire Fitzpatrick," Anne Marie said, in a warmer tone than Claire expected. "I've been thinking about you all day; I'm not surprised to hear from you."

"Have they called you about Knox?"

"I got the call this afternoon," Anne Marie said. "I wasn't shocked, of course. My ex-husband has created quite the deficit of karma, wouldn't you say?"

"Nonetheless, I'm sorry for your loss," Claire said. "Had you heard from him lately?"

"He called me this morning to ask for money," Anne Marie said. "I told him that until after the trial I thought we should limit our communications to those made through our attorneys. I don't want to compromise my case by making what might look like an inappropriate remuneration."

"I guess he didn't like that."

"Patience has never been one of Knox's virtues, if he had any to begin with."

"Did he tell you anything else?"

"He told me Meredith was skulking around town, and that made him nervous. He said Trick was driving him crazy, as usual, and Stuart was distancing himself in a way that concerned him. I think he was finally facing the consequences of his actions and realizing he could no longer maneuver his way out of the destiny he had created for himself."

"Jeremy implicated you and Knox in Mamie Rodefeffer's death," Claire said. "Aren't *you* worried about that?"

"No, darling," Anne Marie said. "My guides tell me not to worry, so I don't. I didn't do anything wrong, and my karma is balanced, so there's nothing to fear. My attorneys are expensive and aggressive, as well, and that never hurts."

"I'm glad to hear it," Claire said.

"I had the weirdest vision of you today, during my afternoon meditation," Anne Marie said. "You were in a small boat on the ocean in a storm, and there were two drowning men, one clinging to each side, begging you to save them. There was only room in the boat for one man."

"What did I do?"

"You were paralyzed with indecision," Anne Marie said. "One man was young and had a family at home who needed him, and the other was old and had no one."

"But what did I do?"

"I don't know," Anne Marie said. "That was all it consisted of, just this horrible choice you had to make, and you being unable to make it."

"Do you see anything else?"

"I'm not really on tonight," Anne Marie said. "I had a veggie pizza with a lot of onions and peppers on it, so my instrument is all wonky."

"Well, thanks for the vision, I guess," Claire said. "Was there anyone Knox was afraid of, particularly, that he mentioned?"

"Other than the FBI, you mean?"

"Yes."

"He was feeling pretty paranoid," Anne Marie said. "He seemed to think the senator's people might be out to get him. Senator Bayard hadn't been returning Knox's phone calls, and Knox said there's been a dark car following him around town. That may only have been his guilty conscience manifesting as a hallucination."

Claire didn't tell Anne Marie she had seen the car up close and personal, and it was very real.

"Anyone else?"

"Oh, you know Knox," Anne Marie said. "He makes enemies like Mother Nature makes dandelions."

"Do you think he will contact you from the other side?"

"Quite possibly," Anne Marie said. "He may not even know he's passed, yet."

Claire shuddered as she thought of Knox as a hungry ghost, wandering around Rose Hill, looking for weak people to take over. What would he miss doing most?

"It's uncharitable to say, but his death may mean the end of my legal problems," Anne Marie said.

"Has the FBI been bothering you?"

"Not a bit," Anne Marie said. "I assume they're listening in right now, so I'd just like to thank them for that."

Claire felt her stomach turn as she realized that Anne Marie was probably right.

"Don't worry," Anne Marie said. "I see a bright light shining all around you. You've got nothing to worry about. Except for that boat thing; that was freaky."

Claire was already in bed when her phone rang. She smiled when she saw Scott's name.

"Hey, buddy!" she said when she answered. "How's it going down there?"

"I leave you all alone for five minutes, and people are running around getting themselves killed," he said. "What in the hell was Pip doing up at Knox's?"

Claire explained it all to Scott, and he was silent for a few moments when she finished.

"Are you still there?" she asked.

"Do you think I should come home early?" he asked.

"No, don't do that," Claire said. "You'll be back on Sunday, and surely things won't get any worse by then."

"How's Laurie doing?"

Claire paused.

"Uh oh," Scott said. "Dammit. I was hoping he would keep it together."

Claire told Scott what she had found at his house that afternoon.

"I hate to hear that," Scott said.

"He needs to go to rehab," Claire said, "but he thinks he'll lose his job if he does."

"He probably would," Scott said. "I wish that wasn't a real possibility, but it is."

"I don't know how to help him," Claire said. "What can I do?"

"I don't know," Scott said. "I'll talk to him when I get back, but I don't know how much good it will do."

"He's not doing it on the job."

"You know as well as I do that job is 24-7."

"I know."

"He starts in Pendleton on Monday?"

"Yep."

"Okay, I'll see what I can do," Scott said. "Listen, the reason I called is that I couldn't reach Laurie, and I didn't want to call Sarah, but I have some information that might help in the investigation into Knox's murder."

"How can I help?"

"When you see Laurie, ask him to call me," Scott said. "A couple of weeks ago I broke up a fight between Meredith and Knox, and she told me she'd like to slit his throat or something of that nature. I don't remember exactly, but when I heard how he died, well ..."

"I'll tell him to call."

"Have you seen Meredith around town this week?"

"I thought I saw someone in the tea room, but I couldn't tell if it was her or just a reflection on the window," she said. "Patrick said she was talking to Trick about selling it, so she must be around here somewhere."

"I wonder if she inherits anything or has any insurance policies on him."

"I don't know," Claire said. "I could try to find out."

"I'm just thinking out loud," Scott said. "Don't get involved in this."

"I know Pip didn't kill him," Claire said.

"Oh, I never thought he did," Scott said. "Pip's a make-love-not-war kinda guy."

"Thank you," Claire said. "I was beginning to think I was the only one who knew that."

"Maggie wants to talk to you," he said, and she could hear him hand the phone over.

"Quit trying to make my husband work," Maggie said.

"Are you pulling your hair out yet?" Claire asked her.

"Oh my goodness," Maggie said. "I don't know who to strangle first. It changes every day. If I come home alone, you'll know why."

"I miss you," Claire said. "I want you to come home yesterday."

"What's going on?"

Claire said, "It's been awful ..." but then she started to cry and couldn't continue.

"Oh, Claire Bear," Maggie said. "Whose ass do I need to kick first?"

Claire laughed, and then wiped her nose and eyes on the sheet.

"Do you have a minute?" she asked.

"I have all night," Maggie said. "I'm going out on the balcony, and I'm closing the door behind me. Okay, it's just you and me and the ocean. Now spill it."

Claire sighed. Somebody did care.

CHAPTER 7

Kay had been determined not to attend Diedre's funeral, but the Interdenominational Women's Society was handling the reception, and with all they were doing to support her mayoral run, she could not turn down their call for help. So it was that she found herself in the kitchen of the Rose Hill Community Center, filling a coffee urn when the Delvecchio family arrived from the cemetery.

Kay felt as if all eyes were upon her as Antonia, the matriarch of the Delvecchio family, entered the kitchen. Antonia was in her late sixties, but she was still a beautiful woman. Tall and statuesque, with an hour-glass figure atop long shapely legs, she had once been told she looked like Sophia Loren and had played that part to the hilt ever since.

Kay stood back and let everyone else rush forward. Eventually, Antonia caught her eye, smiled, grasped both of Kay's hands in her own, and kissed her on both cheeks.

"Darling Kay, mia cara amica, I am so glad to see you here," Antonia said. "Thank you for coming."

"I'm so sorry for your family's loss," Kay said.

Antonia said, "My poor son, a widower now, and so young," out loud but then leaned in and whispered, "but it was not such a great loss, I think."

Kay was shocked but tried not to show it.

"You will come to dinner at our house tonight," Antonia said.

"I wouldn't want to impose," Kay said.

"Don't be silly," Antonia said. "You're like a member of our family, and we want you to come."

"Thank you," Kay said. "Is there anything I can bring?"

"Bring a dessert," Antonia said. "I don't eat sweets, so I never make them."

Antonia smoothed her hands over her hips as if to assure herself that her diligence was still paying off. Kay felt huge and dowdy next to her, as if she came from a different species altogether than this elegant, sensuous woman.

"I'll be glad to," Kay said.

"Six o'clock," Antonia said and then whispered, "I'll set a place for you between Sonny and Matthew."

Antonia's eyes twinkled, and Kay swallowed hard.

"May the best son win," Antonia said and winked at Kay.

All through the reception, Kay stayed busy in the kitchen and fought the urge to eat, not an easy thing to do in a room full of Rose Hill's finest homemade food. She knew she was fat, everyone else knew she was fat, and they had to know that in order to be that fat she must eat a lot, but she'd be damned if she'd let them see her eat anything.

That was the thing about a food addiction if you didn't binge and purge; your weakness was right out there for everyone to see, criticize, or make faux-concerned comments about it.

'You have such a pretty face; it's such a shame.'

'I'm just worried about your health.'

'Have you thought about surgery?'

Worse were the people who didn't pretend to care, who looked at her body with disgust, or made comments and laughed. It made her wish she could disappear, that the earth would open up and swallow her whole. It made her feel as if she didn't deserve to live.

Why couldn't she have been cursed with an addiction she could hide? Were there any like that? She'd have to look into it.

She was blessedly alone in the kitchen when Sonny came in.

"So this is where you've been hiding," he said. "I hear you're coming to dinner."

"I couldn't tell your mother no," Kay said.

"No one can," he said. "She heard Matt came to see you. I told her I was going to give him a run for his money."

"I could tell," Kay said. "She was very funny about it."

"My mother has a great sense of humor," Sonny said. "Not too many people get that about her."

"You're her oldest, so you must be her favorite."

"Not even close," he said. "That would be baby Anthony. No, I'm probably last in line, but that makes me the underdog, and everyone roots for the underdog."

"You're not last in my line," Kay said.

"Kay Templeton, are you flirting with me?"

"I seem to be."

"Good," he said. "That means I'm ahead."

"This is not a race."

"It wasn't until my brother made it one," Sonny said.

Unfortunately, there were others in the kitchen when Matt came back. Kay could see many exchanged looks and surreptitious smiles, which reinforced the sad fact that there were no secrets in a small town, no matter how old the gossip. Matt made a point of thanking everyone, saving Kay for last.

"I'm so sorry for your loss," she said, as she made his attempted hug as brief as possible.

"Thank you so much for coming," he said. "It means so much to me."

His big brown eyes were swimming with tears, and his smile was sad. You could tell he was suffering, and the pull to console him was strong. She could still see the young man she had fallen in love with so many years ago. He had made a big mistake, committed a youthful indiscretion, and had paid for it all these years. Her heart was big enough to forgive that in anyone, why not her childhood sweetheart?

"It was the least I could do," Kay said. "I've known you and Diedre since we were kids; it must have been a shock to lose her in such a tragic way."

He dissolved into tears, and several women came forward to console him. Kay was well aware of the spectacle she and Matt were quickly making of themselves; it would be recounted a dozen times, with dramatic embellishments, before the hour was over.

Kay was so irritated by how foolish and conspicuous she felt that she turned extra brisk.

"I have to go now," she said. "You take care."

Kay patted his arm and left by the back door, not making eye contact with anyone as she went. She was filled with a humiliating shame, as if she were sixteen years old again, running to the girl's bathroom, sobs wracking her body while everyone stared or snickered. That was more than 30 years ago; why did it feel as if it had happened yesterday?

In the parking lot outside the community center, Kay saw Karla, Sonny's ex-wife, getting out of a car. Kay was so emotionally off kilter that she feared what she'd say, so she veered right, pretending she hadn't seen her, only to have Karla run after her, shouting, "Kay, wait!"

Kay took a deep breath and turned around. She plastered a smile on her face and said, "Oh, hello, Karla; I didn't see you there. I guess I wasn't paying attention."

"Do you have a minute?" Karla asked her. "I want to talk to you about Sonny."

"No need for that," Kay said. "Your relationship is none of my business."

"That's not what I heard," Karla said.

Karla was a striking woman of medium height who you could tell took good care of herself. Her tan arms and legs were muscular like a tennis player's, and her hair was shoulder length and dark. She obviously knew her way around makeup and had made the most of her hazel eyes and good bone structure. She was dressed in a short black dress which showed off pert cleavage, and tall heels which were sinking into the lawn of the community center. If Kay didn't know for a fact that Karla was the same age as she was, she would have guessed she was ten years younger.

Karla looked Kay up and down and smirked without trying to hide it.

"I couldn't believe it when I heard it," she said. "I guess Sonny must be pretty lonesome these days."

"I'm not going to talk about Sonny with you," Kay said.

"Then you can listen instead," Karla said and took a menacing step closer. Kay, to her credit, did not back up. Instead, she froze the pleasant smile on her face and looked at Karla as you would look at an obnoxious child who is not related to you, to whom you do not want to appear to be rude.

"Sonny and I should never have got divorced," she said. "I made a dumb mistake, but I paid for it, and I'm sorry for what I did. Sonny and I are part of a family, we have kids. That's a bond that cannot be broken by divorce. You can't understand that because you don't have any kids. You don't know what having a family is like. You take in those orphans or whatever, and you pretend they're your kids, but that's just temporary. That's just play acting. Now you're doing the same thing with Sonny, but that isn't real, either. What Sonny and I have is the real thing, the kind of thing that's for life. Do you understand what I'm saying to you?"

"I think this is between you and Sonny," Kay said, although she was trembling with anger at being spoken to so rudely. "You should be talking to him, not me."

As Kay turned and walked away, Karla laughed.

"Oh, I'll talk to Sonny, all right," she said to Kay's back. "And that's not all I'll do."

Kay's retreat ended in the kitchen of her own little house, standing in front of the refrigerator, looking for something with which to smother the screaming she wanted to do.

There were Girl Scout cookies in the freezer, put there to keep her from eating them all right away. She dumped a whole box of the peanut butter and chocolate ones in a ceramic bowl and stuck them in the microwave. Oops. That was too long. Oh well. With vanilla ice cream on top, it was like a new Ben and Jerry's flavor.

"Girl Scout Heartache," she would call it.

Kay locked the front door and drew the curtains. She curled up on the couch with her big bowl and a spoon and ate as if it were a job she had to finish. As soon as the warm, fuzzy, sleepy feeling came over her, she put on her jammies, got into bed, rolled herself up in a blanket like a burrito, and went to sleep.

Kay woke up with a headache and a horrible taste in her mouth.

She looked at the clock.

Oh my goodness, she had to be at Delvecchios in twenty minutes.

Kay tore off her jammies. After a quick shower and tooth brushing, she put on the first thing she found in her closet that was clean and didn't need to be pressed. It was a sensible-looking navy blue linen jacket which she wore over a sleeveless white blouse and accessorized with pearls. She couldn't button the matching linen pants so she prayed they would stay zipped; at least the hem of the blouse covered the waistband.

Ordinarily, she would have spent hours agonizing over what to wear, would have blown out her hair and carefully applied her makeup. She didn't have time for that. She blew her hair almost dry, pulled it back into a stubby ponytail, and tied it with a white silk scarf. She swiped her face with powder, dabbed at her lashes with mascara, and applied some lipstick. She wore navy blue flats but took the car so she wouldn't be an even bigger sweaty mess when she got up there.

The Delvecchios lived up on the highest point of Morning Glory Avenue, in a large, comfortable home that overlooked all of Rose Hill. The men of the family were all on the front porch, watching Pauly's four boys, ages ranging from four to sixteen, running around on the front lawn.

The patriarch, Sal, was there on the porch, tiny compared to his strapping sons, his rocking chair situated next to an oxygen tank that was connected to his nose by a long thin tube. He looked sad and kind of out of it. He briefly raised his hand and smiled at Kay, but there was none of his old enthusiasm, his hearty charm. This was all that was left of that former man, the one who had loved his life and everyone in it.

Sonny was the first to get to her and hug her.

"You look beautiful," he said.

Matt looked irritated, which made her feel awkward. Pauly and Anthony both hugged her, told her they were voting for her this fall.

"The girls are inside," was all Matt said.

Kay instantly recognized this reminder of the antiquated gender norms by which this household was run. As a guest, she was obligated to observe family protocol, so she went inside. As expected, all feminine activity was taking place in the kitchen and dining room.

In the foyer, Pauly's wife, Julie, greeted her, handed her their newest offspring, the fifth one, who was around twelve-months-old and based on the profusion of pink ruffles in which it was dressed, a girl.

"This is Giada," Julie said. "You have to watch her; she's going through a biting phase."

Kay and Giada considered each other, Giada with a serious frown on her chubby little face. She was drooling, so Kay suspected the issue must be teething.

"Do you bite?" Kay asked her with a smile.

Giada's serious expression collapsed into a big, partially toothy smile. She had her mother's dimples and her father's big brown eyes. What hair she had was clasped on top of her head in a big pink bow.

"I bite," Giada said.

"It's not nice to bite," Julie told her.

"Is Karla here?" Kay whispered to Julie.

"Heavens, no," Julie said. "Their mother would kick her down the hill into the river."

"I bite," Giada said again.

She opened her mouth and showed Kay her teeth.

"Then let's get you something for you to bite other than me," Kay said and entered the kitchen.

Antonia was at the stove, an apron tied around her tiny waist, her high heels kicked aside.

"Kay, welcome," she said and hugged her warmly. "Watch this one; she bites."

"Do you have something frozen she could chew on?" Kay asked.

"Good idea," Julie said.

She rooted around in the freezer, came up with a frozen bagel, and wrapped a paper towel around it. When she handed it to Giada, the baby considered it with a serious expression and then asked Kay, "Bah?"

"She calls everything that goes in her mouth 'bah,' " Julie said.

"It's good," Kay told her. "Yummy."

Giada put it in her mouth, decided it was good, and began to chew on it.

"When my boys were teething, I rubbed whiskey on their gums," Antonia said.

"That explains so much," Julie said while rolling her eyes at Kay.

Matt and Diedre's daughter, Tina, was seated at the kitchen table, cutting vegetables for a salad. She greeted Kay, albeit a bit frostily.

"I'm so sorry for your loss," Kay said.

"My husband stayed home with the kids," Tina said as if Kay had asked. "I don't think children should go to funerals; they didn't know my mom very well and I was afraid it would freak them out."

"Of course," Kay said. "I understand."

"It's a part of life," Antonia said with a shrug. "I always took my children, even the babies; it's a sign of respect."

Tina closed her eyes and gritted her teeth. Kay could tell she was fighting the urge to respond. When she opened her eyes, Kay smiled at her kindly, but Tina looked away as if unwilling to accept anyone's support.

Kay then turned to address a young woman whom she didn't know. She was standing at the sink, peeling potatoes with a paring knife, and cutting off more potato than skin.

"Hello," Kay said. "I'm Kay Templeton; I don't believe we've met."

The girl wiped her hands on a dish towel and shook Kay's; she had a strong, firm handshake.

"I'm Kimberly," she said.

"I'm so sorry," Antonia said. "I should have introduced you two. Kimberly is Anthony's girlfriend."

Kay hoped her shock didn't show on her face.

Julie, standing behind Kimberly and Antonia, pretended to stick her finger down her throat.

"It's nice to meet you," Kay said. "I'm sorry it's in such sad circumstances."

"You're the one running for mayor, right?" Kimberly said.

"Yes," Kay said. "The election is this fall."

"I'm sorry I can't vote for you," Kimberly said.

Her tone was sweetly regretful, but the look in her eyes was not. Kay thought she must be one of Marigold's supporters.

"You're free to vote for whomever you choose," Kay said. "That's the beauty of our democratic system."

"I'm not voting for Marigold, either," Kimberly said. "I don't think a woman should take a job a man is supposed to do."

"You have got to be kidding me," Julie said. "What year is it again? 1955? '56?"

"Miss Julie," Antonia said. "Those are Kimberly's beliefs, and you will respect them in my house."

Kay was used to responding to any outrageous thing anyone said with grace and equanimity. She just pushed her real feelings down and put on a pleasant face.

"I admire the courage you have in your convictions," Kay said. "Julie, I think this one needs a diaper change; I'll be glad to help out."

Julie led Kay into the front hallway and then upstairs to a bedroom, where the diaper bag was stowed.

"Can you believe that Kimberly?" Julie whispered. "Everyone in the family knows Anthony is gay, but they're letting him ruin his life, not to mention that stupid girl's life, as if everything's just fine and dandy."

"It's sad," Kay said. "Poor Anthony."

"I want Pauly to do something about it, but those boys ... that mother ..."

"I know," Kay said.

"I hear Sonny's been calling on you all hours of the day," Julie said with a sly grin. "He's my favorite, you know. Matt seems like the jolly, nice one, but that's an act he puts on down at the IGA. He's really a miserable prick."

"Julie!"

"I'm sorry, but I call 'em like I see 'em," Julie said. "I know he was your high school sweetheart, but he's had his head up his own ass for years. He's still mad at me for being on Sonny's side when he got divorced. And that Diedre, God rest her soul. They couldn't go on vacation on account of her agoraphobia; they couldn't have people over on account of the hoarding; she wouldn't even go to her own daughter's wedding on account of it wasn't in a Catholic church. She held them hostage for all those years, and now we're supposed to be sorry for their loss? I'm glad about it. It's just a shame all that time got wasted."

"Even if they didn't get along while she was alive, they will still grieve her loss," Kay said.

"Well, just so you know, I'm all for you and Sonny getting together. Besides my Pauly, he's the best one of the bunch. Karla made an ass out of herself, and there will be no going back."

"She definitely wants to."

"Sure she does," Julie said. "She's all the time calling me, asking me how Sonny's doing. Left him for some no-good bum who goes around breaking up marriages like it's his hobby or something. She's burned that bridge, though; don't you worry about that. Their girls are on Team Sonny, and they'll be happy as long as he's happy."

"Where are they today?"

"They weren't that fond of Diedre, as you can imagine," she said. "Definitely not fond enough to purchase plane tickets at the last minute, for a thousand dollars a pop."

"Sonny adores his girls."

"They're sweet, like him," she said. "Their mother broke their hearts, but does she care? She calls them selfish for not being happy for her. Can you imagine? She's the type of mother who wanted to be a friend to her kids instead of a parent. She wore their clothes and flirted with their boyfriends; it was embarrassing."

The diaper had been changed, and now they were sitting on the bed, talking. Giada fussed, and Julie started to unbutton her blouse.

"Do you mind?" she asked Kay.

"Do you want me to leave?" Kay asked her.

"Hell no," Julie said. "I don't care. Antonia doesn't like me to do this downstairs; she thinks it might upset someone to see me feed my child in such a natural manner."

The baby latched on and sucked hungrily while looking up dreamy-eyed at her mother.

"How is Sal?" Kay asked. "He doesn't look good."

"He could go any minute," Julie said. "It's going to devastate this family, but look at him; it will be a blessing he won't suffer anymore."

"He adores Antonia," Kay said.

"You mark my word; she'll go back to Italy."

"No," Kay said. "With all her boys here?"

"There's a man," Julie said. "A childhood sweetheart, recently widowed. They've been emailing. She was sixteen when she got married, and Sal was twenty years older. There's a lot of life left in that woman, and I doubt she wastes a minute of it."

"Oh my goodness," Kay said. "Who'd have thought?"

"It might be the best thing for the boys," Julie said, "speaking of hostages."

Antonia called up the stairs that dinner was ready. She sounded irritated. Kay felt as guilty as if she had been caught doing exactly what she was doing, which was gossiping about Antonia and her family.

"You go on," Julie said. "I'll put her down for a nap and then join you."

"Thank you, Julie," Kay said. "I'll keep everything you said in confidence."

"No worries," Julie said. "Everybody downstairs knows exactly how I feel; I don't bottle it up."

Kay reflected that was probably why Julie didn't weigh fifty pounds more than she should, didn't smoke, drink to excess, or gamble away the family grocery money.

Dinner began with grace, during which Kay found herself holding hands with both Sonny and Matthew. In a wheezing whisper, Sal thanked the Lord for everyone, became tearful, and by the end of his prayer, there wasn't a dry eye at the table.

The food was delicious looking, and there was plenty of it, but Kay only took a dab of everything.

"That's a pitiful helping," Sonny said, as she put a few gnocchi on her plate.

"Kay's probably on a diet," Matt said. "We could all stand to lose a few pounds."

Kay felt her face grow warm. She felt as if everyone was looking at her, judging her.

"But not today," Sal said. "Today we enjoy life, for tomorrow we may be gone."

He winked at Kay, and she smiled back at him.

"This is just my first go round," she said. "I'm pacing myself, so I have room for dessert."

It was then she realized, 'Oh my Lord, I forgot to bring the dessert.'

"I'm going to check on Julie real quick," Kay said. "See if she needs anything."

"That's kind of you," Antonia said. "I hadn't noticed she was missing."

"The peace and quiet should have been your first clue," Matt said. "Let's enjoy it while it lasts."

"My wife does not suffer fools gladly," Pauly said, "so unless you're some kind of fool, brother dear, you've got nothing to worry about."

Kay went to the upstairs bathroom and used her cell phone to call Fitzpatrick's Bakery. She was so relieved when

Melissa answered, and said she'd bring something right away.

Kay looked in on Julie and Giada and saw that they had fallen asleep together. Julie's shirt was still open, and Giada was nestled up against her breast, her little mouth making nursing motions in her sleep, even though she was no longer nursing. Kay took a woolen throw off a nearby chair and draped it over them.

'I missed out on this,' she thought.

Kay had provided a safe, loving refuge for multiple foster children over the years. Soon Grace would be her daughter, and she looked forward to living vicariously through her and any eventual grandchildren she might produce. No, it was fine that this was no longer an option. She had made her choices, and if she made up her mind to, she could live quite happily with the consequences.

Back downstairs she could tell there had been an argument; the air was thick with tension.

"You missed the good news," Kimberly sang out, oblivious to the atmosphere. "Anthony and I are engaged!"

She held out her hand, which now sported a modest diamond ring. Kay glanced around the table and absorbed the many emotions she saw reflected in the family's faces. Antonia was irritated, Sonny and Matthew seemed angry, Pauly looked like he might cry, and Sal looked worn out.

"Congratulations," Kay said. "Have you set a date?"

"No hurry," Sonny said. "There's nothing wrong with long engagements."

"It's up to them," Matt said. "We should stay out of it."

Pauly's tears spilled over, and he left the table. Kay could hear him bound up the steps to where his wife and baby slept.

"You must excuse us, Kay," Antonia said. "We're such an emotional family."

To Anthony, Antonia said, "You could have waited a few days, out of respect for your brother and his daughter."

Anthony's face was blotchy with shame, and he hung his head.

"I don't mind," Tina said. "I'm glad somebody's happy."

"We thought it might cheer everyone up," Kimberly said, still determined to get the elated reaction she had anticipated. "We thought you'd be glad to have something to look forward to, didn't we, honey?"

Anthony looked the most miserable of anyone. He looked up and caught Kay's eye. She thought, 'Oh, Anthony, don't do this,' and it must have shown on her face because he quickly looked away.

The doorbell rang, and Kay jumped up, offering to answer it.

"How bad our company must be that she keeps finding reasons to leave it," Antonia said as she left the room.

Melissa was at the door with a coconut-covered chocolate cake in a bakery box.

"It's Sonny's favorite," Melissa said with a wink. "You can pay for it tomorrow."

Kay wanted nothing more than to take the cake home and eat the whole thing. Instead, she took it to the kitchen and looked for a cake plate to put it on. Antonia came in and looked at the box.

"I thought you were going to make one of your homemade specialties," she said, as she removed a cake plate from a high shelf in one of her cupboards. "Sonny says you're quite the cook."

"There was no time today," Kay said. "I promise I'll bring something homemade next time."

"I'm happy to hear you say there will be a next time," Antonia said with a mischievous smile. "I'd like to see my boys all settled before ..."

Kay thought she was about to say, 'before I leave,' and gave Antonia a sharp, questioning look.

"Before their father passes away," Antonia said. "He would like to see them settled and happy. He doesn't care which one you end up with, so long as it's one of them."

"Mrs. Delvecchio," Kay started.

"I know, I know," Antonia replied, waving her hands in the air. "It's none of my business, I'm only their mother. But between you and me, you should take Sonny. He's not much to look at, but neither was his father, and I couldn't have asked for a better husband, a better life. Sonny will dote on you, and Matthew, well, I love him, he's a good boy, but he wants all the doting to himself, you see? He was such a clingy child; always needed the most attention and it was never enough. But my Sonny? He's the oldest, so he never got much, and he's grateful for anything he gets."

"I see," Kay said. "Thank you for being so welcoming."

"A mayor in the family, just imagine," Antonia said. "I can bring you all my parking tickets."

"If you don't mind me asking," Kay said, "I heard you were the only witness to what went on at Knox's yesterday."

"I do my housework, and then I sit on the porch with Sal. He sleeps, and I read. I can see everything that happens at Knox's house; not that I'm a nosy neighbor, but when I hear yelling, I want to know who's doing the yelling."

"You heard yelling?"

"The other mayor woman, what's her name?"

"Marigold?"

"I saw her, wearing one of those horrible outfits she wears; that woman has no sense of style; she doesn't know how to dress for her figure."

Antonia paused as if realizing she was insulting one heavy woman in front of another, and Kay prompted her to continue, saying, "She was at Knox's house?"

"She came, she yelled, she left, boom, boom, boom; it happened quickly."

"I wonder what that was about," Kay said.

Antonia shrugged.

"Did you see anyone else?"

"I saw the little gray wife, the number two wife," she said.

"Meredith?"

"Yes, the tiny one, who also cannot dress," she said. "All that money and she wears old clothes. The cloth is shiny where she sits, you know. You can always tell."

"Did she go in?"

"I did not see her go in," Antonia said, "but I saw her leaving out the back way. She was a carrying a big bag, a shopping bag. Knox put all her things in storage after she tried to kill him, you know, at the same place where Diedre died."

"I didn't know that."

"I knew she was not right in the head, that Meredith," Antonia said. "She had a way of looking at you as if she were measuring you for a coffin."

"Did you know Anne Marie well?"

"The first wife, the stylish one," Antonia said. "Now, her I liked. We would sometimes have a glass of wine together here on the porch, while the husbands were at work. No, she was here last month, but she didn't visit. Not many people visit, now that Sal is so sick; they're afraid to bother him. It's been very lonely."

"Did you see anyone else?"

"The boy with the truck, the hippie."

"Phillip Deacon."

"He's good-looking, but that hair; I don't see how you could keep all that matted hair clean. He came in his truck, and then Claire Fitzpatrick came right after. He left and then the police came."

"Claire told me," Kay said.

"She's a stylish woman," Antonia said. "A little bit of the *buttana*, if you know what I mean, but that's the style nowadays."

"Claire's beautiful," Kay said. "She takes great care of herself."

"You know, I always wanted Anthony to marry Mary Margaret."

"Maggie Fitzpatrick?"

"She's got no style, I know, but she has a good head for business. She's Catholic, too, from a good family. They've had their troubles, but we all have. No one is safe from troubles. She's no beauty, and all that red curly hair is unfortunate, but they would have been a good match, don't you think?"

"The most important thing is if they'd be happy together."

"Why would you think that?" Antonia said. "In life, you make the smartest choice, the one that will provide the best for your children, and then you make do with what you get. It's not because you have romance in your heart, it's because you are willing to work hard to get what you need for the children."

"I hope Anthony is making the right choice," Kay said.

"Kimberly's a nice Catholic girl from a good family," Antonia said. "He'll finally give us some beautiful grandchildren. That's all that matters to his father and me. As far as happiness, that should be enough for him. That's more than most people get."

After the tense dinner was over, Sonny walked Kay to her car.

"That's how we are," he said. "We've never had a relaxed, pleasant meal together as long as I've lived."

"I'm fond of your family," Kay said. "All that drama just means you care what happens to each other."

"Anthony's making a huge mistake," Sonny said. "Nobody deserves to be deceived like he's doing to her. It's wrong."

"I hope he sees the light before it's too late," Kay said.

"He's a good person, a good Christian," Sonny said, "and love is love. I don't see why we gotta go around telling people they can't love each other. That doesn't seem right."

"Come by for breakfast tomorrow," Kay said. "I'll make you some French toast."

"I'm so full of cake that shouldn't sound good, but it does."

He hugged Kay and then kissed her forehead.

"Thank you," he said, "for giving me a chance."

"I should thank you," she said, "for exactly the same thing."

Kay happened to look up at the house as she got in her car. Matthew was standing on the porch watching, and he didn't look happy.

Kay went home, changed into some comfy clothes, and sat on her front porch glider, where she sipped some iced tea. The air was fresh and cool, a classic Rose Hill summer evening. She was about to relax when ex-mayor Stuart Machalvie walked up the front path.

"Evenin' Kay," he said.

"Stuart," she said.

"May I sit with you a spell?" he asked.

"Of course," Kay said, but she did not offer him anything from her kitchen.

This was the same man, after all, who, when questioned by federal investigators, tried to pin many of his misdeeds on her. Luckily, Kay had been smart enough over the years to document any shady behavior she witnessed in the mayor's office and to keep copies of various things locked up in a safe in her bedroom closet in case she needed them.

"Horrible thing, about Knox," he started.

Kay nodded, wondering where this was headed.

"It's being investigated as a homicide," he said.

Kay did not respond but continued looking at him, waiting for him to say what it was he actually came to say.

"Now, personally, I think it may have been suicide," Stuart said.

"What?!" Kay said, not able to contain herself any longer.

Stuart shrugged his shoulders.

"So many of the things I've been accused of," he said, "that we, Knox, Trick, and I have been accused of, have turned out to be things that Knox did without our knowledge."

"Is that so?"

"I think the FBI was getting close to proving that, and the guilt Knox must have felt, well, it was probably too much for him. After his wife's nervous breakdown, leaving the senate race, getting fired from the bank, and the questions about his Aunt Mamie's death ... "

"Knox was such a dear friend of yours," Kay said. "You told everyone he hadn't done anything wrong."

"Well, when that young woman met her untimely end, and it turned out he may have had a hand in that, I had to ask myself what else would a man like that do. I had always considered Knox a dear friend, as you say, but even I couldn't stretch the bonds of our friendship to accommodate crimes such as those. No, he was faced with spending the rest of his life in prison, and he did the honorable thing."

"You didn't happen to visit Knox before he died, did you?"

"No, I had an important meeting with my attorneys to prepare for. I wish I had been there and could have counseled him, helped him face his guilty conscience and confess his sins rather than take his own life at such a low moment."

"I think that version is the most convenient for you, the congressman, and the senator," Kay said.

"Convenience doesn't come into it, Kay. I'm surprised you would even think that. It's a tragedy for his family and the whole community. To die before he could clear his name, maybe because he couldn't, well, let's let the man rest in peace now. Let's all get on with our lives and leave the past in the past. That's the line I'm taking; the line I think we should all take."

"You never cease to amaze me."

"I just wanted to stop by, to see how your campaign is coming along. If I can help, you know, just holler. I know many important people, my dear, people who would help you get elected if I asked them to."

"No, thanks, Stuart," she said.

"I'm extending the olive branch, Kay," he said. "It would help you more than you know, and I would appreciate it, as would Peg. I don't like having bad blood between us any more than you do. I'd like to see us get back to the beneficial friendship which served us so well for so many years."

"I'll decline," Kay said. "I think we had better go our separate ways."

"I'll give you time to think about it," he said. "Time to see how this election plays out."

"I won't change my mind."

"We'll see," he said as he rose to go. "What will you do, Kay, if you don't get elected? Marigold won't let you stay on as city administrator, and we're, none of us, as young as we used to be. It might be difficult for you to find something else."

"Thanks for your concern, Stuart," Kay said.

Kay watched him walk away, whistling like he hadn't a care in the world and then waving to everyone he passed.

Her blood was boiling. Who did he think he was to tell her how to spin Knox's death? Why did he think he could intimidate or coerce her into getting involved with him and his crooked cronies? It was just like Stuart to play upon her vulnerabilities to try to make her think she needed him.

She wished she'd had the courage to ask him why he and Knox had been paying Marigold Lawson so much money over the past two years. Marigold, the same person who had argued with Knox right before he was found dead. The truth was she was afraid of what he might do if he found out she knew.

Kay called Claire.

"I've got to talk to you," Kay said.

"I can't come up," Claire said. "I gave Melissa the evening off."

"Do you mind if I come down?" Kay asked. "It's very important."

"Sure," Claire said. "Come on down."

Kay locked up the house and walked down Peony Street to Iris Avenue, where Ian Fitzpatrick's small brick ranch house sat right next to Ed Harrison's. Claire was sitting on the front stoop, holding her little Boston Terrier, Mackie Pea. A little black cat was poking around in the nearby flower bed.

Mackie Pea was excited to see Kay, and she jumped up over and over until Kay picked her up. Mackie Pea licked Kay's face and wriggled all around.

Kay put her down and then watched her run in circles all around the yard.

"How was dinner?" Claire asked.

"Tense," Kay said. "Anthony announced his engagement to someone named Kimberly."

"No," Claire said. "What's he thinking?"

"Trying to please his parents, I think."

"Sean will be devastated."

"Maybe he won't go through with it," Kay said.

"How were your two suitors?"

Kay gave her a blow-by-blow account of the funeral reception and dinner.

"So we're firmly on Team Sonny," Claire said.

"Seems like it," Kay said.

"You don't seem very excited."

"I am happy about Sonny," Kay said. "But I keep thinking about all the years I wasted wishing I could be with Matthew."

"It's easy to idealize someone you once loved," Claire said.

"Well, I'm seeing him clearly now," Kay said. "By the way, I did get some eye-witness information."

She told Claire what Antonia had seen.

"Marigold's house is right across the street from Knox's," Kay said. "What happened two years ago to make them start paying her, and what happened yesterday?"

"You should tell Laurie about this," Claire said.

"Why can't you tell him?"

"We're not speaking at the moment," Claire said. "He got black-out drunk on his day off yesterday, and I haven't heard from him since."

"Oh no," Kay said. "I thought he had it under control."

"He needs to go away somewhere and dry out," Claire said. "He needs to learn a new way to cope with his grief."

"I can kind of understand it," Kay said. "I dive headfirst into the sugar bowl whenever I'm stressed."

"But you're not likely to crash your car under the influence of a cookie."

"True," Kay said.

"I can't understand the impulse to wreck your life rather than deal with your problems," Claire said. "Why do people do it?"

"You didn't meet my last foster before Grace," Kay said. "Tiffany was a good student, had a beautiful voice; sang in the church choir every Sunday. I was so hopeful for her future, but then she met this boy, a real hoodlum, and started drinking and doing drugs. She stole from me, lied to me, cursed me out; she became someone I didn't recognize. Her counselor tried to get her to go to a rehabilitation program, but she ran away, and now I don't know where she is or what happened to her. Addiction is so insidious, and kids don't realize how little it takes to get hooked; it's a wonder more of them aren't lost that way."

They were both silent for a few moments, watching Mackie Pea tease the small cat and the cat swat at the dog's nose.

"I'm a compulsive shopper," Claire said. "It's like I have to have some addictive behavior to release the pressure, so I use the one that hurts me the least."

"What's the more destructive one you're avoiding?"

"I used to starve myself to be thin," Claire said. "Laxatives, diet pills, throwing up; you name it, I tried it. When I started running, it helped, but I still obsess over my weight; the difference is now I starve myself and exercise instead of binging and purging."

"I've got the binging part down," Kay said, "but I can't purge."

"Listen to yourself," Claire said. "You keep it all inside. Maybe you should let some of your feelings out."

"Not in an election year," Kay said. "I'm living in a fishbowl."

"Maybe being mayor isn't the best thing for you," Claire said. "Maybe you should do something where you can be yourself, and say what you really think."

"Claire, my darling, there are no jobs like that," Kay said. "Unless you're independently wealthy or have a spouse to support you, you have to play well with others in order to stay employed."

"You're right," Claire said. "I should have been nicer to Gwyneth the other day. She probably ran right down the street and blackballed me."

"Her specialty when she had a private therapy practice in Manhattan was eating disorders," Kay said. "But I can't imagine her being compassionate toward me about mine."

"I know that lean-and-hungry look," Claire said. "I'd bet you anything she's got one herself."

"We're all flawed in some way," Kay said. "They say that's how the light gets in."

"I wish some light would shine in Laurie."

"Laurie should have taken this past month to get straightened out," Kay said. "I wonder if we can get him an extra month."

"Scott's a good buddy of the chief in Pendleton," Claire said. "Maybe he would put off his retirement for one more month."

"I'll call Scott when I get home," Kay said.

"Laurie's going to be mad I told on him."

"There's more than Laurie's life at stake," Kay said. "I can't, in good conscience, let him take over at Pendleton knowing he has this problem."

"I hope you and Scott can work something out for him," Claire said.

"You're done with him, then?"

"Until I know he's sober, and staying that way."

"How could you ever be sure?"

"I guess I couldn't," Claire said. "Looks like there's not much hope for us."

"And Ed's going to stay married to Eve?"

"Sounds like it," Claire said.

"You didn't tell him about her affair with the senator?"

"It wouldn't matter," she said. "He wants a son or daughter, and he doesn't care who the biological father is."

"I'm so sorry."

"I'll be all right," Claire said.

"Then why are you crying?"

"Feeling sorry for myself," Claire said.

"Do you want a cookie?"

"No, silly, weren't you listening?" Claire said. "I want new shoes."

When Claire checked her phone before bed, there was a message from her cousin Maggie.

"Hey," Maggie said. "Scott just got off the phone with Kay. I don't know if this will help, but when Theo Eldridge got murdered, Hannah and I did some snooping around up at his house. We found where he kept his blackmail information, and there was a file on something that happened when Knox was in college. His fraternity lost their charter, and Knox transferred to another school rather than be expelled. The folder is at my apartment hidden in my bookcase behind the big art books. If Hannah and I were there, we'd be right in the middle of this thing, so you have to represent us. Get in there, girl, and investigate! Let me know if any of this helps. See you Sunday."

Claire's mind was off and running, so she got on the Internet and went to work. She quickly found out what college Knox had graduated from, but couldn't find any mention of the one at which he started and from which he transferred.

Marigold's online campaign bio listed a different college than the one Knox had graduated from. Could that be the college where the scandal happened? Stuart was much older than Knox and Marigold and hadn't attended either college.

Claire heard a light tapping on her bedroom window. She opened the curtains and found her ex-husband looking in. She pulled up the sash.

"What in the hell is wrong with you?"

"I need some money," he said. "You've got to help me."

"Running away is only making you look guilty," Claire said. "No one thinks you killed Knox."

"But I'm the one who found him," Pip said.

"They just want to question you," Claire said. "I'll go with you."

"Are you sure they won't arrest me?"

"I'm sure," Claire said, although she wasn't. "Let me get Melissa over here to stay with Dad, and we'll go down to the station together."

Claire called Melissa and then got dressed. When she opened the back door, she found Pip smoking a joint.

"Oh for crissakes," she said. "Put that out. You don't have any more of that on you, do you?"

He looked guilty.

"Give it to me," she said and held out her hand.

Reluctantly, he handed over his rolling papers and a small baggie of weed.

"Don't flush it," he said. "It's all I have left."

Claire took it into the kitchen and hid it in the cabinet over the refrigerator, next to the whiskey.

Melissa let herself in the front door.

"Hey," she said.

"Thank you for coming," Claire said. "I don't know how long we'll be."

"That's okay," Melissa said. "Patrick's going to come here when he gets off at two."

"If it's going to be any later, I'll call."

Claire left by the back door, and Pip followed her.

"I can't go back to jail," Pip said. "You don't know what it's like."

"This will keep you from going to jail," Claire said. "Just tell Laurie what happened. He'll help you."

Claire knew Laurie was on the night shift; she just hoped he was sober.

He answered the door of the station when she rang the bell. His eyes were bloodshot, and there were dark circles underneath. He looked at her, then at Pip, and his eyebrows went up.

"Good evening," he said as he opened the door. "Mr. and Mrs. Deacon, I presume."

"Knock it off," Claire said.

"Hey, Laurie," Pip said. "Long time no see."

"Mr. Deacon," Laurie said and shook his hand.

"Pip's here to assist with your inquiries," Claire said. "He's willing to answer your questions without an attorney, provided he's not under arrest. If you arrest him, he wants an attorney appointed before he says anything."

"Yeah," Pip said. "What she said."

"Come on in," Laurie said. "Sherlock and Watson have the night off, so it's just me. I'll make us some coffee."

Pip walked past Laurie toward the break room. As Claire started past, Laurie grasped her by the arm.

"I'm sorry I haven't called," he said.

"That's not why I'm here," Claire said, as she pulled her arm free. "I'm here to help Pip."

"I have to call Sarah," he said. "She's in charge of the investigation."

"Then do it," Claire said. "Let's get this over with."

With deep interest, Claire paid attention to how Sarah interacted with Laurie. If the woman hadn't as much as confessed her deep feelings for him, Claire would never have known. Sarah was curt, insulting, and bossy; in short, she treated him the same way she treated every other member of law enforcement who wasn't in a position to do anything for her career. Laurie was obsequious and accommodating, but the more passive he behaved, the more aggressive Sarah became.

They let Claire stay with Pip while they questioned him. He told them the truth; that he had gone to Knox's to ask for money and found him dead on the stairway inside his unlocked house. He ran off because he was scared they would think he did it.

Sarah was not as hard on him as Claire anticipated she would be. She actually treated him more like a scared child, which he basically was, and asked him the same questions several different ways. To his credit, Pip did not back off of his story and didn't change it. Claire was proud of him.

"He was in shock when he took off. As soon as the shock wore off, he came back to help," Claire said. "He's not going to leave town. He has a paying job here, and his mother's here. If you have more questions, he'll make himself available."

"Are you vouching for him?" Sarah asked.

Claire hesitated.

"Claire," Pip said.

"Wait a minute," Claire said. "I'm thinking."

"Miss Fitzpatrick," Sarah said. "You are under no obligation to guarantee Mr. Deacon remains within the city limits; I'm asking if you truly believe he won't take off."

"I don't know," Claire said. "I hope he won't."

"Thanks a lot, Claire," Pip said.

"Well, what have you usually done, Pip?" Claire asked him. "I can only go on my past experience with you."

"That's all anyone can do," Laurie said.

Their eyes met, and Claire knew he wasn't talking about Pip.

Sarah and Laurie left the room to confer.

"They're probably going to arrest me now," Pip said, "and it'll be all your fault."

"Oh, Pip," Claire said. "What's sad is you truly believe that."

"If you gave me some money, I wouldn't leave."

"If you finish the work on Sean's office, you'll have some money."

"You could give me an advance," he said. "Sean will pay you back."

"Listen," Claire said. "I'll give you twenty dollars, but that's it. Don't ask again."

Claire gave him the twenty.

"Thanks, Claire," he said. "And thanks for coming with me."

Claire took a deep breath.

"I wish they'd hurry," she said. "Seems like they oughta be more interested in questioning Marigold than you."

"Who's Marigold?" he asked.

"The lady who lives across the street from Knox," Claire said. "She was at his house before you."

"So she killed him?"

"They don't know," Claire said. "They just need to talk to her."

"I'm glad I'm not the only one," he said.

Laurie came back in and said to Pip, "You have to write up your statement, and then you can go."

"Thanks, man," Pip said. "D'ya hear that, Claire? I get to go."

"That's great," Claire said.

"Hey, Claire," Pip said. "Would you write that statement thingy for me?"

"No," Claire said. "I'm out of here."

"But Claire ..." he whined.

As Claire left the break room, Sarah came back in.

"Thanks," she said, so softly Claire could barely hear it.

Claire didn't speak to Laurie before she left the station. He had to chase her halfway down Rose Hill Avenue.

"Excuse me, miss," he said as he caught up. "I think you left some of your baggage in our break room."

"Very funny," she said.

"Please stop," he said. "I'd like to apologize."

Claire turned around.

"For what?" she asked him. "For being an alcoholic? For not having it under control like you said you did? For doing exactly what you warned me you would do?"

"Well, yes."

"I should apologize to you," Claire said. "I expected too much, or at least more than you're capable of."

"Ouch."

"It's the truth, though, isn't it?" she asked. "You're not ready to be in a new relationship because you're still in one with your wife."

"My dead wife."

"Yes," Claire said. "Miss whatever-her-name-is, the second one, is only another symptom of your disease, like Sarah and all the other women you slept with. I don't want to be your next mistake."

"I'm sorry," he said. "You deserve better."

"You're damn right I do," she said, and to her embarrassment, she began to cry. "So become someone better, Laurie, but don't call me until you do."

She turned and walked away, but this time he didn't follow her.

The folder with the newspaper clippings was right where Maggie said it would be. Claire sat down at the table in Maggie's kitchen to look through it. Maggie and Scott's cat, Duke, twined around her legs, purring like a motorboat. He jumped up on the table and lay down on the documents Claire was trying to read. He was a big cat, and due to the stories she'd heard about him, Claire was a little afraid of him, so rather than pick him up she found the cat food, took it to the front room, and he followed.

"Don't tell Melissa," she said. "This will be our little secret."

When she returned to the kitchen, she closed the door so she could read uninterrupted.

Knox had been a member of the disgraced fraternity at the college Marigold went to. His name was one of the five listed in the complaint, a copy of which Theo had somehow managed to acquire. Marigold's name wasn't mentioned, but the crime that had been committed against the unnamed young woman was. Claire shuddered; how would you ever get over something like that? And if Marigold was that young woman, why did she wait so long to get back at him?

Claire knew she should take what she had found to Laurie; instead, she called Sarah. She hadn't left the Rose Hill station yet, so she agreed to meet Claire in the Rose and Thorn. Claire went back down Rose Hill Avenue to the Thorn, where Patrick and the stalwart late night locals greeted her with enthusiasm.

"You owe me for the free drinks you gave these bozos," Patrick said. "I had them all house-trained, and you had to go spoiling them with treats."

Claire gave him the money and then went to the far end of the bar to wait for Sarah.

"Can I buy you a drink?" Claire asked her when she arrived.

"No, thanks," Sarah said.

Sarah saw Patrick and yelled, "Looking good, Fitzpatrick. What time do you get off, and can I help?"

Patrick held up his arms and made a bodybuilder pose for her. She whistled, and the locals laughed.

"Your brother's something else," Sarah said.

"He's my cousin," Claire said, "and his fiancée is one of my dearest friends."

"Miss West Virginia?" she asked. "I've met her. I wasn't impressed."

"She's from Tennessee, actually," Claire said, "and stop being such a bitch when I'm trying to help you."

"Sorry," Sarah shrugged. "What have you got for me?"

Claire gave her the folder and told her what she knew.

"Very interesting," Sarah said. "So you think Marigold was the girl who was raped, and that she waited all this time to get her revenge."

"I don't know," Claire said. "I do know that Knox and Stuart Machalvie have been paying money into an account that only Marigold withdraws money from."

"How do you know this?"

"I'd rather not say," Claire said. "I also heard Knox was embezzling his Aunt Mamie's money, and this account may be where that money was going."

"Hmm," Sarah said. "This is all good; what else?"

"Knox started paying into this account two years ago," Claire said. "That was right around the time he married Meredith."

"And decided to run for the Senate," Sarah said.

"Yep," Claire said. "What better time to blackmail someone?"

"The feds took everything we had on Knox when they took over," Sarah said. "I probably should take this to them."

"Whatever," Claire said. "I just wanted someone to know about this."

"Why not Laurie?"

"He's only got another couple of days here," Claire said.

"You could have saved this for Scott."

"I wanted it out of my hands and into someone else's tonight," Claire said. "That's all."

"Purcell's in love with you," Sarah said. "I saw how he ran after you."

"I'm not in love with him," Claire said, and then felt her face flush.

"You're not very good at lying," Sarah said.

"I'm not going to see him anymore," Claire said. "I don't want to get involved with an alcoholic who's not doing anything to get better."

"I see," Sarah said. "Well, thanks for the tip. I heard the 911 call you made about the meth lab at the storage unit facility; I recognized your voice. Thanks for that tip, too. You're single-handedly improving my promotion prospects. If you're interested in being a paid informant, maybe we can work something out."

"Sarah," Claire said. "I'm sorry about Laurie."

"I don't know what you're talking about," Sarah said and stood up.

"Hey, Fitzpatrick," she yelled at Patrick. "Meet me out back for ten minutes; I wanna strip-search you."

"What are you looking for?" Patrick yelled back.

"A way to kill ten minutes," she responded, and the men all laughed.

Claire didn't laugh. It dawned on her that Sarah's sexually predatory behavior was just another version of Laurie's alcoholism, Kay's eating disorder, and her compulsive shopping. Evidently, all bitches not only have sorrows but self-destructive ways to battle them.

CHAPTER 8

Sꜰe, the alarm's not hard to set," Claire explained to Melissa, "and you know how to do everything else."

"Are you sure Sean won't mind me covering for you?"

"I think if he comes back and sees you already know how to do everything, and you're doing a good job, he's more likely to leave things the way they are. If it ain't broke, you know?"

"If it isn't broke," Melissa said.

"Right," Claire said. "Good catch."

"Bonnie's gonna skin me alive when she finds out," Melissa said.

"She's not going to kill you and eat you," Claire said. "She's all bark."

"She's gonna be my mother-in-law someday," Melissa said. "I hate to rile her up."

"Has Patrick proposed?"

"Patrick done asked me to marry him the day I got home from prison."

"So?"

"I've known that man a long time," Melissa said. "I wanna make sure he can be true before I get yoked to him."

"Don't defer your happiness," Claire said.

"That's what your mama's always saying."

"That's where I heard it."

"Eve was in the bakery the other day," Melissa said. "She was downright rude to me just 'cause Ed wasn't there to see her do it."

"I'm not surprised."

"Ed and me weren't right together," Melissa said, "but he's a good man. I hate to see him get hornswaggled like that."

"He's a big boy."

"They're all big boys," Melissa said. "That's the problem."

Claire was headed out the door when Pip arrived.

"Where're you going?" he asked.

"Melissa and I switched jobs," Claire said. "I'm working in the bakery now, and she's working here."

"How come?"

"She needs secretarial experience, and I'm bored out of my mind."

"Hey, could you hook me up with some free food?"

"The leftovers go to the Pendleton City Mission."

"I'm needy," Pip said. "I'm hungry."

"You've got twenty dollars and a job," Claire said. "Count yourself lucky."

Claire turned to Melissa and said, "Don't give him any money no matter what he tells you."

"Aw, Claire," Pip said. "You didn't have to go and say that."

"Don't worry," Melissa said. "I'm not fooled by the likes of him."

"Have fun," Claire told them both and left the office.

Professor Richmond was coming down the sidewalk from the bookstore.

"Claire," he called out to her. "So glad I caught you."

"Hey," Claire said. "Good news?"

"I'm afraid not," he said. "I'm sorry to say they've decided to hire a recent graduate, the unfortunately named Cressida Buttercombe. Apparently, our darling Cress failed to set Broadway on fire in the twelve months Mummy and Daddy allowed her to try, so she's coming back to Eldridge to teach."

"So she's barely got any acting experience and zero stage and film hair and make-up experience," Claire said. "I'm much more qualified for the job."

"I'm so sorry," Professor Richmond said.

"Is this because of Gwyneth Eldridge?" Claire asked. "Or because I can't get Sloan to appear at the film festival?"

"No, not at all," Professor Richmond said. "This is because Cressida's parents are paying to renovate and expand the theater arts facility with ten million of darling daddy's fertilizer export dollars. Imagine with me, if you will, the horror that will be *The Buttercombe Center for the Performing Arts.*"

"So it's about money."

"Fishes live in the sea, as men do a-land; the great ones eat up the little ones," he said. "In this case, I'm afraid, we are but little fish compared to the great white Buttercombes."

"Damn," Claire said. "I really wanted that job."

"And we wanted you to have it," he said. "Torby and Ned will be devastated."

"Oh well," Claire said. "I guess that's that."

"Chin up," he said. "Remember, the robbed that smiles steals something from the thief."

"And what goes around comes around," Claire said.

"We'll still see you for Scrabble, I trust," he said. "And down the pub, as they say."

"Of course," Claire said. "Thank you for coming to tell me in person."

"Fare thee well, sweet ladybird," he said. "Don't let the bloody buggers get you down."

Ruthie Postlethwaite had been helping out at the bakery while the majority of the Fitzpatrick women were at the beach, and she was glad to see Claire show up to relieve her.

"I'm getting too old for this," she said as she left, rubbing her lower back.

Claire spent the afternoon making sales and prepping for the next morning. It was hot, hard work, and by four o'clock her back ached, and her arms were weak from lifting heavy trays. When the four-thirty rush commenced, she raced around waiting on customers and filling phone orders. By six-thirty it was quiet again, so she started the evening clean-up chores.

Claire was filling a box with leftover baked goods for the City Mission when the bells on the front door jingled. She looked up to see Marigold Lawson, her face bright red with anger.

Marigold was a tall woman with strong features and an Amazonian figure. Unfortunately, she dressed in clothing more appropriate to a much more petite and girlish young woman. The end result was that she looked both uncomfortable and foolish.

Claire, as was her habit, mentally cut the woman's hair into a shorter style, dyed it dark red, and dressed her in jewel-toned, long, flowing tunic separates, with bold, chunky jewelry and more subtle make-up. There. That was better.

"Your husband had the temerity to come to my house and ask me for money," Marigold said. "I have half a mind to call the police and have him arrested for extortion."

Claire's whole body sagged, and she moaned.

"Pip?"

"He looks like a dirty hippie," Marigold said. "He's lucky my husband wasn't home."

"First of all, he's my ex-husband," Claire said. "Second of all, I'm sorry, but I can't control what Pip does with his time, or what kind of hare-brained schemes he comes up with to get money."

"He insinuated that he could make things difficult for me with the police," she said.

"He doesn't mean it," Claire said. "Pip has smoked so much marijuana he has brain damage. Just take a broom to his backside and chase him off your porch. If he comes back, tell him you're calling the police, and he'll run away."

"It's bad enough that the police have been to my house," Marigold said. "A squad car parked right out in front, like I'm some kind of criminal."

"I guess you *were* one of the last people to see Knox alive ..."

"He was alive when I left his house," Marigold said. "Not that anyone seems to believe me."

"Meredith was there after you," Claire said. "I'm sure she'll clear things up when they talk to her."

"Unless she killed him and blames me!"

Marigold's face was so red Claire thought she might have a stroke.

"Can I get you a cup of tea or something?" Claire asked her. "I really am sorry about Pip."

Marigold sniffed.

"You're Kay's friend," she said. "You'll probably call her as soon as I leave. I'm sure she's enjoying my predicament."

"Kay's a good person," Claire said. "If you took the time to get to know her, you would think so, too. She hasn't said one unkind word about you to the press, now, has she?"

Marigold looked as if she were about to cry.

"No," she said. "She never has."

Her chin trembled, her lower lip turned down, and the tears fell.

"Come and sit down," Claire said. "Have a cup of tea and eat one of these leftover muffins while I clean up. We don't even have to talk. Just catch your breath. I promise you, Pip cannot hurt you, and Kay is not out to get you."

Marigold sat down, sniffed a few times, blew her nose, and then peeled the paper off one of the muffins Claire had put in front of her. Meanwhile, Claire made her a cup of strong hot tea with a generous spoonful of sugar.

Claire filled three large bakery boxes and stacked them on a table near the door, completely ignoring her guest, and eventually, after she ate four muffins, Marigold regained her composure.

"I saw Stuart at Kay's house," Marigold said as she wiped her mouth with a napkin. "He's supposed to be on my side."

"I wouldn't want him anywhere near my side," Claire said. "That man's one federal indictment away from a prison sentence."

"He said Kay did most of the things he and Knox were accused of."

"Well, he would, wouldn't he?" Claire said. "Fortunately for Kay, she kept documentation that proves she had nothing to do with any of it."

"Really?" Marigold said. "So she's not under investigation?"

"Nope," Claire said. "She's helping the FBI with their investigation."

"That's not what Stuart said," Marigold said. "He said it was just a matter of time before she was in jail and he was exonerated."

"Stuart Machalvie is lying to you," Claire said. "He's lying to everyone. It's what he does."

Marigold was quiet for a few moments as if considering this new information.

"So you don't think Kay is going to use Knox's death to discredit me?"

"What's to use?" Claire asked. "You went to visit a neighbor for some reason, and he died after you left."

"There's more to it," Marigold said. "It'll all come out eventually."

"So tell Kay your side of the story, and ask her to fight a fair fight."

"Fat lot of good that'll do," Marigold said. "She'll probably laugh in my face."

"You really don't know her at all, do you? Kay Templeton has the most well-developed conscience of anyone I know. It's like there's a flippin' cricket on her shoulder. I've known her my whole life, and I'm telling you she's a decent person."

"Except my son spray-painted her house. It was just youthful high jinx that got out of hand, of course, but nonetheless, I'm sure she holds me responsible."

"She doesn't," Claire said. "She holds your son responsible, and she wants him to get counseling, not jail time."

"There's nothing wrong with my son," Marigold said, drawing her shoulders up in a huff.

"We're being honest here, Marigold," Claire said. "Your son is a mean bully, and pretty soon he's going to seriously hurt someone."

"What have you heard?"

"You can kid yourself about him, but not me," Claire said. "I saw what he wrote on those houses. That kid needs an anger intervention."

"I took him to our minister," Marigold said, as her shoulders collapsed. "I've sent him to a private Christian school; I don't know what else to do."

"I don't know, either," Claire said. "But Kay is not your enemy. Go see her. Be honest with her, and she will be fair with you."

"It's probably pointless," Marigold said.

"Here's something you can do," Claire said. "Take these boxes of leftovers to the Pendleton City Mission and make sure someone from the paper is there to photograph you doing it. It'll save me a trip and be good P.R. for you."

"Thank you," Marigold said. "Why are you being so nice to me?"

"Just something I'm learning," Claire said. "You know the saying: be kind, for everyone is fighting some kind of battle."

"Well, I'm touched," Marigold said. "I think after I drop these off I will go and see Kay, and have a heart-to-heart talk with her."

"Maybe you two could go to the mission together," Claire said. "Show the public you're willing to put politics aside to help those in need."

"I won't bother her," Marigold said. "No need to muddy the message."

Claire wanted to laugh but held it in until Marigold left.

Even bitches have sorrows.

Gwyneth Eldridge came in right as Claire was closing up for the night.

"We're closing," Claire told her.

"I didn't come to buy anything," Gwyneth said. "I want to talk to you."

Claire sighed, flipped the lights back on, and sat down.

"I'm so tired, Gwyneth," Claire said. "Could you go ahead and say whatever it is you came to say so I can disagree with you or tell you 'no' and then we can both go home?"

"There's no need to be so rude," Gwyneth said. "I'm offering to do you a favor."

"Do *me* a favor?" Claire said. "And why would you do that?"

"Because I need your help," Gwyneth said. "My back's against the wall on this spa issue, and I've come here, checkbook in hand, to beg you to help me."

"I don't need the money," Claire said, even though visions of online shopping expeditions were dancing in her head.

"But you do need to get rid of Pip."

"What are you suggesting?"

"Nothing like that," Gwyneth said. "Although he did only half-build some bookshelves for me after I paid him for the whole job, and I think he may have stolen an antique silver letter opener off of my desk."

"Cut to the chase, Gwyneth."

"My sister Caroline is living in Hawaii, where she's building a sort of ashram for her spiritual community."

"I heard something about that."

"She needs someone who can do all sorts of handyman work, not only building the place but to reside there afterward as a sort of jack-of-all-trades."

"I'm sure there are people in Hawaii who can do that sort of work."

"Unfortunately, Caroline has made some social gaffs which have alienated the locals. Something about wanting to barter for work using spiritual lessons instead of money. Although she can afford to pay, she doesn't have her non-profit status yet, so she'd prefer not to hire someone. Pip would ostensibly be a volunteer, but she'd take care of him under the table."

"Which would suit him to a tee."

"I'm willing to pay for a one-way ticket, and vouch for him with whatever parole officer is unlucky enough to be in charge of him, so that he can help Caroline with her project."

"And in return, I help you set up a spa in the basement of the Eldridge Inn."

"Exactly."

Claire was tempted. It would be so wonderful not to have Pip underfoot for a while. Knowing Pip, she had no illusions about it being a permanent placement, but it might last six months.

"Can I think about it?"

"I'll give you twenty-four hours," Gwyneth said.

Claire's feet were so sore she wanted nothing more than to go home, take a hot shower, and go straight to bed. As she passed the newspaper office, however, Ed came outside and stopped her.

"Can you come in for a minute?" he asked her. "I'd like to talk to you."

"Is Eve here?" Claire asked.

"No," Ed said. "She's working."

Claire came inside and sat down at the work table in the middle of the front room. She was so tired she could barely function.

"Bakery work is brutal, I'm guessing," he said.

"I'm out of shape," Claire said. "I need to start running again."

"Anytime you're ready I'm ready," Ed said.

"Let's say tomorrow," Claire said. "I may cancel, but let's pretend I'll follow through and see what happens."

"I wanted to thank you for the information you got from Knox's phone. I was able to get to the person he talked to at the bank before Sarah did. He was checking on an application he had made for a loan against his home. He was denied, of course. You don't fire someone for misappropriating funds and coercing a bank board for personal gain and then turn around and give him a loan."

"Only Knox would be arrogant enough to think that could work for him."

Claire told Ed about her phone call to Anne Marie, and he took notes. She did not tell him about the vision Anne Marie had.

"Neither the bank or the attorneys will talk to me, of course," Ed said, "and neither Stuart nor Trick will return my phone calls."

"That leaves Marigold," Claire said.

"She said her call was about a committee Knox and she are on," Ed said. "He didn't answer, she didn't leave a message, and he didn't return her call."

"So we know he was alive at 12:20 p.m., when he called his brother," Claire said. "The call Pip made to Knox was at 12:52. When I called Frieda, she said Pip had left five minutes before, and it only takes about five minutes to get from her house to Knox's, so sometime between 12:20 a.m. and around 1:00 p.m., when Pip found him, someone killed Knox."

"Unless Trick killed him, and then had Sandy call from Knox's cell phone to give him an alibi."

"You don't really think Trick is smart enough to think that up, or that Sandy would go along with it."

"No, I guess not."

"At least that narrows it down," Claire said. "I'd like to know where Meredith was during those 40 minutes."

They were both quiet for a few moments, thinking through the series of events on Knox's last day.

"My brain hurts," Claire said. "I need to go home, take a shower, and go to bed."

"Eve told me about the senator," Ed said.

Claire was taken aback, and it took her a moment to organize her thoughts.

"What did she say?"

"The affair started when she spent a week with him working on a profile piece," he said. "She said she didn't want there to be any secrets between us."

"That's admirable."

"You aren't surprised, I see."

"No, I knew all about it."

"Why didn't you tell me?"

"It felt like tattling," Claire said. "It felt like a petty thing a jealous ex-girlfriend would do, and not a good friend."

"There's still a chance the child's mine," Ed said. "And even if it isn't, I want it to be raised as mine."

"I understand," Claire said. "I do. I understand it, I accept it, and I support your decision, if not 100 percent wholeheartedly, then at least 85 percent, which, I'm sorry, is probably the best I can do."

"I appreciate that you were looking out for me."

"We're friends, Ed," Claire said. "At least I hope we still are."

"Of course we are."

"Before I go, I want to say this, and you can take my advice or leave it," Claire said. "You're more valuable to Eve than she wants you to think."

"I don't know about that."

"It's true," Claire said. "Right now you have all the power in the relationship, and you don't even realize it. If you tell her how you want it to be, and she doesn't agree, you don't have to cooperate."

"But I want the kid."

"Tell her you're prepared to sue for custody and demand a DNA test," Claire said. "That should get her maternity panties in a twist."

"Wow," he said. "You seem very sweet, Claire, but underneath you're actually a cutthroat pirate of a girl, aren't you?"

"There are some things I need to tell you about my own past," Claire said. "Some things I'm not too proud of. Since we're putting everything out here on the table, I'd like to get that over with."

"You're entitled to your privacy," Ed said.

"No," Claire said. "My father used to say you shouldn't complain about being robbed if you make your living as a thief."

"I have a hard time picturing you as even a metaphorical thief."

"That's what I want to address," Claire said. "I want you to know who I am."

"Do you want a beer, first?"

"Yeah, I think I better have one," Claire said. "Bring two, actually; I may need them both."

After she left the newspaper office, Claire went back down Rose Hill Avenue, and just happened to look into the tea room to see if Meredith was there. She had her nose pressed to the window and didn't hear Laurie until he was right next to her.

"Hey," he said. "Find any dead executives lately?"

Claire jumped, her heart thumping, and she must have been down to her last nerve because it infuriated her all out of proportion.

"Been to the bottom of any vodka bottles lately?" she asked him.

"The office was covered."

"You could have died, Laurie."

"It's a lot like Russian roulette," he said. "I just prefer spirits to firearms."

"That's not funny," Claire said. "You can't go on this way."

"A momentary lapse of focus," he said. "It won't happen again."

Claire took a deep breath and reminded herself how compassionate she had planned to be in regard to other people's battles. It wasn't always easy.

"I'm concerned," she said. "What *did* happen?"

"My life," Laurie said. "Do we have to talk about this? Can't I just buy you some flowers or a pair of shoes with some Italian man's name on them, and we can put this behind us?"

"Yeah, because I'm just some shallow, stupid little woman," Claire said.

"I'd apologize," he said, "but what I'd really like to do is change the subject."

"Fine," Claire said. "Your alcoholism is beginning to bore me, anyway."

There were a few moments of tense silence, heavy as a thundercloud. She crossed her arms, sighed, and rolled her eyes. Laurie looked as if he were counting to ten, as if he felt the same. If they were each so mad, so fed up with each other, then why didn't one of them just walk away?

"So, you went up to Knox's house to stop Pip from blackmailing Knox ..." he finally said.

His tone was quiet, detached, and polite, but barely so.

"I thought Knox might do something to Pip, like shoot him and then say it was in self-defense or something. I don't know; it was an impulse."

"Tell me what happened," he said.

"I gave Sarah my statement at the scene, and you got Pip's last night."

"But you didn't give yours to me," he said. "Go slowly, take your time."

Claire took a deep breath and blew it out. She told him everything she could remember, but she didn't mention her amateur detective work. He didn't speak until she mentioned the hundred dollar bill.

"They said there was nothing in his wallet," Laurie said. "Big self-important guy like that probably carried around a big wad of cash, don't you think?"

Claire shrugged. She wasn't supposed to know Knox was broke so she couldn't say anything about it.

"Didn't you talk to Sarah about the case?" she asked.

"She basically said 'Stay out of the way, and we'll handle it.'"

"The county always takes over when there's a suspicious death," Claire said. "That's the way it is here."

"Whoever was driving the sedan wasn't at all worried about being seen," Laurie said. "I think that was more of a harassment tool than a murder-for-hire. Any idea who'd want to kill the guy?"

Claire told him about the conversation she overheard between Knox, his brother, Trick, and former mayor, Stuart Machalvie.

"What a charming fellow," Laurie said. "You think one of the other two might have done it?"

"Stuart's capable, but I can't see Trick doing it," Claire said. "He's more the whiny little brother who always screws everything up but thinks it's just bad luck."

"Sounds like Knox is a bigger liability to the congressman and senator."

"He never cared who he stepped on to get ahead," Claire said. "He made a lot of enemies."

"What about you?" Laurie said. "Any reason you'd like to see Humpty Dumpty have a great fall?"

"He put my parents in a ridiculous balloon mortgage," she said. "When I found out about it I went up to his office and decked him."

Laurie's solemn face broke into a delighted smile.

"You socked ole Roly Poly Rodefeffer?"

"I did," Claire said. "I also rescued his second wife out of his office safe."

"This, I need to hear," Laurie said.

Claire told him the story of how Meredith disappeared and Knox's first wife, Anne Marie, told Claire he used to lock her up in the room-size safe behind his office when he was mad at her.

"Hannah and I went up there, and while Hannah wrestled with Courtenay, the secretary he was having an affair with, I found the safe and let Meredith out. Knox arrived right as I released her, and she attacked him with a coin box; put him in the hospital."

Claire shared what Scott had told her about Meredith threatening to kill Knox.

"So it wouldn't be that big of a stretch to imagine her whacking him on the head," he said. "So this was the same Courtenay who was living with Pip when she was murdered?"

"Anne Marie's assistant said it was Knox and Anne Marie who put him up to it."

"What do you think?"

"I heard Anne Marie tell him to take care of Courtenay, but she didn't say to kill her."

"How did you overhear this?"

"I was hiding under a bed in the Eldridge Inn," Claire said.

"You're going to have to explain that a little more thoroughly," Laurie said. "Can we go somewhere and get a cup of coffee or something?"

Claire hesitated.

"Please," Laurie said. "I know the county has this case, but it happened on my watch. How can I look Scott in the eye when he returns if I haven't at least made an attempt to figure out who killed the big lug?"

"All right," Claire said.

"Your house? My house?"

"The station," Claire said.

"Probably safer that way," Laurie said. "I hadn't realized how violent your temper is."

Back at the station, Skip was playing some sort of Internet game on the computer, and Frank was taking a nap on the sofa in the chief's office. Laurie shut the break room door behind them.

"I hate to disturb Crockett and Tubbs while they're working on a case," he said.

Claire made the coffee, and while it was dripping, she washed two mugs for them to use.

"Just a few more days," Laurie said. "You won't have to put up with me much longer."

"I'm not going to pretend with you," Claire said. "If you don't stop drinking you're going to lose that job, or kill yourself."

"I thought we weren't going to talk about it."

"Fine," she said and told him the story of Anne Marie coming to Rose Hill to hold a seminar at the Eldridge Inn.

Gwyneth had hired Claire to set up a temporary spa space in the basement of the inn, and while working there, Claire had been privy to some private conversations between Meredith and Anne Marie, and Anne Marie and her assistant, Jeremy. It was while Anne Marie was in town that Knox's Aunt Mamie and Courtenay both died under suspicious circumstances.

"I was there when Trick found his Aunt Mamie's body," Claire said.

"You've been back here for four months, and you've found how many corpses?"

"Just four," Claire said. "My friend Tuppy, Mamie, Diedre, and Knox."

"That's more than I've seen in the past four months, and that's part of my job."

"I can't help it," Claire said. "It just happened that way."

"Where is Meredith now?"

"I think she's in town, trying to sell the tea room," Claire said.

"I wonder if she still has a key to the house."

"He probably changed the locks after she tried to kill him."

"I'd like to see what the county has on this," he said.

"Sarah's still sweet on you," Claire said. "Buy her a pair of shoes, why don't you?"

"You still sore about that?" Laurie asked. "I thought you were through with me."

"I've been trying to be through with you. Lord knows why I can't just walk away."

"You love a lost cause? You've always been attracted to the antihero?"

"If you drink because of your grief over the death of your first wife, I can understand."

"I had this problem way before I married her."

Claire was surprised by this confession. She had the urge to snap at him, but he looked so vulnerable and miserable, all her righteous indignation evaporated.

"When did it start?"

"In college," he said. "Everyone partied, some much worse than me. Most of them got it together after we graduated; I just learned to hide it better."

"Why did you start?"

"For some people, all pathetic losers like me, to be alive is to be overly aware, with no filters, no defense, like it's always raining acid and you have no skin. The question then becomes how much awareness can you take?"

"Georgia said it was usually about feelings of anger, shame, and guilt."

"All of the above," he said. "Things I've done in the past haunt me. That's the thing about the past; it won't ever leave you the hell alone. It's noisiest at about three in the morning when I can't sleep for agonizing over the shitty things I've done. In theory, I can atone for my bad behavior, as long as my victims are still alive. Unfortunately, I feel the most guilty about things I didn't do when I had the chance, for people who are now gone. And that's just guilt; we've still got anger and shame to deal with."

"I guess I never thought about the difference between shame and guilt."

"Shame is an unslayable dragon. How can you atone for who you are?"

"But what's wrong with who you are?"

"I'm not blaming this on my parents; you have to know that. I was always the problem. I was the cuckoo's egg dropped in their nest. My father was this tough, manly, larger-than-life loaded gun, filled to the brim with angry, righteous morality. My mother lived in her head, where she escaped into her books, music, and art. They coexisted but just barely, and neither one understood me or knew how to relate to me, let alone each other. I was so lonely growing up; I never felt that I belonged anywhere. I expected to figure it out in college, but that didn't happen. There was nothing I was terribly interested in, nothing that filled me with passion. I graduated not knowing what to do with myself. I took the job working for my father thinking, well, at least maybe I could earn his approval, his respect."

"Did you?"

"I don't know," he said. "My father viewed tender feelings as weakness. I always knew when I'd disappointed him, but the opposite of that was nothing, only the absence of his disapproval."

"And you don't like police work."

"I loathe it," he said. "I'm the lifeguard at a sewage-filled cesspool of the worst examples of human behavior. I've come to detest my fellow man. I expect the worst of everyone."

"Why don't you do something different, then?"

"Like what? I look around, and I don't see any more attractive options. I couldn't work for someone else now; I'd be fired the first day for being such a sarcastic jerk. In this job at least I can be of some use in the world. I'm not actively making things worse for innocent people, and I can sometimes protect them from the bad guys. No, I've made my life into this mess, and it's too late to change it."

"There's nothing else you'd like to do?" Claire said. "Even if there was no guarantee you'd succeed, nothing you'd even be willing to try?"

"Life doesn't work like that, Claire," Laurie said. "There's no magical reward for self-actualization. There's only us, the human race, down here in the mud, ruining everything, fighting over shiny objects, and trying to gain power over each other."

"That's so depressing."

"That's life," Laurie said. "Anyone who thinks differently is a fool."

"So why bother?"

"I think that's the point I was just making."

"Would you consider talking to a doctor about this, maybe try an antidepressant?"

"I don't have a delusion about how awful the world is, Claire, I have an accurate awareness of reality."

"But you still believe good things can happen, don't you?"

"I believe you believe that," he said. "I want to warm my hands by that fire every chance I get."

"You have to find a reason to believe it for yourself."

"What I would give to live in County Claire. I'd swim the moat made from your tears; I'd climb the walls built from the failures of lesser men."

"You're so full of shit."

"I could get better if I knew you were waiting for me."

"I can't save you."

"But you could soothe me, I know you could."

"I think if I let myself love you, you'll pull me down with you."

"No doubt," he said.

To Claire's surprise, Laurie's eyes filled with tears. She reached for his hand, and he pulled it away.

"Abandon hope, all ye who enter here," he said.

He attempted a smile, but it dissolved.

"Laurie," she said.

"Run," he said. "Save yourself."

The plea was there. Claire could feel it pulling her like a natural force, like a whirlpool. The urge to jump in, to embrace him, even if it meant drowning, was so strong it was disorienting, intoxicating.

"I would gladly destroy you," he said, through his tears, "in order to be loved by you."

Claire fled.

Claire ordered a pizza delivered for her father's supper, and he said it was the best he had ever eaten. One convenient thing about taking care of someone with a severe short-term memory problem was that he didn't complain about having the same meal several nights during a week because he couldn't remember that he had.

Claire had deliberately ordered a pizza covered in toppings she didn't like, but still, she found herself picking at the crust. To stop herself eating it, she put the leftovers in the garbage disposal. She ate some celery with fat-free cream cheese, but that did not satisfy her hungry ghost.

"Knox, if that's you trying to get me to eat too much, take a hike," she said. "I'm not going to embezzle money or run for office, either, just so you can get your ghostly rocks off."

"Who are you talking to?" her father called out.

"I'm on the phone."

To distract herself, Claire took a long, hot bath, put on her yoga pants and a T-shirt, and settled in on the living room couch with *Confessions of an English Opium Eater* by Thomas De Quincey, one of the books from Professor Richmond's collection. She kept re-reading a page and then realizing she wasn't retaining a thing. She couldn't get Laurie's tear-stained face out of her head.

She had just begun the first chapter for the fourth time when the house phone rang. Claire ran to grab it before her father woke up, but he kept snoring in his recliner, a small cat and dog tucked in between his legs.

"I need to talk to you," Sarah said when she answered.

"I'm beat," Claire said. "I was about to go to bed."

"I'm right outside your house," Sarah said. "Meet me out back."

Claire slipped on some tennis shoes and quietly let herself out the back door. She sat down at the picnic table in the backyard just as Sarah rounded the corner.

"I need you to do something for me," Sarah said.

"I'm not wearing a wire," Claire said. "One near-death experience per year is my limit."

"No," Sarah said. "I need you to find Knox's wife, Meredith."

"If you can't find her, how in the world am I going to find her?"

"No one in this town trusts me," Sarah said. "But you get to hear all the gossip."

Claire bit her lip.

"You know something."

"I heard something," Claire said. "But I don't remember who told me."

"Fair enough," Sarah said. "Let's have it."

"Meredith went to see Trick Rodefeffer, to contract him to sell the tea room. I heard she needs the money."

"So, you can make an appointment to see the tea room," Sarah said. "Nose around there and see if you can get Trick to tell you where she's hiding."

"I could do that," Claire said. "My cousin is interested in buying the place, so I could take him with me in case she shows up and tries to kill me."

"Let me know when your appointment is and I'll make sure I'm nearby," Sarah said. "And keep this to yourself; I don't want the feds to know I'm tracking her down."

"I really am beat, Sarah. Can we wrap this up?"

"How's Purcell?"

"I'm not his babysitter, Sarah."

"He's going to crash and burn in Pendleton," Sarah said. "There aren't several decades of loyalty to his old man to protect him there."

"I wish him the best," Claire said. "I just don't want to go down that road with him."

"But I would," Sarah said. "And yet he doesn't give a damn about me."

"I'm sorry."

Sarah shrugged.

"That's life," she said. "Nobody lives happily ever after."

Kay came home from a campaign committee meeting to find Marigold Lawson sitting on her front porch.

"I know you're surprised to find me here," Marigold said.

Marigold's hand was trembling as she shook Kay's.

"Come in," Kay said. "I need to get these shoes off, and you look like you could use a glass of wine."

Marigold followed her inside and looked around.

"Your place is so cute," she said, "but Lord, it's tiny."

"It suits me," Kay said. "Why don't you have a seat and I'll be right back."

Kay changed into some casual clothes. When she returned to the front room, Marigold was perched on the edge of the loveseat, dabbing at her eyes with a wadded up Kleenex.

"Whatever it is, a glass of wine and a good cry may help," Kay said.

"I've cried enough tears over Knox Rodefeffer," Marigold said.

Kay fetched two glasses and a bottle of white wine. She poured them both a glass, pushed the tissue box closer to Marigold, sat down, and put her feet up.

"Tell me about it," Kay said. "Whatever it is, it's not worth the high blood pressure."

"Claire said you wouldn't use this against me," Marigold said.

"Unless you killed Knox," Kay said. "I can't keep that kind of secret."

"I didn't kill him," Marigold said. "I don't know what happened after I left his house, but he was alive the last time I saw him."

"Start at the beginning," Kay said.

Marigold drank her glass of wine in one swallow, so Kay poured her another.

"We dated in college," Marigold said. "It was our first semester in the fall. I was in the sister sorority to Knox's fraternity. We were both from Rose Hill, and my dad was mayor at that time."

"I'd forgotten that," Kay said. "You've never mentioned that in your campaign."

"It was only for a short time, as interim, after the incumbent mayor passed away, and only until the next election, which he lost. It was humiliating. He thought he was more popular than he was. He felt betrayed by the whole town. He never got over it."

"I'm so sorry."

"Anyway," Marigold said, "my dad was the mayor, and Knox was impressed with that. He had political ambitions even back then. He dumped me, of course, as soon as Dad lost."

"Jerk."

"Yes, he was," Marigold said. "I was heartbroken. I thought it was something more than it was. I did things I wouldn't have done if I'd known."

"You were young," Kay said. "We all make mistakes."

"I got pregnant."

"Oh, my."

"You went away, back in those days, to a group home in southern Pennsylvania. I had the baby there, gave it up for adoption, and then went back to school the next fall. We told everyone I went to Europe for the spring semester. I got good at acting like nothing happened. Eventually, it felt like it happened to someone else."

"I'm so sorry."

"Knox was gone by the time I came back. Something happened at his fraternity, and they shut it down. His parents paid everyone off and transferred him to another school. I didn't see him again until he came back here after grad school. The glassworks was closed by then, so he went to work for the bank. I was married with a little one."

"It must have been difficult to have him living right across the street."

"He acted like we were barely acquainted, so I did, too. I didn't tell him about the baby," Marigold said. "My parents were so ashamed; they forbid me from telling anyone."

"How hard that must have been for you," Kay said. "How lonely you must have felt."

"I never told anyone," Marigold said. "Not even Ken. When we got married, he thought he was the first."

"He was, in a way," Kay said. "He loved you; it meant something."

"But I lied," Marigold said. "He knows now, of course."

"When did you tell him?"

"Two years ago," Marigold said. "My son got in touch with me, my son by Knox, that is. The adoption agency let me know that he wanted to meet me. I can't tell you how upset I was. I was terrified someone would find out about it."

"Of course you were."

"He was adopted by a family in Pennsylvania, a Jewish couple. He was about to graduate from law school at Penn State and had a job lined up in Pittsburgh, with a law firm where a friend of his father's works. He's a big boy, of course, how could he not be, with my and Knox's genes? He didn't play football in high school, though; his parents said he was more of a bookworm."

"Do you have a photo?"

Marigold was beaming, her face pink, as she scrolled through the photos kept on her phone, and then held it out for Kay to look at. The young man had dark hair and the Rodefeffer nose, but his build was classic linebacker Lawson. Kay could see both his biological parents in his facial features. His adoptive parents, in contrast, were short, friendly looking people who were obviously proud of their son.

"He's handsome," Kay said. "I can see your dad in him."

Marigold broke out into fresh tears.

"My father refused to meet him," she said. "He's ashamed of him."

"That's too bad," Kay said. "Maybe he'll change his mind one day."

"It's the sin, you see," Marigold said. "It's living evidence of my sin."

"If God can forgive you, surely your father can, too."

Marigold shook her head.

"He won't," Marigold said. "My father is a devout Christian, and he has never forgiven me for what I did."

"I would think a devout Christian would be the first person to forgive you."

"Our church is strict on following the literal Word," Kay said. "Sin is sin and will be punished by God, either here on Earth or in hell."

"I'm sorry I can't agree," Kay said. "I believe in a loving God, who has great compassion for all of us."

"Well, how convenient for you," Marigold said. "If you studied your Bible you'd know better."

"There's no point in us arguing about doctrine," Kay said. "Let's just agree to disagree. After your son contacted you, did you tell Knox?"

"I had to," Marigold said. "The adoption agency was going to contact him next."

"How did he take the news?"

"He was furious, of course," she said. "He was engaged to Meredith, with all her political connections, and planning to run for the Senate. It was exactly the kind of thing that could ruin his chances."

"Did Knox meet him?"

"He met the parents, separately from me."

"How did that go?"

"Knox offered to pay them off to keep them quiet, and they were insulted. They refused, and our son never contacted him."

"That's sad," Kay said. "Did your meeting go well?"

"It did," she said. "He's a lovely young man with excellent manners. His mother showed me a photo album of all the growing up years I missed. They invited me to his law school graduation; I didn't go, of course. What if someone saw me there?"

"It was a brave thing you did, giving him up," Kay said. "And look what happiness you gave his parents. That's the most precious gift."

"They were so kind," Kay said. "I didn't know what to expect, them being Jewish, but they seemed so normal."

"Now, Marigold," Kay said. "You know there are many people who don't believe the same way you do, and yet they lead exemplary lives and love their children. They want the same things for their children that you do for your own."

"The way this country is going we'll soon be outnumbered," Marigold said. "I hate to think what will happen to us Christians when the globalists and leftists take over."

"Oh, Marigold, sweetie, have some more wine," Kay said. "I know I'm going to."

"You can stick your head in the ground if you want to, but I know what's coming," Marigold said. "The signs are all around us, just like it says in the Book of Revelation."

Kay took a deep breath and smiled at her guest.

"Tell me something," Kay said, as she poured Marigold's next glass of wine. "After the boy's adoptive parents refused to accept Knox's bribe, what did he offer you?"

Marigold's face turned a deep red, and she sputtered, "Not a thing!"

"I know about the account he set up," Kay said.

"I don't know what you're talking about."

"Stuart was careless with his bank statements," Kay said. "I know Stuart and Knox were depositing money in an account that only you drew from."

"I can't believe you didn't run straight to the newspapers with that."

"I don't run that kind of campaign," Kay said. "I should be elected upon my own merit, not at the expense of someone else's reputation."

"I don't know what to say," Marigold said. "I'm flabbergasted."

"Tell me why you accepted the money."

"Well, I was owed it, wasn't I?" she said. "Breaking my heart like he did, and leading me into temptation, into sins of the flesh. All those years of keeping that awful secret, and not knowing my own son, my own flesh and blood. All those years Knox paraded those horrible wives around town and cheated on them any chance he got. Everyone knew about it."

"So why did you go see him on the day he died?"

"He quit paying," she said. "I went over there to ask him why. He said he wasn't going to give me another red cent; that he couldn't afford to."

"That was it?"

"He took out his wallet and threw a bunch of bills at me, said that was all he had left. I wasn't going to stand there and be treated like that, so I left."

"Did you take the money?"

"I certainly did not."

"Where was he when he did this?"

"In his house."

"Where in his house?"

"He was standing on the stairs," Marigold said. "On the landing, there."

"That seems odd; why would he be up there?"

"I knew he was home; I saw him go in. So when he didn't answer the doorbell, I tried the door; it was unlocked. As soon as I got inside, I called out to him, but he only came halfway down the stairs. He used very vulgar language. When I told him why I was there, he laughed at me."

"So he threw the money down the steps?"

"Yes, I've just told you," Marigold said. "Why does that matter?"

"Everything matters in a murder investigation."

"I'm innocent," Marigold said. "Meredith was in there after me; she probably pushed him down the steps."

"If they can find Meredith," Kay said. "Did you tell the police all of this?"

Marigold shook her head.

"You need to tell the truth," Kay said. "It could save you from going to jail."

"I've been praying about it," Marigold said. "But I haven't got the go-ahead yet."

"Sometimes the Lord trusts us to know the right thing to do," Kay said. "Even if it's hard to do."

"I'm hoping I won't have to," Marigold said. "If they can find Meredith, and she confesses, I won't have to tell anyone anything."

"How likely is that, really?"

"She already tried to kill Knox once. I heard she confessed to poisoning her father and late husband," Marigold said. "Why they let her out of the nut house I'll never know."

"Meredith was mentally ill," Kay said. "I gather they couldn't use anything she said against her on account of that."

"People like that should be locked up," Marigold said. "They should throw away the key."

"You wouldn't like that to happen to Jared, though, would you?"

"My son is not crazy."

"But he definitely has some emotional problems, wouldn't you agree?"

"Some might say he was only calling a spade a spade," Marigold said. "Some might say he was only pointing out what we all know to be true."

"That someone in this house is a homosexual witch?"

"I know for a fact that Grace Branduff reads books about witchcraft," Marigold said.

"Reading *Harry Potter* hardly constitutes devil worship," Kay said.

"Jared told me she's friends with those girls who hold hands in the halls. I heard she had an unnatural interest in Charlotte Fitzpatrick, and after Charlotte's mother put a stop to it, Grace verbally abused Charlotte in front of a classroom full of children. And foul-mouthed! You should have heard that child in the school library; she cussed me out like a drunken sailor."

"Was that the day you gathered up the books you wanted to burn?"

"For the sake of the children!" Marigold said. "Their minds are soft at that age; you can't go filling them up with witchcraft and sexual perversions. Grace Branduff is clearly in the fast lane to hell."

"Grace Branduff is an intelligent, compassionate, brave young woman who has been through a lot in her young life," Kay said, as she stood up. "I will not allow you to disparage her in my home."

"Well, good luck with that one," Marigold said, whilst struggling to get to her feet. "You're going to need it."

Marigold seemed a little unsteady, but when Kay reached out to help her, Marigold pulled away as if she'd been burned.

"You're not planning to drive, are you?" Kay asked her.

"I walked here, and I can walk back home, thank you very much," Marigold said.

"Thank you for confiding in me," Kay said. "I won't tell a soul what you've told me."

"You got me drunk," Marigold said. "That was a dirty trick."

"Oh, sweetie," Kay said. "You're so troubled; I'm sorry I can't help you more. Be careful."

And with that, Kay shut her front door behind Marigold Lawson.

Kay was halfway through a carton of chocolate ice cream when Sonny knocked on her front door. She didn't try to hide it, just wiped her mouth with a napkin and answered the door with the carton in one hand and the spoon in the other.

"Wow," he said as he stepped inside. "Is this what a Kay Templeton bender looks like? I want in."

Kay went to the kitchen and got him a spoon. He sat down at the table and accepted the utensil, along with the carton. He ate a spoonful and then looked at her.

"This needs whipped cream," he said.

Kay got the can of whipped cream out of the refrigerator, handed it to him, and sat down across from him.

"So what brought this on?" he asked as he shook the can and then squirted the whipped cream into the carton.

Kay was tempted to tell him about her visit with Marigold but decided to keep her word instead.

"Politics," she said. "I don't want to talk about it."

"I can see that," he said, gesturing to the carton. "You know, it's only going to get worse after you're elected."

"Thanks," she said. "That helps a lot."

"I'm just saying," he said. "You might want to find a healthier way to deal with stress than diving head first into the ice cream. I think you're beautiful exactly the way you are, mind you, and I could stand to lose a few, myself, but I just got you, and I don't want to lose you to a heart attack or a stroke."

"I know," Kay said. "It's a problem I have."

"What do you say we go for a walk?" Sonny said. "Let's try out that rail trail the folks come all the way from D.C. to walk on."

"I don't want to leave the house," Kay said.

"You're not likely to run into any Rose Hill residents down there," Sonny said. "All that fresh air might get into their closed little minds, might blow out some of the dust they've got in there."

"I'll change my shoes," Kay said.

"That's my girl," Sonny said.

"When we get back I'll make you a nice salad for dinner," Kay said.

"Don't let's go crazy, now," Sonny said. "We're not rabbits."

The rail trail ran alongside the Little Bear River from Rose Hill to Fleurmania.

"I don't think I can make it all the way to the lake," Kay said, as they passed the dam right below town.

"Let's start slow," Sonny said. "We'll walk as far as the old depot in Lumberton and then turn around."

"That's probably three miles round trip," she said, already breathless.

"If we get tired, we'll sit," he said.

"If I have a heart attack, Grace will be an orphan again," she said.

"You'll be fine."

They walked in companionable silence for a while, and Kay was conscious of her heavy breathing and heart pounding in her chest. They passed the soccer fields on the Eldridge college campus, rounded the bend, and turned southeast. As soon as they came to a small park-like setting at the back edge of the campus, they stopped.

"This is nice," Kay said. "I'm embarrassed to say I've never been back here."

"Let's take a break," Sonny said.

They sat on the bench and enjoyed the prospect of the river, shallow in this part, as it cascaded over multiple large rocks. On the other side of the water, rhododendron covered the steep bank in a profusion of purple flowers and deep green foliage. The air was cool and sweet smelling.

"Honeysuckle," Sonny said. "It's one of my favorite things about summer."

"Look," Kay said.

A doe and her white-speckled twin fawns came down the steep bank on the other side of the river, drank some water, and then scampered back up the hillside to disappear into the underbrush.

243

"This is nice," Sonny said. "We should do this every night."

"I'd love to."

"It's nice to have someone to do stuff with," he said. "I gotta tell you, I'm sick of my own company, sitting in that apartment every night, watching television."

"With Grace gone, I've been at loose ends."

"After Karla left," he said, "I was so mad at her that I spent a long time going over and over what she did to me, to our family. I kinda got stuck in a rut being miserable about it. I couldn't get past how unfair it was, how deceitful she'd been. Then I realized I was wasting what was left of my life and, meanwhile, she was going on with hers. Being mad about it wasn't going to change the past. I'm still mad, don't get me wrong, I'm no angel, but now it doesn't hurt so much. It's more like a bad knee than a broken leg; does that make sense?"

"It does," Kay said.

"So I'm wondering if this thing with Matty is more like a bad knee or a broken leg?"

Kay thought a moment.

"It's actually more like an allergy," she said.

Sonny laughed.

"I only notice it when I'm around him, and it's more irritating than painful."

"That's good to hear," he said. "What about this engagement situation you had?"

"Shug was a nice man," Kay said. "His wife died of cancer, and he'd dated around for a while before we met. Looking back, I think he was just ready to get married again when I happened along; I think whoever he met next would've done as well."

"Don't talk about my good friend Kay like that," Sonny said. "That man knew quality when he met it, that's all."

"I don't know," Kay said. "After I broke the engagement he had a new girlfriend within the week; he married her not too much later."

"Why did you break up?"

"I realized I was letting myself get carried along," she said. "I liked Shug; he was a good guy; you would've liked him, too. But I didn't love him, and I didn't feel loved by him. Don't get me wrong; he was wonderful to me, but I didn't feel what I thought I should feel. I think maybe you have to love somebody in order to feel loved."

"Did you regret it?"

"Not for a minute," she said. "As soon as I ended it, I felt a huge sense of relief. I hadn't realized how much I didn't want to marry him until I didn't have to."

"Once you see how wrong it can go, you're bound to take it more seriously," he said. "It's risky to love people."

"Do you want to get married again?"

"I do," he said. "I miss having somebody in my corner."

"Someone you can count on."

"Only if they're not pretending," he said. "I guess I never had that with Karla; I just thought I did."

"I'm sorry you had to go through that," she said. "You deserve better."

"I'm starting to think I've found better," he said.

"We'll see," she said. "Let's walk."

As they started off, Sonny grabbed her hand and held it, swinging it between them as they went.

"This is nice," he said.

"It is," she said.

When they returned from their walk, sweaty and clammy from the cool night air, Sonny said, "I need a shower; do you mind if I run home real quick?"

"Use mine," Kay said. "We'll take turns."

He paused, and Kay looked at him. He was smiling in a way that made him look years younger, and in his expression, she could see the teenager he once was.

"You know," he said. "It would conserve water if we shared."

Kay was shocked, and her face must've shown it.

He winked and nodded toward the bathroom.

"C'mon," he said. "We're grownups. We're neither of us fashion models, and that's okay. Let's do something fun."

"I like to think of myself as a green candidate," Kay said.

"Well then," he said. "Maybe we've stumbled upon a better stress reliever than ice cream."

CHAPTER 9

W hen the alarm clock went off at 4:00 a.m., Claire moaned. She'd been awake for most of the night, obsessing about Laurie and Ed, worrying about what to do with her life, and resisting the urge to mix up some cookie dough.

The sleep she did get was muddled up with dreams about Knox and Anne Marie. In the dream, it was Knox's funeral, and Anne Marie was dressed in widow's black, but she kept flashing everyone with her bright red panties. In the dream, Claire kept trying to get Anne Marie to cover up. "Cover up," she kept telling the woman, but Anne Marie just laughed and flipped up her skirt at all the men in attendance. The words "cover up" were still reverberating in Claire's ears as she got out of bed.

A hot shower helped a little, and two cups of coffee helped even more. By the time her father got up at 5:00 a.m. Claire was dressed and able to form complete sentences.

Claire took Mackie Pea and Junior outside to do their business and found her father's big cat, Chester, asleep on top of the newspapers in the recycling bin. Since Mackie Pea and the kitten had taken over Ian's affections, Chester had taken to living outside. Claire used a broom to protect the kitten from the growling cat and finally got the two little pets back inside safely.

Ed was standing in her living room.

"What are you doing here?" she asked him.

"Ian's going to keep me company while I deliver papers," he said.

"I'm riding shotgun," her father said.

"I thought it might help," Ed said. "I'll take him to the depot for breakfast and then to the station afterward."

"Thank you," Claire said. "But what I really need is to be twenty-two again."

"You and me both," Ed said.

At the bakery, Claire consulted the instruction sheet that Melissa had left for her. She had helped her Aunt Bonnie before, but now that it was up to her to do everything, and not just be the assistant, she found she had forgotten how to do most of it. Consequently, the croissants came out of the oven in interesting, distinctly un-croissant-like shapes, and she must have added too much baking powder, or was a little too generous in filling the muffin papers because all of the muffins had exploded at the top as they baked.

She was a little embarrassed at what she put on display in the bakery case, so she made a sign that said "student driver - everything 10% off today." The customers laughed at her wares, but they still bought them.

"It ain't pretty, but it tastes the same," one of the regulars said. "And the coffee's better, in my opinion."

By the time Ruthie Postlethwaite showed up at noon, moaning about her own back and feet, Claire was more than ready for a break.

"I've got my daughter coming in after a bit," Ruthie said, as she surveyed the array of pitiful baked goods that were left. "Why don't you take the afternoon off."

Claire was so thankful she hugged the woman.

"Why don't we switch tomorrow," Ruthie said. "I'll take the morning shift and do the baking, and then you can do the afternoon."

Claire hugged her again, and as she left, pretended not to see Ruthie slide the last of her overblown muffins into the trash can.

248

Trick Rodefeffer was kicked back in his rolling chair, feet on his desk, sipping a beer, when his wife, Sandy, let Claire into his office.

"Whassup, beautiful?" he asked her, jerking his head back and raising his beer to greet her.

"Richard!" Sandy said. "Put that away and sit up straight. What have I told you about that?"

"Sure, sure, sure," Trick said, as he struggled to comply, only to tip his chair over and fall on the floor.

Sandy left the room shaking her head and muttering under her breath.

When Trick got to his feet, he attempted to brush the spilled beer off his polo shirt and slick his wispy blonde hair over the thinning spot on the top of his head at the same time.

"Well, well, well. Claire Fitzpatrick, you are looking well," he said, in what she knew he thought was a suave manner. "To what do I owe the pleasure of such a beautiful woman's company on this fine morning?"

"It's past noon, actually," Claire said. "I'm interested in looking at the tea room. I understand it's for sale."

"Yes indeedy, yes, yes, yes," Trick said. "Meredith gave me a key if I can find it ..."

He looked through the tangle of papers on his desk, opened and closed drawers, patted his pockets, and looked around the office as if it might be anywhere.

Sandy came back in with a key and handed it to Claire, along with a folder.

"Here's the key and the details," she said. "After you're done, be sure and bring them back to *me*, not him."

"There they are!" Trick said. "Thank you, my dear, my angel, my pet, thank you so very much ..."

He was cut off by Sandy saying, "I'm going to lunch" and slamming the front door behind her.

"Shall we?" he asked Claire and gestured for her to precede him.

As they walked down Rose Hill Avenue, Trick greeted everyone he met with a "what's up?" or "hey, how ya doin?"

"I was so sorry to hear about your brother," Claire said.

"Oh, yeah," Trick said. "A terrible thing, so terrible, for sure."

"So it was an accident?"

"I don't know," Trick said. "The police seem to think someone killed him."

"Any idea who might have wanted to?"

"No idea," Trick said. "I can't imagine."

"Had you seen him that day?"

"No, no, no," Trick said. "I talked to him on the phone earlier, but he was fine then."

"Why did he call?"

"He was reminding me we were supposed to go to a meeting at the funeral home at 12:30, to talk to Stuart about some stuff. He said he was leaving as soon as he hung up, and I was to meet him in the back parking lot beforehand. I made it more or less on time, but then Knox didn't show up. The next thing you know we heard sirens and then the cops showed up."

"When is the funeral?"

"I don't know," Trick said. "Sandy does all that stuff; seems like she said Friday or Saturday; I don't always listen as well as I should. She'll tell me when it's time to go or if I need to do anything."

"I guess this means you'll inherit everything."

"Nothing left to inherit," he said. "There was a little trust money left after Aunt Mamie died, but there are all these debts, apparently, and attorney fees. It's just a huge mess, really huge. Sandy's on top of it; she'll tell me what I need to know."

"You and Knox were close?"

"Yeah, you'd think so, but, no, not really," he said. "I kind of could never do anything right where ole Knox was concerned, ya know? He was the brains of the outfit, and he just told me what I needed to do and when I needed to do it. I'm not that smart, I mean, I know it, Sandy knows it, and Knox sure as hell knew it. I never could seem to dig into anything and make a go of it. This real estate thing, well, Sandy runs the show. I turn up and do what she tells me to do. It's a living, I mean, we do all right."

"Well, it must be awful to lose Knox so soon after losing your Aunt Mamie."

"I don't think either of them liked me very much," Trick said. "But I'll miss them."

His eyes were glassy, and not only from drink. He tried to smile and failed, cleared his throat, stuck his hands down in his pockets, and chewed his lower lip.

As much as Claire disrespected Trick for being such a drunken womanizer, she found herself feeling sorry for him now.

She guessed even rotten bastards could have sorrows.

The tea room was also a gift shop, with a few small round tables and spindly chairs at the back. Meredith's taste ran to pastels, preppy pink and green, and ruffles. Everything was covered in a fine layer of dust, and beyond the combined smell of all the scented candles and tea, Claire smelled something rank. She wrinkled her nose, and Trick noticed.

"Sewer issues," he said. "Easily remedied; don't worry about it."

Claire went behind the counter and through the door to the backroom. Trick switched on the lights, and it was immediately evident that someone, probably Meredith, had been living there. There was an air mattress, heaps of clothing, some groceries, and an open laptop on the floor. Claire touched the laptop touchpad with the toe of her shoe, and the screen lit up, exposing an open browser page. It looked as though someone had recently left.

"I maybe should have given her a call to let her know we were coming," Trick said. "She could have cleaned up a little."

"What's upstairs?" Claire asked.

"Storage," Trick said.

"What's that door?"

"A bathroom."

Claire opened the door and flipped on a light, revealing the origin of the rank smell, along with a makeshift clothesline that had several hundred dollar bills clothes-pinned to it. It looked as though Meredith had bleached them, but even as faded as they were, some were still stained a light pink. Claire held her breath and closed the door, thankful to find that Trick was not paying attention.

"Where's she staying?"

"I don't know," he said with a shrug. "She gave me her cell number. The phone in here's been disconnected."

"Trick," Claire said. "I wonder if you wouldn't call Meredith and ask her to come over? I'd like to ask her some questions about the business."

"Sure, sure, sure," he said. "No problemo."

He patted all his pockets and then grimaced.

"Looks like I left my cell phone at the office; do you mind if I run back over and get it?"

"No, I'll wait," Claire said.

"You wanna beer?"

"No, but thanks."

As soon as Trick left, Claire texted Sarah to tell her where she was. Sarah texted back that she was not far away and would be there shortly.

Claire crouched down to look at Meredith's browsing history. Prices on airline tickets, a moving company quote request page, and her bank log-in page were the last three sites she visited.

"Find anything interesting?" someone said from behind Claire.

Claire jumped up, startled.

It was Meredith.

Meredith was a small, brittle-thin woman with narrow lips and a permanently disapproving expression. She was dressed in her best political wife pearls and a black linen pantsuit. She had smeared some bright pink lipstick on her mouth, and her mousy hair was held back by a black linen headband. She was livid, of course, as Claire could plainly see by her compressed lips and frown.

"I'm so sorry," Claire said. "You scared me."

"Caught you is more like it," Meredith said. "Who are you? What are you doing here?"

Claire blessed her good fortune that Meredith did not recognize her. It was only a few months earlier that Claire had caught Pip and Meredith having a lover's tiff in this very building, and then had been present in Knox's office when Meredith attacked him. Both of those times Claire had been dressed in designer clothing and high heels, her hair expertly blown out and her face covered in what constituted fashionable war paint.

Today Claire didn't have on any makeup, and her hair was pulled back into a messy bun on the back of her head. She wore blue jeans and a T-shirt, which was still covered in flour from her morning's work. In her mother's puffy white tennis shoes, she was several inches shorter than in her heels. Evidently, she didn't look like herself, or more accurately, she finally did.

"Trick brought me to look at the place," Claire said. "I'm thinking of buying it."

Meredith's demeanor immediately changed. Her eyebrows shot up, and her thin lips stretched into a fake smile. Her eyes, however, stayed alert and shrewd.

"I'm so sorry things are such a mess," Meredith said, extending her hand out to Claire. "I'm Meredith Stanhope Huckle Rodefeffer."

"Rebecca Fitzpatrick," Claire said, using her middle name, and wincing under the crushing claw that gripped her sore hand.

A brief expression passed over Meredith's face; only for a split-second, and it did not reflect a positive emotion.

"Are you any relation to the woman who owns the bakery?" Meredith said.

"She's my aunt."

"A stubborn woman, your aunt, but she makes delicious teacakes," Meredith said. "I couldn't afford them for my shop, actually, which was such a shame; she really is a formidable negotiator, and difficult to deal with, but such a talented baker."

"Maybe you could tell me a little about this place," Claire said.

"You get the entire inventory," Meredith said. "Everything you see here conveys. Do you have any retail experience?"

"No," Claire said. "I worked in the bakery when I was in high school, but only helped out in the kitchen."

"Are you married; do you have children?"

"No, it's just me," Claire said.

"What do you do?"

"Well, right now, nothing," Claire said. "I'm looking for something to do."

Meredith's fake friendliness began to slip.

"Have you been pre-approved for a mortgage? I told Richard I couldn't waste my time with local looky-loos who weren't serious."

"I can pay cash," Claire said.

Meredith cast a dubious look over Claire's attire and sniffed a little.

"So you say," she said. "Where is my brother-in-law?"

"He went back to the office to get his phone and call you," Claire said.

"How nice," she said. "Leaving you to pillage the place and snoop on my computer. You look familiar to me. Have we met before?"

Claire scooted around Meredith and backed out into the retail space. She didn't want to be trapped in the back room with someone she had once seen bludgeon a man with a collectible coin box, and she didn't dare turn her back on her.

"Were you one of Knox's girlfriends?" Meredith asked.

"Certainly not," Claire said. "I barely knew your husband."

"He's dead now," Meredith said. "So it hardly matters."

"I'm so sorry," Claire said. "How did it happen?"

Meredith released an unsettling cackle from deep in her chest.

"Money, honey," she said. "Money was the root of all his evil, and it was money got him in the end."

"I don't understand," Claire said. "What do you mean?"

"Never mind," Meredith said. "Listen, I'm leaving town today. Are you actually interested in buying this place? Because I'd like to sign the papers before I go. I don't intend to come back here if I can help it."

"Where are you off to?"

"Back to New England, where I belong."

"Won't you miss the funeral and the reading of the will?"

"Nothing in it for me," Meredith said with a shrug. "That man was broke and headed to the hoosegow. Anything he owned will be sold to settle his debts. So what's it going to be? Are you interested?"

"I am," Claire said. "I'd like to make an offer."

Claire named a figure, and Meredith laughed.

"Ridiculous," she said. "I spent more than that on the renovations."

"The sewer's backing up; I can smell it."

Meredith waved her hand.

"Immaterial," she said. "You're wasting my time. The price is set, and I'm not entertaining any low ball offers."

"What were your sales like?" Claire asked, trying to keep her distracted until Sarah arrived.

"This was a hobby for me, nothing more," Meredith said. "The price includes the building, fixtures, equipment, and the merchandise; what you make of it is up to you. Although with no retail experience and your poor taste in clothing, I can't imagine you'll do very well."

"I'm going to tear everything out and make it into a dance hall with a commercial kitchen," Claire said. "My cousin, Patrick, runs the Rose and Thorn next door; we're going to open up a door between the two places and have live music in here."

Meredith's face froze in a look of distaste and dismay, which quickly turned to shocked realization.

"I do know you," she said. "You're Philip's ex-wife, the hairdresser."

Claire felt a chill as the expression on Meredith's face turned from shocked to murderous.

"You're confusing me with my cousin," Claire said. "There are a lot of Fitzpatricks in Rose Hill, and we all look alike."

"You let me out of the safe," Meredith said. "You were there that day, in Knox's office. You accused me of running over that homosexual friend of yours, what was his name? Toodles? Poodles? Something ridiculous like that."

Claire's blood pressure shot up, and she forgot to pretend to be Rebecca.

"Tuppy," Claire said. "His name was Lawrence Tupworth III, but we called him Tuppy. He was a lovely young man who didn't deserve what happened to him, and his sexual preference is none of your damn business."

"I didn't kill him," Meredith said.

"I know," Claire said. "Your son did."

"Peyton was in the passenger seat," Meredith hissed. "He was an unwilling witness who was too afraid to come forward for fear of reprisals. He has post-traumatic stress disorder. I have a report from a psychiatrist that says he's too fragile to appear in court."

"I met Peyton," Claire said. "He's a spoiled, drug-addicted snot-head who didn't give the tiniest wee damn about the man he and his friend hit with their car and left to die in the street."

"Innocent until proven guilty!" Meredith screeched.

"Guilty, guilty, guilty!" Claire shouted back. "He confessed it; I recorded it."

"It was you!" Meredith bellowed.

Meredith grabbed the nearest thing she could use as a weapon, which happened to be a pink and green floral umbrella. The end was pointy enough that Claire knew it would hurt if she got stabbed with it. When Meredith jabbed it at her, Claire stumbled backward. She bumped into a display of monogrammed stationery, and it all fell onto the floor. Meredith cursed her and jabbed again. Claire pushed a display of Beatrix Potter ceramic figurines over between them, and they crashed into pieces on the floor.

"My bunnies!" Meredith roared, and then let loose a torrent of expletives that would have impressed Claire had she not been in fear for her life.

Claire pulled over another display between them, this time a large spinner rack of handmade lace greeting cards. Meredith stepped over the broken figurines, but her umbrella got caught up in the spindles of the card rack. While trying to disengage it, the umbrella opened up and further tangled her in the display. As she struggled to pull herself free, her necklace caught, broke, and pearls seemed to explode and soar in every direction.

Meredith screeched with rage, slipped on her pearls, and collapsed in a heap.

Claire heaved a stack of candle-wick-embroidered bedspreads over Meredith and scrambled to the front of the room. She made her way to the front door and flung it open just as Trick arrived. He had his phone up to his ear and pointed to it.

"Calling her now," he said.

Underneath the writhing pile of bedspreads came the muffled but distinct sound of a phone ringing.

Claire was in her father's old office at the Rose Hill Police Station, sitting on the green vinyl couch where as a child she used to do her homework. Sarah and Laurie had Meredith in the break room, where she had screeched abuse at them for twenty minutes but was now speaking in a more normal tone, so low that Claire could not make out what she was saying. At the top of the wall behind the couch, there was a heating vent between the two rooms, and Claire was considering climbing up on the back of the couch so she could press her ear to it, the better to know what was going on.

She texted Patrick to say she would be late picking up her dad, and Patrick texted back not to worry about it, that Melissa would take him home and stay with him until she got there.

"Where r u?" Patrick texted.

"Jail," she replied.

"Need bail?" he responded.

"No but thanks," she replied.

Claire texted Ed next.

"Meredith in custody," she wrote. "I'm in jail."

"Be right there," he replied.

Laurie came in and pointed to her phone.

"I should've had Shaggy or Scooby confiscate that," he said.

"Did she confess to killing Knox?"

Laurie rolled his eyes.

"Like I'd tell you," he said. "Why'd you call Sarah and not me?"

"You know why," she said.

"I don't drink when I'm working," he said.

"It wasn't only because of that," she said. "It's more that you don't seem to give a damn about doing your job. Anytime something happens, you either look the other way, or you get someone else to do the dirty work. You didn't even care what happened to Diedre's car after she died."

He was silent for a few moments.

"Well, you're right about all of that," he said. "But Diedre's car, really? You're still hung up on that?"

"You need to take a month, go somewhere they give professional help, and get yourself sorted out," she said. "If you ask the Pendleton Town Council for it, they may give it to you."

"They did," Laurie said. "Kay and Scott got it all arranged. Shep's not going to retire for another month, and I'm taking what everyone's calling a much-needed vacation."

"To rehab."

"Heaven help them," Laurie said. "They've got their work cut out for them."

"But you'll do your best, right?"

"We both know how low that bar is."

"Please, Laurie," Claire said. "Not for anyone else, but for you."

"Oh, him," Laurie said. "Why would I wanna help that jerk?"

"Because you're worth saving," Claire said.

"I'm touched you still think so," he said.

The look he gave her was filled with longing and sadness.

"Where will you be in a month?" he asked.

Claire considered the question, which was both more complicated and more meaningful than it might appear on the surface.

"I'll be here," she said, finally. "Trying to figure out what to do with my life."

"Good to know," he said. "Turns out there *is* a step where I have to apologize to everyone I've wronged and try to make it up to them, so I'll be in touch. There's a long list so it may take me awhile to get to 'F.'"

Ed arrived, and Laurie gestured for him to come in.

"She's all yours," Laurie said and winked at Claire.

"What's going on?" Ed asked. "Are you all right?"

"Yeah, I'm fine," she said and closed the door to the office behind him.

"What are you doing?"

"Hold this couch steady, and I'll tell you," Claire said, as she stepped up on it.

She climbed up to stand on the back of it and put her ear to the grill of the heating vent.

"Claire," Ed said.

"I know, I know," she said. "It's wrong."

"No," he said. "Use this."

He handed her his hand-held digital voice recorder.

"So when you came down through the woods behind Knox's house," Sarah asked, "what was your plan?"

"I knew Knox had just left for the funeral home to meet with Trick and Stuart," Meredith said. "I thought while he was out I would collect the things he stole from me."

"How did you know where he was?"

"I was in his brother's office when he called," Meredith said. "Trick is handling the sale of my tea room.

We were discussing his commission. I feel I am owed a family discount, but Trick does not agree."

"How did you know what they discussed on the phone?"

"Trick put him on speaker," Meredith said. "It's so rude, but both of those boys have terrible manners, so I wasn't surprised."

"What did Knox say?"

"He said he was leaving the house as soon as he hung up, and that Trick should meet him in the parking lot before the meeting so they could go over their strategy."

"Anything else?"

"He said Trick should leave immediately so he wouldn't be late."

"Did Trick say anything about the call?"

"He said he needed to cut our meeting short, so I walked out with him," Meredith said. "He went down Rose Hill Avenue, and I went up Pine Mountain Road, so I wouldn't run into Knox."

"Where did you go?"

"I walked up Pine Mountain Road until I reached the top of the hill, behind Delvecchio's house. There's a deer trail up there that winds around the top of the hill and ends up in the graveyard. I followed the trail until I was behind our house, and then I walked down the hill. The housekeeper was just arriving, so I told her I had accidentally locked myself out, and she let me in. She's from a service, so she didn't know anything about anybody."

"What was your plan otherwise?"

"To use a brick from the flower bed border to break one of the basement windows."

"She didn't question you were who you said you were?"

"I think I intimidated her," Meredith said. "She could tell I wasn't taking no for an answer."

"So she let you in; then what?"

"We found Knox together. She was a young woman, and very emotional, and I told her just to go on home, and I'd call the police."

"But you didn't."

"I did what I came to do," Meredith said. "Knox had stolen some very precious and valuable things from me, and I wanted them back."

"Did it occur to you to call for an ambulance, maybe check his pulse to make sure he was dead?"

"I know dead, honey, and that man was D.E.A.D. dead."

"But did you check to be sure?"

"I may have poked him," she said.

"What did you do after that?"

"Well, if you want to know the truth, I got a little emotional," Meredith said.

"You were upset that your husband had died."

"I was only upset that Knox wouldn't live to see the inside of a jail cell," Meredith said. "I got emotional because it reminded me of my father and my first husband, the senator."

"What did you do next?"

"I got a shopping bag out of the pantry and went looking for my pilfered belongings."

"What did you take?"

"I didn't *take* anything," Meredith said. "I restored my possessions to their rightful owner."

"What did you restore?"

"A few silver items, my mother's tea service, and my father's coin collection."

"What about the money?"

"Knox stole money from me, too; maybe not those exact bills, but money in the larger sense, certainly. I was owed that money."

"Even if it was covered in blood."

Claire could not hear Meredith's answer.

"Did you move the body?"

"Certainly not."

"The money was soaked with Knox's blood. It wouldn't have been if it was in his wallet in his pocket. I'm going to ask you again," Sarah said. "Did you move Knox's body in order to get the money?"

"I may have rolled him over a little."

"When you found him, was he laying on his back or his front."

"On his back," Meredith said. "I rolled him over toward the wall so I could get the money."

"It was underneath his body, on the stairs?"

"Yes," Meredith said.

"Did you remove anything else from his clothing or the area around his body?"

"There wasn't anything else to remove."

"You didn't remove any jewelry he might have been wearing?"

"I'm not a grave robber," Meredith said. "I told you I only took what was mine or what I was owed."

"What did you take from the safe?"

"The coin collection," Meredith said. "My father's coin collection. His name is engraved on the lid."

"Was there anything else in the safe?"

"I don't remember."

"Meredith."

"I only took items that belonged to me, to my family."

"Where are these beloved family heirlooms now?"

"At the pawn shop in Pendleton."

"Not quite so dear to you as you indicated."

"I need the money," she said. "I'll send for them once I get settled."

"Do you know anything about a black Acura with Maryland plates that's been seen cruising around town?"

"That's my driver," Meredith said. "I've engaged him for the week."

"Did you direct him to follow Knox?"

"Just for fun," Meredith said. "Just to mess with his head a little bit."

"Did you know your driver almost hit Claire Fitzpatrick while pursuing Knox?"

"Too bad he missed."

By the time they let Claire go, Ed had hurried back to his office to file the story with the Pendleton paper. Another county car had arrived to transport Meredith, and Sarah followed it in her car. True to form, she had ignored Claire and been rude to Laurie. Minutes after she departed, however, she texted Claire.

"Thanks," it read. "I O U."

Laurie walked Claire home.

"So now you have Marigold saying Knox was alive when she left, and Meredith saying he was dead when she got there," she said. "Whom do you believe?"

"Both of them," Laurie said.

"But how can they both be telling the truth?"

"Unbeknownst to you, I have actually been doing my job," he said. "After Marigold left, Knox called Stuart to warn him that Marigold might be coming for him next. So we know he was alive after she left."

"So who killed him?"

"The coroner says her preliminary examination seems to indicate he slipped, fell backward, hit his head on the sharp edge of the marble landing, and died."

"I didn't think you could get post-mortem results back that fast."

"It was an unofficial communication," he said. "Celeste, the coroner, is an old friend."

"Of course she is."

"If you're gonna get mad every time I mention an old girlfriend, the high blood pressure's going to give you a stroke."

"I hate this about myself," Claire said. "And you're not even my boyfriend."

"Not even."

"So what happened?"

"Marigold said that from her living room window she saw him walk up to the house and go in, but when she called him, he didn't answer. She went across the street and rang the bell, but he didn't answer. The door was unlocked, so she let herself into the house and yelled for him. He came down the upper set of stairs and stood on the landing while they argued. At some point, he threw money at her, so she left in a huff.

"According to Sarah, he must have been working in his study on the second floor when she arrived; there were bills spread out on his desk, a checkbook, a calculator, and his cell phone. After Marigold left, he must have gone back upstairs to his study to call Stuart. At 12:20 he called his brother. At some point after that, he came back down the stairs ..."

"And slipped on the money he threw at Marigold, hit his head on the edge of the marble landing, and died," Claire said. "Meredith told me it was money that got him in the end."

"That's the theory."

"You don't know there was a housekeeper; she could have made that up," Claire said. "After Meredith left Trick's office she had plenty of time to kill him. She could have pushed him back so he fell on the edge of the marble landing."

"We called the cleaning service. There was a housekeeper, and she corroborated Meredith's story."

"She may have killed Knox and then paid off the housekeeper."

"Listen, Knox didn't make the 12:30 meeting because he slipped and died on his way down the steps. If he hadn't died, he would have been at that meeting. The attorneys were going to be present to discuss the federal case against them. Knox told Trick they would know where they stood with Stuart by how he acted at this meeting. Either they would all three be united in their defense, or Stuart would split off and implicate them. Knox was dead when Meredith got there, which was after the starting time for the meeting."

"No, he wouldn't have missed that meeting."

"Here's the thing about Meredith: she's got little or no conscience. She doesn't mind telling us she broke in, stole money from a dead man, and took things she claims were hers. She doesn't mind because she doesn't see anything wrong with what she did. She can justify it all. If she had killed him, she would say it was in self-defense. She would justify that, too, and possibly get away with it."

"That woman has ice water in her veins."

"She also has a prescription for anti-psychotic meds in her purse, if that tells you anything."

"She took her father's coin collection and her mother's silver tea service directly to the pawn shop in Pendleton."

"Along with Knox's Rolex watch, diamond pinky ring, and some other valuable old jewelry, which Knox probably had in the safe."

"You called the pawn shop."

"I know Irv, the owner," Laurie said. "He was a friend of my father's."

"Do me a favor."

"Anything. Everything."

"Don't call me unless you find a reason to get better, and then you get better."

"Besides the thought of you, pining away for me here in Budville."

"Yes."

"I'll see what I can do," he said.

He pulled her into a tight embrace, kissed the side of her head, and said, quietly, "wait for me."

"I won't," she said.

"But you might," he said as he let go.

"No," she said. "I'm not promising anything."

"I'll think of you," he said, as he backed away.

He pointed up at the sky.

"Whenever I see Claire de Lune."

Claire's eyes filled, and she couldn't speak.

He turned and jogged away.

Claire rummaged through the cabinets in her parents' kitchen, looking for something to eat. She wasn't hungry. She was full of conflicting, uncomfortable feelings and didn't want to think about sorting them out. Salty and sweet, that's what she wanted. In the pantry, she found a bag of corn chips, and that reminded her of something she used to love to eat as a child. She found a jar of applesauce in the fridge and poured the whole thing into a bowl. Seated at the kitchen table with the bag of chips, a bowl of applesauce to dip them in and a host of celebrity gossip sites bookmarked on her laptop, Claire felt her worries recede to a comfortable distance, where they hovered, waiting for her.

An hour later, with all the chips and applesauce gone, plus four of her father's pudding cups and what was left of a carton of ice cream, Claire felt the familiar pressure in her upper abdomen signaling her body's urge to throw up. It would be so easy, and then she wouldn't have to absorb all those calories she'd recently consumed.

Her stomach cramped.

Claire never weighed herself, because that woke up her anxiety over her weight, which stressed her, which made her obsess about food, which triggered her eating disorder. She didn't need to weigh herself to know where she stood;

her clothes were all so tight right now that by the end of the week she would not be able to zip up her pants, even if she jumped up and down or stretched out flat on the bed and sucked in her stomach. She needed to undo what she'd done. Otherwise, she'd have to run ten miles instead of five just to break even.

Claire knew there was no "just this once" when it came to binging and purging. Five years ago she had come close to doing herself irreparable harm over her abuse of laxatives and vomiting to control her weight. Living in California among the skeletal elite of the movie industry, Claire had been considered fat even though her clothing size was in the single digits. At her thinnest, she received constant praise and attention. She also occasionally blacked out from low blood pressure and didn't have periods, but whatever. She enjoyed looking like the women she envied and took vicious pleasure in having them consider her attractive enough to be a threat.

Her heart began to beat faster, and her nose began to run, both signs that what had gone down was about to come back up. Her mouth began to water, and she broke out in a cold, clammy sweat. She jumped up and ran, and made it to the bathroom in time.

Afterward, she felt a sense of relief, shame, and inevitability.

The thought that repeated itself over and over in her head was, 'I am broken this way, and always will be.'

As she brushed her teeth, she avoided looking in the mirror above the sink. She didn't want to see what this felt like.

A half-hour later, Claire was jogging down Magnolia Avenue when Georgia and Dottie hailed her from Dottie's front porch. Claire staggered up the stairs and collapsed on the top step.

"Good gracious," Dottie said. "Let me get you some water."

"How far have you run?" Georgia asked while Dottie went inside.

"I have no idea," Claire said, between gulps of air.

Her plan was to run until she felt she had punished herself enough, and she wasn't there, yet. There was a stitch in her side, and she pressed on it. The pad of fat covering her hip bone repulsed her. This disgust manifested itself as a spiritual and physical pain, a wince of the soul.

"Are you okay?" Georgia asked her.

Claire waved her concern away with a flip of her hand.

"Just out of shape," she said.

"You need to take it a little more slowly, I think," Georgia said. "You might hurt yourself."

"I'm fine, really," Claire said.

As she leaned forward to ease the cramp, the small roll of fat between the bottom of her bra and her belly button compressed in a way she hated. She felt repulsive.

"I need to lose a few pounds," Claire said. "No pain no gain."

"You look too thin to me," Dottie said, as she came back out with a glass of ice water.

"Sip it, don't gulp it," Georgia said.

Claire obeyed.

The cold water felt wonderful. She wanted to dive in and swim.

"Do you think I could swim in the college pool?" she asked.

"You would have to buy a pass," Georgia said. "I'm pretty sure they still allow townies to do that."

"Might be easier on your joints than running," Dottie said.

"Is this all about being thin?" Georgia asked her.

"Healthy," Claire said. "Thin and healthy."

"Hmmm," Georgia said. "I wonder."

"None of our business, really," Dottie said to Georgia in a warning tone.

"Hush," Georgia said. "You know, Claire, I've been thinking about our conversation at dinner the other night, and what you said about being addicted to romance."

"Oh, here we go," Dottie said.

"I'm sure there are other things you could do if I'm boring you," Georgia said to Dottie.

"I'm gonna go inside and watch 'Love it or List it,' " Dottie said. "You all holler if you need me."

"Thank you for the water," Claire said.

"You know," Georgia said, as soon as Dottie left, "when you feel attraction or affection for someone, the body releases a chemical called oxytocin, and it's just as addictive as any illegal drug."

"I believe it," Claire said. "I once paid for a good-looking, unemployed actor to get a chin implant. That's not the kind of thing you can ask to have returned when you break up. And by breaking up, I mean I found him in my boss's bed and afterward still thought it might somehow work out. Imagine how humiliating it was to have a jackass like that tell me how pathetic I was being. I mean *he* was embarrassed for *me*."

"We all do stupid things when we're in love," Georgia said. "It's even harder, I think when the person is attractive. We somehow expect more from pretty people."

"I created this fantasy, you see, based on the movies I'd seen and the books I'd read. I was looking for someone to fill the role of the handsome man who falls madly in love with me even though I'm clumsy but whimsically adorable. I didn't actually know these men I dated because they were pretending to be rock star ninjas or deeply intellectual rebels while I was pretending to be the perfect girlfriend:

oversexed, skinny, and low, low maintenance; when actually, I'm not any of those things. I wish I'd had half the good sex I pretended to have over the years."

"It makes me sad what sexualized marketing has done to young women and men," Georgia said. "I know I sound like an old grouch, but I think it promotes the degradation of human dignity in the service of selling things."

"Ed says we're a society of compulsive consumers," Claire said. "Drowning in debt trying to live a fantasy life we feel entitled to but can't afford."

"I think about poor Diedre Delvecchio, done in by her desire to not only acquire things but to keep all of them."

"I'm kind of a compulsive shopper, myself," Claire said. "I'd be ashamed to tell you how many handbags I own, or what I paid for them."

"I have stacks and stacks of books," Georgia said. "Even if I read a book a day for a year I could never read them all. I donate them to the library after I read them, which makes Dottie happy and keeps her off my back, but I can't quit. I'm powerless over my desire to acquire books. I'm obsessed with learning as much as I can, you see, and I don't have an endless amount of time left; maybe twenty years, if my mind stays sharp."

"I can see where compulsive book buying can be an addiction, and that your research is another one," Claire said. "But if an addiction is constructive, is it still bad?"

"If it hurts you or someone you love," Georgia said.

"How could your research do that?"

"If you devote more time to it than you do to your friendships, or become obsessed to the point that you can't think about anything else."

"Does that happen to you?"

"Dottie keeps me from going too far in that direction," Georgia said. "I have a bit of an obsessive-compulsive problem."

"Can I confide something in you?"

"Certainly," Georgia said. "From my ears to the vault."

"I'm kind of, sort of involved with someone who's an alcoholic," Claire said. "He says he has it under control, but he doesn't. There's a chance he may go to rehab and get sober, but then I wonder if he can even stay sober after that. I'm ashamed of myself for not believing in him, and for not being more patient while he figures things out, but I'm also afraid of what might happen to me if I get more deeply involved."

"Do his issues trigger your own issues?"

"I never thought about it that way, but yes, probably."

"So, basically, he's asking you to sacrifice yourself on the altar of his addiction."

"That sounds kind of dramatic," Claire said, "and not like scientific research."

"Dottie says I have the brain of a scientist but the soul of a poet," Georgia said. "One thing I've learned, and not just from books, mind you, but from painful personal experience, is that deeply addicted people are supremely selfish. They feel profoundly sorry for themselves, and when drowning, will always pull you under if you let them."

"I expected you to suggest a support group like Alanon or something," Claire said.

"My best advice to you, my dear girl, is that you wish him good luck and walk away."

"That seems harsh."

"You're getting off on hits of oxytocin every time you're around this man," Georgia said. "When you look at the situation from that viewpoint, does it change the way you think about the relationship?"

"So Laurie's like heroin and Ed's like a nice, healthy fruit smoothie," Claire said. "It does put things in perspective."

"We can get addicted to romantic feelings, to passion and sexual attraction just as easily as we do to drugs and alcohol," Georgia said. "After a while, a healthy relationship doesn't offer those high highs and low lows. There's an element of danger, of the unknown, in a new relationship that doesn't exist in a secure, reliable partnership. A person who's addicted to those feelings might create high drama, or even stray, in order to feel that roller coaster of emotion again."

"That explains so much," Claire said. "I just have to quit feeding my drama addiction so I can have a healthy relationship with someone steady and good."

"I wish it were that easy," Georgie said. "I have come to believe that an addictive personality requires constant vigilance and some sort of support system when, as Aretha Franklin put it best, 'willpower is weak and temptation strong.' "

"Some kind of a Drama Queens Anonymous," Claire said.

"You call me whenever you're feeling weak, and I'll be your sponsor," Georgia said.

"I can't quite picture you as a recovering drama queen," Claire said. "You seem like the most sensible and sane person I know."

"I just hide it better," Georgia said and winked.

"I may just be overdramatizing the whole thing," Claire said. "I'm not actually in a relationship with him."

"You may not be drowning yet," Georgia said, "but you're in the water."

It was hard to sleep with a big, snoring man taking up three-fourths of her double-size bed, so Kay spent a wakeful night over-thinking everything. By 4:00 a.m. she had worn herself out worrying about the possible repercussions of their impulsive sleepover, and how it might impact both her personal life and her mayoral run.

At 5:00 a.m. Kay eased her way out of bed and went to the bathroom to take a shower. A tangle of her and Sonny's clothing was there on the floor, along with two damp towels. She smiled as she picked up the mess and sorted out the clothes. After her shower, she decided it would be better to launder his clothes so he wouldn't leave looking like a wrinkly damp mess. She started a load of laundry and then went out on the front porch to have a cup of tea.

Sonny's truck was parked right outside, leaving no doubt where he'd passed the night and with whom. There would probably be a swarm of early morning walkers just happening to pass by, as many times as it took until they could witness Sonny leaving her house. The drawbacks of small-town life included this proprietary nosiness and the subsequent exaggerated gossip that would follow. Kay cared very much what her neighbors thought, and dreaded what was to come.

It was still dark, but the birds in the trees were already singing. Kay pulled her robe closer around her, drew her feet up onto the glider seat, and sipped her tea. It was so odd to think a man was inside, asleep in her bed. Shug had stayed the night a few times, but he preferred his king-sized bed in his king-sized house, where his housekeeper took care of everything and Kay wasn't allowed to lift so much as a finger. If Kay tried to put a king-size bed in her bedroom, it would be a wall-to-wall bed in there.

Kay was tired and sleepy, but her heart fluttered inside with what felt like happy anticipation. Sonny was in love with her, had said so, and he wasn't the type to use those words lightly. She wasn't worried he would wake up and change his mind, or that he would suddenly decide to give his ex-wife another chance. No, Sonny was exactly what he portrayed himself to be: a good man, a loyal man, a man of his word. Kay realized that what she felt was settled, in the best, most contented way possible.

'So this is what's next,' she thought.

It was a pleasant thought.

By the time Sonny got up, his clothes were pressed, and Kay was making his breakfast. He embraced her from behind as she tended to a pan of eggs on the stove. Kay laughed at the sight of him wearing her pink chenille robe.

"Woman, you are the best thing that's happened to me in a long time," he said.

"You're absolutely right," Kay said. "Now, sit down and eat."

When Kay got to work, word had already spread, and she endured many too-wide and too-knowing smiles. She did her best to act normally, but her face felt warm, and she knew it was pink with embarrassment. Lucille came out of her office as soon as she heard Kay arrive. She poured a mug of coffee, picked up a muffin off the cart in the hallway, and then took a seat in the chair across from Kay's desk.

"Inquiring minds want to know," Lucille said.

"I haven't the slightest idea to what you are referring," Kay said.

"C'mon," Lucille said. "I tell you all my adventures."

"What have you heard?" Kay asked.

"Sonny Delvecchio's truck was parked outside of your house all night, and Doc's wife saw Sonny leave there to go to work at 7:00 a.m."

"All true," Kay said. "Can we get back to work now?"

Town council member Alva Johnston appeared in the doorway and knocked on the door frame.

"Did you see the paper?" she asked and waved a copy of the Pendleton paper at them.

She handed it to Kay, whose heart skipped a beat as she read the headline of the article in question, which was written by Ed Harrison.

"Death of local businessman reveals hidden graft," it read.

"That woman from the FBI has already been to see me," Lucille said. "I told them it was Stuart who signed the checks, and Stuart who told me to code them as consulting fees."

"I gave them a copy of the minutes from the meeting where he stated the contingency fund was being used for consulting fees," Alva said. "There were ten witnesses to that big fat lie."

"What I want to know is why Stuart was contributing to that account," Lucille said. "Was Knox blackmailing him or something?"

"We may never know," was all Kay said.

"Well," Alva said, "if he thought Knox was going to be the next U.S. Senator he probably wanted to be on his good side, and nothing was nearer and dearer to Knox Rodefeffer's tiny little heart than cold hard cash."

The article outlined the diversion of city funds into a bank account in Pittsburgh and revealed that Knox Rodefeffer's name was on the same account. Kay skimmed the rest of the paragraph, looking for Marigold's name, but her name was not mentioned, and the actual intended use of the money was not revealed. Although Kay hadn't told anyone what Marigold had shared with her, it was only a matter of time before it was all known, at the very least because Ed was good at his job and so very thorough.

The article further reported, "Attorneys for former mayor Stuart Machalvie, implicated in the alleged misappropriation of city funds, said that he was innocent of any wrongdoing and would respond to the allegations at the appropriate time to the appropriate authorities."

"I heard Knox slipped on a hundred dollar bill, hit his head, and died," Alva said. "How's that for an appropriate ending?"

"God rest his soul, I know," Lucille said, "but that man was as mean as a snake-bit bear, and he deserved what he got."

"He would have spent the rest of his life in the pokey for murdering his Aunt Mamie," Alva said. "I say he took the easy way out."

"We don't know that's true about Mamie," Kay said. "We need to be careful not to jump to conclusions."

The FBI agent known as Terese knocked on the door frame and all three women were startled.

"Could I speak with you?" she asked Kay.

"Of course," Kay said.

"Just leaving," Lucille said.

"Me, too," Alva said.

Kay took a deep breath and steeled herself for the interview. Terese always made it seem casual and friendly, but Kay knew better.

The interview went pretty much as she thought it would. Terese knew about the bank account, probably from statements found in Knox's office after his death. Kay knew that, with those statements as evidence, there would be no doubt about Marigold's involvement.

"When did you find out about this account?" Terese asked her.

"A few days before the town council asked Stuart to resign," Kay said, "Lucille and I were discussing the contingency fund because I wanted to pay the substitute police chief out of it, and we were speculating about the consultant Stuart was paying so much money. The checks were made out to 'The Mark Nost Group,' but we couldn't find any information about Mr. Nost or his consultancy business on the Internet.

"Later that day, while Stuart was in a closed-door meeting with the town council, I went to his office, found his briefcase open on the desk, and went through it. I found the folder for the bank account. I examined the statements and saw that the dates and amounts of the deposits matched those of the contingency fund checks. I saw the names of the account owners, and the copies of the checks Marigold had written to herself. Then the name made sense: 'Mar' is for Marigold, 'kno' is for Knox, and 'st' is for Stuart. I made copies of everything and returned the originals to his briefcase."

"Did you tell Lucille what you found?"

"I did not."

"Did you confront Stuart, Knox, or Marigold about the account?"

"I did not."

"Were you planning to use this information in your campaign?"

"No," Kay said. "I had heard through the grapevine that Stuart was trying to throw me under the bus, to blame me for the things he was accused of doing, and I wanted to have evidence to use to defend myself in court if it came to that."

"Was Marigold having an affair with Knox or Stuart?" Terese asked her.

"No!" Kay said. "I mean, not to my knowledge."

"Was she performing some service for them?"

"Not to my knowledge."

"Was she blackmailing either of them?"

"Not to my knowledge."

"Why do you think they were paying her?"

Kay hesitated. She did not want to lie to the F.B.I. but she had given Marigold her word.

"Miss Templeton," Terese prompted.

"I was not privy to any conversations between Knox, Stuart, and Marigold that led to this account being set up, nor did I witness any collaboration between the three account owners."

"You may have heard gossip, though," Terese said. "You may have put two and two together."

"If I did, I wouldn't use it as testimony."

"Sometimes gossip has a bit of truth in it."

"Nevertheless," Kay said. "I've told you what I know from my direct knowledge of the situation."

Terese did not specifically ask her about a possible relationship Marigold might have had when she and Knox were young, and that may have been splitting hairs, but Kay did not want to betray Marigold's confidence about her college romance with Knox or their baby. She had given Marigold her word.

"I may need to talk to you again," Terese said.

"No problem," Kay said, although her heart was thumping hard in her chest.

Later that afternoon, Marigold Lawson came to Kay's office. Her face was pale, her eyes red and swollen.

"I won't stay," she said. "I've just been interviewed by the FBI, and I wanted to tell you I'm withdrawing from the mayoral race. Congratulations."

"Marigold," Kay said, as she rose and came around her desk. "Are you sure you want to do that?"

"I told them everything," Marigold said, and her voice shook. "There's no way I can continue now."

"I didn't tell them about your relationship with Knox or the baby you gave up," Kay said. "I kept my word to you."

"It was stupid of me to trust you, I know," Marigold said. "Political battles always bring out the worst in people."

"I swear to you I didn't tell anybody what you told me," Kay said. "They found out about the bank account from the bank statements in Knox's office, and that led them to you."

"I knew you'd deny it," Marigold said. "But I wanted you to know that I know the truth."

"I'm sorry you think that," Kay said. "It looks like there's nothing I can do to convince you otherwise."

"I heard Sonny Delvecchio spent the night at your place," Marigold said. "Lucky for you I'm in such trouble or that would be all anyone would be talking about today."

"I'm so sorry about your troubles, Marigold. Truly."

"It might interest you to know that Sonny's ex-wife has left her husband," Marigold said. "She's telling everyone that Sonny agreed to take her back."

"Marigold, don't," Kay said. "I hope you'll change your mind about running. I think people are kinder and more accepting of youthful indiscretions than you think."

Tears filled Marigold's eyes.

"I will never forgive you for this," she said. "Never."

With that, she turned and left.

Kay sat back down at her desk and felt the energy drain from her body. Lucille walked across the hall and leaned against the door frame.

"I heard arguing," she said. "Are you okay?"

"I'll be fine," Kay said.

"Do you want a muffin?"

"Yes," Kay said. "But I'm not going to have one, thanks."

"What's the story with Marigold?"

"I'm not going to share it," Kay said. "Marigold confided in me, and even though she doesn't believe me, I am keeping her confidence."

"It hardly matters now," Lucille said.

"It does matter," Kay said. "It matters to me."

Later that afternoon, Kay was surprised to see Peg Machalvie in her office doorway. Even though her features had been partially paralyzed through chemical intervention, her expression was like thunder, which in Kay's experience, always presaged a major temper tantrum.

Stuart's wife ran the local funeral parlor, and she tended to dress and apply makeup in a dramatic fashion. Today her coal black hair was teased up into a poofy French twist with crisply curled spirals in front of each ear and bangs that sprouted like spider legs from above her waxy-smooth brow.

On her stick-thin, yet amazingly busty figure she wore a tight, white, form-fitting suit jacket and short skirt with matching platform heels. Her makeup and spray tan had turned her normally pale white skin a deep pumpkin color. Her jewelry was large, sparkly, and complicated. The theme seemed to be nautical; there were shoulder epaulets and gem-encrusted anchors involved.

"Good afternoon," Kay said. "What can I do for you, Peg?"

Peg pulled the door shut behind her, so Kay took that opportunity to push the voice record shortcut button on her cell phone. She set it on top of her desk, not trying to hide it or what she was doing, but Peg didn't seem to notice.

"I need to have a word with you if you don't mind," Peg said. "It's about Stuart."

Peg stretched her mouth into a big rectangular grimace, which was the only version of a smile she could make using the parts of her face that still moved.

"I can't help Stuart," Kay said.

"We're willing to be generous," Peg said. "All you have to do is confirm Stuart didn't know the consulting firm account was actually a front for Knox's slush fund. Knox was the one who deceived Stuart."

Peg's voice quivered, and her hands were restless; she kept touching her necklace, her earrings, and her hair.

"I'm not interested in accepting a bribe from you and Stuart," Kay said, speaking up for the voice recorder. "I'm also not willing to lie for anybody."

"He can't go to jail," Peg said. Her eyes filled with tears, which spilled over, taking dark streaks of mascara and eyeliner with them. "I don't know what I'll do without him."

"I'm sorry, Peg," Kay said. "But Stuart abused the trust of this town, and now he has to face the consequences."

Peg was sobbing in earnest now, and Kay handed her a box of tissues.

"Peg," Kay said. "Please try to get hold of yourself."

"You ... don't ... understand," Peg sobbed. "Stuart ... is ... my ... whole ... world!"

Peg was wailing now. Kay felt sorry for her; everyone in the building could probably hear.

"I'm so sorry for what you're going through," Kay said. "But I can't help you."

"Please!" Peg cried. "You have to!"

There was a knock on the door, and Terese stuck her head in.

"Everything all right?" she asked.

Lucille was right behind her, craning her neck to see inside the office.

"Peg is upset," Kay said, as she stood up and came around her desk. "Lucille, please help Peg to the ladies room so she can get cleaned up, and then take her out the back way so she can have some privacy."

Lucille said, "C'mon hon," to Peg, who allowed herself to be led like a child, still crying as though her heart was broken.

When Peg reached the door, she clutched the arm of the FBI agent.

"Don't take him away from me," she cried. "He's all I have."

Terese looked grim as she removed Peg's grasping hand and stood aside so the two women could get past her in the doorway.

Kay reached out and ended the recording.

"Anything you want to share?" Terese asked her.

"No," Kay said. "Nothing to share."

The last thing Kay wanted to do was face Matt Delvecchio, but she also didn't want to appear to be avoiding him, and her cupboard was bare, so after work, she went down to the IGA to get some groceries. She got as far as the deli counter before he accosted her. There was no other word for it.

"You're not welcome in here," Matt said as he blocked the aisle.

There was a hush as everyone working or shopping in the store stopped to listen.

"Please don't do this, Matthew," Kay said in a quiet voice.

"I mean it," Matt said. "I don't want you to come in here again."

Kay realized that to argue would only make it worse. She took a deep breath, removed her handbag from the shopping cart, turned, and walked out, head held high. Unfortunately, he followed her outside, as did several people who didn't want to miss anything. He grabbed her arm, and she turned.

"You're making a spectacle of us," she said.

"You're the one making a spectacle," Matt said. "What did you think would happen, letting him park out in front? Everyone knows my brother stayed at your house last night."

"Let me go," Kay said, jerking her arm away from his grip. "Unless you lower your voice and speak to me in a respectful way, I'm not going to discuss this with you any further."

"I don't have any respect left for you," he said. "Especially not now."

"I'm sorry I hurt you," Kay said, "but you have no right to treat me this way."

"You can tell Grace she's fired," Matt said. "Tell her she can work for my brother at the hardware store."

Kay turned on her heel and walked away. As she crossed the street, she met Laurie walking toward her on Rose Hill Avenue.

"What's going on?" he asked. "Can I help?"

"Walk with me, please," Kay said. "I could use the moral support."

"You've got it," Laurie said and turned so he could link her arm through his. "What's Mario so upset about? Did Miss Peach dump him for Luigi?"

"Stop it," Kay said. "That's not right, and it's not funny."

"Sorry," Laurie said. "Just trying to cheer you up."

"This has been some day," Kay said. "And now I can't even shop for groceries in my own town."

"His prices are too high," Laurie said, "and they have better produce in Pendleton, anyway. Plus now you have an excuse to come and see me. I'll even let you go 35 in the 25 mile-an-hour zone."

"I've loved having you here," Kay said. "I want you to know I believe in you; you can beat this thing if you want to."

"I appreciate that Kay, more than you know. And I appreciate what you and Scott did for me. I won't let you down."

"See that you don't."

"You know, you would've made a helluva good schoolteacher."

"If I keep making scenes in public places, I may have to retrain for a new career."

"Don't worry about that," he said. "That made him look like a loser, not you."

"I don't even care that much anymore," she said. "It might be a relief to be a regular person again; not always having to worry about what everyone thinks."

"Just be yourself and to hell with what everyone thinks," Laurie said. "Some people will think the worst no matter what you do, but the people who count will always give you the benefit of the doubt."

"Thanks, Laurie," she said.

"Can I ask you a question?" Laurie asked.

"Of course, anything."

"Claire said that I act like I don't give a damn about my job. Did I do okay here?"

"As far as I know," Kay said. "What was she referring to?"

"Well, you know Diedre's car disappeared before or after she died. I wasn't worried about finding it, but Claire thinks it's important for some reason."

"When he was the chief, her father was a stickler for tying up loose ends."

"I still have a couple days," he said. "I bet I could find that car."

"You do it," Kay said. "It'll make Claire happy."

"I can but try," he said.

When Kay got home, Sonny was sitting on her front porch. He rose and met her with a quick kiss.

"How's my girl?" he asked.

"Well, I just got kicked out of your brother's store," she said. "And that wasn't even the worst thing that happened today."

"That pecker-headed son-of-a-bitch," Sonny said. "I'll straighten him out."

"Please don't," Kay said. "It will only make things worse. Let's give him some time to get used to the idea and then I'll talk to him."

"I'm sorry he's such an idiot," Sonny said.

"I'm ready for this day to be over," Kay said. "Let's order pizza and watch a funny movie."

"I'm sorry, sweetheart, but I can't," Sonny said. "I'm afraid I have bad news."

Kay's heart seemed to stop for a moment. Was he about to tell her that he was going back to his ex-wife? Up until that moment, although Kay knew she cared, she didn't realize exactly how much.

"Oh, my goodness," Kay said. "I don't know if I can take any more bad news."

She sat down on the top step of the porch and felt tears prick the backs of her eyes. Sonny sat down next to her and took her hand.

"My dad passed away," he said. "I got the call right as I was leaving work, so I came straight here."

"Oh, Sonny," she said and put her arms around him.

Her tears spilled over, mostly in sympathy but partly in relief that he wasn't dumping her.

"I knew it was coming, but it was still a shock," he said. "I just can't believe it."

"You need to go to your mother."

"I'm headed there next," he said. "I wanted to see you first. I'm so glad about us, Kay. I'm so happy to know I have you. I'm not fooling around, you know. We need to make this a permanent situation, and soon."

"There's plenty of time for that," Kay said. "Take care of your mother. Let me know if I can do anything to help."

He kissed her forehead and then left. Kay decided that in some ways that kind of kiss was even sweeter; it also felt like a blessing.

CHAPTER 10

Claire made it to the top of the hill behind Eldridge College, with Ed's black lab, Lucida, running in circles around her. Claire stopped and leaned over, her hands on her knees, and attempted to catch her breath.

Lucida danced around her and nudged her, as if to say, "C'mon, keep going."

"Stop rubbing it in," she said.

Claire sat down on the ground and then fell back, spread eagle on the dewy green grass. Lucida licked her face and then went off to investigate some nearby bushes. Claire closed her eyes and didn't open them until she heard Ed's voice, calling her name with some urgency.

"Not dead, then," he said when he reached her, out of breath and red in the face. "I'm relieved to know it. You almost gave me a heart attack."

He dropped down and reclined beside her.

His older dog, Hank, meandered up the path and then plopped down next to them, panting.

"I don't think I can do this anymore," Claire said.

"You're out of practice," Ed said. "It's always hard to start back."

"Everything hurts," Claire said, "all the time."

"That bakery work is a killer," Ed said.

"Next stop, rocking chair," Claire said. "Old age is so close I can see its big pores and crow's feet from here."

"You're only halfway there," Ed said. "It's too soon to give up."

"But what will happen when I can't run anymore?"

"You'll walk," Ed said. "We'll walk together."

"You and me and Eve and the baby," Claire said.

"We had a come-to-Jesus meeting last night," he said.

Claire turned over on her side and propped her head upon her hand.

"Do tell," she said. "Don't leave anything out, especially any terribly uncomfortable moments for Eve."

"I have agreed to stay married to her until after the next presidential election."

"Is the Senator running?"

"I'm not at liberty to say," he said, but he nodded.

"But that's two more years."

"In return, Miss Interrupter, I will raise the child here until he is twelve, at which time he can decide where he wants to be, either here with me in Rose Hill or at some fancy-shmancy boarding school for privileged oppressors-in-training."

"Does someone have class prejudice issues?"

"Absolutely," he said. "I happen to think being raised in privilege is more of a burden than a blessing."

"So we know it's a boy, do we?"

"We do," he said, as he sat up. "And I took your advice, which I thank you for."

"God help you," Claire said. "What advice was that?"

"That I should remember she needs me more than I need her right now," he said. "I had all the power; I just needed to realize it."

"I can't believe she agreed to all that."

"She had already submitted a press release about the happy news she shares with her husband," he said. "Rock, meet hard place."

"Oh, my gosh," Claire said, as she also sat up. "What in the world are you going to do with a real live baby?"

"I don't know," he said. "I'm going to need some help."

"I'm in, did I tell you? I'm so in on this action you couldn't keep me out if you tried."

288

"That's good to hear," he said, "because I basically just agreed to be a single dad. Come December I'll have a teaching position, a weekly newspaper to write and edit, two dogs, a teenager, and a baby."

"How could she give him up like that?" Claire asked. "Nine months of carrying the little bugger, twenty-four hours of labor, and then boom, here's your baby, see you in twelve years."

"Of course not," he said. "She'll have maternity leave, and then we'll have a visitation schedule. But here's what I now realize about Eve: her career means more to her than anything, and in the end, she will only be interested in us when she needs a photo op."

"That's kind of mean," Claire said. "Seems to me she wouldn't have had the baby if she felt that way about it."

"Look at it from her point of view," Ed said. "If you-know-who becomes you-know-what, this baby will be a valuable leveraging tool. As a journalist, she will have unlimited access to you-know-who."

"Which also makes life dangerous for Ed Jr.," Claire said. "He may need his own secret service agents."

Ed looked thoughtful.

"You hadn't thought about that," she said.

"I'll get a DNA test," he said. "If it's mine, there's nothing to worry about."

"And if it isn't?"

"I'll make sure he's safe," Ed said. "Somehow, I'll figure it out."

"I know you will," she said.

"What's going on with you and Laurie?"

"You know about that, do you?"

"It's a small town, Claire."

"Do you really want to know?"

"All's fair," Ed said. "We're completely honest about everything, remember?"

"Well, he's going to rehab for a month, and, hopefully, he'll get straightened out and stay sober."

"And then?"

"I'm not waiting for him."

"What if he gets sober and stays that way?"

"I can't stake my life on the probability of that," she said.

"I'm not going to be divorced for two more years," he said. "You told me once you would never get involved with a married man."

"The universe has a way of humbling me in the exact way I am righteous," she said. "Two years is a long time."

"So here we are," he said.

"Walking, not running," she said.

When Kay called Claire to see if she was free to accompany her on a short jaunt to Pendleton, Claire jumped at the chance to get out of Rose Hill for a little while, as long as she was back in time for her afternoon shift at the bakery. Kay picked her up, and Claire got her caught up as they drove.

"So Ed's going to be a single dad," Kay said. "He'll need help."

"I know," Claire said. "I told him I'm all in."

"It's a big commitment," Kay said. "Maybe you should think about it some more."

"Ed's my friend, and he needs my help," Claire said. "What more do I need to think about?"

"You'll get attached," Kay said. "To the baby, to Ed and the baby. I don't think you've thought through what 'all in' actually entails."

"I don't have anything else going for me right now," Claire said. "So why not?"

"Let's say you help Ed raise this child, you and the child form a close attachment, and then, God forbid, something happens to Ed. The child would go to Eve, and you would have no legal recourse."

"I hadn't thought of that."

"What if Ed meets someone else, falls in love, and when the two years are up, the child has a new stepmother. She probably won't welcome you as part of the family."

"You're harshing my baby buzz, lady."

"If you want to be the mother of this baby, you need to make it legal somehow, or I'm afraid you're setting yourself up for heartache. Plus, think of how someone you might get involved with would feel about it."

"There is no one else, and probably won't be. I'm romantically cursed."

"I think maybe you and Laurie might have some unfinished business."

"I know he's your friend and you've gone way out on a limb for him," Claire said. "I wish he would turn his life around, but honestly, I don't think he will."

"I'm surprised," Kay said. "I thought you cared about him."

"I do care about him," Claire said. "It seems like so many people struggle with addiction, and so few actually get better, or get better and then stay better. Laurie doesn't have faith in anything, he doesn't have much of a support system, and he doesn't seem to have any friends left he hasn't alienated. I care about him, I do, but I don't want to board that train. Sorry."

When Kay pulled up in front of the Pineville Hospice House, Claire turned in her seat and looked at her with alarm.

"What are we doing here?"

"You told me you wanted to do something meaningful that helped people."

"What are you talking about?"

"The other day, you said you wanted your life to be about more than what guy you were interested in and other superficial issues."

"What exactly is your plan here?"

"We are volunteering this morning."

"I can't do dead people hair and make-up," Claire said. "It's too creepy."

"These people are alive, they are patients, and some of them haven't had their hair washed and styled for a long while. It's something you can do that will mean so much to them, and to their families."

"What if I hurt one of them?" Claire asked. "How can I even do it? Aren't they in hospital beds?"

"They have a spa with a shampoo bowl, and a nursing assistant will be with you, to make sure everybody's safe."

"Kay," Claire said. "What if one of them dies?"

"Then you won't have to keep reminding them to hold still, now, will you?"

Claire was so nervous she was trembling. The house director took them on a tour; the hospice house looked like an elegant inn but with hospital beds. Claire saw medical staff working at a large, central desk, and going in and out of rooms. Family members were hanging out in various comfortable lounging areas. Through the windows, she caught glimpses of patients being wheeled out into the garden. The atmosphere was peaceful, quiet, and calm.

"This isn't so bad," she whispered to Kay.

"It's actually very good," Kay whispered back.

The spa room was finished in Carrera marble, complimented by white equipment and gray-and-white soft furnishings.

"Everything we do here is to provide our patients with the best quality of life while they are with us," the director said. "The family of one of our former patients donated the money to create this room, and other donors have paid for everything in it."

There was a large, deep tub with a motorized lift bed that patients could be transferred to from their hospital beds, and then lowered into a bath.

"Some of our patients come to us having had only sponge baths for many months," the director said. "It's such a pleasure for them to be immersed in warm water and bathed."

The shampoo bowl and styling station were state of the art, and Claire felt right at home.

"I can work with this," Claire said. "How do we get started?"

"We need you to fill out some paperwork," the director said. "I'll do a quick background check on you, and then we'll bring in the first patient."

"You certainly work quickly," Claire said.

"Kay is one of our favorite volunteers," the director said. "When she told us you were willing to do this, we wanted to get you in place as quickly as possible. She said you could commit to three mornings a week to start."

Claire looked at Kay, who was grinning at her.

"Kay is so helpful," Claire said, although she made a face at Kay the director couldn't see. "Lead me to the paperwork."

Claire only had time to work with two ladies before she had to leave to work at the bakery. Both of them were lovely women, and so appreciative of her gentle touch and skillful artistry, but their family members moved Claire to tears.

"You are so kind to do this," one daughter said. "My mother never went out of the house unless she was dressed up with her hair and makeup done. You're making her feel like a person again."

"Bless you," one's husband said, and then could not continue for crying.

Claire left the building feeling quiet and thoughtful. She had received accolades for her professional work before but never had it felt like she felt right now.

When they got in the car, Kay paused before she started the ignition.

"You're awfully quiet," she said. "What do you think?"

Claire had to blink to keep the tears from falling.

"I want to do this every day," she said. "Thank you for bringing me here."

On the way home from Pendleton, Claire's phone rang.

"Hey, Moonbeam," Laurie said when she answered. "Guess what I found?"

"Diedre's car?" Claire asked.

"The one and only," he said. "I've called for a tow truck. I'm just about to jimmy the lock and call this mystery solved."

"Where was it?"

"Up some godforsaken holler out Hollyhock Ridge," he said. "This morning the owner of the barn it's in reported it, and, amazingly, Skip noticed the posting and told me about it. He offered to come, but I wanted to see this through myself."

"Good for you," Claire said. "Well done, Laurie."

"It smells so strong of piss in here it's making my eyes water," he said. "I haven't used one of these lock poppers in quite a while. I suppose it's like riding a bike."

Claire started to say something, but there was a loud noise on Laurie's end of the call, and it was disconnected.

Claire stared at Kay in shock.

"What is it?" Kay asked. "What's wrong?"

"Pull over," Claire said, as her shock turned to panic. "Pull over, pull over, pull over! Something's happened to Laurie."

Kay called 911 to report an officer in trouble and his general whereabouts. Claire called Sarah and told her what was going on. Sarah was brisk and professional but told Claire to start calling towing companies until she found the one Laurie had given the address to.

Kay drove them to the Pendleton Police Department, where Chief Shepherd let them commandeer an empty office, and he radioed two officers to head out toward Hollyhock Ridge. From the front desk, he retrieved the list of towing companies, tore it in half, and gave Claire and Kay each half the list.

Claire had called three companies when Kay yelled, "Found it!"

Shep called the fire department, and it wasn't two minutes before they heard the sirens start. Then he got on the radio and gave his officers the address.

"Come with me," he told Kay and Claire, who followed him to his squad car.

By the time they got to the mouth of the holler, they could see black smoke rising above the treetops.

"Oh, no," Claire breathed, and Kay grasped her hand.

They started out the narrow, rutted road, but had to pull over to let an ambulance get past.

"This is all my fault," Kay said.

"No, this is my fault," Claire said.

"Ladies, this is most likely the fault of the criminals who stole the vehicle," Shep said. "One of the most recent developments in drug manufacturing is the mobile lab, the better to evade detection by law enforcement. They probably had a shake-and-bake lab in that station wagon, and the chemicals outgassed in the interior, which was sealed. One spark or a sudden influx of oxygen, and the whole thing blows up."

The chief pulled off the road a hundred yards back from the barn, from which flames were shooting high up in the air. Pieces of ash and burning hay were floating on the breeze.

"No, no, no," Claire said.

Kay grasped her hand and held it.

Shep got out of the car, saying, "You two stay here; it's not safe to get any closer."

He spoke to a fireman who was walking their way, and then came back and leaned down to the open window.

"He's alive," Shep said, but his expression was grim. "They're taking him to town and then airlifting him to Morgantown."

Claire dissolved into tears, and Kay put her arm around her.

"He's strong," she told Claire, "and he's still alive. We'll meet them there."

"I'll drive you," Shep said.

A few minutes later the ambulance rolled past, and Shep turned the car around.

"I'll turn on the lights," he said. "We'll be there in thirty minutes."

When they arrived, the waiting room was full of police officers. It took a few moments before Claire realized they were all there for Laurie. Kay greeted the few she knew, and Skip arrived soon after them.

"I came as soon as I heard," he said. "My mom notified the IWS to start the prayer chain."

"Who are all these people?" Claire asked him.

"People who worked with Laurie," Skip said.

Another uniformed officer arrived along with a tall, thin, pretty young woman with long dark hair. She looked familiar to Claire.

"That's his ex and his best friend," Skip said.

The woman was in tears. She went to the desk, showed them an ID, and then was allowed to go back. The officer who had arrived with her greeted his colleagues, who all had grim faces, and then sat a little way apart from them. He put his face in his hands, his elbows on his knees.

"Why was she allowed to go back?" Claire asked. "They're divorced."

"Her license probably still says 'Purcell' on it," Kay said.

Claire felt helpless and frustrated.

"What can we do?"

"Let's go get everyone coffee," Kay said.

Claire followed Kay to the cafeteria, where they were allowed to borrow two trays to take coffee back for everyone. Claire helped pass them around and introduced herself as Chief Fitzpatrick's daughter, which gave her immediate access to their inner circle.

"Laurie saved my life," one officer told her. "I was still a rookie, green as grass. We did a routine traffic stop together; the guy turned out to be a wanted felon. He reached over to take something out of his glove box; I thought it was the car registration, but Laurie saw the gun. He pushed me out of the way and took a bullet in the shoulder. I'll never forget that; the guy could've killed me."

"He drove me to the hospital the night my daughter was born two months prematurely," another one said. "Stayed with us all night, made calls, and drove to Oakland to fetch my mother-in-law. He's been like a father to me."

"I've known Laurie all my life," an older man said. "I worked for his father while Laurie was still in school. Larry was tough on him, but he was the apple of his eye. When Laurie graduated from the academy, his old man cried like a baby. It was the proudest day of his life."

Claire and Kay listened to story after story about Laurie. Everyone had something good to say about him or recounted some generous, kind thing he did for them. As

297

time went on, more and more people arrived, including Laurie's neighbors, friends of his parents, friends of his late wife, church members, sheriffs from two adjoining counties, state police officers, and other people Claire didn't have a chance to meet.

The whole time, the man who had arrived with his ex-wife sat a little apart and stared into space with red-rimmed, weary eyes. Finally, Claire sat down next to him and introduced herself. He said his name was Bobby and shook her hand.

"He was my best friend," Bobby said. "This is all my fault."

"How can that be?" Claire said.

"You don't know?"

Claire shook her head, not wanting to admit all the gossip she'd listened to.

"He left his job because of me," he said. "If I hadn't got involved with Daphne, he'd still be chief, and none of this would have happened."

"You don't know that," Claire said. "I don't think they were happy together."

Bobby shook his head.

"Daphne adored him," Bobby said. "She only left him as an ultimatum, to get him to stop drinking. The thing between us just happened. Too many nights spent worrying about him, looking for him in every sleazy bar he'd passed out in and then dragging him home. We got close because we both loved him. I mean, we do love him. If he dies, I will never forgive myself."

Daphne came through the swinging doors and walked straight toward them.

"You Claire?" she asked.

Daphne's mascara was a little smeared, but she was still a beautiful woman. She had dark brown eyes, so dark you couldn't see where the pupils ended and the irises began. Her fingernails were expertly manicured, and the complicated abstract design exactly matched her toenails. Her hair had been blown out to a shiny waterfall of deep brown, not quite black. Claire felt self-conscious of her own, more casual appearance as Daphne looked her up and down.

"Yes," Claire said.

"Come with me," she said.

Daphne didn't look at anyone else, not even at Bobby; it was as if he did not exist.

Claire got up and followed her back through the swinging doors. If Daphne was worried anyone would stop her, she didn't show it. She held her head high as she tip-tapped down the hallway in her spike heels, her long dark hair swinging behind her, and didn't stop until they reached a curtained cubicle.

"He looks like hell," she said to Claire. "Only one person can be in here at a time; if anybody questions you, show them this."

She peeled off the visitor's sticker that was adhered to her blouse and stuck it on Claire's shirt. She looked Claire up and down.

"He certainly has a type, doesn't he?" she said.

Claire realized then why Daphne looked so familiar. Other than eye color, they could have been mistaken for sisters.

"Thank you," Claire said, and steeled herself to go inside.

"They said he asked for you on the way here," Daphne said. "Otherwise, it would be me."

With that, she turned and walked back down the hallway, wiping her eyes as she went.

Claire parted the curtain and went inside the cubicle. Laurie was in a hospital bed, covered from his feet to the waist with a sheet. His clothes were heaped in bloody tatters on the floor; it looked as if they had been cut off his body. Broken glass sparkled on the floor around his bed. His hands and arms were swaddled in bandages; a gash on his forehead was held together with a butterfly bandage; there was dried blood on his face and neck; an oxygen mask was affixed over his mouth and nose.

His chest, dotted with round rubber stickers holding electrodes connected to wires, was crisscrossed with shallow cuts. The wires adhered to his chest were attached to rolling monitors on one side of the bed. One IV was inserted in his arm, connected to a bag of dark red blood hung up on the IV pole; another attached a port in his neck to a large bag of clear liquid and a smaller bag of yellow liquid.

A nurse was recording his vital signs, and she glanced at Claire's sticker.

"You the wife?"

Claire nodded, her eyes fixed on Laurie.

"He's stable but barely," the nurse said. "They lost him on the way here but were able to revive him. He has an advance directive on file at the state registry that calls for no resuscitation, but in the heat of the moment, emergency personnel are focused on saving people, not checking to see if they have a living will.

"He has chemical burns on his arms and hands. Whatever chemical he inhaled after the explosion may have permanently damaged his lungs and possibly his eyes. He was in so much pain that they've put him on a Roxanal drip; that's morphine. His pulse is too thready, and his pressure's too low to do surgery, so we're making him comfortable and giving him fluids and blood. We'll move him to ICU as soon as there's a bed available; if he stabilizes, then they'll reassess."

"Can I stay?"

"Sure, sweetie," the nurse said. "Someone will be in to clean him up. Press the red button on the remote if you need anything. He's wired for sound in here so if anything happens we'll know it."

Claire sat down. Her eyes went from Laurie's face to the heart monitor. Even with all the noise in the ER, she felt she could hear her own heart beating as well.

A man wearing green scrubs came in and said, "Hey there, campers," in way too loud and chipper of a voice.

"Hello," Claire said.

"I'm gonna get him cleaned up and put a gown on him," he said. "I hear he's headed to ICU soon."

Claire asked if she could help.

The man said "sure" and shrugged his shoulders.

He hummed under his breath, and for some reason, this irritated Claire to no end. He picked up Laurie's pants and shirt. They were stiff with blood and smelled like copper pennies. He threw them in a lined bin marked, "Biohazard." As he worked on Laurie, he was a little too brisk for Claire's liking, and not nearly as gentle as Claire wanted him to be, but she bit her tongue.

Claire took the pan of warm water and sponge he prepared, and gently washed Laurie's face as well as she could around the oxygen mask. There was blood in his hair, and in every crease on his face.

"What happened to him?" the man asked.

"A car blew up," Claire said. "He's a policeman."

"Well, we won't hold that against him," the man said.

Claire gave him a look that conveyed her opinion of that remark.

"Sorry," he said. "I'll just keep my mouth shut now."

Claire bathed his upper body. The man then swabbed his cuts with an orange-red liquid and applied antibiotic ointment to them. Claire noted the puckered shoulder wound where years ago he had been shot saving his fellow officer.

Once he was bathed, with a hospital gown on, and covered with a sheet and several warm blankets, the man quietly took his leave, turning the lights down as he left.

Claire pulled her chair up next to the bed. Using the remote, she lowered the bed until her face was level with Laurie's.

"I'm going to be here when you wake up," she said. "I won't leave you."

Nurses came and went, and each one said he would be moved to ICU soon, but he was still in the ER four hours later. Claire was finally overcome with fatigue, and could hardly keep her eyes open. She put her head down on her arms on the bed for a minute to rest her eyes. She lost track of time. She could hear the ER noise and the beeps of the monitors, so she wasn't quite asleep, but she still couldn't seem to wake up.

She heard someone in the room and looked up.

Laurie was standing at the foot of his bed.

"What happened to this guy?" he asked, gesturing to the bed.

"The car blew up," she told him. "It's all my fault."

"No," he said, shaking his head.

"But I wanted you to find the car," she said.

"It was my job to find the car," he said. "If it hadn't been me it might have been Donald or Goofy."

"Everyone's here; your best friend, your ex-wife ..."

"I know," he said.

"You need to get back in bed," she said. "You need to rest so you can get out of here."

"I am out of here," he said. "Don't you hear that? They're playing our song."

Claire could hear Claire de Lune being played on a piano, faintly, as if from far away. A door opened, one that Claire hadn't noticed before, over in the corner on the other side of the bed. The bright light that streamed in was blinding after sitting in the darkness for so long. There seemed to be a crowd of people in the hallway beyond it.

"They're waiting for me," Laurie said.

There was a new, loud, insistent noise.

"Time to go," he said.

"Wait," Claire said.

"It'll be all right," he said. "You'll see."

Claire awoke with a sucking feeling in her stomach as if she had just gone over the tallest drop on a roller coaster. A nurse rushed in, quickly followed by another.

Claire realized the loud noise was the alarm on Laurie's heart monitor. The display showed a long flat line, unrelieved by peaks and valleys.

"No," Claire breathed. "Laurie."

When Claire got back to the waiting room, there were still many people there from before, and most were crying. Kay reached her first and pulled her into a warm hug.

"Oh, honey," she said. "I'm so, so sorry."

Sonny was there with Kay, and he patted Claire's arm. When Kay let go, he put an arm around each of them.

"It's all my fault," Kay said.

"No," Claire said. "It just happened."

Chief Shepherd from Pendleton came up to Claire and shook her hand.

"I haven't seen you since you were a little bitty thing," he said. "How's your dad doing?"

"About the same," Claire said.

"I've meant to get up there and see him," he said. "You think that'd be all right?"

"He'd love it," Claire said. "Most of his old friends avoid him now."

"Well, there's two kinds of people in this world," he told her, "people like me, and people who wish they were like me. I'll be up to see him this next week. If he feels up to it, I'll take him out in the boat, and we'll see what's biting."

"Thanks," Claire said.

"It's a damned shame about Laurie," he said to Kay. "I wish I'd done more to help him."

"We all do," Kay said.

Daphne and Bobby were picking up their things, preparing to leave as Claire went up to them. Their eyes were red-rimmed and puffy from crying. Claire opened her mouth to speak but then couldn't think of anything to say.

Daphne reached out, squeezed Claire's hand, and said, "You take care."

They walked away, and it was then that Claire saw Ed, standing at the back of the room, his back against the wall, with a cup of coffee in his hand. As soon as he saw her notice him, he put down the cup and came forward.

"I'm so sorry," he said.

Claire had held it together pretty well up until that point, but his kind eyes and compassionate expression undid her. She walked into his embrace and bawled.

Sonny followed Kay home, and it seemed perfectly natural to assume that he would stay the night. For a while, they sat out on the porch in the darkness, swaying to and fro on the glider, holding hands, and saying nothing. Meanwhile, fireflies glowed on and off, frogs peeped, and crickets trilled.

Holding Sonny's hand, Kay silently prayed for Laurie's safe journey to the other side, and that Claire would be comforted, her faith strengthened by adversity. She gave thanks for Sonny, asked that He might overlook their current sleepover arrangement, and would forgive her for being so very human. She prayed for Knox and Diedre, and that Matthew would find a way to forgive her. She remembered Sal then and said a prayer for him and Antonia. She asked that God guide her to do the right thing, and to forgive her when she did not. She gave thanks for all her many blessings. And finally, she prayed for Grace to be protected on her journey home.

It was midnight when a car drew up to the curb. Kay squinted in the glare of the headlights to see whose it was. Someone got out of the back seat and tossed a duffel bag on the ground. It wasn't until the front car window rolled down and Janet called out, "Got her home safe; see you tomorrow," that Kay realized that her last prayer had been answered.

Hollyhock Ridge by Pamela Grandstaff

CHAPTER 11

Claire woke up to a knock on her bedroom door. "Claire Bear," her father said. "You're going to be late for school."

She had a fierce headache. She could feel how swollen her eyes were. It was not going to be pretty.

"Liam's out delivering the papers," her father said.

Claire closed her eyes and tried to draw the strength she needed to deal with her father's dementia, but the well was almost dry. Her little brother, Liam, had died from leukemia as a child, more than twenty years ago.

Oh, and Laurie was dead.

Laurie was dead.

It hit her in the chest like an anvil.

What she would give for some of that memory loss.

"Claire Rebecca," her father said, in his stern voice.

"I'm getting up," she called out and then did so.

It was 6:00 a.m.

When she opened the door, Mackie Pea and Junior came barreling down the hallway to greet her. She could hear her father shaving in the bathroom, so she walked her swollen eyes, aching head, and broken heart to the kitchen, let the animals go outside in the backyard, and started the coffee.

She couldn't bear to think about what had happened the day before, so she focused on the small things she could accomplish without thinking too much: the next step in her day, the next item on her list.

She prepared a tall glass of ice water and took a package of frozen peas out of the freezer. She let the dog and cat back in and fed them. She took a long deep drink of the icy water, and it felt good going down. She wondered if it was possible to become dehydrated from crying.

307

When Ed arrived, she was sitting at the kitchen table, her head tilted back, holding the bag of peas across her eyes.

He put his hands on her shoulders and kissed the top of her head.

"Good morning," he said. "Will you feel like going for a run later today?"

"A walk," she said. "A long walk, but tonight."

He sat down across the table from her. She removed the bag of peas and looked at him, but to his credit, he did not wince at what he saw. He smiled kindly instead.

"I hear the Fitzpatrick Family Circus is coming back to town today," he said.

"Great," she said. "I can hardly wait til Aunt Bonnie discovers I traded places with Melissa."

"If you need to escape, give me a call," he said.

"Thank you," Claire said. "I'll come by the office after I'm done at the bakery."

"No one expects you to work today."

"I want to work," Claire said. "It will keep me from thinking too much."

"I'm writing Laurie's obituary," Ed said. "I told Daphne I'd take care of it, and she's going to email some information and a photo. I gathered so many stories from the folks in the E.R. waiting room last night I could fill a whole issue. Is there anything you'd like to add?"

"He told me he didn't like being a policeman," Claire said. "Turns out he was awfully good at it."

"Everyone says he was a great guy," Ed said. "I didn't know him that well but whenever our paths crossed I enjoyed talking to him."

"I wish I had known him better," she said. "I wish I could have made a difference."

"There was probably nothing you could've done," Ed said. "You can't save someone who doesn't want to be saved."

This made Claire so angry. Who was Ed to tell her she couldn't have saved Laurie? Before the accident, he intended to go to rehab. He could have turned his life around. He was once this great guy all those people loved; why couldn't he have found a way to be that man again? Why didn't he want to? More selfishly, she thought, why wasn't the possibility of being with her enough of a reason?

She wanted Ed to leave, and to quit coming around with his comments about things he couldn't possibly know about. Immediately after this thought, Claire was ashamed of herself for taking out her anger on Ed.

It was Laurie she was mad at, of course it was.

"Anything else you want to add?" he asked.

"He played the piano. He liked to sing old songs."

He didn't have sex with her the night she got drunk, took off her clothes, and begged him to. How would that look in the obit?

'Goes to show character,' Claire thought.

"His ex-wife is quite a bit younger than he was," Ed said. "Pretty lady."

"I heard the first wife was the soul mate," Claire said. "Did you ever meet her?"

Claire had stopped sticking pins in her imaginary Ed voodoo doll and was now sticking them in herself. She didn't want to hear how wonderful the woman was, or how great their marriage was. Claire had shown up at the theater as the actors took their closing night bows; she didn't want to hear how great the run had been.

"I ran into her at fundraisers, walks for various causes," Ed said. "She was a nice woman."

"Of course she was," Claire said.

Laurie's sainted dead wife would have been a better wife even for Ed. Claire begged herself to quit asking questions, but she stuck another pin in instead.

"What did she look like?"

"Tall and thin, with long dark hair," Ed said. "She was pretty."

"Of course she was," Claire said.

If Daphne was meant to be a copy of the original, Claire guessed she was just the smudged, illegible faxed version of the copy.

"You can love more than one person in a lifetime, you know," he said. "You can even love more than one person at the same time."

'Shut up, shut up, shut up,' Claire was thinking.

It hurt too much, and she was too tired to start crying again.

Ed meant well, she knew he did. His expression was full of sympathy and compassion. He had proved his friendship by showing up at the hospital where Claire was grieving over the loss of his rival. He had gathered her up, shepherded her home, tucked her into bed, and stayed until she fell asleep.

"Thank you, for coming to Morgantown last night, and for bringing me home," she said.

"That's what friends do," he said. "We help pick up the pieces and put each other back together."

"C'mon!" Ian said from the front room. "We're late!"

"Will I see you later?" he asked.

"You will," she said.

Kay woke up to Sonny snoring loudly next to her. He had taken up three-fourths of the bed again and all of the top sheet and quilt. Kay slid out of bed and performed her morning tasks. By the time she'd put the kettle on, he was up, and soon she could hear him taking a shower. She checked on Grace, who was still sound asleep in her room.

Kay retrieved the newspaper off the front steps and sat with her tea on the front porch to read it. She immediately wished she'd waited. It seemed like every story inside was something she didn't want to face this early in the morning.

Knox's death had been tentatively deemed accidental, but the names of the three trustees on the secret account had been revealed, and Marigold's name was there in black ink on the front page, as a new person of interest in the ongoing investigation.

The paper also reported that Marigold had formally withdrawn her candidacy for mayor. It said that opposing mayoral candidate, Kay Templeton, had not been available to respond to this bombshell announcement. Kay knew that many of the voicemails that were waiting on her cell phone were probably from someone at the Pendleton paper, asking her for a comment.

Laurie's death warranted a big write-up. Multiple law officials eulogized him and praised his exemplary police record. County Sheriff's Homicide Investigator Sarah Albright stated that he was instrumental in the investigation that resulted in the arrest of several members of an extensive network of drug manufacturers and that he died in the line of duty.

"He will be missed," she was quoted as saying.

Sal's obituary covered half of a page and detailed his long history in Rose Hill. Kay had just started reading it when Sonny came out on the porch and sat down next to her.

"How's my girl?"

"We need a bigger bed," she said and handed him the page with his father's obituary.

"What we need is a bigger house," he said. "My apartment isn't much bigger than this."

"I love my little house," Kay said. "I don't want to leave it."

"Then we'll add on," Sonny said. "I know a guy who'll do it cheap. He'll even work for food."

"Good to know," she said. "Considering I now have to drive to Pendleton to buy food, I'll need to stock up."

"Do you think Grace will be okay with all of this?"

"She was surprised," Kay said. "I was, too."

"It was always meant to be," Sonny said. "It just took us a while to realize it."

"When did you know?"

He paused, looked off into the distance, and then smiled.

"I came to hear you speak at the IWS hospice fundraiser back in June," Sonny said. "You were so eloquent, and gracious to Marigold, even though she was so rude to you. And you were beautiful; I could see the teenager in you, you know, right in there with the woman you grew up to be. I thought to myself that Kay Templeton is one class act. Then I thought, I'm single, and she's single; why don't I call her up and ask her out?"

"Why didn't you?"

"Because what could a woman like you possibly see in a man like me?' "

"Only everything," Kay said. "Everything I love best."

"Well, then," he said. "I have a question for you."

"Yes," Kay said. "The answer is yes."

"We can get a license today," he said. "I'm not kidding around, here."

"Let's do it," Kay said. "Quietly and quickly."

"Good idea," he said. "What with my dad and Diedre, and, of course, Matty. So many tender feelings; it would probably be best."

"We can go down to the Pendleton courthouse and do it," she said. "We'll get Pauly and Julie to be our witnesses."

"My mother's going to flip out," he said.

Kay had a feeling his mother was going to be more relieved than anything else.

"You feel what you need to feel, right?" he asked. "You're not just getting carried along by me."

"It feels right," she said. "I think Dottie would approve. You?"

"I've got no doubts," he said. "We're gonna do fine."

Claire was cleaning the house in anticipation of her mother coming home later that day. As she put the tall stack of paper plates back up in the cabinet above the refrigerator, she rediscovered the bottle of whiskey and Pip's baggie of pot. Overcome with fresh grief, she sat down at the kitchen table to cry and was still there, the bottle in front of her and the bag of pot in her hand, when Ed came in through the back door.

"This looks serious," he said.

"It's Pip's," she said. "I don't know whether to flush it or smoke it."

Ed took the baggie from her and went down the hall, where she could hear the toilet flush.

Claire's phone rang, and she answered it.

"Your twenty-four hours is almost up," Gwyneth Eldridge said. "What are you going to do about Pip?"

"Not a blessed thing," Claire said. "Thanks, anyway."

"But ..." Gwyneth started to say.

"Listen, Gwyneth," Claire said. "What Pip or your sister do or don't do is up to them. We gotta quit trying to control everything. As for me, I'm not going to waste another minute worrying about Pip, and I'm sure as hell not going to decide what's best for him. It's none of my business."

"I assume this means you're not interested in the spa position," Gwyneth said, contempt and condescension dripping from her words.

"Nope," Claire said, "but thanks, anyway."

She ended the call and began pouring the whiskey down the kitchen sink drain.

"I would have helped you drink that," Ed said.

"Nope," she said. "Nobody's drinking this."

Ed sat down at the kitchen table, and it was then that Claire noticed he didn't look like he felt well.

"Are you okay?" she asked him.

He shook his head, and she was taken aback to see he was fighting back the tears.

"Hey," she said, "What's wrong?"

He shook his head, took a deep breath, and wiped his face with his hands. When he looked back up, he gave her a weary, sad smile.

"Have you been on the Internet today?" he asked her.

"No," she said. "Why?"

"Looks like Eve's senator got careless with his emails and texts."

"Uh oh," she said. "What happened?"

"Someone on his staff turned it all over to a reporter at the Washington Post."

"He'll just say his accounts were hacked."

"I don't think he can get away with that. Apparently, he sent naked photographs of himself and certain parts of himself," Ed said. "There's no way he'll be able to run now."

"What's Eve say?"

"She's pretty pissed," Ed said. "Not all of the emails were to her."

"Oh, no," Claire said. "Poor Eve."

"More women are expected to come forward," he said. "More than a few."

"So much for her exclusive access to the next president."

"Not so exclusive, as it turns out."

"Does this change anything for you and her?"

"You might say that," he said. "She's anticipating that her confidential emails to him will be revealed any minute. If they are, her career will be over."

"She can say her account was hacked," Claire said.

"I don't think that's possible," Ed said.

"She sent photos, too?"

He nodded.

"I'm so sorry," she said.

"I don't know why," he said. "You tried to warn me; I just didn't listen."

"Where is she now?"

"She's on her way to Atlanta, to meet with her agent and attorney."

"I guess the baby ..."

"Not mine; never was and never will be."

He looked so woebegone that Claire's heart, or whatever was functioning in its place this morning, went out to him. She sat down next to him and put her hand on his arm.

"I'm so sorry," she said. "You didn't deserve to be deceived like that. You were willing to stand by her and take care of her and the baby."

"Like a chump."

"You don't have anything to be ashamed of," she said. "She's the one who should be ashamed."

"I'm sorry to dump this on you today," he said. "You've got your own stuff to deal with."

"We're friends, pal," she said. "This is what friends do, remember? We pick up the broken pieces and help put them back together again."

There was a knock on the front door, and it turned out to be an express shipping driver delivering the shoes Claire had forgotten she had ordered just a few days ago. She didn't feel excited anticipation like she usually would. Now she felt irritated with the person she had been only a few days ago. She tossed the box into a chair and returned to the kitchen.

She leaned against the doorway and looked at Ed. She felt so fond of him. The sane realness of their relationship was calm and deep and comforting to her. It was what you hoped was on the other side of the intoxication of attraction and the rocky terrain of a new relationship. It felt like home, the one she had longed for from the other side of the world, and from the crossroads under the town's only traffic light, here, in Rose Hill.

"If our friendship can survive this year, it can survive anything," Claire said.

"What will happen to us, though, after life gets through with us?" Ed said. "All our years might be like this one, with one sad thing after another."

"We'll hold hands and walk," Claire said, "or you'll push my wheelchair up and down Rose Hill Avenue so I can still wear my high heels."

"Thank you," he said, as he stood up, "for being my friend."

Ed pulled her into a tight hug, and she let herself sink into it, feeling the strength of his arms around her and the weight of his chin on her shoulder. There was comfort and acceptance there, and all the peace and stability she longed for in the deepest recesses of her heart.

Claire's phone jingled, and she pulled away, saying, "With the whole family on the road today I have to answer."

"Miss Fitzpatrick," a woman said. "This is Susanna; I'm the volunteer coordinator down at Pineville Hospice. First of all, I want to tell you how thrilled we are that you've agreed to volunteer, and how happy you made the two families you helped yesterday. I have several patients that would love to see you, so I was wondering when you planned to be here again."

Claire had forgotten about her commitment to volunteer. It seemed like a week ago that she'd been there, instead of just the day before. She thought about the feeling she'd had when she'd left there. If she was going to be addicted to something, that seemed like a good choice.

"I'll be there tomorrow," Claire said.

They settled on a time, and Claire ended the call.

"What was that about?" Ed asked her.

"I finally figured out what I want to do with my life," Claire said.

"How about who you want to be with?"

"You already know that," she said. "Everything else is just details."

ACKNOWLEDGMENTS

I am blessed with family and friends who love me, support my addiction to writing fiction, and are generous enough to overlook my many faults and foibles. In return, I hope I communicate to them how much I love them. If not, here's the perfect opportunity: I love you people, and everything else is just details.

Thank you to Betsy Grandstaff, Terry Hutchison, Joan Turner, and Ella Curry for their encouragement and feedback.

Because I love my dog family, I want to mention June Bug, who still has the spirit of the young, frisky pup I rescued 13 ½ years ago. Her younger brother George is a new addition, and although it's too soon to tell how he will measure up, we love him dearly, so that's a good start.

Thank you to Tamarack: The Best of West Virginia, for selling my paper books in your beautiful building.

And last, but not least, I want to thank the people who buy and read my books. Thank you so much.

If you liked this book, please leave a review on Amazon.com (Thank you!)

51882736R00183

Made in the USA
Columbia, SC
23 February 2019